P.D. MARTIN
THE
MURDERERS'
CLUB

MIRA

All the characters in this book have no existence outside the imagination
of the author, and have no relation whatsoever to anyone bearing the
same name or names. They are not even distantly inspired by any
individual known or unknown to the author, and all the incidents are
pure invention.

Published in Great Britain 2008.
MIRA Books, Eton House, 18-24 Paradise Road,
Richmond, Surrey, TW9 1SR

ISBN 978 0 7783 0238 4

59-0708

MIRA's policy is to use papers that are natural, renewable and
recyclable products and made from wood grown in sustainable
forests. The logging and manufacturing processes conform to the
legal environmental regulations of the country of origin.

Printed and bound in Spain
by Litografia Rosés S.A., Barcelona

Acknowledgements

Firstly, I'd like to thank my agent Elaine Koster and everyone at MIRA, especially Margaret Marbury, Selina McLemore, Linda McFall, the design team, and the sales and marketing teams.

For their advice and professional insights I'd like to thank the FBI; ex-FBI agent and profiler Candice de Long; forensic pathologist Shelley Robertson; author and medical practitioner Kathryn Fox; Paul Spencely for some IT help; Guy Franklin for his web and video-streaming expertise; Tom Cook (via Aislinn Kerr) for some helicopter facts; and firearms instructor Phil Harden. Any mistakes are mine and mine alone.

I'd also like to thank Gil Broadway of Australian Tiger and Crane Kung Fu for the training; Gillian Ramsay and Momentum Technologies Group for my website (www.pdmartin.com.au); and Sisters in Crime for their support.

Big thanks also go to my test readers – Keir Paterson, Kathryn Deans, Marlo Garnsworthy, Martina McKeon, Avril Baxter, Adele Whish-Wilson and Kirsty Badcock.

I'd also like to thank my fantastic friends and family for their continuing support and faith in me.

PROLOGUE

A few weeks ago

BlackWidow has entered the room.

AmericanPsycho: Welcome, BlackWidow, you're the last of our little group...and the only woman.

BlackWidow: Sorry I'm late. Have I missed anything?

AmericanPsycho: No. We've only been online for a minute or so.

BlackWidow: Good.

DialM: So, how do we start?

NeverCaught: Yeah, let's get down to the good stuff.

AmericanPsycho: Today is mostly orientation.

NeverCaught: Okay, shoot.

AmericanPsycho: First up is security. I've set the system up for our protection, but I need to know you've followed my security demands. Did you all follow the instructions in your member packs?

DialM: Certainly.

NeverCaught: Sure.

BlackWidow: Yes.

AmericanPsycho: Great. That's the first line of our defense—your laptops are all specially fitted out.

NeverCaught: Yup, the instructions are clear.

AmericanPsycho: The rest of the security I've handled
from my end. We can never be too careful.

NeverCaught: Good. I want to stay *never caught*.

AmericanPsycho: I've also set up a filter program that will
pick up certain words, like your occupations, all of your real
names, cities, states, etc. and replace any suspect text with
a random number of ***. There's a two-second delay to
accommodate the censoring.

NeverCaught: Awesome.

AmericanPsycho: Secrecy must be our paramount concern
AT ALL TIMES. No talking, no bragging, nothing, to anyone but us, online. Here you are safe. Here you can say
whatever you want. Feel free to indulge your darkest fan-
tasies in the safety of our select group. All contact must
be via this chat room. Never try to contact me, or each
other, by any other means, including the other chat rooms
we frequent. I'll keep posting news and the site's also got
the online profiles. Plus of course the main feature, video
streaming. Questions?

DialM: Thank you, AmericanPsycho. That seems clear
enough.

BlackWidow: What about the FBI and this site?

AmericanPsycho: The site uses the latest in data security
and encryption and it will be almost impossible for anyone, including the FBI, to hack into it...at least not without me getting an alert. But nothing's impenetrable. If it
comes to that, I've got all sorts of security backups. And
don't forget—if something is up, follow the emergency instructions in your pack.

NeverCaught: Gotcha.

AmericanPsycho: Okay, that's the boring part done. Now we just have to wait…only a few weeks to go. The construction is nearly finished.
NeverCaught: Excellent.
AmericanPsycho: Any other questions? Comments?
NeverCaught: Yes. One. YOU know our names!
AmericanPsycho: Yes, me, and only me. But your secrets are safe with me. I am the President of the Club.

1

I hold my Smith & Wesson 9mm semiautomatic in front of me, legs shoulder-width apart, and line up the gun's sights, aiming at his chest—the heart to be precise. The middle sight is pointed squarely at the target, and the outer sights are horizontally level. I take a breath, hold it and squeeze the trigger. The gun recoils, but after each backward motion I readjust my aim and fire again. I empty my whole magazine—eight shots—and revel in the muffled yet rhythmic click…click…click as my shells are thrown onto the ground near my feet.

"Nice grouping, Anderson."

I jump slightly, instinctively tightening the already firm grip on my gun. My rational mind wins out over my impulses and I resist the temptation to swing the gun around and point it. I turn to see Andy Rivers, the head of the Behavioral Analysis Unit, standing next to me. I relax my grip. Rivers's dark, wiry hair is offset by patches of gray at his temples, the only sign that time—or perhaps stress—is catching up with him. In his midforties, he's been the head of the unit for nearly ten years, and I don't imagine he'll be leaving any time soon. He's too good at his job. I take off my earmuffs and goggles and the muffled world returns to normal.

"Hi, boss." I look back at my target and the bullet holes clustered around the heart. "Thanks."

I'm standing in booth twelve of one of the FBI's firing ranges at Quantico, Virginia. Our unit is part of the National Center for the Analysis of Violent Crimes—NCAVC—and we get to share the FBI Academy's three hundred and eighty-five acres with new recruits and several other active units. The impressive complex includes three dormitories, a dining room, a library, an auditorium, a chapel, a gym, a large running track, a defensive-driving track, several firing ranges and the famous Hogan's Alley—a simulated town. Over the past year, since I started with the Bureau, I've spent a lot of time here...it's home now.

I push the button in my booth that initiates the pulley system and the target sails toward me. The range consists of fifteen booths, each with a pulley system to move the targets backward and forward—from the booth to the twenty-five or fifty-yard mark. When I first came to the States I was constantly converting to metric, but now I'm used to the American way. The targets contain the impression of a person, an outline of someone's upper body in black ink. My paper target arrives and I take a closer look. I've emptied three rounds into the paper and the heart region is just one large hole where bullets have penetrated it again and again.

I was always one for firing practice—and not just in the few weeks before our yearly firearms test like some of the agents. But since one especially intense case I worked, I've been coming here a lot. An awful lot. Sometimes I spend hours in a trancelike state, my gun pulsating as I fire over and over again.

Rivers smiles for an instant before staring at the target. "Anyone we know?" he asks quietly. I know what he's hinting at, but I don't want to talk about it. My compulsory fortnightly sessions with the Bureau psychologist Dr. Amanda Rosen are bad enough. It's been six months; I should be over it.

I shrug. "Just practicing." I'm lying and he knows it, but we both leave it. I bite my lip and reload, distracting myself with the repetitive motion of forcing bullets into the gun's magazine.

Rivers watches my hands. "Practicing," he says with a hint of disbelief.

I release my lower lip from my teeth and consciously alter my body language, acting for my boss. "You know me, I'm a perfection-ist." I force a light tone into my voice.

He pushes his gold-framed glasses higher onto his nose, masking his dark brown eyes. "That's why I wanted you in my team."

I nod and smile genuinely, still humbled by the fact that Rivers handpicked me to work as a profiler in his team. The Victorian po-lice sent me out here for the Bureau's six-week International Program and I wound up with a job offer. Funny how things work out.

"Anyway, I better get to it. I've got my firearms test coming up." He gives me a wink and moves into the booth next to me.

"You don't fool me. I know you come down here more than once a year."

"Maybe. But keep it to yourself, Anderson."

I laugh, put my earmuffs and goggles back on and attach a fresh target to the clips. Once the target is back at the fifty-yard mark, I raise my gun and let him have it.

Today, Dr. Amanda Rosen wears her pinstripe pantsuit—straight, classy pants and a plain white blouse that pulls slightly across her chest. The white shirt highlights her olive complexion, making it seem even richer, darker. Hanging on her chair is the suit's match-ing jacket, a short, bolero-style number. She's covering old ground, crossing her Ts and dotting her Is. The case I was involved with six months ago got out of hand and she needs to know I've dealt with everything that happened.

Usually our expertise is requested for cases the police have been unable to solve. We do most of our work remotely, examining crime-scene photos and reports, which are sometimes months or even years old. Then we draft our profile of the perpetrator and send it to the cops. Occasionally we work in the field, in the thick of it, and this case was one of those times. It was a big case, pursuing a killer dubbed the DC Slasher, and two profilers were assigned to the task force. But things turned bad when the killer targeted the Bureau... and me.

Dr. Rosen's eyes fix on me, trying to read my body language, trying to break through my defenses. If my plan's working, she thinks she's in. Her dark brown hair is cut so it falls around her face in wisps, but today she wears it swept back in a French roll. Small strands have broken free and arc across her face. Her full lips are pursed, waiting for my response, and her dark brown eyes are sympathetic. Her eyes are her most powerful weapon. Sometimes when she looks at me I feel stripped bare as if she can see right through me, through the charade.

"Yes, it's going well," I say.

I haven't told her what disturbed me most about the case, and I never will. I can't tell the Bureau shrink that I had dreams and waking visions that came true. Hell, I can hardly believe it myself, especially given I haven't had any psychic episodes since.

"So you feel you've put the case behind you now, Sophie."

I take a breath, careful not to answer too quickly. Desperation could give me away. "It's hard, of course, but I love my job. I like being part of the fight."

"Yes—" she studies her notepad and then looks up "—the fight. You've clocked up a lot of time on the range and in the gym recently."

I shrug. "I'm keeping busy." A half truth. "I'm not the kinda gal who likes to sit around and watch TV."

"No. That doesn't match your personality profile. But maybe there are other reasons too?"

She leaves the conversation open, prompting me for the response. I know what she's looking for and decide it might be in my best interests to give it to her.

I nod. "It's true. I am more—" I search for the right word "—security conscious these days."

"Does it give you a sense of control?"

"Yes." I answer slowly, pretending to think about what I'm say-

ing. "Being physically fit, strong and a proficient marksperson make
me feel safer."

"How much gym time are you doing?"

I know the summary's right in front of her. We have to swipe our
ID card every time we enter and exit the gym, and that data is au-
tomatically compiled. Same for the firing range.

I shrug, pretending I'm not overtly aware or conscious of my
movements. After a respectable pause I say, "Probably an hour a day."
I keep my mouth shut about the morning runs and the midnight ex-
cursions to my apartment's gym. I haven't told her much about my
sleeping problems either…and I don't intend to.

"Sounds like a lot."

I shrug again. "Not really. It's about routine. And keeping in
shape." I smile, a forced smile. "Besides, gotta keep those calories
off." I pat my stomach, even though I'm in the best shape of my life.
My daily routine includes kung fu exercises and even body condi-
tioning so I can take punches and block harder. Nobody's going to
get to me.

I close my eyes and for an instant I see *him* standing over me.
Memory's a bitch.

AmericanPsycho: These are the last two.
DialM: Susie Dean and Jonathan Cantor.
AmericanPsycho: Yup. We'll get to know them and the
other six real well in the next eight weeks.
DialM: Eight people, eight weeks.
AmericanPsycho: Exactly.
DialM: Very equitable. Two each.
NeverCaught: I can't wait.
BlackWidow: But there are three men—Jonathan, Danny
and Malcolm—that makes three for me!
NeverCaught: She's right. What's up with that?
AmericanPsycho: Six girls and two men might have looked
suspicious.

DialM: You're very erudite, Psycho.

NeverCaught: ***ing big words.

NeverCaught: What the…

AmericanPsycho: My censorship extends to language, Never.

NeverCaught: Whatever.

AmericanPsycho: Back to business. Have you checked out the bios?

DialM: Yes.

NeverCaught: Yup. And man am I loving it. We've got Cindy the Vegas showgirl, Malcolm the hunk, Danny the macho *****head, Brigitte the exotic sexpot, Ling the shy one, Clair the singer, Susie the loser actress and Jonathan the geek.

BlackWidow: Jonathan's cute.

DialM: I like them all. All good choices. You really are spoiling us, Psycho.

AmericanPsycho: I told you it was pure genius.

BlackWidow: Yes, well done. This is so self-indulgent.

NeverCaught: Much more fun than stalking.

DialM: Their ignorance is our bliss.

NeverCaught: Yes. Can't wait for the first kill.

2

It's early, 6:00 p.m., when I swing into the garage underneath my apartment block and park my Buick in my assigned spot. My apartment is in Alexandria, which is perfect because it's halfway between DC and Quantico.

I purposefully load up my left arm with my handbag and the grocery bag from the trunk so my right hand is free. Free to lock the car, press the elevator button, open the door…and get my gun. A girl's got to be prepared, right?

The slight heels on my ankle boots make a clipping noise on the concrete as I walk to the elevator. I press the up button and wait, scanning the garage and looking for anything or anyone out of place. Garages and parking lots are the most likely places for a woman to be raped if the perpetrator is a stranger. I flick my eyes to the display—the elevator's on the fifteenth floor and moving down at a snail's pace. When it finally arrives and the doors open I let out a breath that I barely realized I was holding.

The elevator glides effortlessly to the third floor and the doors open with the usual *ping*. The hallways of my apartment block are painted a blue-gray, with teal-colored tiles on the floor—carpet would be too messy for winter, when everyone's shoes are covered in snow. Coming from Australia, I'd never lived in a city with snow before, and last year was my first white Christmas. Or as they'd say here, my first *real* winter.

I walk down the hall to my apartment, number 310, flipping through my keys as I go. I use a color-coded system: the top lock is the red key, then the yellow key, then the green key, just like a traffic light. Once I've unlocked all three, I turn the handle and shuffle into my apartment, quickly unloading everything onto the kitchen counter and drawing my gun so I can check the apartment. The sad thing is, I used to do this even before the Slasher case.

After checking my one-bedroom apartment thoroughly, I'm satisfied that I'm alone. I reholster my gun and take in the emptiness around me. I sigh, thinking about the recent departure of a fellow profiler who'd been more than just a friend. They say you should never mix business with pleasure, but I thought we had something special. And we did, until that case ruined it all. Can trust, once broken, ever be rebuilt? He said he hadn't asked for the transfer to the Philadelphia field office, but I wasn't so sure. And his comment that "it might be good to have a break for a while" didn't do anything to allay my suspicion. Maybe I should face facts—despite the amazing beginning, things hadn't really been working.

I push him out of my mind and start on dinner. Within half an hour I'm eating grilled salmon with a couscous salad and sipping a glass of wine from a freshly opened bottle of Semillon. Normally I prefer red, but with fish, white is better.

I eat in silence, taking a few sips of wine in between mouthfuls. I top up my glass and twirl it from the stem, gazing at the liquid as it swirls. I certainly won't finish the bottle; in fact, I can't. Except when we're on leave, FBI agents must be fit for duty at all times, and this mandate extends to alcohol intake. This is my third and final glass for the evening, but I could easily imagine myself finishing off the bottle. Maybe then I could relax? I've studied psychology; I know

I'm in a high-risk group to become too fond of drinking. Thank God for the Bureau's alcohol mandate—I'm too much of a Goody Two-shoes to break the FBI's rules.

I recork the bottle, using a wine pump so it won't spoil, and move to the couch. I break the silence by turning on the TV, flicking through the channels to try to find something that will hold my interest and distract me from more sinister thoughts like rape statistics. I fly through the stations, pausing on each one only for a couple of seconds. Nothing captivates me, but maybe that's more reflective of my mood than the programming. I settle on the news and finish my glass of wine before washing the dishes.

Finally I call home.

"Hi, Mum."

"Hi, sweetie." I can hear the excitement in her voice. "Great to hear from you. How's life in the good old US of A?"

"Great, everything's great." I never did tell Mum and Dad about what happened. It would totally freak them out. Then they'd spend all their time trying to convince me to give up the Bureau. At first I didn't tell them because I couldn't deal with reliving those few weeks. Then I realized it would open up a can of worms, with lots of "we told you so" and pressure to quit. And now...well, now it seems too late.

"And work?" Her tone changes. She's asking because she knows it's the right thing to do, because she knows it's important to me, not because she's really interested. They never wanted me in this line of work.

"Love it." I keep it simple. "So, what's news in Melbourne?" I lean back against the couch.

"Mmm." She pauses. "Your dad's still going stir-crazy."

I laugh. "That's old news, Mum." Dad retired six months ago and he's still readjusting to life on the outside. I think life as a retiree is as foreign to him as life on the outside of a prison for a career criminal.

I hear the unmistakable click of another phone being picked up.

"How's my little girl?" Dad's American accent has softened over the years, but you still hear the unmistakable twang of his roots.

"I'm good, Dad."

"Hope you're not working on any dangerous cases." His voice is serious now, concerned.

I draw out my words in a singsong voice. "No, Dad." It's not a lie. I'm not working on any dangerous cases *right now*.

"We do worry about you." Mum follows this with a sigh.

"I'm fine." Silence. "Really, I am." I chew on my bottom lip, catching it and releasing it a few times with my two front teeth.

"Are you looking forward to your holiday?" Dad moves the conversation to a less controversial subject.

I let my head sink back further into the couch and release my lip. "You bet. It's only a week but it will be nice to get away."

We spend the next twenty minutes engaged in our usual chitchat. By the time I hang up, I feel comforted. But within minutes the silence engulfs me again. I look at my watch. Too early for bed. I try channel surfing again, but in the end I opt for reading. I grab my latest Kathryn Deans novel and curl up on the couch, with the heater on low. I fly through the book, turning pages and only occasionally looking over my shoulder.

I wake up with a start and immediately look around the room to make sure I'm alone. I'm still on the couch and my book lies on the floor. A small drop of saliva sits on the corner of my mouth and I notice that the cushion I'd propped underneath my head and shoulders is slightly damp. Nice. Drooling in my sleep.

I change into my gym gear, like I do most nights when I can't sleep, and throw my gun, a bottle of water, a towel and my gloves into a small bag. Up on the fifteenth-floor gym I do a few stretches before jumping on the treadmill. For the first five minutes I gradually increase my pace and then up the speed until I'm pushing myself— hard. An hour and ten miles later I slow the treadmill to a walking pace and guzzle some water. My legs are shaky, and I'm barely able to stand. I ride the slight nausea with more water before slipping into my protective gloves and moving over to the punching bag. I go through my kung fu punches on the bag, starting with straight punches and moving on to hooks, tiger punches—which use the heel of your palm as the impact point—uppercuts, back fists, and leopard punches with bent fingers so you're striking with your knuckles. I finish up with my favorite, scratching face—a tiger strike followed by a sharp drag. In practice you'd strike the person's cheekbone or temple with the palm of your hand, then drag your hand down their face, digging your nails in. Nice.

Back in my apartment I check the place once more, gun in hand, before jumping in the shower. Finally I flop into bed and stare at the ceiling, waiting for the adrenaline to level off. Logically, exercising is not a good move for insomnia, but it seems to be the only thing that calms me, that helps me release the anger.

If I hadn't killed the bastard already, I'd do it now.

NeverCaught: I thought Wednesday would never **ing come.

DialM: Really? I think the first week has passed by quite swiftly.

AmericanPsycho: So, nearly one week down, who do we like?

BlackWidow: Well, you can count me out on Danny. The guy's an asshole—worse than most.

NeverCaught: You are some man hater.

DialM: I personally have grown quite fond of Ling over this past week.

BlackWidow: Is it the accent?

DialM: I do like the Australian accent, but it's more than that. Rare is the union of beauty and modesty.

BlackWidow: What's her story anyway?

AmericanPsycho: Haven't you checked out her bio?

BlackWidow: I haven't bothered with the women.

DialM: She's eighteen years old. She's in the U.S. for six months before she starts studying medicine back in Sydney, Australia. She's adopted from China—both her adoptive parents are from Italian stock.

BlackWidow: Thanks.

DialM: Who do you like, Psycho?

AmericanPsycho: Brigitte.

DialM: She is a beauty, that one.

AmericanPsycho: Yes. It's time.

DialM: What if we go for Danny? I don't like the fact he's got army training.

BlackWidow: Like I said, I'm out. I like to play with them first, and I couldn't DO him.

NeverCaught: Who cares about Danny? It's Brigitte that I want. She's hot.

AmericanPsycho: I think I'm more her type.

NeverCaught: Like she's got a say in it.

DialM: True.

AmericanPsycho: I think it should be Malcolm or Danny first, just to make things more interesting.

DialM: Not much pleasure in it. Well not for me at least.

NeverCaught: Hey, Psycho, do we get to watch the actual deed?

AmericanPsycho: The successful member can take video and still images of the kill, but you mustn't show us your face. Or you can keep it private.

NeverCaught: I like to strut my stuff.

AmericanPsycho: Your member kits included a digital camera. There are instructions on how to post photos to the Web site via your laptops. We also have a house especially set up. Somewhere private you can take them. But there are no cameras in the house.

BlackWidow: You have thought of everything, Psycho.

AmericanPsycho: Of course I have.

NeverCaught: Only a few hours until one of us has the first victim of the Murderers' Club.
BlackWidow: I can't wait.

3

The sound of my phone ringing wakes me up and I look at my watch—8:00 a.m. How did I sleep so late? More to the point, I'm late for work! I give my alarm clock the evil eye, even though it's probably human error, my error.

I take a breath and answer the phone. "Hello." I try to fake an awake, bright voice but don't know if I pull it off or not.

"Sophie. Sorry, did I wake you?"

Okay, so I didn't pull it off. "No. Of course not," I lie.

"How are you?"

My sluggish mind finally comes out of its stupor and I recognize the voice. "Good thanks, Darren. And you?"

I worked with Detective Darren Carter from Tucson Homicide on the DC Slasher case. He's a good cop and a nice guy. In fact, if I hadn't already been involved with someone at the time, our relationship might have extended beyond the professional. But I was taken, full stop.

"Pretty good," he says. "Still planning on heading out this way for some R & R?" His voice is slightly hesitant—maybe he thought I'd cancel.

"Of course." I get out of bed. "Flying out Friday…God, that's tomorrow."

He laughs. "Yes, it is." A pause. "Had any of those dreams of yours recently?"

Darren's the only person who knows about my visions. He saw me "experience" a young girl's murder during a particularly realistic vision. I still remember his words: My aunt had the gift and you've got it, too.

"No, no dreams."

"That a good thing?"

"The jury's out."

"I can understand that," Darren says.

A big part of me feels overwhelming relief that I'm not dreaming about murdered women, not experiencing the perverted feelings of pleasure in the mind of a killer. It freaked me out big-time, even though it helped me solve the Slasher case. And that's where the guilt comes in. It helped me save lives, so does that mean if I was dreaming and having waking visions now, I'd be saving victims from some other sick psycho?

"So, are you working on anything interesting at the moment?" I move the conversation away from the visions.

"We've got a professional hit. That's unusual for us."

"Any leads?"

"None to speak of."

"I guess that's why they call it professional."

He laughs. "The good news is it looks like I've managed to wangle a few days off. I'll show you the sights of Tucson."

"Excellent." I pause. "Well, I better get moving—I'm late for work. I presume your spare bedroom's still on offer."

"You bet. See you tomorrow."

"Nine a.m."

BlackWidow has entered the room.
DialM: Finally she returns. Was it good, BW?

BlackWidow: Yes. He didn't even hesitate when I started coming on to him. Who could resist him, right? Men…your egos truly are out of control.

NeverCaught: I almost feel sorry for Malcolm. Almost!

BlackWidow: What about what you're going to do to Cindy, Susie, Ling, Clair and Brigitte?

NeverCaught: I wish I *could* have them all.

DialM: What's the house like?

BlackWidow: Beautiful. Big, modern, quiet.

AmericanPsycho has entered the room.

BlackWidow: Hey, Psycho.

AmericanPsycho: Nice work, BW. He looked very content. Satisfied.

NeverCaught: Hey, how come we didn't get to see photos?

AmericanPsycho: I didn't see a photo of Malcolm.

BlackWidow: So *you* dumped the body?

AmericanPsycho: He was disposed of in the early hours of this morning in Tucson, just like we agreed.

BlackWidow: And the scene?

AmericanPsycho: Also like we agreed. All the bodies will be found around the same area, with the same marks.

BlackWidow: Malcolm was a great ***. And I did enjoy that body of his. Six-foot-four and all black, rippling muscle. I can see how he got his job.

AmericanPsycho: Nice to know you're a satisfied customer.

BlackWidow: I'm satisfied, all right. And definitely no links to me, right?

AmericanPsycho: I've taken care of everything. Trust me.

I walk through Tucson airport, maneuvering my bag toward the pick-up area, where Darren and I have arranged to meet. I'm annoyed by the slight butterflies I feel over seeing Darren again and I walk faster in a futile attempt to look and feel focused.

Before I make it to the automatic doors, I see him. He catches sight of me at exactly the same moment and walks toward me. My stomach does an extra flip—damn it. Darren hasn't changed a bit—then again, it was only six months ago. He's five-eleven and skinny, with slightly tousled black hair and midnight-blue eyes. His eyes are spectacular and I remember having to pull myself away from them on several occasions. He smiles, and even from here I can see his dimples, which make him look younger than his thirty-odd years. I sigh, trying to work out why I find his dimples so incredibly attractive. Maybe this wasn't such a good idea after all.

Once we're within touching distance things become awkward. A kiss on the cheek? A hug? A handshake? There should be an in-between greeting for these sorts of circumstances. I go for the hug, figuring that's the safest option. A handshake might offend and a kiss may have other implications. Too complicated, even though I guess I'm officially single now.

"Hey, you," he says, his big smile still firmly planted across his face.

"Hi."

His hand reaches down in an offer to pull my wheelie bag.

"It's fine," I say. "It's light." Besides, I'm not giving up my bag when it gives me something to do with at least one of my hands.

We both start walking.

"You're looking well." He glances at me briefly then looks ahead again.

"You too. Fully healed of course." I resist the urge to touch his left arm, which was in a sling last time I saw him.

"A little bullet never hurt anyone." His tone is sarcastic macho bravado.

I laugh. "God, I wonder how many cops have said that."

"Too many."

His unmarked navy-blue Mercury Sable is parked near the arrivals gate, in a no-standing zone. He pops the trunk and I throw in my luggage before climbing into the passenger side.

He starts the car. "It's great to see you again." He doesn't look at me.

"You, too." I follow suit, eyes front.

"How are you?"

"Good. Fine."

He's silent for a few seconds. "Not very convincing." He studies my face briefly before pulling into the traffic. "How are you really?" We move forward slowly, backed up with the other cars leaving the airport.

I lean my head back against the headrest and let out an exhausted sigh. "I don't know, Darren…" I bring one knee up to my chest. "I'm not sleeping."

"Well, no wonder you're not having any *special* dreams." He smiles. "Can't dream if you're not asleep."

"Okay, so I'm sleeping a little bit. But not much."

"And nothing at all?" He's asking for confirmation, perhaps concerned I might be hiding something from him. Truth is, he's the only person I *don't* have to hide from. He knows my secret and he's not going to fire me or write something detrimental in my file.

"No." I move my head off the rest and look at him. "I don't even know if I want to see anything." I flick my eyes back to the road, scared to witness his response.

We follow the stream of traffic onto a highway, and speed up to about sixty.

"What cases have you been working on?" Darren asks.

"The usual—serial killers, cold cases, abductions."

He nods. "But nothing in the field?"

"No." I look out the car window at the trees and notice the branches weighed down by plump leaves.

"I can help you, Sophie. My aunt told me lots of things about her gift. When she first knew, how she controlled it—all that stuff."

I pull myself away from the alluring trees and focus on Darren. "The question is, do I want to know?" I let out another sigh, this time a sigh of relief. Honesty feels good.

"Well, that's up to you."

We're interrupted by the very loud ringing of Darren's cell phone.

"Sure you can hear it?" I joke, relieved to be able to lighten the mood.

"Ha, ha." He flips the phone open. "Detective Carter…right…uh huh." His voice becomes uncertain and he shoots a strange look my way. "Damn. Can't Bolson handle it? All right, all right, I'll see you soon." He flips his phone shut and looks at me. "Sorry. I'm not officially on leave until tomorrow."

I smile. "Duty calls."

He swings the car around in a U-turn. "Doesn't it always?"

4

Darren pulls into the University of Arizona.

"College kid?" I ask.

"Looks that way."

I nod, familiar enough with the territory. I've seen a few cases of a dead college coed. Usually it turns out to be misadventure but there are instances of murder. College students can be high-risk victims: friendly, accessible, sometimes walking around campus by themselves at night, high alcohol intake, and mostly experiencing their first taste of freedom. That's attractive bait for a killer. Bundy's a prime example—he often hunted at colleges.

From the outskirts of the college it's obvious something's not right, with a large crowd gathered about three hundred feet in front of us. We drive closer, until we're about one hundred feet from the group of people, and then Darren parks the car.

He unbuckles his seat belt. "Want to stay here?"

"Nah. You know me—can't resist a good meal or a dead body."

He manages a smile and we both get out of the car.

Darren flips open his phone and hits a speed-dial button. "Stone, it's Carter. I'm on Fourth...uh huh." Darren motions to me, quickening his pace, and I follow him. "Yup…see you in a minute." He snaps his phone shut and turns to me. "Come on. The body's near the stadium." With his badge out in front of him, he leads the way through the crowd. As we get closer I can see that expressions vary from curiosity to horror. Not many of them will have actually seen anything—the area would have been cordoned off pretty soon after the discovery—but the whispers would be enough, spreading and engulfing the onlookers like a runaway wave. For all they know, it could be their best friend or roomie lying lifeless on the ground.

We reach the police crime-scene tape, with a barrier of uniformed cops encircling the area, and the media right up front, with their cameras firing. One camera swings toward us and its reporter shoves the microphone in Darren's direction.

"Detective Carter, what are we looking at here?" Part of a crime reporter's job is to know the senior investigators on sight, so I'm not surprised that this one knows Darren.

Darren maintains his silence.

The nearest cop takes one look at Darren's badge and moves aside for him.

"Detective Carter…" yells the reporter in vain.

AmericanPsycho: Switch on NBC now. They're running a story about the University of Arizona.

NeverCaught: Cool.

BlackWidow: I don't care much about following the media reports on my vics.

NeverCaught: Are you ****ing crazy? That's half the fun. Okay, I've got it on. Gee, that reporter's hot.

AmericanPsycho: I love it when they look all serious like that.

NeverCaught: Yeah, they must practice that look in the mirror. Is that the lead cop?

AmericanPsycho: Yes. The reporter said he's from Tucson Homicide.

NeverCaught: Who's the blonde with him?
AmericanPsycho: Don't know. But I'll find out.

We walk across an open expanse of grass. About fifty feet ahead, the forensic activity is at its height, with several people hovering around some shrubs and others bent over. A woman in her late twenties is in the mix, and I assume she's Darren's partner, Jessica Stone. They've been partners for less than a year and I didn't meet her during the DC Slasher case.

The woman glances our way. "Sorry, Carter. Bolson's on another call-out."

"Bolson's always on another call." Darren looks at his partner. "Stone, Anderson." He looks at me. "Anderson, Stone." And so our formal introduction is complete.

Detective Jessica Stone is short but muscular, around five-three and about one hundred and ten pounds. She has auburn hair that she wears layered around her face, highlighting stunning green eyes. Her face is lightly freckled, mostly on her cheekbones, and her lips are full but her mouth is narrow.

Finally I cast my eyes to the body. The vic lies on his back, his arms tucked underneath him. On his hairless chest and extending down to the first two bulges of his six-pack is a bright-red love heart, about four inches square. It looks like it's been drawn with a marker or body paint.

I feel a slight dizziness and then it hits me, hard and fast like before.

A good-looking African-American man is lying on a bed, naked, handcuffed to the headboard. His body is slicked with sweat and he's smiling up at me.

As the vision fades I make a grab for something, but I wind up hitting the ground with a thud.

Darren's hand is quickly on my arm, helping me up. "You okay?"

I force my eyes open, force them to focus on Darren. "I'm fine." I look around and everyone's staring at me, not the dead guy. This is probably one of the most embarrassing things that can happen to a law-enforcement professional. Now it looks like the sight of a dead guy makes me weak at the knees. I'd almost prefer to tell them the truth than have them think I'm soft. But the truth isn't an option. The vision took me by surprise and I couldn't steady myself.

"Sorry, I must have tripped on something." I look back for the imaginary culprit and then shrug.

Everyone except Darren returns their attention to the body. He moves me away from the main group. "Did you...did you see something?"

"Yes." I bite my lip, puzzled, but Darren takes the confirmation that it was a vision in his stride.

"Was it him?" He looks at me, but motions his head to the body.

Even though I know it was the vic, I look down at him again. "Yes."

"What did you see?"

"He was handcuffed to a bed, covered in sweat." I recall the image. "I think he might have been having sex."

Darren makes a short humming noise.

"Let's go take a closer look," I say.

We move back to the main drag and sidle in next to Stone.

"The love heart is very ritualistic, very specific," I say. "Seen anything like this before?"

Darren shakes his head. "What have we got, Stone?"

She looks up and a longer strand of hair falls into her face, dancing in her eyes before she shoves it back and reclips a small barrette that captures the stray hairs. "Not much. Unidentified African-American male."

"Who found him?" Darren looks back at the perimeter.

"Jack Bode. He's one of the campus cops." Stone points out an older man sitting on a bench with his head in his hands.

Darren scribbles the information into a notebook. "Did he touch him?"

"No. He called it in and stayed with the body to make sure the scene was left intact."

"Good." Darren glances back at the crowd. "Any other witnesses?"

"Not yet."

"Cameras?"

Stone shakes her head. "The only camera that covers this area was smashed a few days ago. The replacement's due to be put up tomorrow."

We look at the body again, watching as the medical examiner moves down to the victim's feet and secures clear plastic bags around each foot to preserve any evidence.

Darren puts Stone in charge of organizing a search team for the immediate area. At crime-scene locations investigators look for things like footprints, a murder weapon, trace evidence, or anything that seems out of place. Stone and most of the others move off, leaving only a few of us hanging around the body, like insects drawn to a light.

"Okay, let's move him," the ME says.

The ME's assistant lays down a large white sheet of plastic about ten feet to the left of the body—an area that would have already been extensively photographed and inspected for evidence. He moves back to the body, crouching at the feet.

"He's tall," the ME says, staring at the vic. "We might need a hand."

Two of the remaining uniforms join in and they lift the body upward and step awkwardly to one side. Once the body is on the plastic, the photographer takes more shots.

Darren kneels down to get a closer look. "Let's turn him over."

They roll him onto his front. His arms are bound together at the back with a pair of handcuffs. The same cuffs from my vision?

The photographer takes several snaps of the victim's back and the ME's assistant bags the hands, just like the feet.

The ME examines the purplish marks on the body's back and buttocks—lividity. When your heart stops pumping blood, gravity takes over and the blood settles. In this case, lividity indicates the vic died on his back or was moved to his back shortly after death. The victim's arms, however, do not show any sign of the red splotches. They were not the lowest point of the body after death.

The ME notices the arms too. "Looks like he was cuffed like this at least a few hours after death." He tries to move the body's arms. "Rigor's still in. We're probably looking at a time of death around eighteen to thirty-six hours ago."

I nod. Rigor mortis begins in the eyelids a few hours after death and spreads to the face and neck, then the limbs. After about thirty-six hours it starts to dissipate until the body is completely supple once more, about forty-eight to seventy-two hours after death. However, so many factors affect the onset and dissipation of rigor that it can be an unreliable measure of time of death.

"Cause of death?" Darren asks.

"The eyes show some signs of asphyxiation but we'll know more back at the morgue."

Darren nods, accepting that, until the autopsy is done, the body can't do much talking. He stands up and turns to me. "Sorry, Sophie."

I shrug. "These things happen."

"We will do some touristy stuff while you're here. Promise."

I laugh, knowing the job only too well. "Let's see how we go."

"Not much of a vacation for you so far."

I look up at the blue sky. "The warmer weather and change of scenery is a break."

Darren's eyes follow the ME and his assistant as they move past us with the body on a stretcher. "I wouldn't mind sitting in on the autopsy," he says.

"The love heart?" I picture the large heart in the middle of the vic's torso.

"Yup." Darren puts his notebook back in his pocket. "It bothers me."

"Me, too." Marking the victim's body is not something most killers would trouble themselves with, not unless it had personal significance to them. "It could just be a message to the vic." That's one alternative. The other is more ominous—serial killers like to mark their victims, too.

Darren sighs and kicks the ground with his foot. "Damn it! I was really looking forward to a few days off."

Silence. If it does turn out to be a serial killer, Darren will want to be involved. Like me, he's particularly drawn to serial cases, where you have a chance to stop the killer and save lives.

He changes the topic. "You feel okay now?"

"Fine. It was just a flash."

"So it's back. The psychic stuff." His blue eyes bore into me.

I'm uncomfortable under his gaze and look away. "One." I hold my forefinger up for emphasis and meet his eyes again. "I've had one vision." I chew on my lip, wondering *why now? Why this body?* "Any chance you could get me into that autopsy?"

"Doesn't sound very touristy to me," Darren teases.

"I need to find out why this victim is so special. Why I got the vision." I can be honest with Darren because there's no Bureau pressure and no repercussions.

5

I put on a mask and place a small dollop of Vicks VapoRub underneath my nose—a luxury the forensic pathologist doesn't have. While I can guard my senses against the horrific odors, they can't because the sense of smell is essential during the autopsy procedure. For example, in the case of Nitrobenzene poisoning, the organs will usually smell of bitter almonds.

The body has been weighed and measured and taken out of its plastic wrapping. The ME starts with the external examination, searching the front of the body for puncture wounds, bruises or any other marks that could form part of our evidence. He starts with the head. In this case the vic already had a shaved head, but under normal autopsy procedures the head would be shaved and the body thoroughly washed down after an initial examination.

He points to a small gash. "Head wound at the top of the cranium," he says for us and for the microphone that's suspended above the autopsy table. He takes a closer look. "The wound is triangular in shape and approximately two inches in diameter. It may have been enough to knock him unconscious."

Darren nods and looks at the body on the slab. "That's one way to make sure he doesn't put up a fight."

It's a common tactic used for premeditated murder. With serial killers, it's usually just to transport the body. They intercept, knock the victim unconscious and then move them to a location of *their* choice. Then they continue on their terms. Generally they like the victim to be awake when they do the actual killing, so the victim is tied up or restrained in some other way. I flash back to my own abduction and instinctively rub my wrists, still sometimes able to feel the tight ropes burning into my skin. I force myself back into the land of the living…or in this case the dead.

The ME uses tweezers to extract a tiny particle of something from the head wound.

"What is it?" I ask.

"Looks like wood." He drops it into a test tube and labels it, putting it aside. He methodically makes his way across the rest of the skull, looking for any other marks. When he finds nothing else, he moves to the victim's face, leaning in close. Next he examines the nasal cavity and then opens the victim's mouth. He takes a swab from inside the mouth and labels it, placing it in another test tube next to the foreign matter. "The victim's nasal cavity is normal and a mouth swab has been taken," he says for the microphone.

He examines the neck carefully, and after a few seconds he puts some extra light on the subject. "Looks like we might have a cause of death." He points to the victim's neck. "It's hard to see bruises on dark skin, but I think we've got something. I'll need to look under the skin to be certain."

We instinctively lean in, while he dissects the skin away from the neck and examines the underlying muscles. "They're bruises all right." He points to some bleeding beneath the skin, the cause of a bruise. "Strangulation it is."

On the victim's neck muscles are several round patches of blood.

"Manual strangulation, judging by the pattern of bruising," the ME adds.

I imagine the man alive with someone's hands wrapped tightly around his neck. All things considered, it doesn't take long to take a human life. The vic was tall and, judging from his physique, very strong, yet he was strangled to death.

The ME continues down the body. At the love heart, he takes scrapings of the red matter and puts it in a test tube for analysis in the lab. Next are the arms. When he turns over the right arm a small tattoo is visible. About one inch long, it's of a single rose, stem and all. The rose has been outlined and colored with black, not red. He takes some photos of the tattoo before examining the arms and hands more thoroughly, which are normally the site of defensive wounds.

"Anything?" Darren asks.

The ME shakes his head. "The hands and arms have no defensive wounds."

"So maybe he was cuffed before death too?" I saw him handcuffed during sex, but that moment in his life could have been just before his death or weeks before.

Darren and I lean in. There are creases in the victim's wrists, like everyone's wrists, but across the creases are definite indentations, about half an inch wide.

The ME dissects the skin again, revealing traces of blood in a band across his wrist. "Slight bruising around the wrists indicates he had the handcuffs on prior to death." The ME is both answering my question and recording his findings on tape. Once the autopsy is complete, he will type up his official report for the file. For me, as a profiler, I usually read the report and rarely get to view an autopsy. But our presence here gives us a heads-up and allows us to ask questions.

"But the positioning of the hands behind the back definitely happened postmortem." The ME clarifies this fact and we nod our understanding. The victim was posed like that after death.

With the hands visually examined, the ME scrapes the underneath of the victim's fingernails. "We've got something here. Looks like dirt rather than skin, though." He transfers the grains into a vial and labels it. Next he takes prints of the victim—hopefully we'll come up with a match. Then again, the University of Arizona may get back to us with a photo-ID match before the forensics even comes through. Presumably our vic was a student there, given that he was found on campus.

We continue down the body, but find nothing else of interest on the victim's front. We turn the vic over and the body positioning at death is obvious. If he'd been lying on his cuffed hands, like he was when we found him, not only would blood have settled in his arms, but he would've also had darker areas on his buttocks where he'd been resting on his arms and hands. Through lividity, you can even get impressions of something the vic was lying on while the blood was settling. But the blotching on our vic is fairly even.

The ME checks for any signs of rape, such as rectal tearing, but the vic's given the all clear on this front.

He examines the back of the neck, again dissecting the skin away. "The killer's hands are very small." He looks up at us. "We could be looking at a woman."

"Really?" Darren's professional interest is piqued. There aren't many female killers, and most of them are victims of domestic violence who finally turn on their long-term tormentors.

The ME nods and points to the bruising on the back of the vic's neck. "The distance between the thumb print that we saw on the front of the vic's neck and the first finger mark here is short." He holds one hand up and stretches it out. "The distance between my thumb and forefinger is about four to five inches. Agent Anderson, do you mind?" He nods at my gloved hand. I mirror the ME's outstretched pose and put my hand against his much larger hand. The difference is at least an inch if not two. Looking at our hands, he says, "I'd say the killer is a small man, a woman, or even a teenager."

"But our vic's big, heavy," Darren says. "How would a woman or teenager have dumped his body?"

The ME shrugs. "I'm just reporting what the body tells me."

We nod. Darren's question is an area for investigators—for us, not the ME.

Once the external examination is finished, we help turn the vic over so he's resting on his back once again. The ME takes samples of the victim's hair—from his eyebrows, face and pubic region—before washing the body and x-raying it in preparation for the internal examination.

The ME cuts a V shape down the midline rather than the standard Y-section. A V-cut allows the front of the neck to be examined separately to confirm strangulation. I watched lots of autopsies back in Melbourne, but I still find my stomach clenches and bile rises in my throat as the skin and muscles are peeled back to reveal the internal organs.

"Blood first." The ME takes a needle and draws blood directly from the jugular vein. Next he makes a small incision in the bladder and takes a urine sample with a pipette. He keeps a running commentary as he progresses. Like the blood, this sample is put into a small glass vial, ready for analysis, and will be screened for alcohol, drugs, carbon monoxide, carbon dioxide, glucose and a range of poisons.

With the blood and urine work completed, the ME moves on to the organs. He slides the stomach away from the other organs and holds it over a metal dish, using surgical scissors to cut the stomach open and empty its contents into the container.

"So what was our fella's last meal?" I ask, glad of the layer of Vicks between my nose and the air.

He peers into the dish. "Not much. His stomach is almost empty. Looks like we have a small amount of meat."

"Just meat?" I ask—not many people eat meat without some other accompaniment, like bread, vegetables, fries or something.

"Uh huh. And not much of it."

Another oddity. Our vic is big and he'd need a lot of food to sustain his body. "Seems strange for a guy this size," I comment.

The ME nods. "I'll send the contents off to the lab for further analysis."

Next he cuts away the small intestine, tying it off at each end before putting it into a separate metal dish, again making comments for the microphone. He examines the chest cavity and other organs, removing and weighing as necessary, before inspecting the throat section carefully.

"The hyoid bone is intact, but I'd expect that given his age."

The horseshoe-shaped hyoid bone in the neck starts off quite malleable and doesn't become brittle and prone to breaking until we reach our late thirties to early forties. In an older strangulation victim, the hyoid bone would usually be broken.

"But manual strangulation is definitely our cause of death," he continues. "Pending anything strange from the lab."

Of course it's possible the victim was strangled *and* poisoned, and then the ME would have to assess which one was the primary cause of death.

"Anything more on the time of death?" Darren asks.

He shakes his head. "Eighteen to thirty-six hours is as good as it's going to get." Forensic pathologists use rigor mortis, liver temperature and the presence of lividity to estimate the time of death, but it can only be an estimate. Another avenue is insect activity, entomology, but it's mostly useful in cases where the body is found days or weeks after death.

Finally, the ME sews the V-section up. "Autopsy finished at—" he checks the clock on the wall "—five o'clock in the afternoon."

Darren and I leave the ME to clean up, and walk through the corridors of the Pima County medical examiner's office. Outside, a water fountain glistens in the spring sunlight and a few people sit around it, enjoying the late afternoon sun. Compared to DC, it's balmy.

"So how's Stone doing?"

Darren shrugs. "Haven't heard from her. If she got a match from the U of A or from a missing-persons report she would have called. Maybe his fingerprints will be on the database."

I nod. "If we don't find any matches..." I leave the sentence unfinished.

"I know. A John Doe." Darren runs a hand through his hair. "I'd like to drop into the station real quick before we head back to my house. Okay?"

"Fine by me."

We head west down East District Street and take a left onto the I-10, heading for Phoenix. We only drive for about five minutes before Darren takes Exit 258. After a few more rights we're driving into the garage underneath the Tucson Police Headquarters at 270 South Stone Avenue.

We catch the lift up to the third floor and make our way through the corridors to the Homicide area. Darren briefly introduces me to the other four detectives in his department, including the elusive Bolson.

"And this is my real home." He motions to a small open-plan cubicle that he and Stone share. Darren's desk is tidiness personified and every sheet of paper, every pen, seems to have its own spot.

"Doesn't look very lived-in to me," I tease.

He shrugs. "Organized on the desk means organized up here." He taps his head. I hope he's wrong; otherwise I'm screwed.

Stone is on the phone, but she looks up and gives us both a smile and a nod. It sounds like she's still tracking down missing-person reports.

With the show-and-tell over, Darren looks up to the far corner of the area and a glassed office. Etched on the door I can just make out the name Sergeant Harris, who is Darren's boss. I didn't meet Harris on my visit six months ago and I hope he doesn't mind me hanging around. The FBI badge can open doors, but it can also close them. Some cops don't like the Bureau on their turf.

"Let's go." Darren makes a beeline for the office and I follow. He knocks once and Harris motions for us to come in. Harris is a big, burly man, with only a few strands of hair that he can still call his own. His face is round and red, and he definitely wouldn't pass the Bureau's yearly physical. Darren makes the introductions. Harris is polite, but I immediately get the sense he's not overjoyed by my presence.

"On vacation?"

"That's right, sir."

"Do you usually go to autopsies for fun?"

I smile. "Not normally, no. Thanks for letting me sit in."

He nods but his face is still impassive.

I look him in the eyes, not challenging him, but trying to make a connection. The truth, or at least part of the truth, often works. "You know what it's like…when a body like that throws itself at you it's hard to keep your distance." We all know that the heart the killer drew on the vic's chest is a message of some sort. The killer's talking, and we just have to listen.

Finally he smiles. "Yeah, I remember." He moves to the front of his desk and props himself on the corner. It creaks slightly under his weight. "Darren tells me you specialize in serial killers."

"That's right."

"Nasty occupation for a lady."

His words remind me of something my mother would say, but I'm guessing he's testing me, baiting me.

"Nasty occupation for anyone." I pause. "But rewarding when you get your man."

"Yes." Again the smile, the hint of nostalgic recognition. "Well, it was nice to get a couple of our unsolved murders off the books. For that I thank you."

The DC Slasher killed three women in Arizona and all three cold cases are now closed.

"Anyway," Harris moves back around his desk, "you're welcome to sit in on this case." He shakes his head. "Especially if you're crazy enough to spend your vacation time on it."

"Thanks."

"We're just getting it started for Stone," Darren says. "That's all."

Harris snorts. "I'll believe it when I see it, Carter."

Back at Darren's desk, he rolls a spare chair over from the corner and we crowd his computer terminal.

"VICAP?" I say, assuming it will be our first port of call.

"You bet."

VICAP stands for the Violent Criminal Apprehension Program and sits, alongside my unit, under the umbrella of the National

Center for the Analysis of Violent Crime. It was created in the early
eighties to investigate serial offences on a nationwide basis and has
two main offerings: the VICAP software and twenty VICAP consultants based in Quantico. The software system is an online database
of violent crimes. Police can log new and old cases in the system,
and can also search the database for any similar crimes. So if you've
just found a young girl whose body was mutilated in a particular way,
you type it into the system and the database will return any matches,
from anywhere in the U.S. It's a great system, the only problem is
that not all cops use it, so similar murders might not be in the database.

The VICAP consultants work both reactively to a department's
request and proactively by continually monitoring cases that are entered by the cops and comparing them to other violent crimes. If
any potential matches are found, VICAP will contact the local law-
enforcement officers and coordinate an interstate, inter-team analysis.

Once Darren's computer is fired up, he launches the VICAP
software. He types "heart shape on chest" into VICAP's search facility, and hits Enter. We wait as the software trawls through the online database.

After a minute or so the search function returns a "no matches
found" screen. This is both good and bad news. On the one hand it
probably means that this is the offender's first homicide—unless the
murder wasn't logged in VICAP—and first-timers are generally easier to catch because they make more mistakes. On the other hand,
it also means we'll only have the evidence at hand, with no other
cases to help us analyze the killer and his or her patterns.

"Let's log it anyway," I say. Logging the murder will take an hour
or two as we go through the extensive online questionnaire, but it
will get the homicide into the nationwide database. Logging it is also
the first step to getting a VICAP consultant to look at the case.

"You sure?" Darren looks at his watch. "It's nearly six o'clock."

I shrug. "May as well get it over and done with." Besides, as part of the same department, it would look pretty poor if I didn't encourage the murder to be logged as soon as possible.

We go through the questionnaire, entering all the details we know so far, including victim information, offender information and crime-scene data. Many fields we have to leave blank, but hopefully in the next few days some of this information will come to light.

"I'll call Quantico and get an analyst on it, too."

"Great."

I look at my watch—just after 8:00 p.m. on Friday. "It'll have to be for Monday morning."

I dial the direct line of the VICAP consultant I've worked with the most, Barry Evans. I get his voice mail and leave a message with the basic details. I include the fact that we could be looking for a female or a younger killer. "He'll look into it Monday morning, as soon as he gets the message." I'm confident Evans will take action on the phone call quickly.

"You jumping the queue?"

I smile. "If you've got the connections…"

"True. Well, let's see what else we've got." He turns to Stone, who's on the phone.

"Yes, okay. Thanks for your help." Stone hangs up the phone. "My aching ear." She rubs her right ear. "What an awesome day."

"What are you still doing here anyway? Go home, Stone."

"Look who's talking." Stone raises her eyebrows.

Darren stands up. "Walking out the door right now. No luck?"

I stand up, too, and stretch.

"Nada." Stone turns off her computer. "Although we now know the guy's definitely not a U of A student."

"Really?" I lean on the partition. "Maybe the doer is."

BlackWidow: Any more news?
AmericanPsycho: No. They're still running the same stories.
BlackWidow: So they haven't IDed him yet?

AmericanPsycho: Not yet, but they will. He's got a record, after all.

BlackWidow: They haven't mentioned the heart either.

AmericanPsycho: You know they don't like to release all the details.

DialM: True.

AmericanPsycho: Our first kill has made its mark.

BlackWidow: You know what they say—it's never as good as the first time. I mean the very first.

NeverCaught: My first was definitely special, but I enjoy it more now.

AmericanPsycho: Sex or murder?

NeverCaught: Both.

AmericanPsycho: My first was fantastic. It was the same person.

BlackWidow: Yes, they're inextricably linked for me. It's hard to have sex with someone and then not kill them.

NeverCaught: I love that moment of realization. When they know they're gonna die. That look is like a drug. You just want more.

BlackWidow: Agreed.

NeverCaught: If it's a straight kill, they may not realize it until the knife penetrates through their rib cage.

BlackWidow: That your weapon of choice, Never?

NeverCaught: Yes. I love knives. What about you, BW?

BlackWidow: Strangulation.

NeverCaught: Really? You must be one butch chick.

BlackWidow: My men are always handcuffed to a bed, and it's during the act so they just think I'm kinky. Besides, it doesn't take much strength if you know exactly where to apply pressure—the vagus nerve.

DialM: The whole process has to be real slow for me. I chain them up and starve them. Can't wait to get my Ling.

6

A woman runs down a corridor, trapped. Someone is close behind her, chasing her, laughing. He catches up to her and grabs her by her long, dark curls. He drags her down the corridor and she screams. They move into a bedroom and her screams become more hysterical.

A knife comes down on top of her. The screams are soon silenced as multiple stab wounds take their toll. Blood spurts everywhere.

She's dead. He's sitting on top of her, straddling her. He leans back and smiles, his eyes gleaming with frenzied satisfaction. He studies the blood splatters...beautiful.

I wake up gasping for air. A violent shudder passes through my body as the last part of my dream swirls around in my conscious mind. What disturbs me most is the lingering sensation of the killer's mind. He thought it was beautiful. Another shudder engulfs me, followed instantly by a wave of nausea. Despite the gore, my mind is still in that strange half-awake, half-asleep place. I give in to the tiredness and remain semiconscious in bed until roused by a faint knocking on my door.

I wake up more fully, but still feel groggy and disorientated. "Come in."

Darren opens the door and greets me with a wide smile. "Morning." Dressed in blue jeans and a long-sleeved white top, he holds a glass of orange juice in his right hand.

"Hi." I look at the bedside clock. It's 8:00 a.m. "Wow, I can't believe I slept so late." That's two mornings this week. And last night I didn't resort to a midnight gym excursion.

"You are on vacation." He hands me the fresh juice. "Straight orange will have to do—I don't have any carrots."

"I'm impressed," I say, acknowledging his memory. I gulp down the juice and hand the glass back to him. "Thanks."

He nods, lingers for a few seconds and then turns. "There's a towel on the chair for you." He motions toward a wooden chair near the door and walks out.

About twenty minutes later I'm showered and I join Darren at his small kitchen table. While he pours two cups of coffee from his brewer, I get myself a bowl of granola and cover it with milk.

A couple of mouthfuls into my breakfast I decide to tell him. "I had a dream."

He sits down opposite me. "I take it we're not talking about a stock-standard dream."

I shake my head.

"So that's two instances."

"Yes." I drop my spoon in the bowl. "And I can't figure out why. Why all of a sudden?"

"Was the dream about our John Doe?"

"No. A woman." I roll my eyes, frustrated.

"Well, I did have a theory on the John Doe." He pours himself a large bowl of Cheerios.

"Really?" I'm relieved Darren can shed some light on it, because I sure as hell don't have a clue. "And?"

He chews quickly and his Adam's apple bobs with a large gulp. "The cases you've done the last six months, you said they've all been from Quantico."

"Yes." I say the word slowly, trying to work out where he's heading.

"This time it's not a photo of a crime scene. It *is* a crime scene. The body yesterday is your first time back at a real-life crime scene."

Darren could be on to something. I finish the thought. "So I'm closer to the case."

"Exactly. Physically and psychologically." He scoops up a huge mound of Cheerios and shovels them in.

"It's a good theory, a great theory…except it doesn't explain the dream last night, unless we're talking about the same killer. But our first victim was male and strangled and the subject of my dream was a woman who was stabbed to death. Plus, it's also different from the way the visions were triggered last time." I voice the discrepancies.

"Oh." Darren seems somewhat disappointed. "So what do you think triggered your psychic abilities six months ago?"

"People I cared about were in danger. The case was personal, even though I didn't realize that at the time."

"And that was your first-ever experience?"

We're starting to get onto shaky ground, painful ground, and I don't know if I'm ready to go there with Darren, not yet at least.

"Yes," I lie.

"So you think you're in danger now? Or someone you care about is?"

I bite my lip. God I hope not. "I dunno."

We finish our cereal in relative silence, both overwhelmed by the thought of the killer being close again.

I drain my coffee.

"More?" Darren offers.

"Have we got time?"

"All the time in the world. We'll finish up breakfast, drop into the station and then do something fun." He pours out two half cups, finishing the jug. "So tell me about the dream."

I try to recollect the images. "A woman was killed."

"And you're sure it wasn't a normal nightmare?"

"When I have one of these visions or dreams it feels different, more real. Plus I always have this overwhelming sense of impending doom afterward."

He nods. "What else do you remember?"

I bite my lip again, trying to force the memories into my consciousness. "I remember a woman. She was stabbed. And I remember the feeling of…" I search for the word "…satisfaction that the killer felt during the act."

"Anything else?"

"His eyes. I remember his eyes."

"That's something. That's good."

"Know offhand what percentage of the population has dark brown eyes?" I slam back into the chair and shake my head. It was like this with the Slasher case—hints of information but not enough to really make a difference. Still, this time I have a clear image of the girl. Maybe I can find her before it's too late. Maybe I can save her.

"You'll get better at it. Try not to get frustrated. And remember what you said to me at the hospital in DC."

"I know, I know."

He reminds me anyway. "That your gift could help others."

But my gift hasn't been helping anyone. Not recently.

Darren glances at the clock. "Let's get moving." He turns back to me. "First stop, the station, and then we're heading for the Arizona-Sonora Desert Museum."

"Really?"

"I told you we'd do some touristy stuff."

I nod, not fully convinced. I know Darren, and I know myself, and I doubt either of us will be able to walk away from a case that's already sucking us in.

"And I'll tell you some of my aunt's tricks in the car," he says.

His aunt's tricks… I wish I knew whether this psychic stuff was back for good. One waking vision and one dream in less than twenty-four hours? Someone or something's trying to get my attention.

I wait until we're on the road before I prompt him. "So?"

He swings the wheel to the left and starts to brake for an upcoming red light. "It's like meditation. You have to open yourself up to your hunches, your second sight, so you can experience it fully and help others. My aunt used to sit quietly by herself every morning as soon as she woke up and every night before she went to bed. In the morning she said it was to access any dreams from the night before, and in the evening it was to unwind and let go of everything she'd seen or heard during the day. Including the bad stuff."

"Did she see murder? Violence?"

"Not very often, no. She was a professional psychic, not in law enforcement. You've got to remember that you're surrounded by crime, by criminals. It's natural that you'd tap into that side of the gift."

I nod, reluctantly.

Darren continues. "When Rose worked on a criminal case she said it was hard. Real hard."

I nod again, this time with enthusiasm. He ain't wrong there.

"You can handle it, Sophie. I know you can."

"I guess," I say, but I don't know if I believe it. I think of the girl from my dream and know I have to try. I breathe deeply, in and out, concentrating on nothing but my breath. After about five minutes, I take myself back to the dream. I instantly see the woman being dragged down a corridor by her hair. She's crying, screaming and I recognize that feeling all too well. It's a moment of pure fear, of all-consuming panic. I take a deep breath in and it feels like I'm choking. But I'm not choking, I'm totally consumed by fear. "I can't." I open my eyes and shake my head. "I can't." I have to fight to gain control of my emotions, to steady my voice and my breathing. All I want to do is run, and keep running.

Darren glances at me and puts his hand on top of mine. "It's okay, Sophie. It's okay." He pauses. "We can try again later."

The thought of later doesn't thrill me, but I'm more distracted by the warmth of Darren's hand on mine. I look down at our hands and Darren immediately withdraws his.

Silence. Then, "You okay?"

"Yeah." I don't voice my concern—that she's lying dead somewhere right now.

When we arrive at the station Stone is already at her desk, and she looks like she's been in for a while.

"Hey, Stone. What's up?"

"Hi, Anderson." She does a double-take. "Carter's got you working? Today?"

"I'm just returning the favor." Darren shuffles some papers on his desk. "Anderson worked me damn hard in DC."

I smile, relieved to be distracted by cop banter. "He took a bullet an' all."

Darren nods and sighs heavily. "Like I said, damn hard." He speaks slowly and lowers the natural timbre of his voice.

Stone and I both laugh. Ironic really—that people brag about getting shot. I guess it is something to be proud of…but it's not the getting shot part, it's the surviving part that's the real clincher.

"Well, you sure as hell wouldn't find me in here on my day off." This time her comment is directed to both of us.

"What time you get in this morning, Stone?" Darren's voice oozes confidence.

She rolls her eyes. "You got me."

"Tell her, Stone." Darren nods his head in my direction.

"I got in at six. But I am on duty today."

Darren sits down at his desk. "You don't make Homicide unless you're a workaholic." He swivels the chair outward, toward Stone. "So, what have we got?"

"*We've* got nothing, given you're on vacation. *I've* got…well not much."

Darren waves his hand in small circles. "Give it up."

"Nothing on John Doe's identity," Stone tells us. "I've moved from the U of A student photos to photos from the missing-persons database, matching our guy on age, height and weight and then reviewing the photos. But I haven't found anything yet and I'm almost done."

Darren shakes his head. "It's damn hard to close them when you can't identify the vic." He sighs, loud and deep. "State or national?"

"National. I've been calling around a bit too. In case he's new and his photo isn't online yet. But no luck."

Darren nods. "They should be running his fingerprints today or tomorrow in the AFIS."

AFIS, which stands for the Automated Fingerprint Identification System, is a computer network that compares fingerprints against a database and returns any similar prints that are in the system. It's then up to a fingerprint expert to manually go through the computer matches and decide if the prints really do match. It's harder to get a match from a victim, because the database mostly holds fingerprints of suspects and convicted criminals, plus those in law enforcement and the defense industry.

"Anything else?" Darren asks.

"Zip. You guys should go and...do something."

"One step ahead of you, as usual." Darren smirks. "We're going to the Arizona-Sonora Desert Museum."

"Cool." Stone is enthusiastic, so I assume the museum is good.

"But first, let's quickly go through this. Make sure you're heading in the right direction." Darren manages to say it without being condescending. After all, Stone is a rookie on murder investigations, comparatively speaking.

We move into a project room to go over the details of the case. Darren writes three columns on the whiteboard—*victim, crime scene* and *suspect*.

"So, the body." He scribbles down what we know about the victim, one row per item.

African-American male

Early twenties

Not U of A student

Cause of death: manual strangulation

Time of death: approximately Thursday

Naked

Handcuffed before death
Head wound
Posed with handcuffs after death

"We'll need to add *lab work* to this, Stone."

She scribbles on her own notepad while she speaks. "Tox screen, blood work, anything forensics gets off the chunk of wood in the guy, and fingerprints. An ID would be real helpful."

"Yup. And fingernails. They found some dirt underneath his nails."

"I know, you told me already." Stone is not resentful of Darren's reminders, more accepting. "And the love heart—it'll be interesting to see what that was painted on with."

Darren moves across to the crime-scene column. "Forensics didn't find much at the scene, so this one could be tricky, especially given it's obviously not our primary scene."

Darren's referring to the fact that the vic was murdered somewhere else and then transported and posed postmortem. There may be evidence at the primary scene, but there's nothing at the university.

"In the meantime," he continues, "I want you to go back to the U of A with a photo of our John Doe and see if somebody hasn't seen the guy before. Take some uniforms with you to help canvass the campus. He wasn't a student, so what was he doing there? And more important, who was he with?"

Stone nods, taking in Darren's instructions. "Don't forget it's Saturday."

"True, we won't have everyone there. But the place will still be busy." Darren moves to the suspect column. "This is an even bigger blank." He writes *Female or small male—teenager* and then underneath that he writes *Body dumping?*

"Body dumping?" Stone questions.

"The strangulation marks indicate a woman or small male, but would they have the strength to dump a body?"

Stone shrugs. "The dump site is very close to the street so they wouldn't have had far to go from a car to our spot."

"True." Darren taps the marker against the whiteboard. "Any ideas on the love heart, Sophie?"

"It could indicate a romantic involvement. Perhaps the killer was with the victim, or wanted to be."

Stone looks at me. "Does that work for a male or female killer?"

"Both. Given there's nothing in VICAP, this could be a one-off. A jilted girlfriend, or a boyfriend with small hands."

"To track down a partner we need to know the victim's identity," Stone says.

"Yup." Darren stops tapping the marker and stares out the window instead. "What about the nakedness?"

"Indicates the killer felt personal about the vic," I say. "Possibly due to a sexual partnership or perceived attraction on the killer's part. It can also be a form of punishment—leaving the body naked and exposed for all the world to see."

"And that leads us back to the U of A." Darren points the marker at Stone. "See what you turn up on campus." He puts the marker back on the whiteboard ledge and hovers awkwardly, silently.

Stone stands up. "Go! You guys will love the museum."

Darren is conflicted.

"If you want to stay here, I don't mind," I say.

He only hesitates for a second. "No, no. You've got to see some of Tucson. Besides, Stone will call me the minute she finds out anything. Won't you, Stone?"

Stone gives Darren an exaggerated smile. "Of course. And I'm sure Bolson will be around to help out the newest kid on the block."

Darren laughs. "Not likely."

On the way down to the car I quiz Darren. "Are you sure about this? You could cancel your leave and work the case. I really don't mind."

"Nope. I'm all yours for the rest of today and all day tomorrow. What's another murder case?"

Despite what he says, I know it's personal for him. It's *his* case, *his* turf.

"Mmm."

"Realistically we're going to be sitting around waiting for forensics to call, or shoving photographs in front of college brats."

"Charming," I say, but Darren's right. There's a lot of grunt work involved in law enforcement, and canvassing the students won't exactly be the most fulfilling or challenging day on the job. Nor will it require our experience. "What about my visions?"

"We can go back to the U of A tomorrow if you like. See if it triggers another one. But today, we need a day off."

"Maybe the woman from my dream is a student there."

We get in the car and he starts it up. "Can you describe the woman?"

I nod.

"To a sketch artist?"

"Yes." My voice quickens with the prospect of finding the girl. I reach across and put my hand on the steering wheel, looking at Darren.

"Monday?" he says, but he already knows the answer. I can't wait two days, not if she's about to be targeted. And Darren wouldn't let it wait either. He sighs and turns the engine off.

"We'll get a sketch done. Stone and the uniforms can show it around at the campus later today. We can also see if anybody in the station recognizes her as a dead Jane Doe or a missing person."

"I'm hoping she's alive and kicking somewhere, not a dead Jane Doe. But I guess we need to cover all bases."

"We do."

"What are we going to tell the Tucson force?"

He shrugs. "We'll lie, of course." He looks pensive for a moment. "There's not much you can do about the timing thing. Rose used to complain about it. She said sometimes she'd have a sense about whether what she'd seen was in the past, present or future, but often that was the one detail that eluded her."

"Great."

"Sorry to be the bearer of bad news." We're both silent as he opens the car door. "Let's get that sketch done."

An hour later I'm sitting with James Powers, the police sketch artist Darren called in, putting the finishing touches on the woman from my dream. A young guy, in his early twenties, Powers is hunched over his sketch pad and his left hand darts around the page. He looks more like a painter, an eccentric artist, than a cop.

He's totally absorbed in his drawing, and at the moment he's filling in the woman's dark curls—her hair's the last thing he asked me about so I assume that's what he's concentrating on. I can't see the sketch from where I sit, but so far he's shown it to me three times, first to check the shape of the nose, then the eyes, then the mouth. Powers wanted to bring the facial features together from description alone, and then to refine it after I see the face as a whole. I've worked with sketch artists before and most of them have their own style. The process can also be done on a computer with an identikit, bringing together predrawn sections until the face looks right to the witness, but I prefer the old-fashioned way. It's definitely one thing that humans do better than computers.

Finally his hand comes to a stop. "I think we're finished."

He seems tentative, and I'm reminded of Darren's description of him. Apparently the guy's only been in the job for a month, and is still lacking in confidence. It doesn't exactly elicit a whole lot of trust in his talents, despite Darren's reassurances.

"There's nothing else you remember?" Hesitation again.

"No. That's it."

Powers reluctantly, and slowly, turns his pad toward me. "The moment of truth," he says.

The girl has come to life on Powers's sketch pad; every detail is perfect. "Wow!" is all I can manage. No wonder Darren raved about the guy.

"So, it's accurate?" He's still unsure. "The face shape? The ears?"

"All spot on. You're really, really good at this, Powers."

He smiles, a wide, relieved smile. "Great." He tears the page off his pad and hands it to me. "So, what are you going to do with it?"

"See if she doesn't ring a bell with someone. Dead or alive." I don't elaborate, I don't tell Powers the lie Darren and I have come up with—that it's a Bureau case of a girl who was seen being shoved into a car near the University of Arizona.

Powers stands up and stretches, reaching his hands to the sky. Then he puts his hands on his lower back and arches slightly. "I've got to learn to sit right when I do these things."

"Good idea. I'd say your services will be in demand."

A slight blush rises in his face. He picks up the tools of his trade—the pad, several pencils of different grades and an eraser. "Thanks, Agent Anderson. You're the first FBI agent I've sketched for."

Perhaps that fact made him more nervous; certainly his relief is evident.

"Well, I'm impressed."

We're in one of the station's project rooms, for quiet and privacy, and I make a move toward the door. He follows and we wander out to the main hustle and bustle of the station.

"You coming up?" I ask.

"Nope, I've got another appointment lined up across town. Rape victim."

I wince. "Good luck."

He nods. "Bye." He turns left, toward the exit, and I head for the stairs and Homicide.

Darren's waiting for me and we get things moving with the sketch right away, making copies. We give a few copies to Stone, who's about to head off to the university with four uniformed officers she's hijacked. We spin the story and ask her to show the sketch with the photos of John Doe.

She gives us both a disapproving look. "Fine. But you guys really should get your asses out of here."

"I'll just show this around," says Darren, holding up the sketch, "and then we'll hit the museum."

But it takes us nearly a full hour to circulate the sketch and get back to Darren's car. No one on duty recognized the girl, but hopefully someone will in the next couple of days. We've also circulated the sketch to neighboring states, hoping someone may recognize her in another state.

"So, are you ready to be riveted by the museum?" Darren tries again.

"Yes, now I am." We've done everything we can, for today at least. And tomorrow, Sunday, it's the U of A and maybe another vision. But I still feel ineffectual, as though I should be doing more for the girl. I clench my fists in my lap, thinking of the brunette's fear. Thinking of my fear.

NeverCaught: Can't believe it's only Sunday. Another four days until I get my next chance.

BlackWidow: You'll just have to wait, Never.

NeverCaught: Easy for you to say. You got the first kill—Malcolm.

AmericanPsycho: Four days will go quick.

NeverCaught: Thank God. I'm good to go now.

DialM: I find our selection quite tiresome at times.

NeverCaught: I think it's fun watching how pathetic they are. Their sense of time is already totally shot.

AmericanPsycho: Yes, that worked well. No watches, no clocks, darkness most of the time. They've got no idea.

BlackWidow: My Jonathan knew their sense of timing was probably off.

DialM: Hmmm... I don't like him. He's too smart.

NeverCaught: Forget about him. Think about the others...like Brigitte. Have you looked at her bio?

Name: Brigitte Raine
Age: 26
Height: 5' 9"
Weight: 130 pounds
Eye color: Brown
Hair color: Brown

IQ: 97

Occupation: Phone-sex worker.

Family: Parents divorced, no siblings. No contact with father, mother in France.

Home: New Orleans.

President's take: Brigitte is stunning. Her heritage—French, Brazilian, American—combines to make an exotic beauty. High cheekbones, voluptuous lips and a womanly figure will make her popular with most members of the club.

She is the woman every man lusts after.

DialM: Yes. You have certainly accurately described her, Psycho.

NeverCaught: Can't decide…the exotic beauty or Cindy the slut. Might just have to have both.

BlackWidow: Cindy's not exactly the sharpest knife in the drawer, but she's hardly a slut.

NeverCaught: Whatever.

DialM: Every person has his own likes and dislikes, Never. That's why we're individuals. Society would crumble without individuality. And leaps in science, math, technology and infrastructure would be impossible. And art, music… they might not exist.

NeverCaught: And you think *they're* boring?

7

Monday morning hits without any developments in the case. Stone had no luck at the university IDing our John Doe or the girl from the sketch and the university was a total blowout for me too. I sat at the crime scene for nearly an hour yesterday, hoping a premonition or a flashback would come to me but, just like before, this gift seems to have two purposes—to frustrate me or to scare the hell out of me. Neither option is appealing.

I'm making my way up the stairs with a tray of coffee when my phone rings. I juggle the coffees and fish my phone out of the back pocket of my jeans. "Anderson."

"Why am I getting a request from you on your vacation?" It's Barry Evans, the VICAP consultant.

I laugh but ignore the question. "Just tell me what you found." Barry would have been able to perform a much more detailed search than Darren and I.

"Nothing."

"Oh. Definitely no matches?" I'm both relieved and surprised.

"Definitely no matches. Are you thinking serial or one-off?"

"I don't know. The body was naked, posed postmortem with the handcuffs behind his back. And there was that heart."

"Yup, I saw that."

"I was kinda leaning toward serial, but I must be wrong." Hunches aren't always right, even mine.

"This could simply be the first kill," he says. "Tucson might get another one in a few months' time."

"True." I pause. "What about hits on female killers, male victims?"

"Got a few on that. Including one killer we've been tracking for some time. But the MO and scene are all wrong. Your vic matches the profile, but this killer takes them to a motel room, handcuffs them to the bed, has sex with them and strangles them."

"Some elements match."

"Yes, but she leaves them there. She likes them to be discovered in some seedy motel room. Plus there's no love heart on the chest, and they're handcuffed to a bed, not cuffed behind their back."

"Yeah, okay." I climb the last step and my breathing is slightly irregular.

"Did I interrupt something, Anderson?" I can hear the innuendo in Evans's voice.

"No! I'm climbing steps, you jerk."

"Just making sure. I know what I'd be doing if I was on vacation."

"Goodbye, Evans." I hang up and make my way through to the Homicide area. Stone sits at her desk looking expectantly at Darren, who's on the phone and looking animated. *News.* He puts the phone down and looks up, his eyes wide with excitement. "We've got an ID on the John Doe!"

Stone and I crowd him.

"The vic's name is Malcolm Jackson. He was arrested on a possession charge in 2003. Marijuana." Darren pauses to pick out his coffee from the tray. "In Chicago."

"Chicago?" Stone says. She also takes her coffee, leaving my caramel macchiato in the tray.

"Could have moved here in the last few years," I say before taking a sip and letting a small amount of the hot, sweet drink trickle down my throat. I know coffee is a stimulant but it's also soothing somehow.

Darren grins, a big grin. "Either way, we've got an ID."

"Now we've really got something to investigate," I say.

Stone shakes her head. "You're not enjoying the Tucson sights? Was the museum that bad?"

"I had a great time," I say, but it's a partial lie. The museum was amazing, but I couldn't keep my mind off the brunette from my dream.

Darren puts his coffee down and his grin disappears. "The parents."

"Oh, yeah." I sit down. No one likes being the bearer of bad news, but telling someone their child is dead...

Darren opens a window on his computer.

"And the ME's office got back with some of the lab work," Stone says. "Blood-alcohol level was 0.05 and no other drugs or toxins in his system. The meat substance in the stomach has been identified as ham, and the heart shape was body paint. The lab compared its chemical composition with some of the major manufacturers and got a hit. It's Stage F/X Tube Makeup from FX Inc. Color's red, obviously."

"Is that a common brand?" I ask.

Stone nods. "Retails at $2.95." She pauses. "The sand and wood are still with trace."

I move my attention back to Darren's computer screen. A couple of seconds later Malcolm Jackson's details come up.

Malcolm Jackson
Illinois driver's license: 4583-1254-5001
Date of birth: 01/15/1985
Brown eyes
6' 4"
215 pounds
212 E Randolph Street
Oak Park, IL 60601-6401
Traffic offences:

Speeding 05/05/2002, 70miles/hour in 60 zone
Criminal record:
10/05/2003 Arrest for possession of marijuana

Darren turns around to face us. "I guess I'd better call Oak Park."

8

The next day we arrive at the station at 12:30 p.m. for the scheduled 1:00 p.m. conference call with Detective Hamill from Oak Park Homicide. Yesterday Hamill was going to inform the parents and gather as much information as he could about the victim for our one o'clock phone hookup. We arrived early to give Darren time to follow up on the sketch of the girl from my dream, even though we probably would have heard from someone if she looked familiar.

He heads off, sketch in hand, while I hang out at his desk. We decided it would be quicker for him to do it himself, given he knows everyone in the station.

"Feel like you're having a vacation?" Stone asks me, with disbelief in her voice.

"Sure. We've even been up to Mt. Lemmon this morning. It was gorgeous."

She nods and seems relieved that the morning was spent on tourism and not the case. "Pretty spot. I go hiking there sometimes in the summer."

I can easily imagine Stone's stocky frame bounding up a hiking track to the summit.

"Are you managing without Carter?"

She snorts. "Well, I'm hardly without him."

"A couple of hours here and there…" I haven't added it up, but since I arrived last Friday, Darren certainly hasn't been full-time on the case.

"True." She leans back in her chair. "It's not too bad actually. I think he's overrated." The sarcasm is obvious.

We both laugh. Darren's a good cop, and no one would seriously contest that.

While Stone continues to work, I use Darren's computer to check my e-mail—both my FBI account and my personal one. I spend most of the time typing an e-mail to a good friend back home, Lisa, who's a TV journalist for Channel 10 in Melbourne. At five minutes to one, Darren appears.

"Any luck?"

He shakes his head. "Nothing." He pauses and moves in close. "Maybe it's time we tried again. Tried to help you remember that dream."

I grimace from the memory of the beautiful young woman's panic. But Darren's right. I had that dream for a reason and I should do something about it. I need to snap out of this complacency. I nod. "Okay. This afternoon at your place."

"Good decision." He gives me one of his best reassuring smiles. Easy for him to say. He doesn't see it all in his head and, worse still, *feel* it.

An hour later, we've got a much better picture of who Malcolm Jackson was, although we still don't know what he was doing in Arizona.

Malcolm lived alone, in a one-bedroom apartment in Oak Park. He worked as an upscale male escort and was last seen just over a week ago. He hadn't been reported missing because he'd told his family, friends and employer that he was going to New York for a few weeks.

Hamill also told us that the parents did not approve of his work at the escort agency, Rendez-Vous, but that he was saving money to go to college.

Darren looks at me. "Think we should fly up to Chicago?"

I shrug. "We need to work out what he was doing here, that's for sure. What the *connection* is." I stress the word connection, hoping Darren will pick up my double meaning—his connection to Arizona and his connection to me.

Darren gives me a quick single nod and then turns to Stone. "Stone, any luck on campus?" Stone had been back canvassing the students yesterday.

"No. No one recognized him or the girl from the sketch. And we managed to get through lots of students."

Darren stands up. "Okay."

A beat of silence.

"How much would it cost to fly to Chicago?" I ask.

With his hands in his pockets, Darren gives me a small shrug. "Couple hundred I guess."

"I've never been to Chicago..."

Stone shakes her head. "You're crazy."

"No, just...involved." If being around Malcolm's body triggered my initial vision, maybe being at his house will be as powerful, if not more so. I haven't exactly got lots of options here.

"It'll be cold in Chicago." She looks up at me and smiles, a genuine smile.

She's got a point. I hope my packing can handle the extra chill.

We drive back to Darren's house, ready to spend the rest of the afternoon off duty...and to try to find out more about my dream. We sit in the lounge and Darren takes me through the relaxation process. After about ten minutes, he gets me to think about the dream, the woman. At first the dream replays in my mind quickly, as flashes: the girl being dragged by her hair, a knife, blood.

"Go through the dream again and try to slow it down," Darren suggests. He waits several seconds, then asks, "What's happening?"

I start from the first point I can remember. She's running. Then he's got hold of her. "He's taking her into a room. Oh God." It's only a memory, a re-creation of the dream, but still panic engulfs me and my heart races. I clench my fists tightly and rub them up and down my thighs, hard.

Darren takes hold of my wrists. "It's all right. You're safe."

He gradually brings my rubbing motion to a stop. "Did you hear anything in the dream? Did he say anything?"

The memory had been silent, but I concentrate on my senses, including my hearing, wondering if maybe the original dream included sound. Suddenly in the re-creation I can hear her screams as well as see and feel them. The noise is a bloodcurdling, desperate but futile cry for help. *Please let the dream be something that hasn't happened yet. Something that I can stop.*

I realize the killer spoke in the dream. "He said something."

"What?" Darren asks in a whisper.

I recall that part of the dream, but his voice is faint. "I can't make it out... Never?"

"Try to remember, Sophie. Focus on his voice."

I try to tune into his voice but the victim's screams drown out everything else. All I can hear are her screams; all I can feel is her terror. "I can't hear him. I don't think I heard him in the dream."

"Okay, go back to the start again. Go back to the girl running."

I hesitate, not wanting to replay the chase, not again. But I do. I have to help her. "Okay. I've got it." The images start from the beginning.

"Is he saying anything now?"

"I can't hear anything." I'm back in the abduction and it feels so real that my skin breaks out in goose bumps and once again my heart races. "He's got a knife." I struggle for air, the fear comes in a strong wave again.

"Keep going."

But what Darren suggests is the opposite of what I want to do. Every part of my body is screaming *run.* It's my natural reaction, and hers, too.

I shudder. "He's running the knife along her body." And for an instant I think I feel the cool hardness of metal on my stomach. Another shudder, followed by an instant of blackness and then she's tied up on a bed. Either my memory has jumped or the original dream jumped. "I've missed something. She's tied up on a bed now. Naked." I start to cry. "He's raping her." I open my eyes, unwilling to witness the rape. I hug my arms around my body and can't stop the tears that trickle down my cheek.

Darren's eyes are fixed intently on mine. "I'm sorry, Sophie." He leans in and gives me a hug and his touch, in the here and now seems to center me, to ground me. My heart slows down, the tears stop as abruptly as they started, and I'm the one who pulls away from the hug.

I exhale loudly. "What are you sorry for?"

"For making you go through it so vividly. Especially knowing what I know, especially after…" He trails off.

We're both well aware of how the sentence would have finished and it's not somewhere I want to go. It was bad enough remembering the dream of the brunette, I don't want to remember what the Slasher did to me. I fight the tears.

"If the visions and dreams are back, I *should* use them to help people. I *want* to help this girl."

He nods. "Are you sure?"

"Yes," I say, even though I'm not sure. Not sure at all. But can I really walk away when this girl is counting on me?

"Was there anything else?" Darren asks. "Anything else you saw or noticed?"

"I'm pretty sure that was the whole dream." I smile. "It worked, Darren. I remembered more of the dream."

He smiles back at me. "Yup."

My heart rate is back to baseline, and I suddenly feel cold. "I'm just going to get my fleece." I go into Darren's spare bedroom and grab the red fleece I bought a couple of years ago in New Zealand. I slip into it and the warmth comforts me. I'm halfway between the bedroom and the lounge when I hear Darren's cell ringing.

He picks it up as I enter the room. "Carter... Really?" Darren stands up and looks at me. "Hold on, I'm putting you on speaker." He touches a button on his phone. "Okay, Stone. Sophie can hear you now too. Go on."

"Forensics came back with something. It's the dirt under the vic's fingernails. They've come up with a very specific match. It's from the desert, from the Mojave region."

New York must have been a cover story, and the Mojave certainly raises more questions. What was he doing in the desert? And how did he get from there to Tucson, Arizona? It would be a hard lead to track down, too. We certainly can't go door-knocking—or tent-knocking—in and around the Mojave with a photo of Malcolm, in the hope that someone will recognize him.

"Anything else?" I ask.

"That's it. No DNA, no prints, and nothing at the crime scene. If there was evidence, it was probably left at the primary crime scene."

"And the wood from the head wound?" Darren asks.

Pages flick in the background. "Here it is." Stone takes a breath. "Walnut, treated with several coats of varnish. They're thinking a piece of furniture."

"Anything more specific?" I ask. It's possible, even if unlikely, that the varnish is some obscure make or that there's some other identifying matter in the wood itself.

Stone dashes my hopes. "'Fraid not."

"Okay. Thanks, Stone. Let me know if anything else comes in." Darren hangs up. "What do you think?"

I shake my head. "I don't know. I mean, how does the Mojave tie in?"

Darren nods. "And where does the woman from your dream fit?"

That's the question I want answered.

BlackWidow: Maybe we've gone too far.
AmericanPsycho: All's fair in love, war and serial killing.

NeverCaught: How true. Those recordings were made for torture.

BlackWidow: Cindy was a mess. The recording for her was evil, Psycho. I don't think I approve of you bringing up her childhood assault.

AmericanPsycho: They were made to disturb. And they did.

BlackWidow: Mmm…

DialM: As Oscar Wilde said, "Wickedness is a myth invented by good people to account for the curious attraction of others."

NeverCaught: Danny's was awesome. What a jerk. Did you see him looking around when he realized we knew about the dishonorable discharge?

DialM: He indubitably did look perturbed. I thought Susie's was clever. "Let me be cruel, not unnatural; I will speak daggers to her, but use none."

NeverCaught: What the? I WOULD use a dagger.

AmericanPsycho: Shakespeare, Never.

DialM: Thank you, AmericanPsycho. Good to know someone in here is properly educated.

BlackWidow: Telling Susie she's never going to make it as an actress is a metaphoric knife.

NeverCaught: She won't make it…she'll be dead.

AmericanPsycho: It's time to choose the next lucky victim.

NeverCaught: I love Wednesdays.

BlackWidow: Let's get rid of Danny.

NeverCaught: The next one should be a woman. Fair's fair. What about Cindy? The dumb **** actually blabbed to her roommate.

BlackWidow: What are you going to do about the roommate, Psycho?

AmericanPsycho: Don't worry, she's already been taken care of.

DialM: Excellent.
AmericanPsycho: Decision time. Drum roll…
AmericanPsycho: Cindy it is. But who will get the honors?

9

Darren and I touch down in Chicago, Illinois, on Wednesday morning. Given I'm due back at work in another few days, it looks like I'll be spending the last of my vacation days in Chicago. We check in for our car and soon we're sitting in a shiny rental with that unmistakable new smell, an overpowering, pungent odor of chemicals.

Darren puts his seat belt on and starts the engine. "So, have you got a picture of Malcolm's killer in your head?"

"Kind of. I need to find out more about Malcolm and write up a formal victimology first. Then draft the profile of the killer."

"Hopefully someone will be able to tell us what Malcolm was doing in the Mojave." We pull out of the parking bay and drive to the airport exit.

"It's a bloody big area." Yesterday I did an Internet search on the Mojave Desert, only to discover it stretches for 25,000 square miles and spreads across four states: California, Nevada, Arizona and Utah. That's some big crime scene.

Darren heads north on South Cicero, like the woman at the rental desk told him to, and it takes us just over twenty minutes to reach Oak Park. Soon we're sitting across from Hamill, an African-

American in his late forties. His head is shaved and incredibly shiny, and he wears a small, trimmed goatee and frameless glasses. His stocky frame is covered by jeans and a Chicago Bears jacket, teamed up with expensive-looking sneakers.

"I've spoken to the Jacksons. They're expecting you to come by later today." He pauses. "They're still real shell-shocked. And they want to see the body."

It's a natural reaction, particularly when the death is sudden. For most people, it's hard to believe their loved one is gone, and it's not until they see the body that they can truly accept that there hasn't been some terrible mistake.

Darren nods. "The ME hasn't released the body yet, but should in the next couple of days."

"You'll tell the Jacksons when you're over there?"

Darren nods again.

"I finally managed to get a hold of Kitty Dow, Malcolm's boss at Rendez-Vous. I've set up a two o'clock with her for you."

"Great. Thanks, Hamill," Darren says. "How do you want to play this one?"

Hamill shrugs first, but then shows his cards. "Your body, your case." He pauses. "Don't get me wrong, I'll help in any way I can."

"That's fine," Darren says. "Thanks."

"Besides, you've got the FBI on it, too. What do you need me for." Hamill doesn't phrase it as a question. He turns to me. "What's your role at the Bureau?"

"I'm a profiler with the Behavioral Analysis Unit." The profilers at Quantico are divided into two teams, Behavioral Analysis Unit 1— counter-terrorism and threat assessment—and Behavioral Analysis Unit 2—crimes against adults.

Hamill scratches the palm of his hand. "We work with the Bureau's profiler in the Chicago office, Sean Field. You know him?"

"No, haven't come across him yet, but I haven't been with the Bureau long."

He nods. "Well, here are the addresses and directions you need for the Jackson family and—" he attempts a slight French accent and raises his voice, mocking Malcolm's employer "—Rendez-Vous."

I must admit, I'm curious. I know nothing about the escort business, and certainly not male escorts. It will be an interesting interview. The Jackson interview, on the other hand, will be traumatic.

We follow Hamill's directions to Naperville, and Wilson Avenue. The Jackson residence is a large two-story brick home on a beautiful street. Looking at the house, it surprises me that Malcolm had to save for college. If the house is anything to go by, his family is wealthy. We out front and open the large iron gate. The small garden looks like it was once very well tended, but now weeds invade the well-designed flowerbeds.

I ring the doorbell and Darren and I wait silently for the Jacksons. Within a minute the door opens and we're greeted by a striking African-American woman in her mid-forties. Her hair is pulled up into a loose bun, which emphasizes her high cheekbones.

"Mrs. Jackson?" Darren flashes his badge.

"No, I'm her sister, Billie. Come in, Officer, we've been expecting you." Her voice sounds ragged, as though she's been crying constantly and could burst into tears again any minute.

She leads us down a long hallway and through the second door on the right. Sitting in a large living room is a woman that can only be Mrs. Jackson. The resemblance between her and her sister is remarkable and it looks like there's only a year or two separating them. Next to her is a very tall, well-built man. He has his arm around her and when we first enter, both of them are staring vacantly at the TV, which is turned off. Once we're inside the room they look up at us.

"You the detectives from Arizona?" The man stands up and towers over everyone in the room.

"I'm Detective Darren Carter with Tucson Homicide." Darren shakes his hand. "And this is Special Agent Sophie Anderson from the FBI."

I shake hands with Mr. Jackson, who's gentle despite his obvious strength.

"Sorry for your loss." My words are totally inadequate but it's better than remaining silent on the subject.

Mr. Jackson gives me a tiny nod and his lips pinch together. Mrs. Jackson stands up and greets us on remote control, her eyes glazed over. Her sister offers us a drink, which we both decline.

"Have you seen Malcolm?" Mrs. Jackson asks, rubbing her hands together.

"Yes. We both have." I don't elaborate, don't tell her that we witnessed the autopsy. That would definitely be too much information.

"And it's definitely our Malcolm?" She looks at a family portrait that hangs on the wall next to the television. The photo depicts Mr. and Mrs. Jackson and four children, two boys and two girls. I recognize Malcolm instantly as the oldest child in the picture.

"I'm afraid it's definitely him."

Mrs. Jackson starts crying and Mr. Jackson tries to comfort her. She sits back down, although it's more of a collapse than a controlled sit, and takes Mr. Jackson with her.

He holds her. "I'm sorry, we still… We just can't believe it's happened to our boy."

Darren speaks for the first time. "That's a very normal reaction, Mr. Jackson." Darren pauses. "And I'm sorry we have to intrude on you now of all times."

Mrs. Jackson suddenly stops crying. "No. I want the bastard who did this to our boy." Her anger takes over.

"That's why we're here, Mrs. Jackson," Darren says.

Mrs. Jackson sits more upright, and leans less on her husband.

Her sister comes forward and sits on her other side. "What can we do to help?"

I take over. "We need to find out as much as we can about Malcolm and his movements before he left Chicago."

They nod and I continue. "Detective Hamill from Oak Park mentioned you thought Malcolm was in New York on business."

Mrs. Jackson winces.

"Yes," Mr. Jackson says.

"But we know from forensics that he was in the Mojave Desert. And he was found in Tucson."

"We just don't understand." Mr. Jackson removes his arm from around his wife's shoulders and holds her hand instead. "Why would he tell us he was going to New York if he was going to Arizona?"

"That's what we're trying to find out." I take out a notepad and start scribbling. "We need to know everything that Malcolm said about his New York trip."

"He didn't say much. He called us about ten days ago and said he was going out of town for a month or two."

"That's all?"

Mrs. Jackson puts her head down. "We haven't been in contact with Malcolm much over the past year, not since he started that job of his." Mrs. Jackson's disapproval is clear, yet it's manifested more as shame than anger.

Mrs. Jackson's sister intervenes. "We were devastated when he told us. We didn't approve."

"He was doing it to put himself through college?" I ask, even though I already know the answer.

"Yes." This time it's Mr. Jackson's shame that surfaces. "Things have been rough for us. I lost my job at an insurance firm a few years back and I haven't been able to get anything much since then. We couldn't afford to put Malcolm through college. If Billie hadn't taken us in . . ." He doesn't finish his sentence.

The family dynamic is becoming clear to me now. Mr. and Mrs. Jackson have been doing it tough and relying on Billie's charity and Malcolm is the family's black sheep. He was selling his services— although exactly what "services" covers is unclear—to create a new life for himself. All this is essential background information to give us a realistic picture of Malcolm. Without info like this, he's just another body on a slab. Although I can never truly think of any murder victim as just another body.

I turn back to the photo. "He's a good-looking man."

"Yes. Very good looking. He always had women chasing him," Mrs. Jackson says with a hint of pride.

"Was he confident?"

Mr. Jackson responds quickly. "Very. He knew he was handsome."

I nod, getting the message loud and clear. There was no hesitation in Mr. Jackson's response whatsoever—Malcolm had an ego.

"How…" Mrs. Jackson takes a deep breath. "How did it happen? The detective from Oak Park said something about strangulation." She spits the words out, the subject matter leaving a bitter taste in her mouth.

"Yes, that's right." Darren looks at me.

I nod. Now's as good a time as any to give them more details.

"It's possible the killer is a woman." Darren says it slowly, reading their reactions.

They're all shocked, but it's Billie who expresses it first. "How could a woman overpower Malcolm? Strangle him?"

Darren gives me a look, so I take over. "Was Malcolm involved with anyone that you know of?"

"No. He had girlfriends in high school and was with one girl from his senior year up to a couple of years ago. But—"

"Do you know how they parted company? This ex and Malcolm?" I ask.

Mr. Jackson laughs, a forced laugh. "Agent Anderson, you're barking up the wrong tree. Angela is…well, she's not involved in this. No way."

Still, I take down her details and add her to our interview list.

"Why are you asking about Angela?" Billie says.

"We believe it was a sexual crime."

My comment is answered by more confusion.

Finally Mrs. Jackson speaks. "Sexual?"

"I'm afraid there are things that we can't tell you, not yet. But there are elements from the crime scene that indicate a romantic or sexual nature."

"It's that damn job of his." Mrs. Jackson stands up. "Lord have mercy on me, but I'll kill that Kitty Dow. Flashing her dirty money in our Malcolm's face!"

I stand up to face her and put my hand on her arm. "Mrs. Jackson, we don't have any evidence that this was related to his job. Nothing indicates that his killer was a client." It's true, we don't have any evidence to back up that possibility, but it's certainly the first line of questioning we'll be following with Kitty this afternoon. "I know this is hard, but we need to focus on Malcolm. The more we know about him and his movements, the easier it will be to track down his killer." I sit back down and let my comment sink in. It has the desired effect and within a few seconds Mrs. Jackson nods and also returns to her seat.

I fire another question at her, hoping to keep her focused. "So, your son was a confident man. What more can you tell us about him?"

Mr. Jackson stands up and crosses to the family portrait. He stares at Malcolm for a few seconds and then looks back at me. "He was a bright boy. Real smart. He wanted to study law at college. He got the marks, but it all happened around the same time that I lost my job. We just couldn't afford it. He worked in a bar for a couple of years. That's where he met Kitty."

Mrs. Jackson intervenes. "She told him how much he could make working for her. And that he'd be helping lonely professional women."

I nod. It would be hard for a young man to turn down. Good money to go on dates, coupled with the prospect of scoring. Most men fantasize about being attractive enough to secure a job like that.

"Was he outgoing?"

"He tended to be a quiet child," Mr. Jackson continues. "But he did change after he'd been working at Rendez-Vous for a few months. His quiet confidence turned to—" he pauses "—well, to be honest, he was quite egotistical. We *asked* him to stop working there, then *told* him to stop."

"We were always fighting about it," Billie says. "Whenever he'd come over. But he wouldn't listen to us. Didn't see anything wrong with it."

Mrs. Jackson nods. "In the end, he just stopped coming over. He'd call us once a month to check in, but we hadn't seen him since his birthday in January."

I nod and scribble the notes down on my pad.

"And what about his friends?" Darren says. "We'd like to interview his closest friends too."

"Sure."

The Jacksons rattle off a few names and we take them all down, with contact details from Mrs. Jackson's address book.

I take a deep breath, ready to ask the next question. We have to explore all options—and it's possible that the killer is a male, albeit a young one or a man with small hands. "To your knowledge, has Malcolm even been involved with other men?"

"What?" It's Mr. Jackson who voices the initial shock.

"We have to cover all bases," I say to the three family members.

Mr. Jackson seems about to say something when Mrs. Jackson puts her hand on his. She answers the question calmly. "No, he's only had girlfriends and he's only ever expressed interest in the opposite sex."

"Thank you, Mrs. Jackson." I give her what I hope is a comforting look. "One more question." I take out James Powers's sketch of the brunette from my dream. If Malcolm's killer is a woman, the dream is unrelated, but if the killer is a man, despite Malcolm's apparent heterosexuality, maybe Malcolm and the girl from my dream *are* related. "Do you recognize this woman?"

Mr. Jackson shakes his head. "No." He looks at his wife and sister-in-law for confirmation. They both shake their heads.

"Do you think…do you think she did it?" Mrs. Jackson asks.

"No, not at all. In fact, she may be a victim too." I don't elaborate, and although Mrs. Jackson seems confused by my response, she doesn't seem to have the emotional energy to question me further.

I look at the sketch again, and the memory of the girl's screams bubbles to the surface of my conscious mind. I repress the flashback and bite my lip—hard—hoping to drive the thought away.

10

Rendez-Vous is in a very respectable twenty-story office building on West Roosevelt Road—but maybe that's the point. The clientele probably comes from the insurance offices, banks and other high-paying employers in the building itself and the nearby area. We catch the elevator up to the twelfth floor and follow the signs. After a few left turns, we wind up in front of a glass door with a large decal featuring the Rendez-Vous name and logo. Wrapped around the "Rendez" and the "Vous" are the profiles of two faces, meeting in between the two words almost in a kiss. It certainly gets the message across.

"Nice logo," I say as Darren pushes the door open.

He glances back at it over his shoulder as he enters. "Uh huh."

Directly in front of the door is a reception desk. A stunning redhead flashes us a toothy but attractive smile. Braces and whitening, for sure.

"Welcome to Rendez-Vous." Her voice is husky, but it's forced not natural.

"Thanks," we both reply.

The place oozes class. The carpet is a thick pile of musky brown, and the walls are a very light grayish blue. Sitting in each of the front corners of the reception area is a leather armchair, and the walls are covered with artistic photos of men and women, mostly dressed in evening wear. Presumably the images are of Kitty's employees.

We approach the redhead and Darren is quick to get out his badge. "We've got an appointment to see Ms. Dow."

The receptionist takes the badge in her stride, presumably expecting us, and picks up the phone. "Your name?" she asks, even though I'm sure she knows. We do have an appointment, after all.

"Detective Darren Carter."

She smiles again and I can picture her sitting in front of a mirror practicing her smile over and over again.

"Kitty, I've got Detective Carter and—" she looks up at me "—his colleague here to see you." She hangs up the phone. "She'll be with you shortly. Have a seat." She motions toward the two armchairs. Darren and I sit down, both aware of the absurdity of sitting a few meters apart from one another. But then again, I guess Rendez-Vous doesn't get many couples coming in.

We wait silently. We're too far away from each other to carry on a private conversation, so I glance around at the photos. Behind the receptionist are two black-and-white pictures: to the left, an extremely handsome twenty-something male wears a tuxedo, and to the right, a slim but curvaceous woman is depicted in a figure-hugging evening dress. As my gaze moves around the room, I see a photo of Malcolm. A color photo, he's wearing black jeans and a maroon skin-tight T-shirt that shows off his physique.

"Darren."

Darren looks up from the magazine he's flipping through. I nod my head toward the photo and he follows my line of sight.

I continue sweeping the room. The men are of all ages, but the women in the photos are all in their twenties. Why would a man pay for a forty-year-old date when he could pay the same for a twenty-year-old date? From the outside at least, Rendez-Vous seems to be a legitimate escort agency. Stylish, good-looking men and women available for hire for that special evening or dull work function. I can see the slogans now.

After five minutes a woman in her fifties appears. She has dyed-blond hair that's piled on top of her head, and sparkling green eyes, possibly contacts. She's petite, at about five feet four inches, and is immaculately dressed in a navy suit with a plunging neckline. Her lips are plump and her skin taut—she's well-acquainted with collagen and the surgeon's knife.

Darren and I both stand up. Darren is closest and he extends his hand. "Ms. Dow, I'm Detective Darren Carter, and this is Special Agent Sophie Anderson from the FBI."

She shakes his hand. "How'd you do." She moves her focus to me and takes my extended hand. "Nice to meet you. And please, call me Kitty."

Her voice is polished and well-rounded, but I get the feeling it's an accent she learnt later in life because, like the receptionist's smile, it's too well-practiced to be natural.

"Terrible. Simply terrible about Malcolm." Kitty gazes at his photo on the wall. "He was one of our best, you know. In high demand." She gives me a knowing look. Any woman can see why Malcolm was in high demand.

She is sad, but it's hard to tell if she feels real sorrow or is thinking more about how his death will hit her business.

"His regulars will be devastated." She shakes her head. "Are you sure, absolutely positive it's him?"

Darren nods. "We matched his fingerprints."

She sighs. "Well, I guess you better come into my office so we can talk properly." She glances at the redhead. "Hold my calls please, Mandy."

"Yes, ma'am."

We follow Kitty through the door, which opens into a large corridor. The office seems bigger than it needs to be, with only a few of the desks occupied—downsizing or upsizing? She walks past the open-plan area and takes us through another doorway into her office. Like the reception area, her office is covered with framed photos. She sits behind her desk and motions to the two chairs on the other side. Darren and I sit down.

She crosses her legs. "I still can't believe it. Malcolm. He was so..." She trails off, unable to find the right word.

"So what?" I prompt.

"So fit and healthy. Such a perfect specimen." She smiles as she says the word specimen.

The intonation arouses my curiosity. Is Kitty a woman who appreciates good-looking men, or does she take her male escorts for test drives?

"He was so full of life." She flips open a folder and runs her hands over the large photo that sits on top. Again, I get a hint of sexuality in the way she touches his photo; it verges on a caress.

She sighs. "This is Malcolm's file." She hands it to us.

I flip through the folder, holding it between myself and Darren. It includes multiple photos, testimonials from clients, his original application form, police checks and a longer form.

"You knew Malcolm had a record?" I ask, scanning his police check to make sure it had come up.

"Yes." She waves her hand in the air, dismissing the charge. "For having a bit of grass in his pocket. Honestly!"

"So you don't have a policy? Regarding an employee's criminal record?"

"I don't discriminate." She holds my gaze. "But I can't expose my clients either. Malcolm's was a small indiscretion, a few years ago. What kid hasn't smoked pot? For that matter, some of my clients probably still do."

I nod.

Darren finishes reading one of the testimonials. "So, tell us about Malcolm. How did he come to work for you?"

"I met Malcolm just over a year ago in Spoon, a bar over on North Wells Street."

Neither the bar's name nor its address means anything to us and Kitty realizes this.

"It's a nice bar not too far from the lake. Popular. Anyway, I saw him behind the bar and knew he'd be fantastic in this line of work.

I gave him my card and told him how much he could make. He called me about a week later. He came in, we got along real well, and I decided to take him on."

"So how much *could* Malcolm earn?" I ask, out of both curiosity and professional thoroughness.

"Our official charge-out rate is $600 for an evening function. Of that, my boys and girls get $450."

I nod slowly several times, absorbing the information. I certainly couldn't afford Kitty's service. "And how many gigs did Malcolm get?"

"He was *extremely* popular." Again she gives me a knowing look. "Fridays and Saturdays were always booked up and he'd get one other night during the week, too. And more during holiday periods."

Darren whistles. "Damn, that's a lot of cash. Especially if you're under thirty with no college education."

Kitty nods. "That's what most of my kids think."

"Were all his clients women?" I ask.

"Some of my boys service both women and men, but not Malcolm. He was as straight as they come. Only available to women."

I nod.

"And what does the fee include?" Darren asks tactfully.

"Not sex. That is what you're getting at, isn't it, Detective?"

"Yes." Darren clears his throat. "So your employees and clients never have sex?"

She puts her hands up. "I can't guarantee that. But it's not part of the service, not part of the fee." She pauses. "To be honest, I do give them advice on that subject and I'm afraid I'm not much of a feminist. I advise my girls against it. I think it cheapens the experience and the male client will then expect it from all his escorts. For my boys, though, I tell them to do whatever they like. We still live in a world of double standards. I know that, and I make sure my kids know it, too."

As much as I hate to admit it, it's a fair call.

"What was Malcolm's last job? The one that took him to New York?"

Kitty raises her eyebrows. "There was no job in New York. At least, not through Rendez-Vous. Malcolm told me he was going there on vacation. That he would be gone for a few weeks, maybe even six or eight."

Darren and I exchange a glance. So the story to the parents was a lie. Unless Kitty's the one lying.

"Are you sure?" Darren's tone is forceful, almost threatening. He's going for the anything-you-say-can-and-will-be-held-against-you tone.

Kitty gazes at him coolly. "Of course, Detective. There was no job. Malcolm was on vacation."

I watch the exchange, keenly observing Kitty's facial expressions and tone of voice. She's either a damn good liar or she's telling the truth. "So, who were Malcolm's regulars?" I lean forward. "And what services did they get from him?"

"I'm afraid my client list is confidential." She crosses her arms.

"Of course." Darren stands up and looks past Kitty, out her window. "Do you do well, Kitty? From this business?"

She hesitates. "I do all right."

"Profiting from others' loneliness." Darren's voice has a hint of accusation in it.

She shrugs. "I provide a needed service. I don't hear anyone complaining."

"Except, perhaps, Malcolm." He says it slowly, sadly. I know it's an act, but Kitty doesn't.

She stands up to face Darren. "His death has got nothing to do with this agency."

"You sound very sure of that."

"I am. My employees and clients are thoroughly screened. There is no danger."

I come into the conversation. "You're probably right. But we do need to eliminate his clients as possible suspects."

She shrugs. "Not my problem."

Darren gives a long, loud sigh. "It'd be a pity really."

"What?" Kitty's uncertain.

"If the press found out. A scandal like this could ruin your business." Darren stares at Kitty.

"Are you blackmailing me, Detective?"

"Of course not. I was just expressing my hope that this case and Malcolm's occupation stays out of the newspapers."

Kitty's not happy. "Don't you need a subpoena to access a client list?"

"That's one road we can take. *The public road*." Darren has a forcefulness in his voice that I haven't heard before.

She shrugs, but also shoots Darren a disdainful look. She sits down at her computer and types in a few commands. Within a minute her personal printer is whirring into action and paper's spitting out. "That's his last six months of activity. The report includes the date of the job, the name and the person's contact details."

"Perfect. Thanks."

Kitty lets out a small snort. She isn't exactly doing this out of the kindness of her heart. She matches Darren with a threat of her own. "You better show my clients respect and privacy when you speak to them. Otherwise I won't mind contacting your superiors and telling them that you threatened me."

As the more neutral party, I step in. "Don't worry, Kitty. We just want to find Malcolm's killer. We'll play nice."

She nods. "Thank you." She says it to me, not Darren.

"I do have one more question for you, Kitty." I hand Darren the printout and take the sketch from my bag.

"Yes?"

"Is this woman one of your clients or employees?" I show her the sketch.

She only studies it for a couple of seconds. "No."

"She's definitely not one of your girls? Or a client?" I press.

"No. I've never seen her before."

I slump backward a little, unable to hide my frustration. I glance at Darren and sigh. We're about to leave but I feel compelled to flick through the photos of Malcolm once more. There's something about the photos, something not quite right. The photos show Malcolm in different styles, with different looks. There are a few of him dressed in a tuxedo, a couple in more casual suits, a few in jeans, and several that show off more of his body—Malcolm in only his boxers. Darren waits patiently as I study the pictures. Finally, I realize what's missing. The tattoo. There are three photos that show off his body to the maximum and in all three the tattoo is missing. "The tattoo was recent?" I ask Kitty.

"What tattoo?"

"Malcolm had a small tattoo of a rose on the inside of his wrist. Here." I point to the place on one of the photos.

"Not that I know of. And my kids are supposed to talk to me about piercings and tattoos. Some of our clients don't like that sort of thing." She smiles. "And some love it. But I need to know." She's silent for a moment. "Are you sure? Malcolm's not the tattoo type."

"He definitely had a tattoo," I say.

She seems puzzled by the revelation, but leaves it. So why didn't Malcolm ask Kitty about getting a tattoo? By all accounts he had a carefree existence, funded by Rendez-Vous. Why would he break the rules and risk his livelihood?

Malcolm's apartment is in a small, rundown block of ten. Guess he didn't want to waste too much of his college tuition on rent, or maybe he spent more time at his clients' homes. In his one-bedroom, top-floor apartment I walk around, trying to get a feel for him. The place is tidy and sparsely furnished—almost cold, but without the modern sleekness you see in some bachelor pads.

I linger in the bedroom, studying the bed. After much consideration I decide it's not the one from the vision I had, not the one I saw him having sex on. I lie down on it and I'm instantly hit by a stream of images. First my mind is replaying reality: the photos of Malcolm from his Rendez-Vous file, images of his body at the University of

Arizona, a flash of him lying on the ME's slab. But then, amongst it all, I see a brief flash of a black rose. But this time it's not a tattoo and it's not on Malcolm's wrist.

Darren stands in the doorway. "Anything?"

I sit up on the edge of the bed. "Maybe." I close my eyes and can see a clear image of the rose. If only all my visions consisted of flowers.

"What did you see?"

"A black rose." I say it slowly. "Like Malcolm's tattoo, but it was a real one." I sit on the bed, silent for a minute or so, and Darren leans on the door frame, watching me.

"Why didn't he tell Kitty?" I say.

Darren shrugs. "Maybe he just got it done." He smiles. "Hell, I wouldn't tell Harris if I wanted to get a tattoo."

"No, but Malcolm's livelihood depended on Kitty. Surely he'd play by the rules." I pause. There must be something to it.

"Hey, if he got it done recently, it should have been all red and scabby."

"You're right," I say. "And I don't think it was."

Darren moves into the room. "Time to call the ME's office and get someone to have a closer look at that tattoo." Darren punches a number into his phone and relays our concerns. Darren looks up at me and covers the mouthpiece. "Johnson, the ME's assistant, is on duty and he's getting a lab technician to check the tattoo out right now."

Great, instant results.

Darren keeps his hand over the phone but listens intently. Eventually he looks up at me. "Johnson said a recent tattoo should be quite obvious, that there'd be scab formation and inflammation for a couple of weeks. It's also possible it's a fake tatt, but he doubts the ME would have missed that."

I nod. "What are the other options?"

Darren shrugs.

Several minutes pass before Darren says, "Yup, I'm here…really?

Okay. So there's no way it could have been done recently?…
oh…oh. Okay."

Darren hangs up the phone, an odd expression on his face. "It's a
real tattoo, but no inflammation or other indications that it's recent."
He pauses. "Johnson said there was one other explanation…it could
have been done postmortem."

I raise my eyebrows. "That rose means something." I pause. "And
if the killer put it there, it's part of his or her signature."

Darren sits on the edge of the bed next to me. "Why don't you
see if it means anything to your VICAP guy?"

"Good idea." I punch Evans's number into my phone and he picks
up on the second ring.

"Evans. Anderson here. Can you do a search for me on a black rose?"

He's silent.

"Evans?"

"I don't need to do a search. That's the case I was telling you
about. The woman who kills her victims during sex in the motel
room. A black rose left on the bed, next to the dead body…it's part
of her signature. What have you got with a black rose?"

"That case from Tucson that we entered. The vic had a tattoo of
a rose on his wrist and it's possible it was done postmortem, which
means by the killer."

"Shit, Anderson, if you've got this woman in your sights…"

"We have to assume we do. It certainly throws a whole new light
on Malcolm Jackson's death."

"I'll say."

I organize for Evans to send the details of the female perp's earlier cases to Tucson before hanging up and filling Darren in. "I think
we should go back to Tucson."

Darren nods, and then pulls out his notebook and examines the list
of Malcolm's clients and friends. "We should be able to get through some
of these this afternoon and tonight and then head back on a late flight.
I'll fax half the list to Stone and she can kick off with phone interviews."

I nod. "Let's do it."

BlackWidow: It'll probably be twenty-four hours until we hear from Psycho. It's pretty intense in that house. Good intense.
NeverCaught: I can imagine.
BlackWidow: Poor Cindy.
NeverCaught: Here we go…
BlackWidow: Well, I liked her. She'd had a rough life.
NeverCaught: Do you ever feel sorry for your male gigolos?
BlackWidow: No, but that's different. They deserve it.
NeverCaught: They all deserve it.
DialM: I wonder what Psycho's doing to Cindy right now.
NeverCaught: I bet he's **ing her. Unless she's already dead.

11

Back in Tucson the next morning, we pull into the police department, ready to review the files Evans sent to Stone. Waiting on Darren's desk is a large pile of printouts. He whistles, a long slow whistle, measuring the stack against his torso—two piles, each easily reaching his belly button.

"She's been busy," I say.

"Stone or the killer?"

"Well, I was talking about the killer," I reply, "but it applies to Stone too."

Stone's on the phone…again. She gives us a quick wink.

Darren hands me one of the piles. "I'll go halves with you. Let's set up in the project room down the hall." He looks in the direction of the ladies bathroom. I take one pile and make my way down the corridor, with Darren hot on my heels. I manage to prop the heavy files up between my body and the wall and open the door with the hand that's underneath the stack.

"I thought you said you've been working out," Darren teases, pushing the door open. "I gave you the smaller pile, you know."

"Yeah, right."

He switches the light on and releases his pile of files with a thud on the table. "So we're definitely looking for a woman. Hard to believe."

"Yes. It's—"

"Kind of exciting?"

I unload my files next to Darren's. "Well, yeah. I've never gone after a female killer. You?"

"Nope. This is a first."

We both sit down and take a file from the top of the stack. I wonder if a photo of the brunette from my dream is sitting in a file on someone's desk. What I dreamt could have happened years ago, yesterday, or maybe it's about to happen. Or maybe it was just a nightmare, a figment of my subconscious. No, as much as I hate to admit it, she is, or was, real. Somehow I just know.

Before I've even flipped open the first folder, Darren stands up. "I'll just go get us some notepads." He disappears and I study the stack of files. It could take us days to go through them properly. The vacation is well and truly over. This case is too important to work on it part-time anymore.

Darren returns with a small arsenal of stationery: two large notepads, two four-color pens, highlighters, Post-it Notes, two pencils and even a ruler.

Stone follows him. "You gotta give the man some cred. He knows his supplies."

Darren lets the stationery spill onto the desk.

Stone closes the door and takes a seat. "Where are we at?"

"Files." Darren nods toward the two piles. "What about you, find anything in Malcolm's client list?"

"Not yet. I'm waiting on a few return calls." She holds up her cell phone.

Darren takes about ten files from the top of his batch and tosses them onto the table in front of Stone. "In that case, have fun."

She flips open the first one. "Cool." She only reads for a few seconds before she reaches into her inside pocket and takes out some sheets of typed paper. "And this is the profile Agent Evans from VICAP e-mailed through."

The Bureau has been tracking this woman for a while and one of the profilers from my unit had already drafted a profile for the VICAP consultants and the relevant cops, but it was before my time.

"I'm going to start with the case files, then the profile." I hand it to Darren who starts reading it immediately. I prefer to establish my own picture of the killer first, then see what another profiler has come up with. It can be dangerous to start making psychological assumptions before you've got all the information, all the facts. If you start doing that, you can get sidetracked, forcing your mind down a certain path. Then you can become too attached to one theory, one image of the killer.

I look back at my first file, the first kill, Cameron Michaels. I always like to spend time on a killer's first victim. I look at the photos of a naked man handcuffed to a bed. Soon, I'm buried in her world, the killer's world.

By 5:00 p.m. we've completed an initial pass of the files, horrified that this woman has been at large for so long, taking so many lives.

"How has she gotten away with it all these years?" Stone asks incredulously.

Darren leans back in his chair. "Beats me. She's certainly racked up the numbers."

"And you definitely think this is the same woman?" Stone looks at me.

"The black rose detail wasn't released to the press or families. She's made changes, some unusual changes, but the manual strangulation with small hands, handcuffs, it's a match."

"But the heart shape isn't," Stone says.

Darren plays devil's advocate too. "And we've still got a woman carrying all two-hundred and fifteen pounds of Malcolm to the campus dump site."

"The love heart is new. Unusual," I concede. "And as for dumping the body, like Stone said, it wasn't far from the road to the dump site. Difficult, yes. Impossible, no."

We move on.

"My stack had some of the older ones." Darren pats the top file. "We've got DNA in three of the cases from the nineties, but no sample to match it against."

"The DNA evidence will be good for a conviction when we track her down," I say.

"Now that's confidence." Stone points at me.

I smile. "Hope is probably a better word. I'm stubborn. I like to get my man...or woman."

"Don't we all." Darren stands up to stretch. "But some perps get away."

I hide my reaction by moving my clenched fists under the table. There's one that got away that I don't like to think about, the man who kidnapped and murdered my brother when I was eight. The guy was never caught. "But maybe one of these days something new will surface, something to catch them out," I manage to say.

Darren thinks I'm talking about this case, the VICAP files, but I'm thinking more about my brother's killer, and my never-ending hope that something new will surface in his case. Then I'd be on the first plane home.

Every year since I became a cop and got access to his case file I go over it. But nothing new ever strikes me. Maybe I can use my psychic abilities to crack the case. Until now, it's never occurred to me to try.

"Let's get these babies in order," Darren says, bringing me back to the case at hand.

All in all we've got twenty murders that VICAP attributes to the one killer, this femme fatale. Malcolm makes twenty-one.

Once we rearrange the files into chronological order, the killer's base usually becomes obvious. But in this case, the pattern seems to be random. We've got murders in California, Texas, Nevada and Colorado, but the locations chop and change between the four states with no obvious pattern. "She moves around a bit," I say.

Stone leans forward. "Maybe she moves for work." She flicks through the spines of the files with a short fingernail. "Twenty-one murders over the past fifteen years. I wonder if she's planning on retiring any time soon."

"She's been around for a while, but hardly retirement age," I say.

Stone's hand rests on the top file. "How old do you think we're talking here?"

I take a breath and do the math in my head. "Let's say she started in her late teens or early twenties, like most serial killers do—that would place her in her mid-thirties."

"She sure doesn't have a problem attracting good-looking young men."

Stone's right. It's one thing the victims all have in common. They tend to be attractive, well-built and in their late teens or early twenties.

Darren shrugs. "Men are suckers for sex."

Stone crosses her arms. "Men. Your dicks sure do get you into trouble." She takes a file off the pile and flicks through it randomly. "So, where to next?"

Darren takes the file from her. "You're going home, Stone."

She glances at her watch. "It's only six."

Darren glares at her.

"I do my best work after six."

"What time were you here till last night?"

"Late," Stone admits.

"So, vamoose." Darren waves the file in a shooing motion.

Stone stands up, somewhat reluctantly. "All right already. I'm going." She loiters in the same spot. "What about you guys? You should call it a night, too."

Darren smiles. "Goodnight, Stone."

She stays still for a few seconds before heading off.

Darren puts the file back on the table. "She's a good kid."

"She's hardly a kid, Darren. What is she, twenty-six?"

"Something like that." Darren walks over to the project room's whiteboard and flips it around so he's got a fresh board. He starts scribbling notes, talking as he writes.

"So, 1992 to now." He puts an arrow on the end of 1992 to indicate continuing action. "Twenty-one...so she's averaging, like one and a quarter every year." He writes *Victim type* on the whiteboard. He looks at me, but starts the process off himself. "In their late teens and early twenties. Across races."

"Yes, I noticed that. Our girl's politically correct."

Darren closes his eyes, trying to recall the case details. "Caucasian, African-American, Hispanic."

"And don't forget the Swede who was out here on holiday."

"How could I forget that poor bastard? Not much of a vacation."

"No." According to the file, he'd come out for a one-month trip in July 1998 and was found dead two days before he was due to fly back to Stockholm. Sometimes this job really makes me believe in fate.

Darren adds the different ethnic backgrounds to the list. "All the victims were last sighted in bars, but in most cases no one can remember seeing them with a specific woman." Darren writes *Bars* on the board.

"Now that's the strange part. Surely she must have picked them up in those bars. Spent time with them before they moved on to a private location."

"You'd think so. For the ones when the vic *was* sighted with a woman on the night of his death, the descriptions of that woman vary significantly."

I flip through the files, scanning some of the descriptions. "People can change their appearance. If she wears wigs, for example."

"But the height varies too."

"Heels," I say. "The height only varies by a few inches. That could easily be the difference between flats and high heels. Then on top of that, factor in different people's estimates. A person's actually five-eight, but I guess five-seven and you guess five-nine."

"True." Darren writes *Disguises* on the board with a dash and *Wigs* next to it. Next he writes up *Heels*. "So her normal MO is basically that she picks them up, takes them to a motel, handcuffs them, has sex with them and strangles them during the act."

I nod.

Darren writes *MO* on the very right-hand side of the board, and catches up with our conversation, scribbling down the details.

I look at the whiteboard. "The real question is, why was he dumped at a college instead of found in some motel room? That discrepancy concerns me."

"It is a major departure from her MO." Darren taps the marker against the whiteboard.

I stand up and stretch. "Actually, it's stranger than that. The motel room and the way she leaves them, still naked and handcuffed, that's more than MO, that's signature stuff. Not to mention the rose. She has to see them like that, lifeless, handcuffed to the bed. To her it represents ultimate power over them and their sexuality. Perhaps male sexuality in general." I pause. "Our guy doesn't fit. He was in the open, and naked, but why not in a motel room?"

We're both silent, unable to come up with an explanation.

"And don't forget the love heart," Darren says. "Another anomaly."

Again, a depressing silence.

Darren glances at the wall clock. "Maybe we should call it a day, too."

It's not exactly late, but I am wrecked. "I don't feel like we've got very far."

Darren sits down again and leans back, hands behind his head. "What about the profile, then? You want to talk about that?"

"Sure." I search for the folded pages on the table among the chaos and eventually find them. I read through the pages but find my mind wandering—a sign of my tiredness.

Sex:	Female
Age:	Chronological: 30-35 Emotional age: 25-30
Race:	Difficult to determine. Shows preference for African-American victims so perhaps African-American?
Type of offender:	Organized—well-planned murders, MO and signature remain consistent over time and crime scenes. Highly intelligent. Low risk—murder seems to occur under pretence or during a one-night stand.
Occupation/employment:	Killer is hunting across all socioeconomic groups, making it difficult to pin down her own status, but the fact that she easily attracts white-collar guys indicates she's probably white collar herself. Travels with her work. Sales a strong possibility.

Marital status:	Single but very sexually active. If she travels with her job it's possible she's married and the men she has sex with are affairs, one-night stands on the road.
Dependants:	No—under-developed sense of responsibility make it unlikely she's a mother.
Childhood:	Probably the youngest child—acting on sex and power drives rather than having a developed sense of responsibility. Indicates an older sibling looked out for her. But that older sibling was absent in later life—rift or maybe even death. Very smart, so probably good at school. Sexually active from an early age and saw sex as power. This is her motivation—power over men. May have been sexually abused and wants to turn that around—her victims also represent her childhood attacker. Victims also give her attention—something she craves. This may be due to emotional abuse growing up or a sense of a sibling being the favored child, particularly in her father's eyes.
Personality:	Charming, extroverted, flirtatious.
Disabilities:	None.
Interaction with victims:	Victims are victims of opportunity. No stalking prior to night of murder, but some stalking on the night of attack. MO indicates she chooses vulnerable victims at bars—those who are on the lookout for sex and/or who are intoxicated.

Remorse:	No—victims left out in the open, still handcuffed on the motel-room bed. She doesn't respect the men she chooses and possibly has no respect for any man. She wants others to see the men in their final stages of degradation. They paid for their sexual desires with their lives.
Home life:	Lives alone if single, or possibly with partner. Lives in small house.
Car:	Sports car? Enjoys a "racy" life and this could be part of her image. She also doesn't need a more practical vehicle for transporting bodies, because she leaves them in the motel room.
Intelligence:	High IQ.
Education level:	Not clear. She may be able to pick up educated men through her looks and the promise of sex rather than them seeing her as an equal. Victims cross all education levels—from not finishing high school to college-educated.
Outward appearance:	Well-presented and groomed. Overtly sexual in her clothes and appearance.
Criminal background:	Long history of murder. No adult criminal record but probably a juvenile record.
Modus operandi (MO):	Watches the victim at a bar. Uses disguises while she's targeting a victim. Picks up the victim either inside the bar or outside—less witnesses. Takes the victim back to a motel room with promise of sex. Checks in under a false name.

Signature:	Handcuffs. Strangulation during sex. Leaving body in the open, handcuffed and still naked. Black rose draped across bed.
Post-offensive behavior:	Posing elements of the signature—rose. Leaves the motel as soon as he's been killed. She likes to see the victims in their shame, but doesn't need to stay in the room with them.
Media tactics:	Don't think this killer will follow the media. She's not overtly egotistical and doesn't need to relive the kill through the media's reports. Will only show minimal interest in coverage of her crimes.

"Well, what do you think?" Darren's now standing and twisting from side to side.

"Sore back?" I ask.

"A little."

I know how he feels. My shoulders and lower back are both tender—not surprising given the amount of time I've spent on airplanes in the past few days.

"The profile's good. But we may need to make amendments for Malcolm and why she's changed her MO and signature." I start a yawn and stand up to stretch. After about a minute I force myself back into the seat. "Let's go through this now." There are a few areas I'd like to revise, the first is race. I lean over and point to it on the profile. "The original profiler suggested maybe African-American, but I'm not so sure given the cross-section of her victims." In general, male serial killers hunt within their own race: if the victims are all black women, you're looking for a black man; if the victims are Caucasian, the perp usually is, too. But we don't have many stats on female killers. The victims fall across different races but there are more African-American men than any others. But does that mean *she's* black? Lots of white women are attracted to African-American men.

Darren's with me. "It is unusual. I guess not all the serial-killer rules apply, given she's a woman?" He turns the last part into an open-ended question.

"We're not in totally uncharted territory, but we don't have detailed road maps either."

The analogy seems to make sense to Darren. "So we can't assume she's black."

"Definitely not." I pause. "And some of the standard victim rules don't apply either. These guys—" I point to the files "—are all high risk."

Darren raises an eyebrow. "But—"

I put my hand up. "I know, high-risk victims are traditionally women who are easier to target. Prostitutes, or younger girls who just aren't streetwise. But the fact that the guys she targets want sex and are under the influence...that makes them high-risk when a predator like our girl is around."

Darren slowly nods. "Okay, I can see where you're going with this. We've got to think backward because she's a woman."

"Right. The factors that make a woman a high-risk victim are different than what makes a man a high-risk victim." I let out a small breath. "But the crimes themselves are low-risk. She's got her motel setup, she uses disguises, in most bars she'd have lots of men to choose from, and once she gets them back to the motel room, she handcuffs them. Her risk of exposure is low, as long as her disguises are good."

"Which they appear to be, given our different descriptions."

I move back to the profile and the next area is type of offender. Based on the way a crime is committed, we usually classify perps as either disorganized or organized offenders. In our case the crimes are well planned, the murders are controlled to an extent, restraints are used and the killer's obviously smart. All add up to an organized offender. I don't go through this with Darren—he's worked a few serials and he's seen profiles before. He knows the drill.

I put my finger on the next part of the profile—employment. "This part's a little blurry."

Darren reads it through. "She's hunting across different socio-economic groups." He pauses. "A builder, a barman, a sales exec, a doctor, a computer geek, an escort…"

He rattles off only six of the twenty-one victims in terms of occupation, but it demonstrates the issue. Like the race, it's difficult to cross-match her against her victim type. Male serial killers tend to target specific types of women.

Darren reads the last part of the category. "I like this. She travels for her work. So maybe she hasn't lived in the states she's killed in. She's just gone there on business."

"It's a strong possibility."

"Sales would fit perfectly," Darren says.

"It fits in with other parts of the profile as well. She's an extrovert, well-groomed, and she can fit in anywhere."

"You agree with the troubled childhood?" Darren moves on.

"Yes. She likes to be in total control of her victims sexually, and also physically, through restraints. This is to make up for not having control in her earlier life, during a traumatic sexual event. She's also overtly sexual, based on descriptions of her, and that's a trait we often see when women are sexually abused. They think of sexuality as something they have to offer, something that all men want. And often their self-esteem is so low they think it's the *only* thing they have to offer. In our girl's case, she uses sex to entrap them."

"Her motivation is power over men?" Darren reads from the profile.

"Yes. She overpowers them sexually and physically. She has no respect for men, and in some ways she sees her murders as justice. The men had it coming…the hunter became the hunted. She likes to reverse the roles."

He nods and then points to the next section. "The profiler described her as charming, extroverted and flirtatious, which also ties in well with the sales occupation."

"True. Sales people usually know how to talk the talk."

We're momentarily silent until Darren stands up and looks over the whiteboard. "She leaves her victims in the open, for everyone to find."

I nod. "Which indicates she feels no shame or remorse over her actions."

"She sounds like a real man hater."

"She certainly has no respect for men. She uses them to sexually gratify herself, and part of that gratification includes strangling them. She sees a man handcuffed to a bed, killed by a woman he hardly knew but wanted to sleep with, as pathetic. And she likes to leave them like that—naked and still handcuffed."

"Nice. I'm never even gonna think about having a one-night stand." His eyes widen slightly. "Not that I would anyway…I mean one-night stands aren't my thing."

"Nice save," I say sarcastically, even though I believe him.

He reddens and diverts my attention back to the case. "She mates and then kills them. Like that spider…what's it called?"

"Black widow. Other insects do it too. Like the praying mantis."

Silence again. We're both exhausted.

"Forensics indicates she uses a condom, but takes it with her," Darren says. "But at least we got fluids at three of the earlier crime scenes."

"Yes, before she got really careful." I pause. "She takes them back to the motel room, a little bit of foreplay and the handcuffs."

"Which the men probably think is kinky."

"Yep. And next thing they know they're dead." I stand up as well, too sore to sit in the seat any longer. "High IQ. Fits the organized offender and the relatively clean crime scenes." Most organized offenders are one hundred and twenty plus, and serial killers are often even higher.

Darren nods.

"I'd like to review the education level. The victims cross all education levels, so it's difficult to know if she's hunting within her own level, below or above."

"She has a level of sophistication though," Darren says. "To have been doing this for so many years."

"Go on."

"She's at least high-school educated."

"Okay, so let's say she's middle-of-the-road, which means she's probably at least high-school and maybe university educated." I mark up the slight change to the profile.

"Sounds good." Darren looks over my shoulder and takes us to criminal history. "What sort of juvenile record?"

"I think she may have got into some trouble when she was younger—shoplifting or a DUI charge."

"The abuse?"

"Yeah. She's pretty screwed up, obviously, but I think in her adolescence she had no control over her behavior. She's bound to be on the system somewhere. Probably with a big brother or big sister bailing her out." The last three elements on the profile are MO, signature and media tactics. "MO and signature, we've already covered."

"Yup, pretty obvious."

I sit down again. "The media's a little different because of her gender. She's not egotistical like many organized male serial killers. She doesn't need to read about her handiwork in the paper or hear it on the news. She kills for her own pleasure and each kill satisfies her until she chooses her next victim. I don't think we'll be able to use the media on this one."

"Okay." Silence engulfs us again.

I'm filled with thoughts of the killer, impressions that have nothing to do with psychology, nothing to do with profiling. Imagination or psychic abilities? I see our girl, woman, as having long, slightly wavy black hair, a slim yet curvaceous figure—and the profile tells me she'd play on that—and fine facial features with full lips. I envisage her as a woman who exudes sex without trying too hard and yet also has a sophistication about her—perhaps an Angelina Jolie meets Andy McDowell. Fact or fantasy?

Another thing I can feel is her anger. Her predatory nature bubbles through me and I don't like it one little bit.

Darren stands behind my chair and shakes the backrest slightly. "Come on, we really do need to get some sleep."

His hands brush against my shoulders and I'm instantly back in the real world, my world.

AmericanPsycho has entered the room.

NeverCaught: Finally! So, how was Cindy?

AmericanPsycho: Mighty fine.

NeverCaught: Did you get to experience that flexibility of hers?

AmericanPsycho: Yes. I got her drunk on the chopper ride and she jumped me as soon as we got in the house. Had her legs up around her head.

NeverCaught: Really? You lucky ****. So you got to do her more than once?

AmericanPsycho: Yup. Once before she knew our little secret and a few times after. Best of both worlds.

NeverCaught: You lucky **ing ******. I love it when I'm ***ing them and they realize. I like watching the ***es' faces change from desire to fear.

AmericanPsycho: Here's a pic of Cindy.

NeverCaught: This rocks.

DialM: So the body's been dumped?

AmericanPsycho: Yes. And with the second body, the press will declare the birth of a new serial killer.

NeverCaught: **ing excellent.

12

A man's hand reaches down into a shaft and he pulls a girl up, a blonde. She moves closer to him and together they walk toward a chopper. His arm is around her and she wiggles her hips as she walks. In the chopper they drink champagne. Her giggling becomes louder, more frequent.

They touch down at a large house and the girl runs forward. She's running on gravel, and on the way to the front door she passes an ornate fountain. Inside the house she flings her arms around him and pushes her lips against his. A lustful kiss, which ends only after they spin around several times and wind up against the wall. She rips his shirt off and runs her fingers along his muscled chest. She kisses his nipples. He hikes up her skirt and she undoes his button-fly jeans. She wiggles herself on top of him and he pushes her further up against the wall.

Several minutes later they unlink. He grabs her hand and leads her upstairs to a bedroom. She jumps straight on the four-poster and immediately sees the handcuffs. She lies down, rolls onto her stomach and puts on the first handcuff. He kneels on the bed to secure the other one. She pulls her leg into her chest and then extends it so her shin is touching her handcuffed arm, in a display of her flexibility.

He runs his hands down her leg and to her crotch but soon brings her leg back down to the bed, where he cuffs it. He clamps the final handcuff over her ankle and then stands up and moves away.

He tears her clothes off and moves himself on top of her. But this time there's only fear in her eyes.

She is dead, a heart drawn on her chest.

I wake up, disorientated. A man hovers in the darkness beside my bed. I scream and reach for my gun, my hands closing around my weapon. I swing it toward the shape.

"Sophie, it's me!"

My eyes focus and I realize Darren is standing beside my bed. That's right, I'm in Darren's spare bedroom.

I lower my gun. "What happened?"

"You were screaming. I knocked, but...sorry, I didn't know what else to do so I came in, hoping I could wake you."

My pounding heart isn't showing any signs of slowing down. I put my gun back on the bedside table and swing my legs out of the bed so I'm sitting on the edge.

"Another dream?" Darren asks tentatively.

"Yes."

"What did you see?"

"Another body. A woman, but not the brunette. She had the love heart on her chest." I pause. "There was more, but I can't remember it." I guess I've repressed it already. One thing's for sure, death is not pretty.

"Another woman?"

"I know, it doesn't make sense." I stand up and start pacing. "Okay, so Malcolm was killed by this woman who's been screwing men and killing them for fifteen years. But is the brunette related? And this new woman...she had the love heart."

Darren remains silent, realizing I need to vent.

"Why has our female killer suddenly changed her MO and introduced this new signature, the love heart?" I collapse back onto the bed. "Why can't I figure this out?"

"Sophie, it's confusing. Confusing as hell." Darren sits down next to me. "I mean, if the rose tattoo wasn't there, we wouldn't have linked Malcolm's death to the other ones at all."

"The other question mark. Why go from leaving the black rose out on display to hiding it as a small tattoo on the victim? It's like she was hoping we wouldn't notice it."

"Maybe that was the plan *exactly*."

I run with Darren's train of thought. "She's worried about getting caught so she stages it to look like a different killer. Yet her compulsive nature means she has to leave the rose somewhere at the crime scene."

"That's what I'm thinking."

I let it sink in. "It's the only explanation that makes sense."

Darren nods. "Unless someone knew about the rose and is setting our girl up." From the other room Darren's cell phone rings. We both instinctively glance at our watches—it's 3:00 a.m. A phone call at 3:00 a.m. can only mean one thing: a dead body. We look at each other briefly in silent acknowledgement of this fact before Darren bolts into his bedroom to pick up the phone.

I pull my jeans on, whip off my pajama top and slip into a sweater. There's no doubt in my mind we're going out to a crime scene.

Darren comes back into my room, in jeans and pulling on a sweater. He only appears moderately surprised to find me fully dressed.

"Well?"

"A blonde. U of A again."

It's all too familiar. The body of a young woman lies naked, wedged into a dark corner. This time the vic has been left next to a Dumpster on the University of Arizona campus. Temporary floodlights illuminate the crime scene as police, forensic investigators and a representative from the ME's office comb the area.

"Is it her?" Darren whispers as soon as we're close enough to see the woman's face.

I don't speak, I simply nod.

"Hi, Carter." It's not the ME at the scene this time, it's his assistant.

"Morning, Johnson."

I keep my eyes on the woman. She's about five-seven, perfectly toned with long, long legs. Her blonde hair is shortish, to her earlobes, and has a gentle wave. Her eyes are open and glassy—there's no mistaking she's dead.

"What have we got?" Darren asks, getting down to business.

"Looks like manual strangulation as the cause of death." Johnson points to some bruising on her neck, which is quite obvious. This girl is not only Caucasian, but very, very fair, making it much easier to see the strangulation marks than it was on Malcolm. "I'd say she's been dead for less than twenty-four hours. And then of course there's that." He gestures to the marking that partially covers the woman's breasts. The love heart.

"Anything on the inside of her wrists?" I ask.

Johnson looks at me. "You're the FBI agent?"

"Yes, that's right. Agent Anderson." I put my hand out, suddenly reminded of the formalities. I saw Johnson when Malcolm was discovered but we weren't introduced.

He shakes my hand. "Johnson. No tattoo of a rose, if that's what you're looking for."

"And it's not anywhere else on her body?"

"Not that I can see. Not yet, at least."

I notice Stone making her way through the perimeter. She looks like I feel—wrecked. Her auburn hair is sticking out at odd angles and beneath her jacket I notice her shirt is half tucked in.

"Bed hair, Stone?" Darren gives her a boyish grin.

She rakes her fingers through her hair, then gives Darren a lighthearted glare. She looks down at the body. "Another one."

"Might not be related," I say.

Stone points to the love heart. "Not related?"

"No tattoo. No rose. Female victim." Now I'm playing devil's advocate, going against both my instincts and visions, which are telling me that the deaths are connected, somehow.

Stone gives us a thoughtful nod. "Maybe Malcolm wasn't killed by the motel woman."

She's got a good point and it's exactly what Darren was alluding to before we got the call. It's possible our killer somehow knew about the rose and wanted to throw us a curveball.

Darren bends down next to Johnson. "Who's our first responder?"

"O'Grady." Johnson motions to one of the cops who's at the perimeter.

Darren, Stone and I move toward O'Grady. It only takes us a few minutes to learn that the body was found by a student from the Yavapai Residence Hall around the corner. He couldn't sleep because his French roomie had thrown a slab of ten-day-old blue cheese in the bin, stinking up the whole room. Our plain-food-loving guy had stormed out, trash in hand, just before 3:00 a.m., only to discover he had more things to worry about than the stench of smelly cheese.

13

By the time we got back from the crime scene it was the ungodly hour of 5:00 a.m. and we both decided to try to get a bit more sleep.

Thankfully, the second time I wake up is way nicer than the first. Instead of a horrible nightmare about a dead girl, I wake to a bird chirping outside my window. I roll over and look at the bedside clock—11:00 a.m. I stretch first before gradually easing myself out of bed. I've only jogged two mornings over the past week and I'm both disgusted with myself and proud that I've been able to resist my obsessive exercise regime. But today, it's definitely time. Jogging helps to clear my mind and release tension—two things in demand at the moment.

I throw on my running gear and tiptoe into the kitchen, conscious of waking Darren. I pour myself a glass of water and notice a small piece of paper with Darren's handwriting on it pinned to the fridge by a magnet. *Didn't want to wake you. I've gone into work. Give me a call when you're up. There's a spare key on the table.*

I fish my phone out of the back pocket of my tracksuit pants and dial Darren's number. After much debate I manage to convince him that I'm coming in—again—despite the fact that I'm on holiday. He seems relieved, or perhaps just less guilty, when I tell him I'll be a couple of hours because I'm going for a jog first.

I put my MP3 player on full and I'm soon pounding the pavement. At first my legs feel heavy, perhaps because I've broken my routine and haven't been running, or perhaps because of the disrupted sleep. It's not until the fifteen-minute mark that my body seems to slide into its normal rhythm.

By the time I make it to the Tucson police station it's 1:30 p.m. When I reach Darren's desk he's on the phone, a worried expression on his face. After less than a minute he hangs up and looks at me. "She's definitely related to Malcolm. Johnson found dirt deep under her fingernails and they got a rush on the soil. It matches what we found on Malcolm—from the Mojave region."

I shake my head. "What the hell's going on out there?"

"Damn good question."

"ID?"

"Yes."

"Wow, they have rushed it."

"You know what it's like with serials. They jump the line. We need to get something on this perp before the press goes berserk."

I nod. "So, the ID?"

"She's got a criminal record like Malcolm, so we got a fingerprint match. Cindy Star. A dancer from Vegas." Darren punches Cindy's name into the system. "Yup, here it is. Busted for shoplifting when she was seventeen, four years ago. It was her third offence. She got off with a warning the first two times."

I look over Darren's shoulder at Cindy Star's Nevada driver's license on-screen. The bad photo can't hide her attractiveness.

I stare absently at the computer screen, trying to bring Malcolm and Cindy together. "Okay. So, we've got two people with criminal pasts in the desert."

"Doing what?"

"Maybe they were abducted and taken there."

Darren nods. Then a second later stands up. "Oh my God." He

turns to me. "What if we're looking at a male-female team? They pick up Cindy and Malcolm, take them somewhere in the Mojave Desert, kill them, and then get rid of the bodies."

"That's brilliant." I let the concept sink in. "It would explain why our female killer's MO is different to her previous crimes. Why she didn't do Malcolm in a motel room." The profile pegged her as either single or in a long-term relationship with other men and murder on the side. We may need to revise it. "It could also explain the love heart on the bodies. It symbolizes the killers' love for each other."

"Sounds like a perfect match," Darren jokes.

"Perfect for them, not their victims."

"Ain't that the truth. It would also mean the male could have carried Malcolm's body." He crosses his arms. "There have been a few serial-killing couples. It's not like this would be the first."

I think about some of the famous ones. The Moor murderers Ian Brady and Myra Hindley, Fred and Rose West, and Gerald and Charlene Gallego. The woman's involvement tends to vary, from passive conspirator to active murderer. Our case would certainly be an example of the latter. After all, she was killing *before* she met her new beau.

"It also ties in with the sexual nature of both murders," I say.

"We've had confirmation from the ME's office that Cindy was raped, but a condom was used."

"Not surprising. Sex may even be part of the killers' ritual together."

Stone makes her way to her desk. "What are you two so excited about?"

Darren fills her in on the latest developments and our hypothesis.

"It certainly fits." She sits down. "So where to next?"

I twist the ring on my little finger. "The killers are moving unusually fast, two victims in the past week—plus we're crossing jurisdictions. I think maybe it's time my involvement, and the Bureau's, became official."

"I'd be happy with that," Darren says. "Will the Bureau go for it?"

"Evans in VICAP was almost gagging when I told him about the tattoo of the rose. The Bureau's been tracking this woman for years, they've got a vested interest in this case. I'll call Rivers." I look back at Cindy's photo. "And we might have to go to Vegas."

"Is the Bureau paying?" Darren gives me a wink.

"Don't know about that."

He smiles. "We'll phone first. We might not need to make the trip."

I nod. "I also want to see Cindy's body again. Maybe it will trigger something." I'm talking about a psychic something and Darren immediately picks up on my hint. I must learn how to induce my premonitions more reliably. I had success of a sort at Malcolm's apartment and I'd like to repeat that process.

"Good idea."

"Rivers," I say, getting myself back on track. First things first. I move into the project room for some privacy and dial his number, only to find out I was beaten to it. The head of VICAP has already filled him in, and Rivers was deciding whether to suggest I stay on in Tucson or assign someone else from the team. My offer makes the decision for him.

Back in Homicide I deliver the good news to Darren.

"Welcome to the case," he says with a smile. "So, what shall we do first? Cindy's body or her family and friends?"

"Someone notified Cindy's next of kin?"

"Stone rang it through this morning." Darren looks over to Stone. "Hey, Stone, heard back from the Vegas cops?"

She looks up. "No, I'll call them now." She picks up her phone and punches in some numbers. "Detective Cross?… Detective Stone here from Tucson Homicide. How'd you do with Cindy Star this morning?… Really? Hang on, I'm going to put you on speaker-phone." She puts the call on hold first and looks up at us. "You're not going to believe this."

We gather around Stone's desk.

"Detective Cross, I've got my partner Detective Carter here and Special Agent Anderson from the Bureau. Can you please repeat what you just said?"

"Sure. After I spoke to Detective Stone I mentioned Cindy Star's death to someone here. He thought the name sounded familiar and it turns out he was at Star's apartment just last week. Her roommate, Janice Dust, ODed. Heroin."

Darren and I exchange looks. Surely this can't be a coincidence. Both girls dead?

I lean on the desk. "Did her death look suspicious?"

"No. I pulled the file and had a look at it myself first thing this morning. Looked like a standard OD. She had a heroin habit. Friends say she kicked it a couple years back, but junkies often relapse."

"What were her veins like?"

He pauses and I can hear papers shuffling in the background. "Actually, the ME could only find the one injection site." Cross knows it sounds bad. "There were no defensive wounds, no bruises. Nothing whatsoever to indicate it wasn't self-inflicted."

That's fair. In isolation it looks innocent enough, but in conjunction with Cindy's death...

"If it's murder, they did a good job," Cross adds.

"Was Cindy reported missing by Janice or anyone else?" Stone asks.

"No. Dust worked with Star, as a dancer in Hugo's Femme show. Cindy told her boss at Hugo's that she was having a medical procedure and would be out for several weeks."

I look at Darren. "So both Malcolm and Cindy were covering their tracks. If they were abducted by a serial-killing couple, they wouldn't prepare for it."

"Malcolm?" Detective Cross is in the dark.

Darren explains. "Cindy's murder is related to another murder victim here. Malcolm Jackson."

"Related how?"

"The crime scenes indicate the same killer." Darren doesn't go into detail. "And they both had remnants of sand on their bodies that has been positively matched to the Mojave Desert. They were both there before their deaths, possibly together."

I stand up straight, the events becoming clearer. "Maybe Janice knew what Cindy was doing. And that got her killed."

"So that would make it three murders. All related." Detective Cross sighs noisily on the other end of the line.

"Uh huh." Darren starts pacing. "Cross, I think we better come pay you a visit. We'll bring what we've got on Malcolm and Cindy, see if we can't figure out what they had in common."

"Sure. Let me know when you're arriving." He pauses. "What about time of death?"

"Malcolm was killed last Thursday and Cindy yesterday."

"Exactly a week apart," Cross says.

Darren, Stone and I all look at each other. We knew Malcolm was killed last Thursday, but we hadn't verbalized or fully realized that the deaths are separated by exactly a week.

"And when was this Malcolm last seen?"

Darren doesn't need to check the file for this fact. "Two weeks ago, March 20. What about Cindy?"

"Bingo. Hugo's said her leave started on March 20," Cross answers.

Darren puts the file down. "Thanks for your help, Cross. We'll be in touch. Can you fax or e-mail us everything you've got on the roommate? We'll add her into the mix and see what we come up with."

After booking our flights to Vegas for tomorrow morning, we arrive at the ME's office with his official report in hand. One of the on-duty techs takes us into the holding bay, where they keep all the bodies that have been autopsied but haven't been released yet. For now, both Malcolm and Cindy are in this room, but soon, Malcolm will be released to his parents and flown home to Chicago.

The tech looks up Cindy's name. "Cindy Star, bin number 24." He moves over to one of the stainless-steel holding areas, or bins as they unkindly call them. He pulls hard on the handle and the slab rolls out. A dark plastic sheet is placed across her body and the lab tech's hand reaches toward the top of it. But before he pulls it away, I see a flash of Cindy, alive. All four limbs are tied to a bed, spread-eagled. It reminds me of something else...parts of my dream from last night. I chew on my bottom lip and my muscles tense. I don't remember much of my dream about Cindy and, given my reaction to the dream about the brunette, I'm thinking my subconscious is doing some major repression.

The lab tech pulls the plastic off. "Mind if I leave you to it?"

"Sure," Darren says.

"Just roll her back in when you're done."

Darren nods and the tech goes back about his business.

I pull the plastic sheet all the way off, uncovering the whole body. "I just got an image of Cindy, tied to a bed."

"Really?"

"Yeah. I can't remember everything I dreamt about Cindy last night, but this looked familiar. I definitely dreamt about her cuffed to a bed."

"Restraint is in the autopsy report."

"Let's go through it." I look down at the report.

Darren nods, reading from the first, summary page. "Cause of death is strangulation, but she also had a blood alcohol reading of 1.8. That's a helluva lot."

"I'll say. Enough to make her very sluggish, maybe even unconscious."

"Yes, if it wasn't for the restraint marks..."

I nod. You can't struggle if you're unconscious.

Darren flips the first two pages over. "Page three. She was restrained."

I flick to the same spot. "Handcuffs." I finger Cindy's wrists and ankles, looking at the definite indentations. "She pulled hard against the cuffs. She may have been drunk, but she still fought."

"Think back to the dream, Sophie. You're trained to take in every little detail. Do it with your visions." Darren says it gently, but I take it like a slap in the face. He's right of course. I should be noticing everything, picking up all sorts of information, just like I do when I examine a crime scene or crime-scene photos. This is no different.

I nod. "I think I've got a major case of repression."

"I understand that. I do. But you've got to try. Try to get past it."

I sigh and force a small upturn of my lips. "Okay." I close my eyes and try to picture the scene, but my body tenses, scared Cindy's fear will overwhelm me. I take a deep breath and force myself through the fear. "The bed's a big four-poster number. Like an antique bed. Made of a dark wood. Maybe mahogany? It looks kind of familiar." Then I realize. "It's the same bed I saw the other woman on. The brunette."

"But Malcolm and Cindy were both strangled and you saw the brunette stabbed. How can they be related?"

I stand firm. "It's the same room." I let my frustration out in a groan. "But that doesn't make sense either. If we're talking about a serial killer, the male in our team, he either strangles his victims or he stabs them. Not both."

"Okay, let's go back to Cindy. Tell me about the room."

I sigh, still frustrated but I close my eyes again and play back the image, simply visualizing elements from my dream. "Four-poster, mahogany bed," I repeat. I pause, concentrating. "Plain, dark gray bedclothes. Floorboards and a dark red rug on the floor near the bed. An antique-looking bedside table. It matches the bed. And the walls are painted white. I'm only seeing one corner of the room."

"Anything on the bedside table?"

"Just a lamp. Again, it's antique-looking. It's got a brass stand, a balloon-shaped shade, frosted glass."

"Okay. So our killer, or killers if this guy's teamed up with our femme fatale, is into antiques and either owns or rents this place."

"Yep." I groan again. "That's not going to help us."

Darren reaches his hand out to me and touches my arm. "Everything helps. You know that."

I nod, again distracted by his touch. After everything that happened with Josh I'm just not ready to get involved with Darren. And it's still hard to let any man touch me after what happened on the Slasher case. And we're in the morgue...not exactly a suitable ambience.

Darren senses my discomfort and withdraws his hand. He looks down at Cindy's body. "Cindy," he says, moving back to the front page of the report. I do the same.

"So, we've got cause of death as strangulation, time of death as yesterday and the high blood-alcohol level." Darren scans the report, reading out the most pertinent details. "Handcuffed."

"And the rape." I flip to the next page.

"There were traces of nonoxynol from the vaginal swab, so certainly sex with a condom took place. Bruising was minimal." Rape victims often have bruising on the inner thighs and around their genitals. Most of Cindy's bruises are where the cuffs were.

"If all four limbs were restrained before the rape took place, she wouldn't have been in much of a position to struggle."

Darren nods. "He gets her drunk and she wakes up tied to a bed, basically unable to move."

"Exactly. Besides moving her hips a little bit and pulling on the cuffs, she wouldn't have been able to offer any resistance. That might account for the lack of bruising." I read down the report. Her organs were all normal, and the only thing under her fingernails was minute traces of sand.

I look at Cindy's face again and wish I could do more, see more. But the vision of the brunette was so intense and I don't know if I can handle that again.

I move back to the report. The ME found no other signs of trauma. Before her death, Cindy was an extremely healthy young woman. I shake my head, morbidly captivated by the fresh, pretty face on the slab. Someone will pay for taking her life.

NeverCaught: I should have gone higher for Cindy.
AmericanPsycho: Another five days. It'll fly by. Then someone might be yours.

NeverCaught: *Five days? Might?* I beg you to make it Brigitte and let me have her now. Look at the way her long legs are draped over the milk crate and parted ever so slightly so I can see her lacy red pants. I need a kill now.
AmericanPsycho: You'll just have to wait.

14

On the second leg of our Tucson-L.A.-Vegas flight, Darren and I manage to get three seats. I'm on the window, he's on the aisle and the middle seat is occupied by our files.

"I'm looking forward to getting to Vegas," I say.

Darren looks past me, out the window. "Take in a show? Play a bit of blackjack?"

I smile. "No, I'm looking forward to getting to the bottom of this case."

"Oh. Almost as exciting as playing blackjack." He pauses and looks at me. "Have you ever been to Vegas?"

"No."

"Well, you've got to go to at least one production and put a quarter in the slots."

"You want to show me a good time?" I smile.

He looks away. "Something like that."

I shift uncomfortably in my seat and fall back on what I know best—work. "This case seems so disorganized." I flick through the files we've brought with us: Cameron Michaels, the femme fatale's first vic all those years ago, Malcolm Jackson, Cindy Star and Janice Dust.

Darren stares at the files on the seat between us, seemingly also happy to be back on the more solid ground of the case. "All the leads are pulling us in different directions. We need about five to ten cops on this, full-time. You, me and Stone doesn't cut it."

"A task force." I nod. "It'd be nice." I stare out the window, avoiding the decision of which file to review first, which lead to follow. "I bet Evans is rallying for one. It might happen."

"We'll need it if the gap of one week between victims becomes our pattern."

Darren's right—one victim a week is both bizarre and frightening. "The Bureau might assign someone from our field office over here."

Darren leans across, closer to me. "You know, more dreams or visions could help. Then we mightn't need any extra resources."

I turn away from Darren to hide my slight annoyance. I know it's irrational, but it feels like he's pushing me and I'm putting enough pressure on myself without him adding to it. The truth is, having psychic stuff happen again brings up painful memories, memories I don't want to relive. "It's hard, Darren," I say.

Darren puts his hand on top of mine, tentatively. "I'm sorry. But it's not going to just disappear, you know. You went through—" he searches for the word "—hell. Pure hell. And that's not going to change, no matter how much you want it to."

My annoyance disappears. How can I be annoyed when he's being so sweet? I smile. "God, you're worse than the Bureau shrink."

He smiles, but it's only a small smile. "Nice diversionary tactic."

"A girl's got to try."

I pick up Janice's file. It's the one I've spent the least amount of time on but it definitely holds my interest. Janice wasn't in the Mojave, but she knew something, that's for sure. "I'll take Janice."

Darren nods. "I'll give Cindy's another going over, then swap you."

I review the photos, re-creating the crime with different routes to the same end—Janice, in the kitchen, slumped on the floor. I study the photo of her body. To her left is the kitchen table and slightly be-hind her is a chair that lies on the ground. She must have been sitting in that chair when she took the hit. Then, as the heroin engulfed her, she fell onto the floor, taking the chair with her. I flick through the other photos, getting acquainted with the girls' home, and then take another crack at the autopsy report. No crime-scene photo is a sub-stitute for the actual location, especially if it is the tactile nature of the real-life crime scenes that helps trigger my psychic abilities.

When I move onto Cindy's file, there are stark differences. Her body was discovered outdoors, in the early hours of the morning, and the photos contrast dramatically to the daylight, indoor photos of Janice. I flick through the file again, but nothing sticks out.

With only fifteen minutes to touchdown, we decide to go over the way we see the events one more time.

Darren starts. "So, Malcolm leaves Chicago, lies about what he's doing and where he's going. He takes off, presumably for the Mojave, but isn't registered on any of the airlines, buses or trains. Nor does he hire a car."

I nod. We got confirmation early this morning that Malcolm Jackson wasn't a registered passenger on any flights out of Chicago. We also couldn't link him to a train or bus, but it's possible he paid cash and used a fake name. "Cindy also goes to the desert and lies about what she's really doing, except she tells her best friend and roommate, Janice."

Darren rests Janice's file on his lap. "So, at some stage when Cindy and Malcolm are in the Mojave, somebody finds out that Janice knows where Cindy is. Knows what she's really doing."

"Information they didn't want anyone to have."

"For the moment we have to presume 'they' is our femme fatale and her new boyfriend, Cindy's killer," Darren says. "But who killed Janice?"

"The murder is totally different than Cindy's and Malcolm's. Cindy and Malcolm were pleasure. Janice was business."

Darren runs with it. "She was killed quickly and the murderer wanted to make it look like a drug overdose. Janice wasn't one of their normal victims."

"No. She was just damned unlucky that Cindy talked."

"And that the killers found out about it."

I look across at a photo of Janice. "I wonder if Cross has told Janice's family that her death is now suspicious." I stare out the window. We're closer to the ground, but I can still mostly see desert.

Darren leans over slightly, looking at the view too. "Janice's family might be happy to know she didn't relapse."

"Maybe. But they'll want answers. They'll want revenge."

"Family always does."

The pilot comes over the loudspeaker and announces the impending touchdown. The plane banks and I glance out the window again. Now I can see Vegas.

In my imagination, Vegas is a surreal city—neon everywhere, shows, slots, blackjack and Elvis impersonators—and from up here it looks even more toy-like than I'd imagined, almost as though it was built as a movie set. A bloody big movie set.

I turn back to Darren. "Speaking of families, we should call the Jacksons."

"And tell them we've got no leads?"

"I think they'd rather hear that than nothing." I stack the files neatly on the center seat and then put them back in my briefcase. "And what about Cindy's family?"

"Dunno. I guess we'll find out soon enough."

We touch down and as soon as we're out of the gateway I turn on my phone and pick up my one message.

"Rivers wants an update," I tell Darren.

"Great, see if you can get some more bodies on this case."

"I'll give it a go."

He smiles. "And find out if I'm getting reimbursed for this," he jokes. His smile fades. "I'll call the Jacksons."

We move into a quieter corner of the airport to make our calls.

I dial Rivers's cell and after three rings he picks up. "Hi, Anderson."

"Hi, boss," I manage before a boarding announcement comes over the PA, drowning out my voice and temporarily putting a stop to our conversation.

As soon as the announcement finishes, Rivers speaks. "Where are you?"

"Vegas airport."

"Vegas?"

"The latest victim—the woman—well, we found out her roommate died of an overdose only last week."

"Sounds suspicious."

"That's what we thought. So we're here to check it out." I pause. "Actually sir, I wanted to talk to you about resources. This case is taking off and I think we need more people on it."

Rivers doesn't respond.

I trudge on. "What do you think?"

Rivers starts talking but another boarding announcement drowns him out.

"What's that, sir?"

"Things are tight here at the moment. I did contact the Arizona field office, but they're overloaded, too." He pauses. "See what you turn up in the next week. Then we'll look at it again."

"But in a week someone else could be dead."

"We don't know that, Anderson. Two murders don't make a pattern. We wait."

"What about Evans?" I ask as a last resort. Evans isn't field trained, but he knows the case.

"Keep Evans in the loop but you're our only full-time resource on this. For the moment."

I can tell his decision is final.

"Well?" Darren asks, coming over.

I shake my head. "No go. Rivers wants to wait another week and see what happens."

"But—"

"I know. I told him. It's the same old story. Too many crimes and not enough of us." I'm angry as hell but I understand. Every case is important, not just the ones I'm working on. I put my phone back in my purse. "How'd it go with the Jacksons?"

"They're still in the denial phase."

I nod. "What about Malcolm's body?"

"It's being flown back to Chicago today."

"That'll help them accept their son's death."

"Nothing like a dead body to hit you with a dose of reality, right?"

"Exactly." I grip my bag tightly and try not to think of Mr. and Mrs. Jackson being shown their son's body.

Twenty minutes later we're driving out of the Vegas airport, in our dark green Chevrolet Classic rental. We head for the Las Vegas Metropolitan Police Department and Detective Cross.

The airport is pretty much in the center of Vegas, and we can see the world's gambling capital in all its glory. Darren takes a couple of rights and within less than five minutes the over-the-top casinos are looming.

"This is the famous strip, *The* Strip," Darren says. "Las Vegas Boulevard."

I nod, overwhelmed by the number and extravagance of the casinos. I'm not sure whether this is the most direct route or if he's taking the scenic route for my benefit.

"So, what do you think?"

"Wow." It's actually the number of people that shocks me more than the spectacle of the town itself. I was prepared for the glitz, the neon and the sense of a darker underbelly, but the number of people flocking to be part of Vegas… "My God, look at all the people!" This sure isn't a place for someone with demophobia. Or claustrophobia for that matter. The crowds move en masse, leaving only small spaces to move through.

We pass the welcome sign in the middle of the highway but it doesn't simply say Welcome to Vegas. No, it says Welcome to the Fabulous Las Vegas, Nevada. They had to put "fabulous" in there! I smile and keep looking ahead and to the left. Now we're really in the core of it all, hit by swarms of tourists. The casinos are more tangible, but there's still something so over-the-top glitzy about them that I have to remind myself they are real. On the left is a plainer one, Mandalay Bay, but directly next to it is the first themed casino, Luxor, in all its Egyptian glory, shaped like a pyramid, with an almighty sphinx guarding its entrance.

"Oh my God," is all I can manage.

"Impressive, isn't it?"

I'm speechless for a few seconds, already focusing on a miniature skyline of New York up ahead. "What the...?" I stammer.

Darren follows my gaze. "Ah, New York—New York." He pauses. "It's the name of the hotel."

"Of course it is." I laugh, and look at the addition to the New York skyline, a roller coaster that loops its way around the Statue of Liberty and the Empire State Building.

"But we're not just about America." Darren points to the right-hand side of the road, which I've been neglecting as I ogle New York—New York. Rising up only a block down is a mini Eiffel Tower. "That's Paris-Las Vegas." He pauses. "Oh, and we just passed Hugo's. Where the girls worked." Darren points backward and to the right.

For a minute or two I actually forgot what we were here to do. I'm not here to take in the sights, I'm here to solve a murder. And hopefully save the brunette from my dream. I turn around to the front again and take in the rest of the Vegas skyline, but without the same enthusiasm. We pass the very regal-looking Caesar's Palace—complete with columns and a fiery chariot at the entrance—Mirage, Circus Circus and finally the Stratosphere. New York—New York isn't the only casino with a ride built into its impressive architecture.

Eventually we take a left off Las Vegas Boulevard onto Stewart Avenue and arrive at the police station. I'm still focused on the case, but my senses are overloaded with Vegas stardust. Stardust... "Hey, I just realized Cindy's last name is Star and Janice's last name is Dust. Stardust."

Darren starts laughing. "I get it. They must be stage names. A Vegas specialty, like the Elvis impersonator who changed his name by deed poll to Loveme Tender. It's Vegas, baby!"

We clamber out of the car and head for the front desk. Within a couple of minutes a burly detective in his fifties comes out. The desk sergeant points toward us and Cross comes over.

Darren puts out his hand. "Thanks for seeing us, Cross."

"Nice to meet you." He turns to me. "And you're from the FBI."

I introduce myself and shake his hand.

"So, why's the Bureau taking an interest in this case?" From Cross's tone of voice, it's hard to tell if Cross is appreciative of the Bureau's presence or if he resents it. Cops, like most people, can be territorial.

Darren answers the question. "It looks like these recent murders are linked to a female killer that the Bureau's had their eye on for quite some time." Coming from Darren, it shows Cross that Darren asked for our assistance, rather than us trying to push the local forces around. Plus it lets Cross know that Darren's playing ball with me, and so Cross will be more likely to follow suit.

"Ah." Cross smiles. "Terrific." His tone is genuine.

He leads us through to the station proper. "I'll tell you this much, this case has got me now."

I follow him. "It's intriguing all right."

"The more I think about Janice's death, the more I can see the characteristics of a professional hit. Are you guys checking the mob angle?" We come to some stairs and Cross slowly climbs them.

"No. But I guess that's a factor in this jurisdiction," Darren says as he catches up to us. We stay level on the stairs, letting Cross set the pace. Wouldn't want to give the guy a heart attack, especially when he's probably only a few years from retirement.

"You betcha. But what Janice and Cindy have got to do with the mob…" Cross trails off and shakes his head slightly.

It's an interesting take, but I don't think the mob rings true. "Cindy's and Malcolm's murders are both sexual. Classic serial-killer stuff."

Cross looks at me. "That your specialty, serial killers?"

"Yeah. That's what I mostly concentrate on."

"That why you came to the States? Not enough serial killers in Australia?"

I'm impressed that he picked the accent. Many Americans think I'm South African or even English because I don't have the broad Paul Hogan accent.

"I came for the profiling, for the Bureau. But yes, I do enjoy working on serial cases."

Cross nods. At the second floor he takes a left. "Do you have many serial killers in Australia?"

"We've had a few." Several is more accurate. "But nothing like here. It's largely a population thing. We're not even twenty million. About one-fourteenth the size of the U.S."

He makes a small grunting noise as he takes another left. "But I bet you don't have one-fourteenth the number of serial killers."

He's right. The stats are high in the U.S. I remember the first time I read the Bureau estimate—it sent chills down my spine. They think the U.S. has more than two-thousand serial killers at large. I do the arithmetic in my head of what the comparative number would be in Australia, given our population difference. I come up with around one hundred and forty. Australia doesn't have anywhere near that many—and certainly not at large.

Cross doesn't wait for a response. "How'd you get past the U.S. citizen thing?"

All FBI employees must be U.S. citizens, so it's a good question.

"My dad's American," I explain. "I hold dual citizenship."

Cross takes a right, into an open-plan office. "I see." He walks toward a desk in the far right-hand corner. "This is me," he says as he takes a seat behind the desk. There are two chairs on the near side, which I can only assume he's set up in anticipation of our arrival.

Darren and I sit and Cross flips open a file. The chitchat is over. "Well, I thought first we'd go out to the house where the girls lived. Then I've got us set up for an interview with their boss at one."

I smile, thinking of Hamill's approach in Chicago. What a contrast Cross is. Hamill was helpful, to a point, but Cross is efficiency personified. Something I wouldn't have guessed if I'd judged him solely on his rather shabby appearance.

"I tracked down Cindy's parents. Her real name is Cindy Bass and she's from Yucca Valley. Interestingly, not that far from the southern tip of the Mojave. One of the locals went out and informed the parents. Apparently they hadn't seen or heard from their daughter since she was sixteen."

"Really?" I say, curious about what caused the family rift. That's something else Malcolm and Cindy have in common.

Darren looks at me "What's up?"

I must have the light-bulb look on my face. "Both Cindy and Malcolm were estranged to some degree from their parents."

Darren purses his lips. "You think it means something?"

I shrug. "Who knows? But it is a link between them and interesting in terms of the victim profiles."

Cross moves it along. "I also spoke to Janice's parents. They live in L.A. Told them that we'd had a break and that we were now investigating Janice's death as suspicious. As you can imagine, they had lots of questions."

"I'll bet they did," Darren says.

"Anyway, I told them that her roommate's body had been found in Arizona, and that it seems like too much of a coincidence that both girls should wind up dead."

Darren takes out his notebook. "It's *possible* it's a coincidence."

Cross scratches his nose. "Possible, but what are the odds?"

"Were they surprised?" I ask.

"No." Cross shakes his head. "Not at all. I spoke to Janice's mother and she said she knew Janice hadn't ODed. Knew her daughter was off the stuff for good."

It makes sense and ties in with our hunch that Janice knew something.

He places one file down and pulls out another. "So, Cindy. I pulled what I could on her and had a look through it yesterday. Don't know if it's worth our while actually going to the Yucca. I mean, her family hasn't seen her for over five years."

I nod. "I doubt they'll know much about her life."

"What's she got in common with Malcolm?" Cross asks us. "Other than a falling-out with her parents?"

Darren hesitates, but only for a second. "The signature elements at the crime scene are a perfect match—"

I interrupt Darren. "Almost."

Cross looks at me, waiting for the explanation.

"They both had a red love heart painted on their chests, but Malcolm also had a rose tattooed on the inside of his right wrist. That's how we linked him to these other cases that the Bureau's interested in. Cindy didn't have the tattoo."

"Seems odd," Cross comments.

Darren takes over again. "We think we're looking at two killers. A couple."

"Really?"

We both nod.

"So which one was responsible for Janice?"

"It could have been either of them. Like you said, Janice's murder was carried out like a professional hit. In my opinion, Malcolm and Cindy were killed for pleasure." I pause to let this sink in with Cross. "But Janice's murder was business. Quick and quiet, the killer didn't get off on it. Janice knew something and had to be silenced, full stop."

We're quiet for a little while, before Darren continues with the victim comparison. "Both Malcolm and Cindy left around the same time. Both lied to those around them about where they were going and what they were doing. And forensics tells us that both were in the Mojave Desert."

"Anything else?" Cross asks.

"Occupations." Darren and I haven't spoken about it, but I see a similarity between being an escort and being a dancer. Both traded in their bodies, albeit at the upper end of the market.

Darren raises an eyebrow. "Maybe." He turns to Cross. "Malcolm was an escort. High-class."

Cross looks at me. "But they were killed by different people."

"Yes. We've got the original profile on Malcolm's killer." I pull the photocopied report, with my small changes, from my briefcase and hand it to Cross. "This was drafted two years ago by the FBI and we've made a few updates."

"What about cause of death for Malcolm?"

I take the question. "Strangulation. Female killer who seduces her victims and strangles them during the sexual act. Been active for fifteen years."

Cross's face crumples. "No wonder the FBI's been looking for her."

"Exactly," I say.

Cross's eyes go back to the sheets of paper in his hand and when he's finished reading the profile he looks up. "Never tracked a female serial killer before. Y'all——" he looks at me, but obviously refers to women in general "——tend to murder for love or in self-defense."

He's right. When women kill——and we certainly do kill——it tends to be because we've been jilted or cheated on by our lover or because we're in a domestic violence situation that escalates to the point where it's "him or me." Everyone who works this case will be slightly enthralled by the presence of a female serial killer.

We're silent again. After a few beats Cross gathers his coat from the back of his chair. "Let's visit our crime scene."

15

We leave our rental out front and Cross drives. The ride is quiet, and I use the down time to take in my surroundings. I can't really experience Vegas, not this trip, but I can look at it from afar, as a visitor if not a tourist. We drive out of the station and along Las Vegas Boulevard until Cross jumps a few lanes and lands us on the I-515. We get off at the airport exit, and after a left and then a right, Cross pulls up in front of a small brick house in what seems like a very nice neighborhood, more family orientated than trendy. A red PT Cruiser sits in the driveway.

"Whose car?" I ask.

Cross switches the engine off. "Janice's."

Darren gets out of the car and looks at the Cruiser. "Nice wheels."

The garden is sparse, but well-maintained. No weeds, several shrubs that are just starting to sprout spring buds, and about ten rose-bushes evenly spaced along the front of the house. The entrance is enclosed by a small porch, just the width of the door, and crime-scene tape stretches across the porch's outer posts. Cross unsticks one side and takes out a key from a small plastic money bag that's labeled "Dust: 275 Calliope Drive." The door is dark wood with only one lock. Obviously the girls weren't too security conscious, although it's probably also reflective of the wholesome neighborhood they chose. It makes me wonder if the traffic-light system I use for my apartment is paranoid rather than cautious.

We enter the house and I can see instantly that it's a home not a house. I find it difficult to understand how any cop believed Janice ODed. The home is about as far removed as you can imagine from a typical heroin addict's house. One look tells you that Cindy and Janice took pride in their surroundings and had a well-developed nesting instinct. They'd worked hard to create the right atmosphere, and unless dancers get paid a helluva lot more than I think, most of their money went into their home, not hits of heroin for Janice.

The doorway opens into a large living room and to the left is the kitchen. The living-room carpet is worn in spots, but the girls have added three plush rugs. Two new-looking leather sofas adorn the back and right-hand walls, and in between them is a glass coffee table. Near the doorway is a modern, large-screen television, at least a couple of grand's worth.

I put on a pair of latex gloves—every good investigator carries at least a couple of pairs in their bag—and move toward the photos adorning the walls. Most of them feature Cindy and Janice, and it's obvious they were very close. They worked together, lived together and socialized together. A few of the photos have other people in them, and some of the photos are of the girls in costume.

"You know who all these people are?" I ask Cross.

"Yeah. They're mostly from the show. Cindy had been in Vegas for five years, since she left the Yucca. She worked as a waitress in Circus Circus for two years, then in Caesar's for a year, before she got the dancing gig. She spent her first three years auditioning, with no luck until Femme."

I nod. "Janice is a bit older." The age difference tells me that either Cindy was mature for her age or Janice was immature.

"Yup. Cindy was twenty-one, Janice was twenty-six. Everyone down at Hugo's says they were inseparable."

Darren also peers at the photos. "Not many men in their lives."

"We wondered about that, too."

"You think they were lovers?" From the way Cindy poses in the photos and the clothes she wears when not working, it would surprise me. Everything about her cries out for male attention. She wears the same cheeky grin in all the photos, pushes out her boobs ever so slightly, and seems to go for short skirts and plunging necklines. She wouldn't need to try so hard to catch the attention of another woman.

"We looked into it, but everyone we spoke to said no way. Both girls had casual male partners, but no one special."

I nod and move into the kitchen. Darren goes the other way, presumably toward the bedrooms. Cross seems unsure which way to go, but in the end he follows me. The kitchen is larger than it looked in the photos. In one corner is a dining-room table, the table Janice was sitting at. She was sitting on the chair nearest the door but it's now back in its place, rather than toppled over on the floor.

"We think she was sitting down when she took the hit." Cross, now also with gloves on, puts his hand on the back of the chair nearest the door. "She slumped to the side and fell to the ground." He uses his toe to point to the place where Janice's body lay.

"Have the lab techs been back?" I ask, knowing they wouldn't have dusted for prints or looked for other trace evidence in the original overdose investigation.

"Yeah. They've got everything they need for the moment."

"Good." That means I don't have to be quite so careful with the crime scene. I sit down in the chair. "So, let's say the perp made his or her way in here under false pretences. Janice sits at the table…why?"

"Maybe she had a drink with him."

It's possible, but at some point he must have been behind her to take out a syringe, prepare it and then catch her by surprise and inject her. All without her putting up a fight. She must have been preoccupied by something, something engrossing enough that her attention was diverted.

"What if he had something for her to look at? Like a catalogue." I grab the profile from my bag and put it on the table, leaning over it as if I was reading.

Cross plays along. "He's watching her, maybe every now and again pointing something out to her." He leans across me from behind, pointing to a line of the profile. "When she's sufficiently occupied, he prepares the syringe. He quickly grabs her arm from behind and sticks the syringe into her vein." Cross grabs my arm and simulates the interaction.

"It's pretty risky. We must be talking about a very confident killer. She could have taken a swipe at him, he could have missed the vein."

Cross obliges and replays the arm grab. This time I sit up and take a pretend swipe at him with my right hand, but he manages to duck and keep hold of my arm.

"If he was strong——" Cross says, coming in from underneath my outstretched right arm and taking another shot at my vein "——he had her right where he wanted her. If something went wrong with the heroin, I'm sure he had a backup plan. It's a real professional job."

I think about Cross's argument. I've been trained to fight, trained to defend myself, but most women haven't. Back in my Tiger and Crane kung fu classes in Melbourne, I'd been one of only a handful of girls in the class. In fact, sometimes I was the sole representative of my sex. This isn't about what *I'd* do, it's about what Janice would do...how *she'd* react. Janice might have been too shocked to even think about trying to hit him. Or maybe she was just too slow——the killer was prepared for a response, just like Cross was. I could have taken a second go at Cross then and got him. Hell, I don't train a couple of hours a day for nothing. But this is about Janice. She wouldn't have been ready. Cross is right.

"I like it. It rings true with the boldness of coming to her house."

Cross wanders back into the living room and leaves me to snoop around the kitchen for a bit, but nothing holds my interest or is particularly helpful. I close my eyes and try to focus on Janice and what happened in this room. But I'm too distracted by the sound of Cross only a few meters away. If he came back in, it would look pretty strange me standing in the middle of the kitchen with my eyes closed and taking deep breaths.

I move through the living room on my way to the bedrooms. I meet Darren and Cross on the way. "Anything?" I ask.

Darren shakes his head. "Maybe *you* will have some luck." He puts a very slight emphasis on *you* and I get the hint. He'll keep Cross occupied for me.

"Okay," I say.

Cross doesn't seem to notice the hidden meaning in the exchange.

"Cindy's is the first room." Darren points up the hallway.

"Thanks," I say, hiding a grimace. "Janice died in the kitchen. Cross can show you how we think it went down."

I continue down the hallway into Cindy's room, and I'm immediately hit by the central piece of furniture, a large four-poster. I shake my head at the irony. But unlike the one in my dreams and waking visions, this one is modern. Made with wrought iron, the posts stretch straight up and are connected to one another by curves of iron. The artistic work also makes a heart on the headboard. Again, the symbolism hits me: Cindy slept under a love heart and she died with one painted on her chest. The bedclothes are simple, plain light blue, with four large pillows at the head of the bed. Two metal-and-glass bedside tables take up a small space on either side of the bed and a large chest of drawers is against the wall, next to the door. The far wall has a built-in closet, overflowing with shoes and clothes. I flick through the mostly designer labels, all skimpy and size four.

I sigh and look back at her bed. My stomach clenches. I should be trying to induce a vision, but I'm afraid of what I'll see and feel.

I think about the Jacksons. Justice. My job's about justice. It's too late for Malcolm, Cindy and Janice, but their families will want justice. I have to at least try.

Even though I'm confident Darren will keep Cross busy, I still close Cindy's door so I've got some privacy. Sitting on the edge of Cindy's bed, I roll my shoulders back trying to relax them, and then move my head from side to side. My shoulders and neck are tense from lugging my heavy briefcase around, but the small movements loosen them somewhat. I take a deep breath in and focus on a point on the wall. I think about the pure whiteness of that point. A constant stream of thoughts flow into my already crowded mind, from the serious to the mundane. A tug of war goes on for a few minutes before finally my mind is quiet. Once the canvas is blank, I bring an image of Cindy into my mind and concentrate on her. Nothing happens at first, but then finally, after a wave of dizziness, it comes. But it's not what I was expecting or hoping for.

Cindy walks through a tunnel, a long tunnel, carrying some luggage. She climbs a ladder, struggling with the bag. Then a man's hand reaches down and pulls her up to the surface. She's surrounded by sand, the desert.

She's dead, lying near the Dumpster with a love heart drawn on her chest.

Then she's standing in the desert. She looks at me. "Help me!" she mouths, but no sound comes out. She's naked and a large red heart covers her chest. Her hair is blown in all directions and the sand whips around her ankles, pounding her body.

In the back of the car, I stare out the window and chew furiously on my lip. I can't get the image of Cindy in the desert pleading for help out of my head. I keep recycling it, over and over again. What the hell was that? Why did I see her like that?

I'm shaken out of my dark thoughts when the car comes to a halt. I look up and realize we're at the main entrance of Hugo's. We pile out and Cross flashes his badge to the parking attendant. Focus. The case.

Within seconds of the badge making its appearance, a woman in a business suit hurries our way. She's a tall, lanky woman, the kind who could probably eat a cow—and fries—for dinner every night without gaining an ounce of weight. Her suit is navy, and a perfect fit—tailored, unless her measurements happen to correspond exactly to a shop size. A white shirt pokes its way over the lapel of her jacket. She was obviously waiting for us; no doubt to ensure the badge is pocketed as quickly as possible, away from the prying eyes of tourists and guests who may spend less money in her complex if they think something is amiss.

"Detective Cross?"

"Yes."

"I'm Beverley Vander, Hugo's entertainment manager. If you'd like to come this way."

Cross puts his badge away, but doesn't even have time to introduce Carter or me. Instead we all have to hightail it to keep up with Ms. Vander's long strides as she takes us across the casino floor. I don't mind the pace, because it's a surefire way to avoid thinking about the vision of Cindy. Instead I absorb my surroundings. We pass card tables, a couple of roulette wheels, craps tables, and then come to a huge section of slot machines. The casino's guests cover the full spectrum—from retirees to families to young couples. It takes us several minutes to navigate through the gaming area and into another foyer.

Finally, Ms. Vander slows down and turns back to us. "I'll take you backstage."

Cross uses the opportunity to talk. "Ms. Vander, this is Detective Carter from Tucson Homicide and Special Agent Anderson from the FBI."

She nods and gives us both a quick handshake before moving down a corridor that leads backstage. She continues her frenetic pace until she reaches a door with Chorus written on it. "This is where the girls get ready." She opens the door. On the back corner of the room is a long clothes rack, overflowing with costumes. The two side walls are covered in stage mirrors and desks, five on either side. The narrow bench is cluttered with makeup and some of the mirrors have photos stuck to their corners.

"Which are their stations?" I ask, but my voice sounds slightly dreamy, even to me. Darren shoots me a questioning look but I ignore it.

"Umm." For the first time, Ms. Vander is not the picture of authority. "The stage manager will know."

Cross walks along the mirrors and points to a photo of Janice and Cindy. He peers at it more closely. "This must be one of their areas."

I look at the photo over Cross's shoulder, but I don't see Cindy smiling for the camera. Instead I remember how she looked standing in the desert, dead. What did I actually see? It's not the past or the present or the future. Are we talking…are we talking a ghost here? Is Cindy trying to give me a message?

I'm brought back by Cross's voice and I focus on him, on where I am right now. I don't want to think about the desert.

"Where's the stage manager?" Cross asks Vander.

"I've got the whole team assembled in the theater, waiting for you."

Cross moves to the doorway. "Let's talk to them first, then we'll come back here."

Vander nods and leads the way. As soon as I'm clear of the stage curtains I see about twenty people gathered in the front-row seats. An older man hoists himself onto the stage.

"Rodney will give you everything you need, but please, don't hesitate to call me if there's anything I can help you with." Vander fishes a business card out of her suit pocket and hands it to Cross. Now she's covering her ass. She wants to come across as cooperative. She moves closer to Cross and lowers her voice, but I can just make out what she says. "Please, Detective, we'd appreciate it if you could keep this incident as quiet as possible. We at Hugo's don't want any negative press."

Cross nods. "We'll do our best."

I doubt Cross cares about the press, but like Vander, he's covering his ass and smoothing the waters. If we need the press for the case, Cross won't hesitate to use them.

"Thank you, Detective." She gives Darren and me a quick nod and within a few strides she's out of view.

Rodney brings our focus back to the group. "I still can't believe it. Both Janice and Cindy."

The distress in his voice is obvious. To Ms. Vander, Cindy and Janice were names on a list, employee numbers, but to Rodney and everyone else here they were colleagues at the very least, and possibly friends.

I turn to Rodney. "It's a terrible tragedy." My voice is full of emotion, still having a strong visual of Cindy's dead body. Too much emotion for a straight investigator.

He welcomes the empathy by keeping his eyes on me as he shakes his head slowly. "Cindy murdered and Janice overdosing."

Cross steps forward. "Actually, Mr…"

"It's Rodney Sands, but just call me Rodney, everyone does."

Cross continues. "Actually, Rodney, Janice's death looks suspicious now. In light of Cindy's murder."

"I knew it! I knew Janice wouldn't have gotten into heroin again." He sighs. "We were close, Janice and I. I worked with her for four years on this show, and another year before that over at Caesar's. I knew her when she was using. She got off—for good. I can't imagine anything making her use again. And I mean *anything*."

That's two people close to Janice—her mother and Rodney—who vouch for her complete reform.

Cross nods. "Both her and Cindy…it is too coincidental."

"Yes," Rodney says. His eyes are still watery. "So what can we do to help?"

"We'll start off by interviewing everyone. Are all these people in the show's chorus?" Cross motions to the front row.

"No. That's our whole crew. Chorus girls, feature artists and the stage crew."

"I'll interview the girls," I say before Darren or Cross has time to beat me to it. Personally, I think I'll be able to focus on the investigation more easily than a man could. At least I won't be distracted by the skimpy costumes.

Cross seems a bit disappointed, but nods nonetheless. "I'll take the stage crew," he says to both Rodney and us, "and Carter, you get the feature artists, whatever that means."

I take up my position in the back row, and keep myself occupied with the facts of the case, questioning my girls one by one.

Three hours later Cross, Darren and I leave the theater.

"Well?" Cross looks at us.

I go first. "Not much. A few of the girls commented that Cindy seemed a little bit excited, happier than usual." I fidget with my ring, thinking of her distressed face in my desert vision.

"Really?" Darren raises an eyebrow.

"What's the big deal?" Cross asks.

Darren turns to him. "One of Malcolm's friends said the same thing. Apparently Malcolm hinted that when he came back from his *vacation*—" Darren makes air quotes "—he might have a bit of money."

Cross makes an interested grunt.

"Her sister, Laurie, also visited her a little while back," I say.

Both Darren and Cross nod, so obviously Laurie was mentioned to them too.

"How'd you guys do?" I ask.

"You got more than me," Darren says. "All I got was that both girls seemed nice. No one saw or heard anything out of the ordinary. It seems that the feature artists don't socialize much with the chorus."

"Oh," I say. "And one girl said that Gary, one of the stagehands, was sweet on Cindy." I look at Cross.

"Yup. He told me himself. I don't think there's much in it, but I'll still check out his movements over the past couple of weeks. Just to be on the safe side."

We look at him, waiting for more.

"Rodney was the most helpful," Cross says. "He spent a lot of time with Janice and Cindy. He said he was suspicious of Cindy's story about medical treatment. Said she was never a good liar. He thought maybe she was going back home. To try and mend things with her folks."

"Did he say why it needed mending?"

"Yeah. Nasty business by the sounds of it." He pauses. "She was raped by some family friend, Ronald, when she was sixteen. Rodney didn't know the guy's last name. Anyway, she didn't tell anyone until she found out she was pregnant. Then she went to her folks, told them what happened."

I shake my head, already getting the picture. My empathy for Cindy just shot through the roof and my hands clench into fists.

Cross continues, "They didn't believe her. Told her she was a slut and ordered her out of the house. She came to Vegas, had an abortion and started work." He shakes his head. "Tough start in life."

"Tougher finish," I say.

16

Finally Darren and I are alone, having checked into a rather seedy motel off The Strip. It was all we could get on such short notice, unless we wanted to pay for a ritzy suite in one of the main hotels—we'd never get reimbursed for that. We sit in my room, case files unpacked on the small table.

"You saw something at Cindy and Janice's place, didn't you?"

I lie. "No." I stand up and start shuffling the files. I can feel Darren's eyes on me.

"Sophie, what's up?"

I don't respond.

He stands up and spins me around so I have to look him in the eyes. "You've been acting weird ever since you were in Cindy's room. What happened?" He takes both of my hands. "What did you see?"

That is the question...what did I see? "I—I don't know."

"Look, Sophie. I know you saw something. Why can't you trust me?"

I shake my head. "It's not you I don't trust."

"Then who is it?"

I look down. "It's me."

"What do you mean?"

"It just doesn't make sense." I drop into the chair behind me and Darren kneels down in front of me, keeping hold of my hands. "I must be…I must be seeing things." I take a deep breath. "I mean hallucinating."

He smiles and it almost turns into a laugh. "That's all this is about?"

I snatch my hands away from him. "That's all? I'm questioning my sanity here and you're making fun of me?"

"No, no." He shakes his head. "That's not what I meant. Sorry. Okay…" He grabs my hands again. "You're right, it *is* about trust. It's about trusting yourself and trusting this gift of yours. I don't know what you believe, if you believe in God or some other sort of higher being. But one thing's for sure, this *is* a calling, a calling that puts you in touch with all sorts of things. I know something you saw at Cindy's has frightened you, but you have to trust it."

The intensity in Darren's compassionate blue eyes sucks me in. I do trust him. "I saw Cindy."

"Yes?"

"She was dead…but she was talking to me."

"Oh, I see." He moves from his knees onto his haunches. "She came to you."

"So it was…it was her ghost?"

"My aunt believed in spirits of the dead. And even if she didn't see a ghost as such, sometimes she felt it was spirits who were guiding her, sending her the messages."

I nod. It felt like Cindy was trying to get my attention. "She asked me to help her."

Darren sits down. "You are helping her."

I shrug. "Am I?"

"Of course you are. That's what we're doing now. And that's why you tried to induce a premonition in Cindy's bedroom today, even though it scares you."

"I…I don't know."

We're silent for a little while. What Darren says makes sense, but sometimes logic and emotion are light-years apart.

"Have you spoken to Stone?" I change the topic.

Darren looks at me and I know he's deciding whether to pursue the conversation. But after a couple of seconds he stands up. "No. I'll call her now. See if there's any news from Tucson." He punches the speed-dial button on his cell. He holds the phone out from himself and talks into it like a walkie-talkie, converting his cell into a speakerphone. "Hey, Stone."

"Hi, Carter. How's Vegas?"

"You know. It's Vegas."

She laughs. "Don't sound so excited. I'd rather be in Vegas than Tucson."

"You've got a point there. Sorry I couldn't call you earlier. We've been on the road all day with Cross."

"How'd it go?"

"It seems both Malcolm and Cindy were excited about wherever they were going. And neither was close to their folks. Other than that, we've got nothing to tie these vics together...yet."

"And Cindy's roommate?" Stone asks.

"Everyone who knew her is convinced she wouldn't have been into heroin again."

"So the three deaths are related."

"Looks that way," Darren says. "What about your end?"

"I've spoken to all of Malcolm's clients but nothing suspicious. A few of them fit the profile in terms of age, occupation, et cetera, but they've all got alibis for the Thursday Malcolm was killed."

"Mmm. Okay. Let us know if anything else turns up."

"Will do. And have a hand of blackjack for me."

"Maybe I will, Stone." He hangs up and looks at me.

The silence and his look make me uncomfortable. I stand up and stare at the files on the table.

"I'm starving. You?" Darren says.

I'm relieved he's kept the conversation away from my vision of

Cindy. "Sure," I say, happy with the prospect of the distraction. "And maybe Stone's right. Maybe a round of blackjack would do us the world of good."

"Really?" Darren is clearly shocked.

"Hey, I may be a workaholic, but I *can* have a good time, you know." It's only the second flirtatious thing I've said to Darren since I got here and already I'm stressing about it.

He's halfway through my motel door. "Meet you in the foyer in twenty minutes?"

"Sure," I say, even though part of me could easily just roll into bed and sleep for twelve hours.

Exactly twenty-one minutes later I rush into the foyer. Darren's sitting on one of the stained lounges reading the paper. He's wearing black jeans, cowboy boots and a red sweater.

"Where we going?"

He looks up and closes the paper. "Thought we might try a casino."

I laugh. "Gee, thanks for the clarification."

We join the masses on The Strip. "Do you like rides?" Darren asks.

"Love 'em."

"Great." He looks up.

I follow his gaze. We're standing outside the Stratosphere, one of the northern-most places on The Strip. "Oh, no. No way!"

He shakes his head. "You're telling me an FBI agent is scared of a little-bitty ride?"

"You bastard!" He's got me. I have to go on the stupid ride now—my pride won't let me refuse. I sigh. "Let's go."

We make our way up to the top of the Stratosphere and Darren selects Insanity as the ride.

"Three Gs, at one-hundred stories up. You ready?"

"Uh huh," I say with more gusto than I feel. The rides are all on the rooftop but we get in line a few levels down. I watch the video promos and am relieved I haven't eaten yet. Insanity consists of an arm that extends from the top of the Stratosphere tower over the edge, so you're literally hanging in mid-air. It's certainly aptly named. The ride takes ten people at a time. Eventually they send us up to the rooftop. In real life, the ride looks even scarier than it did in the posters and video promos.

The expressions of the people getting off vary from exhilaration to horror, with some looking very green around the gills. I'm shooting for the first look.

Now that we're up close, even Darren looks worried. "Mmm, they really should set it up so you can't see it before you get on."

I laugh. "A big Homicide cop like you, afraid of a little-bitty ride."

He shoots me back a challenging yet cheeky look.

By the time we're ushered over to Insanity's tentacles, I'm shaking slightly and my stomach feels like it's in my throat. In fact, it's not that dissimilar to the feeling I get when we're on a bust. Adrenaline. You'd think I'd be used to it by now. Oddly enough, I think I'm more scared of the stupid ride.

I strap myself in and prepare to be scared shitless. I glance around and the other passengers all have similar looks of anticipation and fear. The ride starts off with a fairly gentle spin that lulls me into a false sense of security. This isn't so bad, right? But then the speed picks up and the arms extend upward and outward so we're suspended in the middle of nowhere.

I look down and scream, a combination of excitement and fear. Darren's grinning at me but his smile is misshapen from the g-force. I grin back. After a couple of breathless, terrifying minutes the ride slows down again and the arms retract, returning us to the safety of the rooftop. I unbuckle myself and slide out of the seat, my legs slightly wobbly, perhaps not convinced that I really do have solid ground under me. After all, I'd just been dangling one-hundred stories in the air.

"That was amazing," I say.

"I knew you'd love it."

"You did not. You hoped I'd be scared."

He grins.

"I'm just glad I haven't eaten in the last few hours," I say.

"I'm with you there." He pats his stomach. "Although give my stomach another few minutes and I think I'll be hungry again."

We decide on an Asian restaurant in the Stratosphere complex, and enjoy some sushi and noodles before hitting The Strip again. If anything, the street is more crowded now, at 10:00 p.m., than it was at 8:00 p.m. We're jostled along with the crowd, me ogling all the way.

"Time to experience the real Vegas." Darren points to the Mirage and we make our way through its doors and into the belly of the casino.

"Well, what's your game? Slots, blackjack, poker?"

"Blackjack." I pause. "Small limit."

"Suits me."

We make our way through the busy slot machines, with their lights and sound effects, to the card area. The first table is a ten-dollar minimum bet, so we move on until we find a spare seat at the one-dollar table. Darren motions me into the seat.

"What about you?"

"I'll watch for a start."

I hand the dealer a twenty—big spender—and get my twenty chips in return. I'm in the game. Before the first hand is even over, a waitress is asking Darren and me what we'd like to drink. Darren orders a beer and I order a piña colada. When in Vegas...

I'm on a winning streak, up by ten dollars after only ten minutes, when Darren manages to get the seat next to me. The dealer hands out the cards. I've got a ten and a five—tricky. The general rule I was told with blackjack is to sit on sixteen or more. I stick with the rule and ask the dealer to hit me. He deals a five and I sit, unable to wipe the smile off my face. One good thing about casinos—you don't have to worry about bluffing.

"Having a good time?" Darren asks.

"Great time." I take the last sip of my drink, which was delicious but served in a very small glass.

Darren sits on his hand and the dealer busts, making us both winners.

Multiple hands blur into one, broken up with a couple more drinks and lots of laughter. When I finally look at my watch I almost fall off my stool.

"It's 2:00 a.m.!" I say. "That's incredible."

Darren looks at his watch too, needing visual confirmation. "Wow! I guess we better call it a night."

"I'll say. What time is Cross expecting us in the morning?"

"First thing."

"Great." I count my chips—thirty-two in total. Not bad. I've won twelve dollars, been entertained for a few hours and had four free piña coladas. Darren's down, but only by a few dollars.

The walk back seems to take forever and the people and lights now seem overwhelming rather than magical. That's what tiredness will do to you.

"What a great night," I say to Darren as we walk down the corridor to our rooms.

"I'll say. You needed some R & R. To take your mind off things."

We stop outside my door. "I guess I did." I rummage through my handbag for my key card. "It's in here somewhere." My hair falls into my face and I push it back before resuming the search. Once again, a few strands of hair fall into my eyes. This time it's Darren who smoothes my bangs back, gently touching my face. I pause, momentarily forgetting what I was doing. But I don't look up at Darren. Looking at him now would be too dangerous.

I resume the search. "Found it."

Darren runs his hand along my face, and finally I can no longer resist the urge to look at him. As soon as our eyes meet he bends down and kisses me. Although a large part of me wants him, I only half respond. The kiss is brief and we're both aware of the awkwardness. He drops his hand and the rest of his body seems to slump a little too. "Well, I guess I'll see you in the morning." He spins around and walks the two doors down to his room without looking back. He's in his room before I've even unlocked my door.

Once inside I lean on the door. Shit! I really have a knack with men. Darren is a great guy and I am attracted to him, but it's too soon. My last relationship is unresolved. Are we having a break or have we split up? And the whole thing's complicated by the damned Slasher case and the uneasiness I still feel when I'm around any man. Will that ever go away? Darren's perfect for me in so many ways, but it's not right. Not yet.

BlackWidow: I'm surprised Danny shared that pizza.

DialM: Yes, very out of character for him.

AmericanPsycho: It's also lucky for him.

NeverCaught: Why?

AmericanPsycho: Let's just say the pizza's not going to agree with them.

DialM: This latest scheme is devious, Psycho. What did you use?

AmericanPsycho: A nasty strain of salmonella.

NeverCaught: Lethal?

AmericanPsycho: Maybe…if he'd had the whole thing.

BlackWidow: Wonder why he did share?

NeverCaught: He might be sick of everyone hating him.

BlackWidow: Maybe. But I think his motives are more strategic than that. How long until we start to see the effects?

AmericanPsycho: Food poisoning's usually four to six hours, so any minute now. Danny's already starting to look a little queasy.

BlackWidow: Yes.

NeverCaught: Check out Clair and Jonathan. I think they're sweet on each other.

DialM: They're actually quite compatible. They're both into music—if you could call it that. Did you try to match anyone? For our viewing pleasure?

AmericanPsycho: As a matter of fact…

NeverCaught: Hope they ***. That'd be cool. Then I can get all my viewing pleasure in one package. Right here.

DialM: Look at Danny now. He's certainly looked better.

NeverCaught: The others aren't so hot, either.

AmericanPsycho: Here we go, the first run to the toilet. Danny.

DialM: He did eat the most pizza.

BlackWidow: Oh, I'm turning my speakers down.

DialM: Agreed. The sound's getting to them, too.

NeverCaught: Here goes Susie. This is gross, man.

AmericanPsycho: Well, you can always log out.

NeverCaught: Yes, but I might miss something. Something other than puking.

BlackWidow: Can you imagine the stench in that toilet?

DialM: I'd rather not!

AmericanPsycho: This is fun! Did you hear Jonathan's plea?

NeverCaught: Medical help. Please!

BlackWidow: It's sweet that he's worried about Danny. I wouldn't be.

NeverCaught: But you're a cold-blooded killer.

17

The alarm goes off at 6:30 a.m., but the radio is drowned out by the deathly thud in my head. I moan, turn over and hit the snooze button. I don't think I'll be going for a run this morning. I only had four small piña coladas! What's with the hangover? I guess my tolerance is low these days.

Finally, I get up at 7:30 a.m. Bloody Darren. I'll kill him. Then again, I could have said no to the drinks he ordered for me. Vegas and its free alcohol is a damn effective way to keep people at the tables. I struggle out of bed over to the bar fridge and guzzle the only bottle of water. Time to phone Darren. I hesitate, my hands hovering over the keypad. The kiss. This is going to be tricky. Okay, I'll pretend nothing happened. That's always a good strategy—kind of.

"Hello." His voice sounds fuzzy. "Detective Carter," he adds, at the last minute.

I manage a laugh. "It's me. You up?"

"Yup. Yup, I'm up."

"I'll see you at the front desk in thirty minutes?"

"Mmm." His voice is still foggy. Unlike me, Darren didn't have to limit his alcohol intake.

"Thirty minutes," I repeat before hanging up. When it's self-in-flicted, it's nice to know someone is suffering more than you. Teasing Darren might also be a good way to avoid the awkwardness of last night's kiss.

When I arrive at the reception area, just over thirty minutes later, I am surprised to see him already checking out. I stand still and watch him from a distance, knowing I'm out of his field of vision. Darren is a great catch, a great guy. Maybe I'm a fool. Will he still be free if I wait? I take a deep breath, trying to quiet the tornado of but-terflies in my stomach, and walk casually over to the front desk.

"You weren't really up, were you?" I ask.

He turns to me and the look on his face shows me his attraction. "Of course," he says, but shakes his head at the same time. "I don't need much work in the morning." He runs his hand over his face. "Shower, shave…"

I'm glad of the light mood. "You and those piña coladas."

He waves a dismissing hand in front of me. "They were tiny and they're watered-down in Vegas. Don't tell me you're feeling under the weather."

I'm conscious of how close we are. "I have a slight headache." I raise my thumb and forefinger and pinch them together, indicating how small the headache is.

"Man, you agents are sissies."

"In my day I could have drunk you under the table."

"Dream on."

"I actually used to be able to hold my drink in my early twenties." He laughs. "Didn't we all? Slippery slope, you know."

Darren and I are both in our midthirties. I'm thirty-five, and I'm not entirely sure exactly how old Darren is, but he's definitely be-tween thirty-four and thirty-eight, despite his baby face.

He signs his American Express receipt. "Breakfast?" He scoots over so I can sign out, too.

I hand the clerk my key. "Definitely," I say to Darren, already feel-ing more at ease, despite the kiss. In fact, I'd say the tornado of but-terflies has downgraded to a gentle breeze.

The guy at the reception suggested two places within walking distance, and we opt for the closest. It's plastered with pictures of "The King" and other memorabilia. I order two poached eggs and Darren orders the "Big Breakfast", which comprises of eggs, bacon, sausage, hash browns and toast.

"Tell me you're not going to put maple syrup on your bacon."

"You betcha." He winks. "Have you ever tried it?"

"No. But I can imagine the taste and that's enough for me."

"Don't knock it till you try it."

Nothing will ever get me to try it. "What are we going to work on today?" I say, now fully at ease with him. This is for the best. Friends…we can be friends.

"Good question."

"How far is Yucca Valley?"

"Cindy's hometown. About three hours by car, or twenty minutes by plane. You think it's worth going? I mean, she hasn't been home in five years, I don't know if they'll be able to tell us much."

"Her sister came and stayed with her. Maybe they're in regular contact."

Darren follows my line of thought. "And if she told Janice something—"

I nod. "She may have told her sister."

"Let's try her on the phone first. See if we can't save ourselves a trip."

Generally it's better to interview people face-to-face. You can read their body language and tell if they're lying; they're also more likely to open up to you in person. But with Cindy dead, her sister's probably going to do everything she can to help us. "Okay, we'll give it a go. I'd like to speak to her though. I think she's more likely to open up to a woman, given what Cindy went through."

Darren grimaces. "The rape."

I nod.

The waitress arrives with our coffees—straight filtered coffee. I miss my lattes in the States. Here you have to go to Starbucks to get an espresso. Still, the bottomless cup ain't all bad.

Darren stirs in sugar. "We can make Cross's office our base. He's expecting us anyway."

"I wonder if the re-examination of Janice's case will turn up anything."

"Maybe the apartment will have something for us." He puts his spoon back on the saucer. "Forensics swept it before we arrived yesterday. Nice to get a print."

I take a sip of coffee. "Nice, but unlikely. Like we said, the job on Janice was professional. Professionals wear gloves."

The waitress arrives with our breakfasts. "That was fast," I say, half to her, half to Darren.

She smiles. "Most people like it fast. So's they can get back to the slots or tables."

Vegas is a conspiracy.

Darren picks up the maple syrup and waves it in front of my face. I put my hand up, blocking out the view of him pouring it over his toast and bacon.

"Man, that's disgusting," I say.

"Over two-hundred-million people can't be wrong."

I smile. "So, why don't you eat with chopsticks? Over two billion people can't be wrong."

When we arrive at the Vegas police station at quarter to nine, Cross is already at his desk and looks settled, like he's been there awhile.

"So, did you get to sample Vegas or did you work the case?"

"Bit of both actually," Darren says, even though we hardly spoke about the case.

I furrow my brow, guilt-ridden. We should have worked on the case last night. I should have been going over the files and trying to induce a premonition, despite being freaked out by the thought of Cindy's ghost or whatever the hell it was…. I shudder.

"So you up or down?"

"Down a few bucks," Darren says.

I come back to the conversation, forcing myself to at least appear normal. "And I won twelve bucks."

Cross looks at Darren. "Better luck tonight."

"We hope to be on a plane by tonight," Darren says. "We're checked out and all. Any word from the ME?"

"They're taking another look at Janice's body before lunch today."

Darren nods. "Great. And forensics?"

"Nothing yet. We probably won't have anything back from the lab today. They're pretty backed up down there."

It's the same the world around, the scientists can't keep up with the criminals.

"Family?" Cross hits the nail on the head—family is our only real starting point.

"Yeah." Darren puts his briefcase down. "Anderson wants to speak to Cindy's sister."

Cross looks at me.

"I'm hoping her visit a couple of years back wasn't the only contact between Cindy and little sis," I say.

"Well, state troopers informed the family two days ago, and I haven't heard boo from them. That's some falling-out if murder hasn't even brought them together. Normally parents would be calling every hour."

I shake my head. "I guess they still believe their friend, not Cindy."

Cross opens up one of the files on his desk and writes down a phone number on a Post-it Note. He hands it to me. "I'm going to make sure Gary's alibi check outs and then catch up on my other cases. My weekend's coming up." Today's Sunday, but obviously Cross's shift work has him rostered off Monday and Tuesday this week. Besides, there's not much more to do until the ME and forensics come back.

"You can use that desk today." He points to a cluttered but vacant desk.

Cross leaves as we settle in. Darren fishes out a file from his briefcase. "I'll go over these files again while you're talking to the family."

"We also need to go back to the woman's first victim, Cameron Michaels."

Darren nods. "Call first."

I lift up the phone and dial.

"Hello." It's a woman's voice, but it sounds older. Probably Cindy's mum.

"Hello, this is Special Agent Anderson from the FBI. I'm working on the murder of Cindy Bass." I use Cindy's real last name, as the parents may not even know she changed it to Star.

"Yes?" The voice is tentative.

"Is that Mrs. Bass?"

"Yes. I'm Cindy's mother." The tone is cold, detached. Like she's ashamed of admitting Cindy was her child.

"I'm sorry for your loss, Mrs. Bass."

"Thank you."

"I'm not sure how much the state trooper told you..."

"Just that Cindy was dead. That she'd been murdered." Cold again. So much for maternal instincts.

"That's right. We've linked the case to some other murders, too."

"Oh." A hint of surprise and curiosity in her voice.

"How did you think Cindy died, Mrs. Bass?"

"I don't like to speak ill of the dead, may the Lord forgive me, but Cindy was trouble. And I figured she'd got herself into trouble with some man."

It's hard to believe she's talking about her own daughter. I also notice the phrase she chose, "got herself into trouble," like it was Cindy's fault. Even if Mrs. Bass believed part of Cindy's story, that she was pregnant by their family friend, she could have easily assumed Cindy brought it on herself. I clench my fist, digging my fingernails into the palm of my hand. This kind of ignorance drives me crazy.

"It looks like Cindy was the victim of a serial killer," I say.

"Oh." This time perhaps a hint of sorrow—or maybe that's wishful thinking on my part.

"When was the last time you saw Cindy?"

She pauses. "Five years ago. When she left Yucca. She got herself into trouble here."

"Really?" I want to hear it in her words.

"She...she was pregnant." She lowers her voice, and I'm not sure if it's because she thinks someone will hear or because it's still a source of shame for her. "The baby must be about four years old now." This time she's definitely a little sad.

I hate to break it to her, but she should know. "Cindy had an abortion, Mrs. Bass, here in Vegas."

"No. No. Impossible. Cindy was...lots of things, but she would never have an abortion. Her religious upbringing wouldn't allow it."

"I'm sorry, Mrs. Bass." I decide to let it all hang on the line. I feel sorry for Cindy. Like Darren said, she had a tough start in life and then she got mixed up in...well, whatever the hell this is. Her family should know the truth. "It's very common, when the pregnancy is the result of rape," I say.

"Someone's been filling your head with lies." She's no longer angry about the abortion, now her emotional energy is fixated on Cindy's "lies." It's possible Cindy did lie, possible that the sex was consensual or that the baby's father was someone in her school. But my gut tells me Cindy was traumatized. When people make false sexual assault allegations it's usually for revenge or attention, and Cindy's behavior shows neither. Rodney was the only one from work who knew about the rape, which shows me she was ashamed...she didn't want attention. Mrs. Bass and her husband are fools.

"We're finding out as much as we can about Cindy, in the hope that something will lead us to her killer." I try to keep the anger out of my voice.

Silence.

"So you haven't had any contact with her at all in the past five years? No phone calls, Christmas cards?"

"No."

"What about your husband?"

"Certainly not." There's a hint of mocking in her voice.

"Can I speak with him?" Ideally I'd like to talk to all family members.

"He never speaks her name. He won't talk to you or anyone else."

"What about your other daughter and your son?"

"What about them?"

"Well, maybe they've been in contact with Cindy." I damn well know that at least her daughter Laurie has, but from the mother's reaction I'm not game to get Laurie into trouble. It wouldn't surprise me one bit if her visit to Vegas was a secret.

"No. Neither of them has spoken to Cindy since the day she left."

"Can I speak to your other daughter please?"

She hesitates. "I don't see the point."

"It's just procedure, Mrs. Bass." I sigh loudly pretending I'm bored. "You know, red tape. I'm supposed to talk to everyone in your family, including your husband and even Cindy's aunts and uncles." I pause, letting it sink in. I bet she doesn't want her extended family finding out about Cindy's pregnancy and abortion. "But I don't want to bother you with all that. I don't want to disturb you any more than I have to, so if I could just speak to your daughter and then your son, I'll leave you alone. If I've got at least three family members on my form here, my boss won't give me grief."

She pauses. "I guess...I guess I can get Laurie for you. Hold on." I hear a slight rustle.

"Laurie!" she yells.

The rest of the conversation is muffled, so I assume Mrs. Bass has put her hand over the receiver.

A minute later a voice comes on the line. "Hello?"

"Hi, Laurie. I'm Agent Sophie Anderson from the FBI. I'm working on your sister's case."

"Uh huh."

"We could really do with your help."

"Mmm."

I can picture what's happening on the other end of the phone: her mother is standing right next to her, making sure she doesn't say something she shouldn't, and for no other reason than it might damage the family's reputation. This is going to be tricky.

"We know you visited Cindy here in Vegas."

A small intake of breath.

"Don't worry. I didn't tell your mum."

"Okay." Relief in her voice.

"Is your mum standing right there?"

"Yes."

"You can't get away?"

A pause. "No."

"Okay. But I really need to talk to you. For Cindy's sake. Have you got a cell phone?"

"Yes."

"Okay, I'm going to call you on your cell in about half an hour." Somehow I have to get her number. "It would take me quite a bit of tracking down this end to get your cell number, but I know it starts with seven-six-zero." I say her area code. "I'm going to run through numbers and you stop me when I get to the right first number. One…two…three…four…"

"Yep."

"Okay." I repeat this process until I have all the digits of her cell phone. "Great, thanks, Laurie. Now pass me back to your mum."

Mrs. Bass comes back on the phone. "I told you we couldn't help."

"Yes. You're right. Well, I guess there's not much point talking to your son. I'll tell my boss that two names on my form is enough." I pause. "And I'll let you know when we find your daughter's killer."

"Yes. Do."

So she is interested.

"Thank you, Mrs. Bass. Goodbye." I force a pleasant tone into my voice.

"Bye now."

I hang up.

Darren looks up. "Sounded painful."

I shake my head. "Don't get me started. I'm glad we didn't visit in person. I think you would have had to hold me back."

"That bad?"

"Oh, yeah. I'm calling Laurie back on her cell in half an hour. Let's hope she can get out of the house."

"Mom keeps the apron strings tight?"

"It's a miracle Laurie even managed to visit Cindy."

Darren doesn't respond. Instead, he holds up the Cameron Michaels file. "Ready?"

"Ready as I'll ever be."

18

I dial Laurie's cell phone number.

"Hello."

"Hi Laurie. It's Agent Anderson."

"Hi." Her tone of voice is totally different than half an hour ago. Now she sounds relaxed and more like a normal teenager. "Thanks for that," she says cheerily. "You totally saved my ass."

"Your folks that bad, huh?"

"What do you think? We can't even mention Cindy's name in the house."

"You know why she left?"

"At the time I didn't." The cheeriness fades from her voice with each word. "For a couple of years I even believed all the crap my folks told me about Cindy tarnishing our good family name." She's using her parents' words, not hers.

"Then what happened?"

"Ronald." She spits the name. "But I was luckier than Cindy. My brother came in just at the right time. He pretended he didn't see anything and wouldn't even talk to me about it, but that fuck Ronald must have been scared, 'cause he hasn't tried to touch me since."

I pause, suddenly feeling a little nauseous.

An older man's on top of a younger-looking Cindy. Cindy's crying, but he doesn't stop.

I push the repulsive image away, shoving it deep down to wherever it came from. But I'm left with anger so intense that I want to slam my fists on the table and start throwing anything and everything I can find.

"Are you there?"

Laurie's voice brings my attention back the interview, back to my job.

"Yes, sorry. Hold on a sec." I take a deep breath. Back to the questions. "Did you know Cindy was pregnant?"

"After Ronald tried it on me I knew something was up. I managed to find Cindy in Vegas and she told me the whole story." She pauses. "That bastard. I tried to tell my folks, but they wouldn't hear it and my brother wouldn't back me up. I had to drop it. I'd seen what happened to Cindy when she told the truth." She sighs. "Another six months and I'm out of this dump."

"Really? Where you going?"

There's silence for a moment before I hear the unmistakable sound of tears. "Cindy." A sob breaks her voice. "Cindy's been saving for me all this time. Saving for me to go to college. It won't pay for everything of course, but it's enough with me working part-time."

"Sounds like she loved you a lot."

"Growing up we were so close. I was devastated when she left. Then I got confused. Started to believe the lies."

"It's hard not to believe your parents."

"Uh huh." She sniffs. "I went to visit Cindy in Vegas just under two years ago. Told my folks I was going on a religious retreat. God, if they knew I was going to sin city itself…" She trails off.

"And you've been in contact with Cindy since then?"

"Sure. We talk on the phone a couple times a week."

"What about in the last few weeks?"

"No. She was away."

"Did she say where she was going?"

"Sure. She tells me everything."

"Yes?" I actually lean forward in my seat. The movement catches Darren's eye and he studies my facial expression intently.

"She was going into the hospital. To get her wisdom teeth out."

My shoulders droop. "But wisdom teeth don't take a few weeks."

"She was getting her teeth done and then going to New York for a few auditions. She was trying to get a Broadway gig." There's pride in Laurie's voice.

Another lie. Both Malcolm and Cindy said they were going to New York. Coincidence? And why wouldn't she call? If she was in New York, or anywhere else for that matter, she still could have called her little sister for their weekly chats. Wherever she was, she knew she wouldn't have access to a phone. That ties in with the desert, somewhere isolated.

"So when was the last time you spoke to her?"

"Um, let me see. She was going into the hospital on March twentieth and she called me the night before. So it must have been the nineteenth."

I write it on my notepad. "Did she seem different the last time you spoke?"

"She was excited. About the audition. She said the job was real good money and that if she got it, she'd be able to put me through college, totally. Everything paid for."

Bingo. We've got the money again. And a much more definite reference than Cindy gave her workmates.

"Must have been some job," I say.

"Cindy was going places." The pitch of her voice drops at the end of her sentence, reflecting her grief.

"What about Janice? Did you know her very well?"

"Janice is fabulous."

I pause. Laurie just used present tense. Shit. "Laurie, your mum did tell you, didn't she?"

"Tell me what?"

Oh God. I take in a deep breath. "Janice...Janice is dead."

"What?"

I'm silent, letting her digest this additional tragedy.

"But...how?"

"She died of a drug overdose."

"Drugs? Janice doesn't do drugs." Her denial is shocked but authoritative.

"She used to. Did you know that?"

A pause. "Cindy said Janice fell on hard times a few years back. But she never said what it was."

"Heroin. She was a user for a couple of years."

"But not now. Not since I've known her."

"We're actually investigating Janice's and Cindy's deaths together. As related."

"What do you mean?"

"I don't know how much your mum has told you. Maybe it's not my place."

"Cindy's my sister. You've got to tell me. I'm not some kid."

She's right. Laurie's eighteen, and she should know. I tell her about her sister's death and the suspicious circumstances she was found in, without going into too much upsetting detail.

"I...I don't understand. This doesn't make sense. And Cindy wouldn't lie to me."

"People do strange things, Laurie."

"No, not Cindy."

"What if someone threatened Cindy? Told her that if she didn't do something, they'd hurt you. And that if she told you, they'd kill you. Would she lie to you then?"

She pauses. "Yes." She's got the point. Sometimes it's not as simple as lying or not lying. Other factors get in the way. Cindy obviously had a *reason* to lie. As did Malcolm. We've just got to work out what that reason was.

"So, are you sure she didn't say anything unusual in the weeks before March twentieth?"

There's a long pause. Laurie is probably replaying the conversations she had with Cindy. She would have already done this—it's part of what we do when we find out a loved one is dead. We replay our last moments with them, over and over again. But now she's looking for something different, something special.

"No," she says finally.

"There was definitely no hint of fear in her voice?"

"No way. I would have known. I would have been able to tell. Like I said, it was the opposite. She was excited."

I try to put myself in Laurie's shoes. Would she lie to me? And if so, why? "Laurie, you know that if you're in any trouble, any trouble at all, you can tell me. We'd be able to protect you."

"I swear it's nothing like that. I wish I did know where Cindy went. I really wish I did."

Part of me wants Laurie to be the answer, wants her to know. But part of me is relieved, because if Laurie did know something, chances are she'd already be dead.

NeverCaught: Now that's brutal. Even by my standards.
BlackWidow: Yeah, stop picking on my Jonathan.
AmericanPsycho: It's for the greater good.
BlackWidow: Don't know about that.
DialM: Ah, this is old world. Right up my alley. Nothing like a bit of good old-fashioned torture.
AmericanPsycho: It's only an isolation chamber.
BlackWidow: And the rest.
AmericanPsycho: What are you worried about, BW? Thought you said Jonathan was smart, cool. Strong despite the geek exterior.
BlackWidow: He is. But I don't want him ruined.
NeverCaught: I'm enjoying the brutality of it. I vote you keep going.

AmericanPsycho: We haven't broken him yet.
DialM: Yes, he's doing remarkably well. I'm impressed. And worried.
NeverCaught: You're always worried, old man. Live a little.
DialM: I do live...and they die.
AmericanPsycho: Yes, they always die.

19

"Well?" Darren asks.

I shake my head. "She doesn't know anything. And to be honest, if she did, I think she'd already be dead."

Darren nods. "Maybe you're right. Our perps haven't made many mistakes so far. Our only real lead would have been Janice."

"And look what happened to her." I lean my elbows on the desk and put my face in my hands, rubbing my forehead.

"I take it you had no luck with the family?"

I look up and am greeted by Cross's bulk.

"No. It's a dead end. They don't know anything."

He nods.

"How'd you do with Cindy's admirer at Hugo's?" I ask.

"Dead end, too. All his movements check out. He hasn't been out of Vegas." He sighs. "So, what are you guys going to do? Head back?"

Darren and I look at each other. I shrug, he shrugs, he nods, then I nod.

"Guess so," Darren says to Cross.

Cross shifts his weight from one foot to the other. "Not much more you can do here. I'll call you with the autopsy results and forensics as soon as I get them."

"Thanks, Cross," I say.

"Yeah, thanks for all your help." Darren forces a smile.

"Never let it be said that the Vegas force isn't cooperative." Cross puts his hands on his hips.

"Hey, what about your days off?" I ask, worried about missing two days of investigative time while the results sit on Cross's empty desk.

"The ME and lab know to call me on my cell. Don't worry, you won't be waiting for me to come back on shift."

"You'd fit right in on the Tucson team," Darren says.

"Any Homicide team," I add.

It's hard to completely clock off when you know lives are at stake. This case is no exception. In fact, if we're right, we've got four days until the next kill. Maybe someone's already holed up in the Mojave Desert, at the hands of our femme fatale and her new partner.

I zone out of the conversation as the men swap Homicide war stories, and lean back in my chair, ticking off a mental list of leads. One thing we haven't checked are the victims' financial records. I interrupt the male bonding. "Cross, have you looked at financials for Janice?"

"Not yet, and the detectives before me were investigating it as a straight OD so they didn't either."

"Back to the basics?" Darren says to me.

I give him a wink. "You know what they say, follow the money."

Darren smiles. "An oldie but a goodie."

Cross walks over to his desk and picks up a file. "They found one Visa card and one ATM card in Janice's wallet, plus a checkbook on the kitchen table. They filed all their bills and bank statements. I'll get them sent over from evidence." He picks up the phone and starts dialing.

"I'll call Hamill," Darren says. "See what we can get happening for Malcolm."

I look up Cindy's file. Her wallet was never recovered.

Cross finishes on the phone first. "They've got the last twelve months' worth of statements for both girls. That should do us."

Darren hangs up. "Hamill's going to look into it and get back to us."

"Was there anything else to indicate serious money? In the apartment?" I'm asking both Darren and Cross, while also trying to trigger my own memory.

"A neighbor..." Cross says. "One of the neighbors saw a limo a couple of weeks back." He starts flipping through Janice's file. "It was from that nosy neighbor opposite them. It didn't seem like much at the time. Limos in Vegas are commonplace."

"A couple weeks back," Darren says. "Like around the twentieth?"

Cross starts flipping through his notebook. "Could be." He flips another two pages. "Here it is." He reads, then looks up. "She couldn't remember the exact date or day, but it's definitely the week Cindy left Vegas."

I scribble on a new sheet of paper. *Excited, money, limo, Mojave Desert, New York.* These mean something.

Darren looks at my list but doesn't comment on it. Instead, he says, "We may as well still head back to Tucson."

"Yeah. We can fly back this afternoon. We'll have the bank records today and an autopsy update tomorrow. For now, let's work on our time line." I grab a sheet of paper from the nearest printer and turn it horizontally. I draw a line across the sheet of paper.

"So the twentieth is the day Malcolm said he was leaving." I use a red pen and write *Malcolm, March 20* on the very left-hand point of the line.

"And the twentieth for Cindy too."

I nod and use a blue pen for Cindy to mark in her "disappearance" date. The next date is red, for Malcolm. "Malcolm was killed on or around the twenty-sixth."

"Then Cindy a week later—around April second," Darren says.

I go back to blue and mark in Cindy's murder date. "Then we've got Janice. She was found on the first, but the ME said she'd been dead for about twenty-four hours." I use a black pen to mark in Janice's death. "So Janice was killed a couple of days before Cindy, around March thirty-first." I flick the marker back and forth between my fingers. "The cat was out of the bag," I say. "Janice knew where Cindy really was and our killers found out."

Darren leans back in his chair, studying the fledgling time line. "So if Cindy mentioned that Janice knew where she was, then obviously Cindy didn't feel threatened in any way at that point in time."

"No. Not unless it was beaten out of her." I pause. "But there was no indication of torture or physical trauma."

Darren nods. "So she didn't think she was in danger, and she certainly didn't realize Janice was."

AmericanPsycho: Congratulations, Never. Brigitte is all yours.
NeverCaught: Thank God for Wednesdays. I'm stoked...soon I'll have her.
DialM: I'm jealous.
AmericanPsycho: What are you going to do with her?
NeverCaught: Take her to that special house. Tie her up. Play with her for a while, then introduce her to my knife.
AmericanPsycho: No knife! I told you the rules when you joined the club. She must be strangled.
NeverCaught: I know. But I can still show her the knife...and run it along her body.

20

Since we got back from Vegas three days ago everything's been a dead end. Nothing suspicious in the financials, the second autopsy on Janice didn't reveal anything new, and the Vegas crime lab came back with the big zilch from Cindy and Janice's house. No suspect prints, no fibers, no hair, no nothing.

Darren stands up and stretches, having just gone over the bank statements again. "So why did Malcolm and Cindy talk about getting money? Wherever it was coming from, they hadn't got a down payment."

It's not the first time we've asked ourselves this question, but the answer is still elusive. I shrug, but then a thought pops into my head. "Could they have known they were going to die?"

Darren gives me a strange look, but I continue. "Maybe the serial killers promised them money. Cindy was planning to give it to her sister and Janice. And Malcolm's parents sure need money."

Darren's brow furrows. "I don't know…"

"Stranger things have happened. Remember that case in Germany? The cannibal who advertised for a victim. He had no problems finding willing subjects." I shudder at the thought. "It turns my stomach just thinking about it. How could you eat another human being?"

Darren's face crumples in disgust and he moves uneasily from foot to foot. "That case creeped me out."

"And everybody else," I say.

"But Malcolm was saving for college, not for his folks. And I don't see someone as confident as Malcolm giving up on life."

Darren's got a point.

"You're right. And Cindy had been through hell and come out on top. Why would she give up now, of all times?"

It leads us back to nowhere—again. Time's running out. For the next victim it's probably already run out.

"If the killers stick to their pattern," I say, "the next victim is either already dead or will be in the next twelve hours or so."

"Don't remind me." Darren runs a hand through his hair.

"Case going that well?" Stone asks as she enters the project room. She's been around Darren long enough to recognize when he's frustrated.

"Pretty much," Darren replies.

A beat of silence.

"If it's a weekly pattern it's going down soon," I say. "It's been six days since the last victim was found." I stand up too and stretch my neck and shoulders gently.

Darren's staring at the whiteboard, which has still got the info about the femme fatale on it. "We may be too late for this one." His voice is steely.

NeverCaught has entered the room.
DialM: Never. What's happening?
NeverCaught: Hi all. One more person knows our little secret.
DialM: How did Brigitte take it?
NeverCaught: How do you think, M?
AmericanPsycho: So she's still alive?
NeverCaught: For the moment. I stopped playing with her to chat with you guys.

DialM: Photos?

NeverCaught: Yeah, I've got photos.

AmericanPsycho: Well, let's see them.

NeverCaught: Check it out.

AmericanPsycho: Oh, yeah. Gotta love that fear.

DialM: Look at her body. That skin.

NeverCaught: Yes. Dough well spent.

DialM: Have you…

NeverCaught: Oh, yeah. She gave it up like there was no tomorrow. I took her gag off for that. She's skanky.

DialM: I do wish she was mine.

NeverCaught: I almost feel sorry for you, M. It's truly **ing fantastic. This club is the best thing that's ever happened to me.

21

The U of A is crawling with undercover cops, and two SWAT teams lie low, hopefully out of our perps' view. With no real leads to follow, we've taken the only option open to us—staking out the university in case the killers repeat the one-week gap between victims and try to dump the body somewhere on campus tonight.

Posing as a student, I carry several books and walk my designated route. It's probably still too early for the killers to make an appearance, but we couldn't risk missing them so we came in waves as soon as dusk hit.

We are too late to save this victim, but if we catch the perps in action tonight at least we'll put an end to the killings. I walk through the main mall and take a right at the library, just opposite where Malcolm's body was found. From there I cut through the grounds to Fourth Street and west along it. It's a coordinated effort and we've all got certain routes we have to follow so that the whole campus is covered.

By midnight my legs are aching and I'm tired. I had an afternoon nap, ready for an all-night stakeout, but it wasn't enough and my eyelids are heavy. At least the walking is keeping me warm. I make my way to my meeting point. Now that midnight's hit and the campus would normally be getting quieter, we'll take it in shifts to monitor certain sections on foot, while the rest of the teams take higher ground. My first position is on the northwest corner of the main library's roof.

The next four hours pass slowly, with the highlight being my scheduled 2:00 a.m. move from the library to the architecture building on Speedway Boulevard. But I see nothing suspicious on the way over, and nothing from my vantage point on the southwest corner of its roof. At 4:00 a.m. Sergeant Harris's voice comes over the comms link, calling us back to the university services building that we'd set up as our on-site base.

On my way I call Darren. "What the hell's going on?"

"I was just about to call you." Darren sounds disheartened. "They've found a body."

"What? Where?"

"Himmel Park. Less than a mile east of the campus."

"Damn!" I hang up and run the rest of the way to join the cops and the SWAT teams in the services building.

"What's going on?" I ask when I reach Darren, Stone and Harris.

"A 9-1-1 call came in about fifteen minutes ago," Harris says. "I dispatched two officers to the park to investigate, and sure enough, we've got our third body. You three get your asses over there while I debrief this lot." He motions with his head to the cops and SWAT teams.

"The ME's office been notified?" Stone asks.

Harris nods. "On their way. And the crime-lab guys too."

"Is the vic male or female?" I ask. If the killers are taking turns, it should be a man.

"Woman." Harris moves to the front of the room to start the debrief and the three of us make a quick exit.

I give Darren a look and bite my lip. God, I hope it's not the brunette.

We drive over to Himmel Park in Darren's car and move quickly toward the crime scene, but I'm more eager than the others. I need to see her face.

I flash my ID at the uniform who's standing guard over her body until all the players arrive. She's been dumped underneath a bush, face down with her arms raised above her head—different from the others. She's also lying on clear plastic but it's not the ME's plastic; this is how the body's been dumped. I pull a small flashlight out of my back pocket and shine it over her body for a closer look. Her hair looks like that of the girl from my dream, but until I see her face I can't be sure. I want to lean in and roll her over now, but until the ME and forensics arrive and set up their night equipment to do a first pass of the scene, the body can't be moved. My skin crawls, literally feeling like thousands of bugs are piercing my flesh. I need to see her face. Darren stares at me with soft blue eyes, but his sympathy makes it worse, not better, and I look away, focusing only on *her*.

It takes another five minutes or so before the ME, Ray George, arrives. He must have been close to get here this soon. The call would have gone out immediately, but even so, he managed to get here in about fifteen minutes. The lab guys arrive hot on his heels, and within five minutes the crime scene is floodlit, but also crowded. Darren and I direct the cops and forensics assigned to the case, getting them moving with their tasks as quickly as possible. I look back at the body, which we can see much better now. George is preparing to turn the girl over. I hover close to him, waiting.

After many photos have been taken and everything's ready, they gently roll her onto her back. Darren moves in, too, and I know it's to support me as much as anything else. Her body weight eventually drags her over, but her brown hair is draped across her face. I lean in and carefully part the rich locks…to reveal her face. I ride the nausea, fighting the need to puke. "Shit!" I say. It's her. I back away from the body. I wanted to protect her. I wanted to save her and now…she's dead. I was too late. I know this feeling all too well.

The nausea threatens to beat me so I focus on distancing myself and regaining my investigative objectivity. In my vision the woman was stabbed, yet to be one of the killers' victims, she should have been strangled. I bend down and run the flashlight over her body, even though the main lights are already illuminating her. The love heart's there, of course, but there are no stab wounds. She looks just like the others, except for the different posing of the body. Why did I dream about her being stabbed so violently?

"It's the woman from your sketch," Stone says.

"Yes," I manage.

I move into the background, torn between wanting to see her and not being able to bear it. Every time I look at her, or think about her, I can see her being dragged through the house by her hair, fighting her attacker every step of the way. And I saw it before it happened. Before she was dead. Why couldn't I stop the killer in time?

Eventually the body is ready for transportation. Darren and I ride in the back with the vic, leaving Stone in charge of the scene. I stare at the body bag and Darren looks at me.

"You okay?" he asks.

"Not really."

He doesn't respond at first. Then: "We can't always make it in time. No one can."

I nod, although without any enthusiasm or sense of absolution.

"It's not our job," he continues.

I look at him. "Of course it is!"

"We find the killer. As soon as we can. That's the best we can do."

I keep my eyes firmly planted on the body bag, not on Darren. I'm in no mood for logic. I can see her face, just as if the black plastic wasn't between her and us. Flashes of the dream ride me. I try to fight it again, but it's futile. I'm no longer looking at a body bag, or even her body lying on the stretcher in front of us. Now all I can see is her past, or more specifically, how she died.

> *She's being dragged by her hair across a hallway. She's screaming, kicking, fighting for her life every step of the way. But he's bigger, stronger than she is and he takes physical control of her easily. He*

drags her into a bedroom, flings her onto the bed and cuffs her hands to the headboard. She screams and screams until her voice is hoarse and she's got nothing left.

I close my eyes trying desperately to repress it, but the onslaught continues.

Her screams start again. He's running the thick blade of a knife across her tanned skin. He runs it from her bare breast, down her abdomen and down onto her inner thigh. Then he traces the mirror line up the other side of her body, until the knife's resting on her face.

"What's happening?" Darren puts his hand on mine. I jump at the contact and open my eyes again, hoping it will stop, but it doesn't.

He raises the knife above her and brings it down in a forceful arc, penetrating her skin. Blood sprays everywhere, across his face, down his naked chest, onto the bed…everywhere.

I put my hands up in front of my face, trying to stop it, trying to deflect the attack.

Darren squeezes my hands tightly, covering both of them with his. "Sophie. Sophie!"

The psychic episode releases its viselike grip on me and I'm staring at Darren's face. He's crouched down in front of me. My hands shake uncontrollably within Darren's firm grip and I realize I'm breathless, like I've run ten miles.

Darren gives my hands a squeeze. "What did you see?"

At first I can't answer him. I'm still shell-shocked, frightened the images and fear will come again. Eventually I manage to speak. "Her death." My breath evens out and I no longer feel like cowering in the corner. "But it was the knife again." I shake my head, confused.

Darren looks down, then back up at me. "There are no knife wounds, Sophie." He pauses. "Maybe the vision is wrong."

"No." I shake my head again. "It was so strong. Besides, you're the one who told me to trust them."

He doesn't have a response and so we ride in silence.

Ray George decides to process the brunette straightaway, and lets her jump the line. Not surprising given it's a serial killer—who's working on an incredibly accelerated time frame. Weekly killings—even Rivers can't deny the pattern now. And it's a far cry from the female killer's average of roughly one a year.

In the autopsy room I stare at her, but I just feel numb.

"Any tattoo?" I ask. If our killing couple was taking turns, a male victim would be lying on the slab and I'd expect a rose to be tattooed on him somewhere. But it's a female victim.

The ME turns her wrist over and brushes off some dirt, being careful to preserve it for analysis. It'll probably turn out to be earth from Himmel Park. But there's nothing underneath the dirt, no tattoo. He does a sweep of the rest of the body and comes up empty-handed—no tattoo.

"Time of death?" Darren asks.

"Based on rigor and body temp, I'd say twelve to twenty-four hours." He removes the plastic bags from her hands and feet and continues the visual examination. He draws our attention to small bruises on her legs, about eight all in all.

Darren looks at me. "Maybe from kicking, trying to escape."

I nod. I try to stop it, but I can't help but visualize the woman being dragged down the hall by her hair, thrashing. She probably knocked her legs against furniture and the walls as she went.

"The bruising was just coming up before she died, so the trauma would have happened only a few hours before death," the ME says. He turns her hands over and examines the fingernails.

"Anything?" I ask.

"They've been scrubbed clean. She may have got a sample of her attacker but he removed all traces of himself. I'll take some swabs anyhow. See what comes back."

He continues up her body, spending more time at the neck.

"Strangulation?" I ask.

"Looks that way." The ME fingers the woman's bruised neck. "Internal will verify that." He moves to her head, which hasn't been shaved yet. "The scalp shows some distress." He runs his gloved hand through her hair, and a handful of broken strands come out. "Looks like hair pulling was used to restrain her."

Again I can't escape the image of her kicking and screaming with the killer dragging her down the corridor.

Next the ME checks for rape. "She was raped," he confirms. He points to bruising on her inner thighs. "This is quite severe—" he examines her pelvic region "—and we've got vaginal and rectal tearing. Looks like he raped her several times."

Darren winces. "Fluids?"

"I'll do a rape kit. See what we find." He starts the swabbing procedure.

"The rape's very different from Cindy," I say.

Darren nods. "Guess he lost control."

I have an instant to feel disturbed by the different rape styles, before I'm taken over by dizziness. I try to resist what I sense is about to happen, but it's no use.

A woman's body is wrapped in mud-streaked but clear plastic, and dumped in long grass. She's lying on her stomach, but her legs are splayed apart slightly and her arms are over her head. On her back are several gashes, deep knife wounds.

I come to and Darren's staring at me, but thankfully the ME's still absorbed in his work. Darren gives me a look but I just shake my head at him, confused by the vision—it wasn't even the brunette. I focus on the body on the slab in front of me and take in every detail. But the rest of the autopsy is uneventful besides a small amount of dirt that the ME finds in her inner-ear canal.

"No doubt soil composition will show it's from the Mojave," Darren says.

"No doubt."

We leave the pathologist to finalize the body. Outside, Darren calls Stone and they swap information.

"Well?" I say.

"They've found a footprint near the dump site, but nothing else. It could be our perp's or it could be the gardener's."

The next afternoon we sit in the project room, going over the autopsy report and the crime-scene photos.

"Anything on the rape kit?" Stone asks.

Darren looks up from the photos. "No DNA. He used a condom."

Stone continues to read the autopsy report. "Scalp trauma?" She looks up.

"No surprise there," I say.

Stone waits for me to expand.

"She was pulled by her hair." As soon as I say it, I regret the certainty in my voice.

"Doh. Sorry." Stone rolls her eyes. "Even rapists use the hair-pulling technique."

I nod, relieved Stone assumes my confidence is based on stats not the fact that I saw the girl's murder. "It's a quick and easy way to subdue a victim with long hair," I add. "And very effective."

Darren continues. "All her organs looked fine, but obviously we're waiting on the tox screen." He flicks to the next page. "The X-rays showed an old injury, a broken arm. She's never given birth."

Probably not a very useful detail for us, but for female victims the ME's report usually includes comments on any obvious gynecological issues such as childbirth.

"Any word on the fingerprints?" Hopefully they've rushed the ID through the system.

"They've run the prints, but no matches from the database," Stone says.

"So unlike Malcolm and Cindy, no criminal record." It's a point of difference, but probably not significant.

Stone sighs. "A woman who's broken her arm and never given birth...not exactly narrowing down our options here."

"No."

We're silent for a few minutes.

"The footprint?" I ask hopefully.

"Matched to one of the contractors employed by Himmel Park," Stone says. "And nothing back on the plastic yet."

"Is the Bureau going to give us some more resources now?" Darren asks.

"No." I sigh. "I called Rivers, but he just doesn't have anyone to spare."

Darren doesn't say anything, but I can tell he's annoyed.

We go back to the hard facts and I try to absorb the case details. But no matter how much I try to ignore it, I'm drawn to two things—the plastic at the crime scene and the new vision I had yesterday. That victim, whoever she was, was posed just like our brunette, face down and covered in plastic. I think about what Darren said in Vegas, about this being a calling. I can't ignore the vision—it's like ignoring a piece of evidence.

"Mind if I use your computer for a bit, Carter?"

Darren looks at me a little quizzically, but says, "Sure."

Until I can piece this together, or at least make some sense of it, it's too early to share the vision.

At Darren's desk I open up the VICAP software and run a search on stabbings where the victims have been found wrapped in clear plastic. To narrow the search I also add in the body positioning from the crime scene: the girl lying on her stomach with her arms posed above her head. Within a few minutes the online database returns seven hits that all have the exact crime-scene elements as my scenario.

I click on each result and find one file that's got scanned photos attached. I open that one up and print out the full file, including the crime-scene report, the autopsy report and the photos. I also print out the files on the other six murders, even though they don't include photos. Photos and other scanned images can be attached when the initial VICAP questionnaire is logged, but scanning can take time—time most cops don't have.

After I've spent an hour going through them, I'm convinced that somehow the brunette is related to these seven cases. The body positioning, the plastic—they're clues to this killer. And the fact that I saw her stabbed in my vision certainly supports that. But it's also so different than Cindy.

I take the files into the project room, to Darren and Stone. "I think I've got something here."

They both look up.

I spread the color printouts of the photos across the table, on top of the current crime-scene photos.

"A stabbing?" Stone is confused.

"I know, I know." I hold my hand up. "It sounds off base. But I was thinking about Malcolm. He had the rose tattoo and the rose is a signature of our killer. Someone's leaving us clues. So, what if the body positioning and the plastic are clues?" I don't mention my vivid premonition. I can't in front of Stone. "Anyway, I did a VICAP search on women who've been wrapped in clear plastic like that found at the latest crime scene. And this is what came up." I motion to the photos. "There are seven murders that match in total, but this is the only one with photos on the VICAP database."

Stone and Darren pick up the printouts and review them. The first picture is of the crime scene as it was when the police first arrived. The body is about thirty feet off the path, and barely discernible through several layers of clear but mud-streaked plastic. Just like my vision. Nothing lies near or around the body. No murder weapon, none of her personal effects, nothing. The photos of this stage cover all angles, and some are taken from a distance while others are close-ups. Next in the sequence are a few photos as the examiners removed the upper layers of plastic. The killer created a sandwich effect by placing her on one doubled-over sheet of plastic, before draping a larger one that'd been folded in three over her body and tucking it in at the sides. It's almost as if he wanted to preserve her. Next are some shots of the victim's back, exposed and showing five knife wounds in total on her back. The final series shows what the investigators found when they turned her over. Her front had been stabbed multiple times in a frenzied-style kill. They are deep stab wounds, where the knife has been plunged into her flesh and then extracted. There are also some smaller cuts on her stomach and breasts. These cuts remind me of a suicide's hesitation cuts, the trial cuts they do while they're gathering enough determination to make the lethal wounds. But our killer isn't indecisive or tentative. He was probably playing with her, all part of his power trip.

"So you're thinking...?" Darren says.

"These are related." I point at the nearest printout. "The pose and plastic are classic signature stuff."

"Agreed," Darren says. "But why would our couple leave clues to lead us to past crimes? The tattoo of the rose, the plastic?"

He's got a damn good point. Why would they?

Stone pipes up. "They could be taunting us. Think they're so much smarter than us."

Darren stands up. "Unless..."

We look at him expectantly.

After a couple of seconds he says, "Have you seen a movie called *Copycat?*"

"Sure. Harry Connick Junior, Sigourney Weaver," I say.

"Well what if this isn't our female killer and it isn't this guy?" Darren points to the new files I've placed on the table. "What if it's someone else trying to set them up?"

"Do you think it's possible?" Stone asks.

"Anything's possible," I say. "But if we do have a copycat killer, how would he know about the rose, the plastic? Those details weren't released."

We're stumped again.

"And what about the second victim, Cindy?" Darren rubs his chin. "There was no special clue on her."

"Not that we found," I say.

Stone breathes in, about to say something, but then abandons it. Darren and I both look at her.

"Go on." I'm assuming Stone has an idea but isn't confident enough to voice it.

"Well, it's just…what if we've got three killers? The woman—" she points to the whiteboard still covered in scrawl about Malcolm "—a second killer for Cindy, and then this third one."

Darren and I are both silent.

"Sorry, dumb idea," Stone says.

"No, not at all. In fact, it would also explain something else that's been bothering me. The rapes. Cindy was raped, but there was no bruising in her thighs, or around her groin. But this latest victim's rapist was much, much rougher. It looked like a different perp, because it *is* a different perp." I say. I twist the ring on my finger, piecing it all together. "But why would three killers team up? The couple I get, but three?"

We're silent again.

Darren runs with it. "So we've got three killers working together? Maybe Janice's killer makes four?" He looks at me for my opinion.

"The OD could be someone's standard MO. It might not be an isolated case." I pause. "They could be working together, comparing their techniques. Maybe it's some kind of competition. See who can kill the most people."

"That's sick," Stone says.

I bite my lip. "It's always sick. This is just…" But I'm unable to think of a truly appropriate word to describe such depravity.

BlackWidow: So, Never, did you have fun?

NeverCaught: Of course. Do you want to see the last photos of her?

BlackWidow: The XXX-rated ones from last night were enough for me.

NeverCaught: So you don't swing both ways, BW?

BlackWidow: No, I drive stick.

DialM: I wouldn't say no to a photographic update.

NeverCaught: I'll upload them.

DialM: Was it more exciting than a regular kill?

NeverCaught: Yes. Brigitte had no idea, either.

AmericanPsycho: Neither did Cindy. You should have seen her face when I told her. She sobered up real quick. But by then it was too late...she'd already willingly slipped into the handcuffs.

DialM: You're all too quick and nasty for my taste.

AmericanPsycho: I've got the video stuff organized for your special chamber.

DialM: Thanks, Psycho.

NeverCaught: What special chamber?

AmericanPsycho: M's still going to strangle his victim, but I'm going to let him have longer with his girl. He's not going to the house.

BlackWidow: That's not fair.

AmericanPsycho: Come on, BW, you prefer one-night stands, anyway.

BlackWidow: I guess. But Malcolm was fine. Fine enough for a few nights.

NeverCaught: Brigitte was fine. And she's headlining on all the local news shows.

AmericanPsycho: Well done on restraining yourself, too, Never.

NeverCaught: Thanks. Nice to know it's appreciated because it was ***ing hard.

DialM: I would like to be next. But I want Ling. I have standards. People used to have standards, you know. The youth of America are lazy and ungrateful. And I'm sure our IQ as a nation is dropping. And whatever happened to manners? Good, old-fashioned manners?

BlackWidow: He's right. I see it when I'm out hunting. Chivalry is dead.
DialM: Could you give it up, BW? Not kill?
BlackWidow: No. Definitely not. You?
DialM: No. Although I do wonder how I'll manage when I'm seventy.
AmericanPsycho: You'll have to get yourself a sidekick.
DialM: Not a bad idea.
NeverCaught: I've got years of killing left in me before I have to worry about retirement!
AmericanPsycho: I'll never stop. Never. How could you stop such a beautiful calling?

22

The next day we focus on the VICAP files of the stabbing victims wrapped in plastic, to which we've added all the crime-scene photos that we'd requested from the local forces. I'm glad one of my visions actually produced something useful, a lead we can follow, but even just thinking about the vision of the brunette's murder makes me nauseous. It also makes me never want to experience another vision again.

We start with the crime that originally had photos attached to its VICAP file. In this case the body, or Vic A as we start referring to her, was found in the Black Hills National Forest in South Dakota.

Darren, the closest to the autopsy report, leads us through it. "So, cause of death is confirmed as a stab wound three inches long. It was deep and severed the carotid artery." We go to the photos of Vic A on her back. The knife wound the forensic pathologist was talking about is obvious. It starts at her left collar bone and spreads three inches across her throat.

"That wound was meant to kill," I say.

"She would have bled out anyway." Stone points to some of the other cuts on her body.

"Oh, yeah. But these are his idea of fun." I point to all the cuts on her abdomen and breasts. "And this one is to finish the job." I point to the throat wound. "The business end of the kill." The knife patterns remind me of the DC Slasher.

Darren flicks through the report. "No fibers, no hair, no bloody prints on the body. Tox screen was normal and nothing from the vaginal and anal swabs except a small amount of condom lubricant."

"Nothing else in the autopsy report?" Stone asks hopefully.

Darren flicks through it. "Not unless you want to know what her heart weighed."

"I'll pass." I reach across Darren to the first set of pictures and pick up one with her covered by the plastic. "Was he hiding her?" I'm asking myself more than Stone and Darren.

Stone looks at the picture. "The snow was about to come in, and apparently that track doesn't get used in the winter months at all."

"But could you expect *nobody* to go there?" This is the real question as I see it. Did the killer expect his handiwork to go unnoticed until spring?

"Probably not, no," Darren says.

"It's interesting." I keep studying the picture. "Dumping her there was like pretending he was trying to conceal her. And it's the same with the plastic. He covered her up, but with clear plastic. I think he wanted to be able to see her, right up to the last moment."

"Or maybe he was planning a visit...if she wasn't found," Stone says. "Clear plastic would mean he could see her without having to disturb the scene."

Stone's got a good point. Many killers like to relive their kills by visiting the victim's grave or body. "True," I say. "Or maybe he's the one who discovered her." It's an obvious suggestion, but it's surprising how often it happens. Again, it's all part of the killer's need to relive the crime, to be involved in its discovery as well as its execution.

Darren shuffles some papers in the file. "She was found by two hikers, Simon Creaser and Jim Torr." He flicks through the file's contents again and fishes out their official statements and related paperwork. "Simon's thirty-four and Jim's thirty-eight. They work together in a plumbing business in Rapid City." He pauses while he reads the statements before giving us a rundown. "Average stuff. They took a shortcut through the grass back to the track and saw plastic flapping in the wind. They went to investigate and found her. They were eliminated as suspects though, based on time of death."

We move to the other files, the other six murders, hoping to find something. All the women were raped multiple times, stabbed to death and then posed in the plastic and dumped around wooded areas in North and South Dakota. No DNA, no trace evidence—the killer's good at what he does.

We're silent for a moment, staring at the files spread over the table.

Stone breaks the silence. "We still haven't decided if we've got three killers or four. Was Janice murdered by one of the killers of Cindy, Malcolm or body number three, or are we dealing with a fourth killer?"

I sigh and shrug my shoulders. "Either's possible." I walk toward the whiteboard and flip it over, back to our jottings on Malcolm. The whiteboard is one of the electronic ones that allows you to print what you've written, so I take a printout of our Malcolm jottings for later review before wiping the board clean. I divide the board into four columns: *Killer 1, Killer 2, Killer 3* and *Janice*. I start with Killer 1. "So killer one is our lady killer. Our femme fatale." Giving a line for each point, I write: *Female; Early to mid 30s; Uses sex to lure victims; Strangulation during sex; Handcuffs; 21 victims from 1992 to present.* Then I write *Victim profile* and underline it, before listing attributes of her victims—*Early twenties; All races; Athletic build; Good looking; Bar patrons;* and *Variety of socioeconomic groups.*

I move over to column two. "So killer two is Cindy's killer. We don't know much about him at all. If there was a clue to his normal MO or signature, we missed it." I jot down *Male* but leave the rest of the column blank for the moment.

We move onto killer three, the brunette's killer. "So we're talking male again, probably in his twenties given the first murder was only five years ago."

"Restraints for his previous vics were ropes, so that's another change in his MO," Darren says.

I nod and write it up. It's not surprising that all our killers restrained their victims. It's one of the traits of an organized serial killer, as are transporting the victim, high IQ and stalking. In fact, no restraints would probably lead you to raise an eyebrow. "And cause of death in this case was strangulation, but his normal MO is the knife." I write *Strangulation/Stabbing* on the board.

"Seven victims in VICAP, from 2002." Darren pauses and I write it up.

"Victim profile is women in their twenties, mostly in the lower socioeconomic groups," Darren continues. "No physical similarities. Although…" he flips through the files and newly acquired photos, "they're all quite big-breasted."

I smile. "Thank God for you, Darren. I'm sure neither Stone nor I would have noticed that detail."

Finally we come to the Janice column, but it is even emptier than column number two. A VICAP search on staged OD as a murder technique came up with no hits—not surprising. Even if there were similar cases they'd be classed as suspicious not murder, and therefore probably wouldn't have been logged in VICAP.

"Well we know Janice and Cindy are linked. Janice knew something she shouldn't have," Darren says.

"And we know for sure that Cindy's, Malcolm's and this third woman's murders are related," Stone says. "The traces of soil from the Mojave and the hearts on their bodies tell us that."

I draw arrows between Janice and Cindy's killer, and arrows between the killers one, two and three. "So, how do the killers know each other? And how are they communicating?"

Darren drums his fingers on the table, Stone sits perfectly still with her arms crossed and I stare out the window—we're all thinking in our own way.

Stone uncrosses her arms. "Well it's not letters or phones, so we must be talking e-mail."

Darren stops drumming. "Or instant messaging."

"True…mmm…" I pause. "That means I might be able to get the Cyber Crime Division of the Bureau involved. I'll call Rivers and see if I can't convince him to assign a tech person to us. It may be easier than getting a field resource."

"No complaints from me."

Rivers picks up after one ring, and after a brief exchange he suggests I contact Agent Daniel Gerard, Senior Computer Forensics Analyst for the FBI's Cyber Crime Division.

Gerard answers the phone after the fourth ring. "Agent Daniel Gerard." His voice sounds distant, like he's distracted.

"Hi Agent Gerard, it's Sophie Anderson from the Behavioral Analysis Unit."

"Yes?"

"Special Agent Andy Rivers, one of the heads of the BAU, said I should give you a call about a case. Can you speak at the moment?"

"Um, just hold on a sec."

I hear a keyboard tapping furiously and then he comes back to the phone. "Sorry, just had to finish that. Shoot."

"We're working on a case that looks like a group of serial killers."

"Nasty."

"Yes. And we think they might be communicating via e-mail or instant messaging."

"Interesting."

"So, is there any way we can track down suspect e-mails?"

"You heard of Echelon?"

"Sure." After much denial in the 80s and 90s, the existence of a network of satellites specifically tasked to intercept suspect key words in telephone conversations, e-mails, and the like has now been widely accepted. It's a contentious issue. Is it invading our privacy or protecting us? Everyone's got a different opinion. My own thoughts swing on the matter. Knowing what people are capable of,

I think it's great to have a tool that acts as an early-warning system. Then again, I also know that discretion isn't always a government's best feature. If the wrong person was behind the wheel...

"Well, that's set up to listen for key words, mostly focused on terrorism, but it also includes other suspect words, some of which may be in your killers' e-mails."

"Great." I lean forward, excited by the prospect of having a way to track down our killers.

"Problem is there are a lot of e-mails to sift through."

"Oh."

"Tell me a bit more about the case so we can set up dedicated search."

I take Gerard through the basics of the case, including the love heart on the victims' chests and the evidence pointing to the Mojave.

"Okay, I'll get someone on this and let you know. No promises, but we'll see what we can do."

"Thanks, Gerard." I hang up, not sure whether to feel hopeful or disappointed.

AmericanPsycho: Next time we need to take out Danny or Jonathan. They seem to have gotten past their initial hatred and are talking. Too much.

DialM: I concur with AmericanPsycho on this one but I think Danny should be next. I don't like his military background. Then again, I have been waiting a long time, and I think I deserve to get my girl. Ling.

AmericanPsycho: You have been very patient, M. But we need to fit Danny into the schedule, and Wednesday is only a few days away.

NeverCaught: Do two next time. What the ***?

DialM: NeverCaught, I think that's a stupendous idea. AmericanPsycho, please consider this possibility.

BlackWidow: Go on, Psycho. Then we'll kill two birds with one stone...so to speak.

AmericanPsycho: Mmm.

DialM: It would be proper for me to go next, yet I see your point regarding Danny. This will solve both issues.

AmericanPsycho: Okay. This is a democracy...sort of. I'll do Danny—nothing fancy—and the other person will go the normal way. I'm happy to grant M's request and make it Ling. Yes?

BlackWidow: Fine by me.

NeverCaught: Me too, I guess.

AmericanPsycho: Ling and Danny it is. But we'll all have a chance at Ling.

23

I put my head in my hands. Time is moving faster than we can, faster than the evidence. We haven't made any progress in the past few days and the next murder is closing in on us. If the killers keep on schedule, we've only got a couple of days to go and we're still no closer to finding *one* of the killers, let alone all three—or four—of them. Agent Gerard drew a blank on the e-mail searches, which means they're either not communicating via e-mail or they're running a heavy-duty encryption program. With our normal investigative techniques drawing a blank, I know I should be trying to embrace my gift rather than reject it. And while there have been a couple of times when I've experienced the early-warning indicators of an oncoming vision, each time I've shut myself down hard, frightened of what I might see.

Darren's cell rings. "Carter, Homicide... Excellent." He covers the mouthpiece and looks up at me. "The lab results are back from our Jane Doe," he whispers. He uncovers the phone and grabs a pen from his top pocket.

"Well?" I ask when he hangs up.

He goes over his notes. Tox screen was negative, no semen and no DNA. The plastic has been identified as manufactured by Lee Light Industrial Products Co. Ltd. of Hong Kong.

"And no ID yet?"

He shakes his head. "The dental X-rays have been e-mailed for matching."

"I'm going to draft a profile of her killer. See if that doesn't help us." To date, we've been following leads on the case and discussing the killer's MO and basic personality, but that doesn't replace a full psychological profile. Now that we've received the complete files from the Dakota forces, including the essential photos, I'm in a position to draft the profile.

"Take the project room again if you like."

"Okay. What about you?"

"I'm going to run the case files one more time. But there's not much more to investigate. Not until we get our next murder."

"The thought of another murder sickens me."

"I know."

We're silent for a moment—there's nothing else to say on the subject—so I pick up my laptop. "See you in a few hours."

In the project room, I spread the seven files across the desk but before I've had a chance to open them up Darren comes in. His face is blank.

"What's up?" I say.

He opens his mouth then shuts it, and then fidgets, smoothing his hands along his jeans.

"What's up?" I repeat.

He takes a breath and speaks slowly, his voice controlled. "It's been a few days now, Sophie."

I give him a puzzled look.

"Since your last vision."

"Oh." I lean over the table and open up the files, revealing the top photo for each murder, each victim.

Darren takes my right hand. "Sophie."

I look him in the eyes. "Yes, it's been a few days."

"And you haven't had another vision? Or a dream?" There's a hint of disbelief in his voice.

I gently pull my arm away from him. "No, I haven't."

He shakes his head. "Are you sure? You didn't tell me about the one of the girl wrapped in plastic straightaway." Now his voice goes from mild disbelief to accusatory. "What else are you hiding?"

I lean both hands on the desk and stare at him. "Nothing."

"So they've just suddenly stopped?" His voice is controlled again, too controlled.

I pause, teetering between being angry and confessing. I could tell him that I've actively been repressing the visions, that I've been too much of a coward to let myself see anything, but I'm ashamed.

"Yes. They've stopped," I lie.

He lingers for only a few seconds, before giving a quick nod and leaving the room. I don't know if he's pissed with me or not, but when one of the photos from the file catches my attention I no longer care. I've got a job to do, and that's profiling, not becoming our resident psychic. I spread a selection of photos around each file, and the crime scenes are identical. The seven victims that VICAP turned up were all found in North or South Dakota, so our killer has either moved to Arizona or he's here specifically for this murder. On a piece of paper I write down the rough dates of all the murders. In some, the body was discovered very late in the game, so they've estimated time of death based on when the person disappeared.

1. May 2002
2. January 2003
3. November 2003
4. December 2004
5. June 2005
6. January 2006
7. February 2007
8. April 2007: Jane Doe

The only pattern is that most of the murders occurred in the winter months, which did, in fact, buy the killer extra time. The bodies were all found in woodlands that are covered by snow in winter. The snow not only hid the victim until the spring thaw, but also helped to slow down the decomposition process.

All victims had multiple stab wounds—from twenty-one to forty-three per victim—and while there were a few knife wounds on the victims' backs, most were concentrated on the front of their bodies, specifically around the breasts and abdomen. The wound locations reflect the sexual nature of the killings, with the breasts and abdomen representing womanhood and perhaps fertility.

All victims were brutally raped, repeatedly, and all were restrained with ropes—except Jane Doe, who was cuffed. In each case no semen or other fluids were present. This evidence would normally indicate either the offender's inability to perform sexually or the use of a condom. In our perp's case, small traces of nonoxynol were found in the vaginal swabs, indicating the latter. The victims' pose is also sexual—their arms raised over their heads and their legs slightly parted. He obviously doesn't have sex with the women in this position—in my nightmare about the brunette she was tied to the bed, arms and legs at different angles—so this postmortem position must have some significance for him. Exactly what is difficult to say. It could represent his first sexual position, or it may have been something he saw, perhaps in a magazine or a skin flick, the first time he saw a sexual act. Either way, this posing gets him off.

I look at the photos that were taken of the women before their deaths and given to police for their records. Darren's right, they are certainly on the larger size in terms of their breasts. Most of the women would be a C-cup at least, curvaceous, with a definite indent at the waist. I check the files for the victims' height and weight. They range from five-seven to five-ten, and one-hundred and thirty to one-hundred and sixty pounds. He's obviously not intimidated by taller women, so it's likely he's tall himself. I also notice that none of the women are blonde, none are fair-skinned. His type is more exotic-looking. To my piece of paper with the dates, I add some more victim information.

1. May 2002: 19YO waitress, black hair, Italian descent

2. January 2003: 22YO chicken-factory worker, brown hair

3. November 2003: 17YO high-school student, black hair, quarter Native American

4. December 2004: 18YO supermarket employee, black hair, Greek descent

5. June 2005: 24YO barmaid, dark brown hair

6. January 2006: 20YO McDonalds employee, dark brown hair

7. February 2007: 19YO stripper, black hair, Asian descent

8. Jane Doe: April 2007—dark brown hair, occupation unknown, descent unknown

For some of the victims I can glean their heritage from the file, and for others it's obvious by their names—the Greek girl's last name was Mykonos. I find it interesting that he picks these types of victims. The cross-section indicates that he doesn't belong to one of these groups himself. He's seeking out difference, which means it's likely he's not only Caucasian, but fair.

A more complete profile is starting to form in my mind, so I fire up my laptop, open Word and create a new document using my standard profiling template.

Sex:	Male
Age:	Chronological: 20-25 Emotional age: 16-20
Race:	Caucasian—but hunts across non-Caucasian races and is attracted to difference.
Type of offender:	Organized—well-planned murders, transports victims before and after death, intelligent. Knife attacks are frenzied, but still organized—similar knife wounds from victim to victim and clean crime scenes forensically. Frenzy is indicator of youth.
Occupation/employment:	White collar but likes his victims to be lower than him in socioeconomic status and intelligence. Office worker in middle management—has some power but not enough to satisfy him.
Marital status:	Single but sexually active with casual partners. Sexual partners more likely to be his equals—college-educated.
Dependants:	No dependants—stereotypical bachelor.
Childhood:	Quite a privileged upbringing—knife wounds and savagery of the rapes indicate a spoiled brat who's used to getting his own way.

Personality:	Charming, but also very manipulative of others. Can be impulsive if things aren't going his way. Needs to exert power through rape and murder because he cannot exert this violent power onto his peers. Hides his own sense of inadequacy by acting like an egotistical playboy. Channels these inadequate feelings into murder.
Disabilities:	None.
Interaction with victims:	Keeps his victims for a day or two—based on forensics. Long enough for multiple rapes and for him to feel in control. Stalks his victims and knows their routines. Nabs them at night, when they are in vulnerable positions—the barmaid disappeared on the walk home from work—something she did every night. Spends time with them postmortem—elaborate positioning of the body.
Remorse:	The plastic wrapping indicates some feelings of remorse because he's symbolically covering the victims. Yet the fact that the plastic is clear shows that he's not overwhelmed by shame. Positioning a body facedown is normally done by a killer who doesn't want the victim "looking" at him or "judging" him but in this case the face-down position is more about the sexual pose. He poses the victims in what he feels is a provocative stance.
Home life:	Lives alone in a modern apartment or townhouse—classic bachelor pad. Would spend a lot of his wealth on his home, which would have the latest gadgetry and be decorated with a modern, yet stark feel.

Car:	He transports the victims, so he must own a van or SUV. More likely an upmarket SUV to tie into his wealthy bachelor look. Also possible he has two cars—one for show, and one for dealing with his victims.
Intelligence:	High IQ.
Education level:	College-educated—although he probably spent more time partying at college than studying. Takes education for granted because his family is wealthy.
Outward appearance:	Highly educated and well-groomed—all the girls seemed to go willingly with him so he must look trustworthy in some way—although women are more likely to trust a man in a business suit with a nice car than a man covered in tattoos on a motorbike. Well-dressed at all times—designer suits or more casual wear.
Criminal background:	Probably no criminal record but it's possible he was charged with something at college like drug possession or DUI—wealthy boy away from parents.
Modus operandi (MO):	Stalks the victims, getting to know their routines. Lures the victims into his car but then takes them to a remote location—not his house. Ties them up and repeatedly rapes them before stabbing them to death. Transports victims to wooded location for dumping—not much blood at dump sites, so he transports them postmortem.
Signature:	Frenzied knife attack. Posing of body postmortem, with plastic.

Post-offensive behavior:	May revisit the dump site and look at his victims—clear plastic facilitates this.
Media tactics:	This killer will follow the media very closely and will want to see his actions in the paper. He uses the media reports to fuel his ego—and cover up the underlying sense of inadequacy. This could be dangerous—if he gets lots of media coverage, this will excite him and may propel him into action in terms of taking his next victim.

I look over the profile and one thing becomes clear: it would have been pure hell for this killer not to take the knife to the brunette. That shows me he can exercise control over his kills—a dangerous ability for any killer.

AmericanPsycho: Sold, to the man with a film fetish.
DialM: Thank goodness.
NeverCaught: Film fetish?
DialM: My username. It's from the movie *Dial M for Murder.*
NeverCaught: Oh, yeah. Michael Douglas.
DialM: Not that one. The original. 1954, starring Grace Kelly and Ray Milland. Classic film.
NeverCaught: Take your word for it. Congrats, M, you finally got one.
DialM: No thanks to you, Never. You love driving that price up.
NeverCaught: If you can't afford it, you shouldn't be in the club.
DialM: I can afford it. But I do like to make sure the girl in question is worth it.
NeverCaught: Ling's worth it, and you know it.
DialM: True.
NeverCaught: So, M, what are you going to do with her?
DialM: Chain her up in my personal dungeon. What else?

24

I sit at a spare desk in Tucson Homicide and work on the profile for another case, something Rivers sent me. The case here is on the go-slow, with no victim last week and no leads left to follow. The fact that we never got our next victim makes me both happy and nervous—could it be over and the serial killers are now inactive? Or is the next victim simply waiting to be found? They changed locations once for the dump site, maybe they've done it again. We had teams at the university and Himmel Park last Thursday night, but nothing happened.

The room starts to swim a little bit, but I concentrate on reading the file in front of me, focusing on something else until the sensation passes. Another vision avoided—good. I let out a heavy sigh and check my watch: it's 8:00 a.m., which makes it 1:00 a.m. at night in Melbourne. I decide to check *The Age*, my hometown newspaper, before concentrating on work again. I often check the news a couple of times a day. It gives me a taste of home and helps me keep up-to-date with what's going on. That, with phone calls to my parents and friends, is my connection back to the homeland.

The Age homepage loads and the top headline instantly sends chills down my spine: Online child-porn ring prosecuted. It's a horrific story, true, but there's some other reason it bothers me so I read the full article. It is an international case, with simultaneous raids in Australia, Germany, France, America and Singapore, capturing more than thirty individuals. The perps range from organizers who held victims against their will and forced them to do sexual acts while they took photographs, to the passive recipients of the pictures. The ring communicated online, in a specially set up chat room. Nowadays most child pornography happens online—it's all too easy.

I go back to the paper's homepage and stare at it vacantly. I vaguely notice that the weather's going to be twenty-two Celsius and that the footy season has started. I think back to the story, the online porn ring. We thought about e-mails and instant messaging, but what if they've set up a Web site with a chat room, just like the pornographers did?

I walk over to Darren's desk. He's also working on other cases. He looks up. "Hey."

"What if they're communicating via a Web site chat room?" I say.

"That's a definite possibility." He pauses for a couple of seconds. "That means one of them is very, very technically minded."

"Hadn't got that far, but you're right. They would have had to build the Web site and presumably they've got security in place."

"Exactly. Unless they got someone else to set it up and then killed them."

A potential avenue has emerged from the swarm of dead ends. "I'll give Agent Gerard another call. See what he says."

"We need something." Darren pauses. "You know what today is, don't you?"

"Yeah," I say. "April twenty-second, two days until our next body's due." I've been trying not to think about it.

"Uh huh. Maybe they're getting more careful now, dumping the bodies better."

"If that's the case we might not find anything in two days' time either."

"Maybe not."

Back at my temporary desk I dial Gerard's number. The phone rings several times and I'm just about to hang up when he answers. "Morning, Daniel Gerard." He sounds a little breathless.

"Hi, Gerard. It's Agent Anderson."

"Hey, Anderson. What's up?" His breathing is still uneven.

"You sound like you just ran a marathon, Gerard."

"Hardly. I just got in and had to run for the phone."

I look at my watch—just after 8:00 a.m., which makes it 11:00 a.m. in DC—very late to be getting in. "Do you want me to call back later? Let you settle in first?"

"Nah, shoot."

"What if our killers are using some sort of secure Web site? Or maybe a chat room?" I'm no computer whiz, but I'm not computer illiterate either. Lots of sites use security systems and have areas that can only be accessed by members with a log-in. "You could set up a Web address so that the site wasn't visible at all unless you logged in, right?"

"Sure. Your initial homepage would be a blank page, with a log-in box for a username and password. If you don't have log-in details, that's all you'd see."

"Okay. So how would you find this site?"

"That's the tricky part. If someone set it up without search stubs, it would be virtually impossible to find without the URL."

"Virtually?"

He laughs. "The Bureau runs a special computer program, more like a virus really, that might pick it up."

"Go on."

"Last year we developed a software tool that does a similar thing to Echelon but on the World Wide Web. It searches Web sites, looking for suspect text."

"So why haven't we caught and prosecuted every kiddy-porn ring in the country? In the world?"

"The Web's just too big. My system spits out URLs which we investigate, and we have caught and prosecuted quite a few people in the past year. But if you've got someone in the know on the other side, they move their site around every couple of weeks and set up shop with a new Web address that promptly gets e-mailed to all the members."

"I see."

"So we just have to wait until Betsy picks them up again."

"Betsy?"

He clears his throat. "I named it after my dog."

I suppress a laugh.

"Go on, laugh. Everybody else does."

"Sorry. So you actually built this thing?"

"I wrote the code, yes." There's a hint of pride in his voice—and rightly so. It sounds awesome.

"Agent Gerard, mind if I ask what you did before the Bureau?"

Now he laughs. "Got a theory, huh?"

"Sure do."

A computer start-up sound comes bursting through the phone line. "Yup, I was a hacker."

This happens in both the government and corporate worlds. In fact, for some hackers breaching a high-security network is like a job interview. In the corporate world, as long as no damage was done, instead of filing charges the company hires the hacker on some ridiculous six-figure salary. But Gerard works for the government, which can mean one of three things: he never got an offer from a private company, he's "doing time" in the system, or he decided to work for the government out of a sense of justice or national pride.

"So, is working for the Bureau part of your court order?"

"No, nothing like that. I did get into the U.S. Army's network when I was sixteen, but they never found me."

"Sixteen!" Shit, he's one of the good ones all right.

"But a couple years later I came across some real bad guys online. I called the Bureau and somehow wound up working here. Go figure. My folks sure were happy."

"I bet." They probably saw jail on the horizon for their son. Jail or working for the FBI. "So, Betsy. Can she search for particular words?"

"Sure. What's the word?"

"How about murder or victim?"

"She searches for those words now, she searches for all words related to violence. But it's a big bad world out there."

"You're telling me."

"And I'm afraid it's not that simple. Lots of sites would have those words. Even sites without sinister motivations. Think about the FBI Web site itself."

I hang my head back. He's right. The FBI site would mention murder and victim hundreds if not thousands of times. I'm silent. There must be something else we can search on. "What about Mojave Desert?" I say, but as soon as I finish the sentence I realize that will be the same. Too many hits.

"Might not narrow it down." Gerard confirms my suspicions. "Sorry, I'm not giving you much hope, am I?"

"No. But I appreciate you telling it like it is." I pause.

"Combining the words would be a better search. So I could search for *murder* and *Mojave Desert*."

"That sounds great. What sort of time frame are we talking about?"

"The search is quick, but it's sorting through the results that's the problem. It could take weeks to manually review every single Web site."

"Shit."

"Sorry. Looking for a specific site is like trying to find a needle in a haystack. Betsy's set up to perform blanket screens, to monitor and report all the nasties she finds, rather than search for one site."

I don't respond, disheartened.

"I'm real sorry, Agent Anderson."

I come to my senses. "That's all right. It's not your fault."

"I'll still start the ball rolling this morning and let you know as soon as we find something."

"Great, thanks." I try to sound enthusiastic, but it's hard when we don't have weeks.

We get back to Darren's place at 7:00 p.m. I have offered to cook a Thai prawn curry, so I get moving on that while Darren showers. Fifteen minutes later the curry's bubbling on the stove, the rice is on and Darren emerges in shorts.

"Shorts?"

"I cranked the heater up for you. You'll feel it soon."

"Thanks." I'm genuinely touched. Even though I've been in the States for just over a year, my body still hasn't fully acclimatized to the northern hemisphere. Probably never will.

"Smells good." He hovers over the pot. "Man, I'm hungry."

"Me, too. But it'll be at least another fifteen minutes."

He shrugs. "I can wait." He opens the fridge and emerges with two beers, opens both, and hands one to me without even asking if I want it. It feels comfortable, natural.

I think back to Vegas and our fleeting kiss at the motel. Will Darren try to kiss me again? Do I want him to? Maybe I should be the one initiating. No, I'm sensible enough to know I'm not ready. And Darren's not a rebound guy; he's a keeper. Nervously, I begin talking about the case for a distraction. "This case is frustrating the hell out of me."

"Me, too." He laughs at first but then pauses. "Who'd have thought we'd be complaining about not getting another body?" The comment sounds flippant, but I know he doesn't mean it that way. This job has just as strong a hold on Darren as it does on me—well almost. At least as far as I know, Darren's sibling wasn't kidnapped and murdered when Darren was a child. I turn away, hiding the emotions that always come up when I think about my brother, John. And then I remember that Darren's aunt was killed by the DC Slasher, so it's personal for him, too. The only difference is that Darren was already a cop when she was killed; he'd already chosen his career. Not me. John's murder is *why* I became a cop and it's shaped me in so many other ways.

"You okay?" Darren walks toward my line of sight, and I fight the desire to turn away from him again.

"I'm fine. Sorry."

"Did you see something?" His voice is hopeful.

"No, nothing."

"So still no visions? No visits from Cindy?"

I turn back to the stove and focus on the pot. "No."

"And you're still not going to try and induce something?"

I take a swig of beer and give the curry a stir. "No."

He's silent for a little while. "We're dying here, you know."

I bite my lip. "I know." Two more days until the next victim's "due." Could my visions save him or her? I shudder as excerpts of my dream about the brunette, and Cindy standing in the desert, play in my head. Dammit, leave me alone!

The images seem to obey my wishes and they subside. But within seconds they're replaced by flashes from the DC case, then flashes from my brother's disappearance. I'm reminded of Darren's words in Vegas again—it's a calling. And the calling isn't casually tapping me on the shoulder for attention; it's violently shaking me.

"It's hard for me, Darren."

He leans against the kitchen counter so eye contact is guaranteed, even though I'm hovering over the stove.

"It reminds you of DC? Of what happened?"

"That, and..."

"Yes?" His voice is eager.

I stir the curry some more, stalling. Finally I say it. "The Slasher wasn't the first time I saw things."

Darren doesn't seem at all shocked.

"You're not surprised?"

"No." He picks at the label on his beer bottle.

"But—"

"I know you've been hiding things from me, Sophie." Unlike our conversation in the project room, this time there's no hint of accusation in his voice, just acceptance and perhaps hurt.

I feel like I've betrayed him. "I'm sorry, Darren." I touch him lightly and quickly on his upper arm.

He forces a smile. "My aunt knew lots of psychics. She said it nearly always starts in childhood."

I let myself look into his eyes properly and nod my head. "I had...I had a brother. He was taken from our house when I was eight. They found his body a year later, but they never caught the guy who did it. And for a week before his abduction I had nightmares—nightmares that John was in danger." I say it quickly, with a forced detachment.

Darren puts his beer down and moves closer. He rubs his hand up and down my arm. I can feel his breath on my skin. "I'm sorry, Sophie." It's a standard response, but I can hear the sincerity and emotion behind it.

I drop my head. "The first time I had visions someone I loved was in danger, and the second time that's how it played out, too." And that brings me to another huge area of avoidance...is someone I know in danger? Someone I care about? I look at Darren—what if it's him? I couldn't stand to lose anyone else.

"I don't think it's that simple," he says.

I give him a puzzled look.

"You were always psychic, Sophie. Always. You probably just didn't realize it."

"But—"

"Let me finish." Darren holds up his hand. "Could you find stuff when you were little? Did you know stuff? Like maybe the phone would ring and you'd know who was calling? I'm talking about *before* your brother's murder."

I take myself back to that wonderful time *before* it happened. It's hard to navigate through the memories, so many of which I've repressed over the years, but finally I reach my early childhood and realize that Darren's right. "Little things, yes. But coincidental stuff."

"No. It wasn't coincidental, it was normal for you." He pauses. "And then, when John's life was in danger, your gift became more intense."

"Yes." I remember seeing John from the killer's eyes.

"And when he really was taken, when you knew he was dead, you repressed your gift. It was always there, waiting to surface, waiting for you to let it out. And you did, when you needed it the most. Don't forget, Sophie, your visions broke the Slasher case. They did save lives."

I nod, unable to find fault with his theory, unable to deny the truth. "But that means someone I care about is in danger now. Why else would they resurface after six months of silence?"

He shakes his head. "Like I said when you first got here, I think the visions were triggered by you being at a crime scene. The more I think about it, the more it makes sense." He moves us across to the table and we sit down. "Rose used to do long-distance readings for people, but she said it took her a while to refine her gift enough that she didn't need the person physically present. And I think that's what it's like for you. You've been looking at photos back at the Bureau and nothing happens. But you come here and see Malcolm's body, in real life. You have a connection to the case because of your physical proximity. And once that connection's established, the floodgates open."

He's right there. I've been fighting them but they're still coming. I stare into his blue eyes across the table, ready to hear what else he has to say.

Darren continues. "I'm sure at some stage in the future you won't need that physical connection—just like Rose trained herself to do long-distance readings."

"I don't know if that's a comforting thought." The intensity of the past few weeks has been incredibly draining. Imagine if that happened with every single case I profiled.

"Eventually you'll have to accept that this is part of you—it always has been."

I let the thought sink in, trying to imagine accepting the visions and not fighting them. It's hard to argue with Darren's reasoning.

* * *

AmericanPsycho: We need to vote for Jonathan this time. He's acting weird. He may be catching on to what's *really* happening.

DialM: The sooner he's dead, the better. He's seen me! I still can't believe he carried Ling's bags up to the surface for her.

AmericanPsycho: There was nothing we could do, M. If I'd told Jonathan over the speakers to return to the main area, he may have been suspicious. Besides, I was busy with Danny.

NeverCaught: How did you do Danny?

AmericanPsycho: It was a quick one. No real pleasure in it really.

BlackWidow: I would have liked to have seen his face. Good?

AmericanPsycho: He was an interesting one. His face showed surprise rather than disbelief.

BlackWidow: Do you think he had guessed?

AmericanPsycho: No, definitely not. But he was more aware of what other humans can do. As a soldier he'd seen war crimes and murder in his daily life. I think he was more surprised that he was part of it, rather than that it was actually happening.

NeverCaught: Bummer.

AmericanPsycho: It was disappointing.

DialM: Back to Jonathan. I want him gone. Dead. Now.

AmericanPsycho: Okay, okay. Jonathan will be dead soon enough. Won't he, BW?

BlackWidow: I'm tingling with anticipation. And don't worry, I'll find out if he's suspicious, and if he's discussed it with anyone.

NeverCaught: How? Torture?

BlackWidow: It's not always about pain…it's amazing what a man will tell you to ensure his sexual satisfaction.

NeverCaught: Lucky guy.

AmericanPsycho: How's Ling, M? Having fun?

DialM: You better believe it.

AmericanPsycho: The live feed of Ling will stay up on the Web site until M kills her. Then her body will be dumped just like the others.

NeverCaught: It's boring to watch. She just cowers in the corner of that bed all the time.

DialM: I love watching her.

AmericanPsycho: Back to the business at hand. Jonathan.

25

We sit in the project room, staring at the board blankly. Tomorrow's the day and we've got nothing. I tried to induce a vision after dinner last night, but no luck. I finally decide to go for it and that part of my mind shuts down.

"Do you want to try again?" Darren says.

"I guess. We've got nothing else, right?"

I move from my upright position in the office chair, trying to move down into a more relaxed body shape, but with no luck. Finally ergonomics has got it right, making it impossible to sit in this chair in anything but an upright posture. I make do with the body position, but try to relax into it more, sinking into the chair itself, as though my flesh was melding with the chair.

I take a deep breath in, then out, and with each outtake of air I focus on releasing tension from my body and clearing my mind. I find both hard to do. Nearly every muscle in my body contracts, unwilling to do my bidding. My thoughts flutter, constantly on the move. Asking me to relax and clear my mind is like asking a biker to get up on stage and dance the lead role of Sleeping Beauty…in a tutu. I push the bizarre thoughts away and go back to my breathing. I've just got to do this. No excuses, no distractions. Our options have run out and this is the only alternative left. I can't wait weeks until Special Agent Gerard finds the Web site.

Back to the breath, back to the breath. In and out...in and out. Finally I gain some control over my rebellious mind.

> *A man's in a tunnel, running. But he doesn't know what he's running from. It's dark with only bare lightbulbs every twenty feet or so ensuring he doesn't fall. He looks up, toward something in the corner, and that frightens him more than the dark, more than the thing behind him.*

Darren's cell phone interrupts the vision and I come to with the man's fear still running through me. My heart pounds and my breathing is no longer steady and smooth. Darren puts his hand on my knee and leans forward. "You okay? What did you see?"

"I—" Darren's cell phone is getting louder with each ring. "I'm fine. Take the call."

He fishes his phone out of his pocket, looks at the number and then puts the phone on the table. "They can leave a message."

"Who is it?" I ask.

"Dunno."

A strange sensation hits me in the pit of my stomach. "Darren, I think you better take that call."

"It can wait. This is more important."

My spider sense is tingling. "Darren, you *need* to take that call."

"Okay," he says, but his voice is hesitant.

I'm a ball of nervous energy and my stomach is doing flips at a million miles per hour. Something terrible has happened. Who's on the phone and what are they saying? I stand up and pace. I glance at the clock. Darren is mostly silent, taking in the caller's information, but I can tell from his face that he's being told some shocking news.

Finally, after what seems like an eternity, he hangs up. There's silence.

"Darren?"

"Sorry." He sounds shaken, dreamy.

"Who was it?"

"It was a uniform from the Pima County Sheriff's Department over at Catalina Foothills." His voice is still vague.

"Yes?"

"About an hour ago a man called Jonathan Cantor walked into their station." Gradually, Darren seems to be coming out of his stupor. "Sophie, you won't believe this. You won't believe his story."

Three hours later Special Agent Daniel Gerard arrives at Tucson by charter plane. I sure as hell wasn't going to wait for him to come in on a commercial route, not after Darren's news. And when I filled Rivers in, he assigned Gerard to the case, full-time.

I'm full of nervous tension, energy and, I hate to admit it, excitement. If Jonathan Cantor is telling the truth, the scheme is just so...so diabolical it's hard to comprehend. The organizer truly is brilliant. Terrifying, but brilliant. And we'll need to move quickly—there are more victims being held captive in the Mojave.

Within twenty minutes of Gerard touching down, he's standing with us, peering into Jonathan's interview room. Through the two-way mirror we can see Jonathan pacing, wildly clutching a laptop under his arm. He refused to hand over the laptop, refused to talk to us anymore until we had a computer expert on site. He told his story to the officer on duty at Catalina, and since then hasn't spoken except to demand someone with IT expertise.

Jonathan's by himself, but the adjoining room is full—Stone, Darren, Gerard, me and Harris.

Harris's eyes fix on me. "Do you believe this story?" His voice contains shades of doubt.

Normally I'd be hesitant to make any judgment call before personally speaking to Jonathan, but he's the man from my vision, the one in the tunnels. And I did see Cindy in a tunnel in one of my visions. She was trying to lead me somewhere, to show me where she was before she died, but I couldn't follow her then. And Jonathan's story fits with the many anomalies in the cases. "It wouldn't surprise me," is all I say.

Harris turns back toward Jonathan. "Maybe he's one of the perps. Working his way into the investigation."

"It's possible," I say, because that's what I'd say if I hadn't seen Jonathan in my vision, if I hadn't seen any tunnels.

Harris shakes his head. "If he is involved he's one hell of a good actor," he concedes. "It's just…I've seen a lot of things in my day, but this…"

"I know." I look at Jonathan through the two-way. "I know."

Jonathan's hair is dark and the same length all over, roughly one-inch long. It looks like a shaved head on its way out. His face and arms are a reddy brown, indicating he's seen a lot of sun recently. His face is angular, the most striking feature his bushy dark brown eyebrows that come together across his defined brow. Normally I imagine it would give him a natural brooding look, but today he's clearly distressed and the bushy eyebrows give him a manic, slightly mad look. But if his story's true and he's actually been through what he claims, then he has a reason to be slightly insane.

His skinny frame does an abrupt turn and comes toward the mirror. "Come on!" he shouts. "What are you people doing in there?" He shakes his head and moves again.

Darren turns away from the pacing figure and looks at me. "What do you think?"

I continue to look at Jonathan. "He's suffering. Very, very anxious and frustrated." I turn to Darren. "But who wouldn't be?" I take out a notebook and pen from my bag. Sometimes we take a couple of huge files into the room—even if they're filled with blank paper—to make a suspect think we've got a load of evidence on him. But today, for the moment, a notebook and pen is enough. I also take out my Dictaphone. The station's recording equipment will video the interview, but I want easy and fast access to whatever Jonathan has to say.

"I'll go in by myself initially," I say to everyone. "I need to see how he reacts to me alone, first." Even though I believe Jonathan, I need to treat him like I'd treat anyone else in this situation, even if it's cruel to Jonathan given his mental state. Besides, to accept his story instantly may arouse suspicion, especially from Harris and Stone. It's normal procedure to treat anyone who comes forward with information as if they could be a witness or a suspect. "Once he's settled, Darren, you might want to help with the questioning. Then we'll bring Agent Gerard in." I look back at Jonathan. "At the moment, he's hanging on. Let's see what his responses are like."

"You call that hanging on?" Harris motions to Jonathan, who's rubbing his free hand up and down his face, almost clawing his skin.

I know how he feels. I know what it's like to be targeted. "He's hanging on."

When I enter the interview room, Jonathan jerks his head my way. "Thank fucking Christ! I've been in here for hours. Are you the computer expert?"

I'm not surprised that I'm greeted by this barrage of anger. He's right; it has been hours. More than three hours, to be precise. Of course he's angry. He's angry at the people who did this to him and he's angry at us for making him wait. And these feelings will be amplified by the fact that he's been effectively held prisoner twice now. But Jonathan's the one who set the rules, who wouldn't talk to Darren or me or anyone until the computer forensics person was on hand.

"I'm not the computer expert, but he's here now. I'm sorry about the delay, but we wanted to get the best."

"Well bring him in!"

"I need to ask you some questions first."

He shakes his head. "The clock is ticking. People's lives are at stake." He waves his hands wildly, then looks down at the laptop in his left hand and stops. "Shit. I can't afford to screw this up." His voice is soft now, hushed. "Can't afford to crash the hard drive."

I press record on my Dictaphone and put it, my pen and my

notebook on the table. I fish out my ID from my jacket pocket. "Mr. Cantor, my name's Special Agent Sophie Anderson from the FBI."

His face relaxes slightly. "The FBI?"

"Yes. I'm sorry you've had to wait so long, but I've flown in one of the Bureau's top computer analysts from the Cyber Crime Division." I sit down.

"What's your role in this?" he asks, but his voice is open, no longer defensive. The FBI's got a reputation, and at this moment that reputation alone has calmed Jonathan down.

"I'm a criminal profiler. I work at FBI headquarters drafting psychological profiles of different criminals. I've been working on profiles for the murders of Malcolm Jackson and Cindy Star." I mention the victims' names, even though my statement isn't entirely accurate—I only reviewed the profile of Malcolm's killer and I don't have enough info to profile Cindy's killer yet. The only profile I actually drafted is of the brunette's killer, but I don't know her name.

Jonathan puts the laptop gingerly on the table and sits down. He drops his head into his hands. "So they are dead?"

I can see that he'd come to this conclusion himself, yet a very small part of him had not fully accepted their deaths, had hoped that maybe he was wrong. "Yes. I'm afraid so. Malcolm Jackson was the first victim we found."

"Yes, he was the first voted out."

"Voted?" I ask. Even though I've heard the basics from Darren, I want it in Jonathan's words.

"Oh, God. What about the others?" He no longer looks insane, just defeated.

I glance up at the two-way mirror, and feel my gaze lock with Darren's even though I can't see him. This is what we were afraid of. We haven't found them all. "We found one other body that we haven't been able to ID. It was a woman, long dark curly hair, darkish skin—"

"Brigitte." He shakes his head. "Brigitte Raine."

"Do you know the spelling on that?" I ask mostly for Darren and

Stone. One of them will look her up while I'm questioning. Any relatives will need to be notified.

"Um…I don't know." He's distracted, not thinking straight. "You haven't found the others?"

"How many have there been?" I bite my lip, scared by what his answer might be.

"Malcolm was first. Then Cindy, then Brigitte. Then Danny and Ling went the same week, then me. How could we be so stupid? They said it would be the biggest thing to happen to reality TV."

I concentrate on the names he mentioned. "Do you know Danny's and Ling's last names?"

"Yeah. Danny Jensen and Ling Gianolo. Danny moves around a lot." He corrects himself. "Moved around. He used to be in the army. But his homestate is Texas. At least that's what he told us. And Ling's an Aussie, like you." He says Aussie with an S sound rather than a Z sound—like most Americans do. "She got voted out the week before me."

I nod. I am intrigued by the Web site, by the computer, but we need to approach the investigation in an orderly manner. Get the names of the others and confirm they are, indeed, missing. This will validate Jonathan's story. "You said Ling's last name was Gianolo."

"Yes."

"Italian," I state. I grew up largely in Melbourne, a multicultural city with lots of Italian migrants from the fifties.

"Kind of."

I look up at Jonathan. "Kind of?"

"Ling was adopted from China," Jonathan continues. "She was out here for six months before she started college." He rubs his hand across his forehead. "She was only eighteen, for God's sake." He puts his head in his hands and I give him the space of silence. A few seconds pass before he looks up with hope in his eyes. "Could she still be alive? I mean, if you haven't found her…"

"I'm afraid it's unlikely, Jonathan." I pause. Jonathan could be right. The first three bodies could have been about getting our attention, and weekly kills guaranteed that. Now they could slow things down a bit. But most killers don't break their patterns. "The killers have followed a strict pattern with weekly kills—I think they've just changed what they do with the bodies." It's about control for them. Controlling the contestants and, more importantly, controlling what we find. But Jonathan's put a spanner in the works for the club.

Despite my bad news, Jonathan is now calm and cooperative. I want to put him at ease as much as possible, and I don't want it to occur to him that there's any doubt in our minds that he's the victim, rather than part of the perpetrating team. "Do you want a coffee or a cold drink? Something else to eat?" Stone had given him a sandwich and a coffee as soon as he arrived from the Catalina station, but that was a while ago.

He looks at me with overwhelming gratitude and excitement. "God, I'd kill for another coffee. No, a Coke. And maybe something sweet?" He runs his hand over his short hair. "Except for a pizza during a reward challenge, they've had us on Spam and baked beans."

Spam—the contents of Malcolm's stomach makes sense now, and I guess he left before the "reward challenge." I nod at the two-way mirror, a sign for someone to grant Jonathan's wish. Making people feel comfortable is a common interview tactic. For victims it helps them open up and tell their whole story, and for perps it can throw them off guard. They relax and let some detail slip, say something incriminating. In this case, it has the added benefit of hopefully reducing Jonathan's paranoia, of building trust between us. His hand still rests on the laptop in a protective manner.

While we wait for Jonathan's food I focus on the computer. "I'll take that if you like." I put my hand out but don't make a grab for it. Trust.

He hugs the laptop closer to himself, but the wildness does not return. "Like I said, people's lives are at stake and this is the only thing that could save them. Someone who knows what they're doing could get Internet log files from this, view the chat-room logs, hopefully track down the video-stream sources and Chester."

"Sounds like you know what you're talking about."

"I studied computers for two years at college. Before I dropped out."

"I see," I say, before backtracking. "Who's Chester?"

"He was the one that came to the bunker. The only face we ever saw."

"You never saw anyone else? Did that make you suspicious?"

He shakes his head. "Not at first, no. By the time I started getting suspicious it was too late. We were trapped. Not even Susie, my best friend, believed me." His eyes widen and he stands up again. "We're wasting time. We need to get moving."

The door opens and Stone comes in with a Coke and a tray of Krispy Kreme doughnuts. Jonathan can't take his eyes off the food. He dives for the can of soda and pops the top, guzzling for a few seconds before taking a breath. Next he shoves a glazed doughnut into his mouth in two goes. He's certainly eating like a man who's been living on beans and Spam for four weeks. In fact, within seconds he's managed to switch from demanding we take action to being focused on eating. That's consistent with food deprivation, as is his skinny frame, even though I can tell from his shape that he's naturally a slim build.

He shoves another doughnut into his mouth and halfway through looks up. His eyes show panic. He puts half of the doughnut back in the tray and sits down, head in his hands. "What the hell am I doing? Susie and Clair are waiting for me."

"We've got a computer forensics expert here, but first, you need to tell me everything that happened. From the start."

He shakes his head. "That's not important. We need to get moving. To find the bunker and Susie." He stands up and starts pacing.

I stand up too. "There is method to the madness. Some minor detail of your story could help us find them."

He pauses, processing the info. He's a smart guy; he knows it's true.

He nods. "Okay." With the acceptance of the fact that he has to retell his story, Jonathan focuses on food again and picks up his half-eaten second doughnut. He bites down consuming most of the doughnut, and then takes a deep breath.

* * *

AmericanPsycho: I wonder if BlackWidow is having as much fun with Jonathan as I had with Cindy.

NeverCaught: I bet Jonathan's getting the ***** of his life.

AmericanPsycho: I'm glad he's gone. I never liked him.

NeverCaught: You were just jealous of him.

AmericanPsycho: Don't be ridiculous. He's…a nothing, a nobody.

NeverCaught: Maybe, but not to Susie. I've worked it out, dude. You're hot for Susie.

DialM: You're right, Never. It would explain all the rough treatment you gave Jonathan.

AmericanPsycho: I admit I like Susie. But regardless, I never liked Jonathan.

DialM: Where are you going to dump his body?

AmericanPsycho: I'll see what the U of A is like. If the police presence is too much I'll find somewhere else.

NeverCaught: But they're not in order!

DialM: Ling will still be killed and dumped in the same manner. There's just a slight delay while I have her.

26

"It all started a few months ago, when Susie showed me an ad in the *Los Angeles Times*."

I cut in. "What's Susie's last name?" He's mentioned her a couple of times and is obviously close to her.

"Dean. Susie Dean." His eyebrows come together and his brow furrows. He's worried about Susie.

Darren, who joined us as planned, leans forward. "Is she your girlfriend?"

"No. She's my best friend."

"What do you remember about the ad?" I ask.

"Everything." He looks at me like I've insulted his intellect. "It said: Hot new reality TV show looking for contestants. Everyone welcome. Send a five-minute video about yourself to PO Box 556, West Hollywood by December twentieth."

It sounds like Jonathan's trying to repeat the ad word for word, rather than summarizing it, yet he didn't stumble. Very unusual. Most people would paraphrase it and would have difficulty remembering it. December was five months ago.

I let it go for the moment and Darren takes the next question.

"So for the past few weeks, you and several others have believed you've been contestants in a reality TV show?"

Jonathan nods. "Yup. Competing for a million dollars."

I shake my head. Over our history, humans have used just about everything to lure potential victims—from candy for the kids to faking an injury—this is just one more. For a wannabe TV star, national media exposure and a million dollars would be too good to pass up. But Jonathan certainly doesn't strike me as someone who'd want fame. There's more to him than meets the eye, but what it is I'm not sure yet. And his recounting of the ad bothers me. How can he remember from months ago, word for word? What if he is playing us? Maybe my vision was wrong, or simply misleading. He could have been down there, but as a conspirator, not a true victim. "What did you say the ad said?"

He repeats it again, word for word. I remembered it, but I only had to remember it for a few minutes and I've trained my memory for recall. You need it in this job. "And you remember this exact wording because…?"

He taps his head. "Photographic memory."

I write down the address so we can check it out. A post-office box could have been registered by anyone, and it's likely they used fake ID.

Darren scribbles it down, too. "Anything else about the ad?"

"It was short but big, taking up a quarter-page spot. There must have been similar ads in Vegas, New York, Boston, and New Orleans, given where all the contestants come from. I figured there were probably more, in other states, but those people didn't make the final eight. Didn't get on the show." He shakes his head. "I don't know how Susie got me into it. I hate reality TV. I think it's pathetic."

Now that rings true to me. "So why were you involved?"

"Susie was auditioning and insisted I send in a video, too. She can be very persuasive and I didn't think either of us would actually get in. But then we were both picked for the next round of applications. And suddenly we were waiting for the limo to arrive out in front of our dump in West Hollywood."

"A limo?" Darren asks.

Just like Cindy. "We might be able to get something on that, especially if they hired it." Then again, how many limo companies would there be in L.A.? Plus they managed to avoid detection in Vegas, so no doubt L.A. will be the same.

Jonathan nods. "It picked us up around 2:00 p.m. on March twentieth."

"Pickup address?"

"Three-fifty-two North Ogden Drive, West Hollywood."

"Okay. Then what happened?"

"It was Chester who picked us up in the limo. He took our bags, which were supplied by the show, and drove us to a helipad."

Darren looks up from his notebook. "When did you get the bags?"

"About a week before the pickup date. With the bags came a set of rules of what we could and couldn't take. No cell phones, no PDAs or pocket PCs, in fact no electronic gadgetry at all. That's when I wanted out."

"Why?" I ask.

"Me without a PDA or computer?" He shakes his head. "It made me twitchy just thinking about it."

I look at the two-way mirror and imagine how Special Agent Gerard would feel if his gadgets were taken away from him. I don't know him very well, but I know he wouldn't like it. No computer fanatic would. Hell, even I don't like being without e-mail for more than a day.

"So why didn't you back out?" Darren's voice has a hint of accusation to it.

Jonathan turns his attention from me to Darren and his gaze hardens. "I'd signed a contract and the paperwork had been real clear about what would happen if you bailed. They'd sue you. I'm not exactly living in the lap of luxury, you know."

"What *do* you do for a living, Mr. Cantor?" Darren looks away, like he's bored.

"I DJ two nights a week and work in a bar four nights. Like I said, not exactly thriving here."

I lean forward. "Where was the helipad?"

He shakes his head. "I was so damned distracted I didn't even pay attention. Not like me at all. There was champagne in the limo so we were drinking and looking for hidden cameras." There's self-disgust in Jonathan's voice. I want to reassure him, but I resist my natural instinct. This is an interview, not a therapy session. I need to concentrate on the facts.

Back to the limo. "Did you find any cameras?"

"Sure. I spotted one in the interior light." His hands clench. "They were watching us. Watching our excitement, watching us making fools of ourselves. This was supposed to be Susie's big break."

"She's a singer?" Darren continues to act disinterested.

"Actress." Jonathan's voice is defensive, which indicates he has a real relationship with Susie, swinging me back to thinking of him as purely victim, not co-conspirator. "There were three people in it for their performance careers. Susie, Cindy and Clair."

"Clair?" I ask.

"She's still in the bunker. Still alive…as far as I know."

"Actually, let's do this now. Who's still in there, besides Susie?" My pen hovers over my notepad.

"Just Clair Kelly. It's down to the final two."

I write down the names *Clair Kelly* and *Susie Dean*. Final two— that's reality TV talk. Then again, I guess they *are* the final two—the final two survivors.

Darren looks at me and I nod. As far as Jonathan's concerned, the nod could mean anything, but Darren knows it's my signal to him that I believe Jonathan. That we no longer have to treat him like a potential suspect.

"We're going to do everything we can to find them." This time I let myself reassure Jonathan. I stand up and Darren follows suit. "We'll be back in a second."

I leave before Jonathan has time to protest verbally—although the look he gives me is enough. We kept him waiting for hours and now I'm leaving when he's really only just starting his account of the past few weeks.

In the viewing room it's Harris who speaks first. "Okay, let's track down these names."

I hand him the full list—Danny Jensen, Ling Gianolo, Clair Kelly, Susie Dean. "I'd like to find out as much as we can about these other 'contestants.' See how they compare to Cindy and Malcolm." My guess is there'll be a pattern, in terms of victim type. Neither Cindy nor Malcolm had strong family ties, which makes them ideal choices for this type of scheme. It's a safe bet that all the victims are isolated in some way, and that was why they were chosen. "I'm going back in."

Harris nods. "I want you two to stay here." He looks at Darren and Stone. "I'll assign these names to someone else." He moves toward the door.

"Do you want me to wait?" I call after him, hoping he'll say no. I don't think it's a good idea to keep Jonathan waiting for too much longer. He's calmer now, but leave him by himself for more than five minutes and that will probably change.

"No. Go ahead."

"Thanks."

I enter the room. "Sorry, about that, Jonathan. I needed to get someone on those names, to start contacting the relatives."

"Families. You won't find much."

"Really?" I sit down again and Jonathan follows suit.

He nods. "That's one of the things that first made me suspicious. We were all from nonexistent or dysfunctional families. I started thinking maybe it was no coincidence. Plus we were missing the real high achievers. No lawyers, no scientists. It didn't sit right with me."

I nod. Jonathan sure as hell is smart. Lucky for the others, and for us. If Jonathan hadn't been suspicious, hadn't escaped, it's quite possible we'd never track down the killers. Most of our leads have turned into dead ends—just what the perps want. But Jonathan is no dead end.

"Let's pick it up from the helipad. What did the pilot look like?"

"The pilot was Chester."

I wonder how many registered helicopter pilots there are in the U.S. "So he left the limo there?"

"Yeah, he parked it in a garage and then blindfolded us. He said the bunker location was secret, and it seemed plausible at the time."

"What was the area like? I presume it wasn't an airport."

"No. It looked like a factory or warehouse. I didn't see anyone else around."

"How long was the flight?"

"About two hours."

"The Mojave Desert." I know this is where they must have been held, where some of them are still being held, but I still verbalize it.

Jonathan shrugs. "It was definitely desert, but I don't know if it was the Mojave Desert or not."

"So what happened after you landed?"

"Chester took our blindfolds off and pointed us in the direction of the bunker entrance, a trapdoor in the sand. It needed a code to open it—5413. He must have taken off after we went down."

"And what did you find inside?"

"We climbed down a series of ladders until we got to the bottom and a long tunnel."

I'm immediately reminded of my vision of tunnels.

Jonathan continues. "At the end of the corridor was another door, but before that was an electronic gate and a conveyor belt. Like you see at the airport."

"Sounds expensive."

"The place would have cost a fortune to set up. The technology and construction were both intense."

I nod.

Jonathan moves on. "When we went through the last door and into the bunker the others were waiting for us."

"All of them?"

"Yes. Susie and I were the last to arrive. Once we were in, the door shut and locked behind us. We were trapped down there."

I control a shudder. Trapped underground and being picked off by serial killers one by one—not a nice way to go. I'm not sure if it was better or worse that they had no idea of their predicament.

"What was it like in the bunker?"

"There were six rooms—a large central room containing the living and kitchen areas, two bedrooms, a bathroom, a separate toilet and a soundproof room they called the blue room. The walls were earth with some concrete and the ceiling had steel girders across it. The cameras and a few lights were mounted on the steel girders. Later we found some hidden cameras—spycams.

"It was real basic. Milk crates for seats, a trunk as a table, camping gear in the kitchen. The kitchen also had a large ceramic sink and a pump hooked up for running water."

I keep taking notes, and check that the Dictaphone is still rolling as Jonathan continues.

"The two bedrooms were small, each with four army cots. The bathroom had another sink with a pump and water outlet, and a small makeshift shower cubicle. The toilet was simply a camping-style pit toilet."

I nod and keep scribbling summary notes. Once my hand catches up, I ask him the next question. "How did they communicate with you?"

"There was a speaker in the bunker that a voice came over, but most of the communication was through Chester."

"So he came back?"

"Oh, yeah. He was responsible for the challenges."

"Challenges?"

"Like on other reality shows—the winner got immunity and was safe from the vote. Safe inside the bunker." He shakes his head. "Talk about a double meaning. That voice, that creepy voice over the speaker, I knew there was something about the way he said *safe*. There was more to it, you know? Like he was in on some joke."

"Was it Chester's voice?"

Jonathan is silent for a moment, thinking. "It's hard to tell. The voice was run through some sort of computer distortion program, so it sounded computerized. It was deep though."

"Chester's voice is deep?"

"Yeah, you could say that."

I look at him questioningly, waiting for him to expand.

"His voice is real deep and gravelly, like he's just had ten shots of whisky and chain-smoked a pack of cigarettes…on two hours' sleep."

I can't help but let out a little snort at Jonathan's description. "I get the picture." I smile. "What does he look like?"

"He's African-American, about six feet five, and built like a brick house. But to tell you the truth, before I realized what was going on, I thought he was kinda nice." Jonathan shakes his head. "Guess it was all part of the act."

"Probably. Although it's possible he was following orders. Who knows what's going on behind the scenes."

"True. Anyway, his head was shaved smooth and shiny and he wore a gold earring in his left ear."

"We'll get you together with a sketch artist later today. Hopefully we'll get a match."

"You're thinking Chester has a criminal record?"

"He could do. We might get an ID from the sketch, but at the very least we can circulate it to the LAPD and a few other areas for them to keep an eye out for him."

"Okay."

"So, then what happened?"

"Not much. We sat on our asses and waited for the challenges. It was pretty boring. In between we'd read, talk to each other, and sometimes we looked for cameras. That's when we found the spy-cams."

"Tell me about the challenges."

"They always held them on Wednesdays. It was our only way of knowing what day it was, especially with no light down there, no way of knowing when it was nighttime."

"What about watches?"

He shakes his head. "They weren't allowed." He pauses. "Whoever won the challenge had immunity. Then we all went to the blue room and told the viewers—" he makes air quotes "—who we thought should go that week, and why. Then they announced who was voted out and that person had to leave the bunker immediately."

The bodies were found Fridays. Fits with the first three victims perfectly.

"How did you know challenges were on Wednesdays?"

"The voice told us at the start. But you're right, I guess it could have been a lie."

"Wednesdays would correspond with the evidence." I scribble down Wednesdays and then look up at Jonathan. "What were the challenges like?"

For the first time, Jonathan freezes up. Finally he speaks. "Some bad shit happened down there."

"The challenges?"

He shudders. "The first one seemed pretty standard—a paintball challenge. But I thought the second one was cruel, personal. It was individual recordings we had to listen to over and over again, but they were nasty."

"Is that when you became suspicious?"

"Partly. I guess it was a gradual thing. The challenges got progressively worse and that didn't sit right, but I still didn't know what was going on. We still could have been on TV, but maybe it was like *The Truman Show* and the joke was on me. Susie is an actress, and I wouldn't have put it past her to be a conspirator, as a career move." He puts his hand protectively on the laptop. "And then came the food challenge. It was for reward this time, and the reward was a pizza and a six-pack of beer. Both very tempting."

"I can imagine," I say, remembering the way Jonathan devoured the doughnut.

"Danny won and he actually shared some of his winnings with us, which surprised the shit out of us, because he was pretty much an ass. But then we all got sick. Food poisoning. Danny was real bad."

"You think it was intentional?"

"At the time it crossed my mind. But I dismissed it. Thought I was being paranoid."

"But now?"

"Now I'm sure those bastards did it on purpose."

I'm inclined to agree with Jonathan. The killers have been playing with the contestants all along, and food poisoning would fit. Another form of torture.

"Then, I think maybe they knew I was suspicious or something, because the next challenge was an isolation chamber, only I got different treatment than the others. They wanted me out of the bunker. All of us were light-deprived, but when I was inside my chamber, I had blasts of bright white lights."

"It's a form of torture."

"Yup, I know. But when I came out, everyone else thought I'd been hallucinating, and I started to believe them." He lets out a small snort. "Susie calls me the great conspiracy theorist. And, I have to admit, I do get carried away sometimes."

"Enough to doubt your feelings this time?"

He nods. "Enough to think that my instincts were just paranoia." He grabs my hand, switching from reflection to desperation in an instant. "You've got to find them. We've got to find that bunker. If it wasn't for those fucking blindfolds!" He stands up and his chair is thrown backward and over by the force.

I'm not alarmed. Having been through it myself, I know exactly what Jonathan's experiencing. I don't expect him to be calm and rational, certainly not all the time. And mood changes are natural as his mind cycles through the multitude of emotions—from disbelief and shock, to anger. At least he's experiencing them all. It's a helluva lot better than shutting down.

He looks at me. "Fuck, I wish I knew where that damn bunker was."

We all wish he knew where the bunker was, but I don't say that. "Tell me what happened after you got voted out."

Jonathan tenses. "I said my goodbyes and left Susie and Clair in the bunker."

I nod.

He takes a seat. "Waiting on the surface was a woman and the chopper. She said she was with the show, but there was something about her that was off."

"Off how?" I ask, but already I'm assuming Jonathan met Malcolm's killer, the femme fatale. I can imagine her predator eyes feasting on Jonathan's innocence.

"She was very—" He stops and is silent.

I complete the picture for him. "She was hitting on you."

"Yes." He seems relieved that he didn't have to say it himself.

"What does she look like?"

"She's got black hair, about shoulder length, with a wave and bits falling onto her face. She's about Susie's height, so that makes her five-seven, and she's in good shape. Attractive and very sexy. I'd place her in her thirties."

I nod. It matches the vague descriptions we've got on her from the VICAP files, and my impression of the woman, too. "What was she wearing?"

"Black leather pants and a tight T-shirt with a Super Girl emblem on it."

The sexualized clothes—part of her look, and part of the profile. "Did you respond to her advances?"

"Not really. I was confused. And to be honest, her actions made me even more suspicious."

I look at Jonathan. "Why?"

He smiles. "Well, maybe I don't hang out in the right circles, but in my experience, beautiful female strangers don't tend to hit on me. Let's face it, I'm not exactly model material."

"Okay." I scribble on my notepad. "So what happened?"

"We got into the chopper."

"Was Chester the pilot?"

"I'm not sure. I couldn't see the pilot this time. The chopper was facing away from us when I crawled out of the bunker, and there was a divider between the cabin and the pilot area."

It strikes me that if Chester was the pilot, he was hiding his identity not from Jonathan but from the female killer.

"Both the woman and I had to put blindfolds on."

"So chances are she doesn't know where the bunker is either."

"I thought it odd at the time, but she said only a couple of people on the show knew the actual location." He laughs, a cynical chuckle. "That they didn't want a leak and the press or fans descending on the location."

"How long was the chopper ride back?"

He shrugs. "After weeks in the bunker, my sense of time is shot. I don't have a clue."

"Take a guess. Do you think it was more like fifteen minutes or three hours?"

"Two hours, maybe." He fidgets and his voice is uncertain. They really did a number on him.

"What did you and the woman talk about during the flight?"

"Not much. For most of it we didn't talk, but when we did, we talked about the bunker. The other contestants, the challenges, you know. She told me how much she hated Danny and how we were all saints for putting up with him for so long."

"Did she say anything that sounded strange? That made you suspicious again?"

"No. In fact, it felt very natural. She'd stopped with the aggressive come-on, and we were just chatting."

"And you landed...?"

He's already told the cops this part of the story, but I want to hear it again, and in his words.

"Some fancy house. Big house, helipad, fountain at the entrance. The chopper took off and we went inside."

A fountain? A blurry memory of my dream about Cindy surfaces. I saw her run past a fountain. I focus on Jonathan again. "And then?"

"She said we'd chill at the house for a day or two, before a camera crew and the show's psychologist arrived to debrief me. Then they'd take me to a live TV appearance on *Letterman*."

"You believed her?"

"I didn't know what to think at that point."

I nod. "Go on."

"We sat down and she brought out a six-pack of beers. Man, I wanted that beer."

Back to her MO. Get the victim drunk, vulnerable. And given Jonathan hadn't had anything to drink for a few weeks and hardly anything to eat, it wouldn't have taken much.

He continues. "We chatted while we drank and she got flirty again, but not so aggressive. I guess I liked the attention." He hangs his head in shame, but I don't know why. Not many men, particularly single men, would resist the attention of a beautiful woman.

"So then what happened?"

"We kissed some but I was still uneasy, something felt wrong. So I quizzed her about the show, but she didn't like it one little bit. Eventually she got real pissed at me. She started muttering something about none of the others having this problem. I knew something was off, but I truly didn't believe my life was in danger. Didn't know the others were...dead." He gulps and his large Adam's apple bobs up and down. "I mean, there are conspiracy theories and then there's this." He shakes his head. "It's...evil. I never believed in that word until now."

I nod, I've believed in evil for years. "What happened next?"

"She pulled out a gun." He takes a deep breath. "And I could tell she got off on the shocked expression on my face. She held the gun on me and had the gall to tell me that it would have been better if she'd been fucking me. That's when she told me how it all went down. That she was part of a group called the Murderers' Club and that the president had recruited them from chat rooms and set this whole thing up." His hands clench into fists. "She told me that after each immunity challenge, the members of the club voted someone off, and then that person—" he gulps again "—that person was auctioned off to the highest bidder in the Murderers' Club." He pauses. "I still can't believe it."

"That's a natural reaction, Jonathan. Most victims of crimes find it hard to accept that it's happened to them. And this one is so...so bizarre that it does seem surreal. Too evil to be possible." I use his choice of word: "evil."

"Well, with a gun pointed at me, I didn't feel like I had many options. Part of me was still waiting for someone to pop out and tell me I'd been *Punk'd*, but I guess part of me knew. My survival instinct took over. I still can't believe I did it." He puts his head in his hands, disturbed by his own actions as much as by those of the members of the club. "I mean, I'm not a killer. I don't believe in war, or guns, or any of that stuff."

He's silent for a little while, and I let him sit with his thoughts before prompting him again. "What happened?"

He sighs again. "First I tried to talk my way out. I told her that if I was going to die, I'd rather fuck a beautiful woman first. She hesitated and came real close to me. Like she was going to start kissing me again." He stood up. "I was standing near the wall, and she was only about a foot away from me. I thought she was falling for it, but then she declined the offer. Once she did that, I knew I had to act fast. I thought I probably only had seconds left to live. I didn't think much of Danny Jensen, but I've got him to thank for my life."

"How so?"

"During the paintball challenge, he disarmed me in a couple of seconds. I recalled the moment and rehearsed the move a couple of times in my mind, and then I did it."

I nod, encouraging him to continue.

"I darted to the left and pushed her arm with my left palm. The gun went off, but I was no longer in the bullet's path and the gun flew across the room. I grabbed her wrist with my right hand and tried to restrain her." His nose curls up in disgust. "But she still came at me. I punched her, hard. And I kept punching her, over and over again." He wrings his hands together. "I finally stopped when I realized she was out cold—or dead. I don't know which. I came to my senses and backed away from her. I don't know how long I stood there. A while, I guess. Then I started to calm down, to think straight. I stopped looking at her bloodied face and got her handbag. There were some handcuffs in there, so I cuffed her to the railings of the staircase.

"I checked the phone, but it was dead. I did a quick search of the house, but didn't find anything except the laptop. I wanted to log on there and then, but I know how important it is for the computer to be in its original condition, not tampered with. I packed up the laptop and ran. I was out of my mind. I didn't know what to do, but I knew I had to get out of that house and I had to find the cops."

"Do you think you could find the house again, if we take you back to the station you came into?"

He rubs his hand across the laptop. "I was...wild. Panic-stricken. I can't even remember how long I was running for."

I bite my lip. He needs to remember. "We'll help you."

"I've got to remember. If someone from the club comes to that house and finds that woman handcuffed to the stairs, Susie and Clair are dead."

27

In the observation room, we discuss our options. One thing's for sure, it's time to act, and fast. Somebody, presumably Chester, will be back to pick up the woman and Jonathan's body. And then the only thing we currently have going for us—the element of surprise—will be gone.

Harris turns to Gerard. "What do you need?"

"I'd like to speak to Jonathan, and get that laptop. Then we'll be able to log on to this site and—"

"We can pretend to be our female killer," I suggest.

Gerard nods. "We need to get a few copies of the hard drive first. The moment we use that laptop, it becomes dubious as evidence." He pauses, and then elaborates. "We'll be corrupting the evidence. Any time the computer is fired up, files are changed."

"It's your call." Harris looks at Gerard and me, handing over official authority. Now that the Internet is involved it's federal law, under our jurisdiction, rather than state law.

I take the lead. "Gerard and I will look after Jonathan. Maybe you guys can start looking at locations where this mystery house could be. Hopefully there aren't that many fancy houses in the Catalina Foothills."

Harris, Carter and Stone exchange a look.

"What?" I ask.

Darren sighs. "Catalina Foothills is full of fancy houses."

"That'd be right," I say. "It's the story of this case." I turn to leave the observation room and Gerard follows me. As we're leaving, Harris starts divvying out tasks to Carter and Stone.

In the interview room I introduce the pair. "Jonathan Cantor, this is Special Agent Gerard."

Jonathan looks Gerard over and shakes his hand. "So, you're from the Cyber Crime Division?"

"That's me." Gerard takes out his ID. "I'm sure you'll want to have a close look at this." He hands the folder to Jonathan.

There's an underlying communication, a knowledge between the pair, but it's lost on me.

Gerard turns to me to explain. "Jonathan will want to confirm my identity. Just to make sure he's not being socially engineered."

My cases have never taken me far into the IT world, and I'm still none the wiser.

Gerard explains. "Lots of hackers and IT experts are into social engineering. That's how they get into a company's network, steal your identity or whatever—by pretending to be someone they're not. Think of a social engineer as a con man who uses IT as his predominant tool."

Jonathan examines the ID closely, even taking it out of the cover. Something he didn't bother to do with mine. "So, you're the expert, Agent Gerard?" Jonathan still keeps the laptop huddled close to his body.

Gerard sighs. "I joined the Bureau just over six years ago. Before that I was into hacking. Big-time hacking."

"Such as?"

Jonathan is grilling Gerard, not willing to hand over the laptop until he is satisfied Gerard won't foul it up. And in Jonathan's eyes, credentials aren't about Gerard's job history, they're about his life before the Bureau.

Gerard narrows his eyes slightly. "I think you've got more than two years of college experience in computers."

Jonathan doesn't respond.

Gerard sighs again, resigned to the fact he has to prove himself. "You're younger than me, so I'll start with the most recent. Did you hear anything about the alleged breach at Microsoft in 2000?"

"Yeah." Jonathan chuckles. "Rumor has it that some wizard took over Bill Gates's machine for an hour before the IT boffins could shut him down."

Gerard translates for me. "Wizard refers to someone very high up in the hacking chain, someone who has advanced skills." He turns back to Jonathan and gives him a little wink.

"No!"

"Yup."

"So you're CommMaster?"

"Uh huh."

"CommMaster?" I ask.

Gerard turns to me again. "My hacker name." He clears his throat. "Back in my pre-Bureau days."

"I wondered why you disappeared into thin air. Thought you must have been in prison, with one of those no-computers orders."

"Well, that was one path. But I decided to steer away from the dark side."

I roll my eyes. Typical, a *Star Wars* reference. "Okay, this is getting way too geeky for me, guys."

Gerard smiles. "Point taken." He turns to Jonathan. "So, did you notice anything unusual about this baby?" Gerard glances at the laptop, but doesn't try to take possession of it.

"I've gotta admit, man, I just grabbed it. Had a quick look around for any other gadgets but didn't see anything," Jonathan replies. "It's got a cellular modem card, so better security and no need to be tethered to a modem or dial-up connection to get online."

"But you haven't started it?" I ask, still unable to believe Jonathan didn't fire it up, even for a few minutes.

"No!" both men reply emphatically.

I hold my hands up. "Whoa."

Gerard looks at me. "It's possible to install a fail-safe on a computer that wipes the hard drive if you don't follow certain commands at the start."

"Like what?"

Jonathan responds for Gerard. "You may have to hold the shift key down during the whole start-up process. You don't do that, and the hard drive is dust. That's why I resisted the temptation."

"I see."

Gerard nods in Jonathan's direction. "You did good. Especially, given…" Gerard motions to the mirror. "Well, I've heard everything." He leaves it at that—no need to remind Jonathan of what he's been through in the past few weeks, especially the past twelve hours.

Gerard unzips his bag of goodies and starts taking various gadgets out. Most things I recognize—a few external hard drives, a couple of memory sticks, cables, CDs, floppy disks. But I'd still like more information. As they say, knowledge is power.

"What's all that stuff?" I ask.

"Think of it as the first-aid box for computer forensics." He grins. "My doctor's bag. I've got sanitized hard drives, a few essential software programs and boot disks like Safeback, EnCase, Forensic Toolkit, Net Threat Analyzer, DataLifter, The Password Recovery Toolkit—"

I hold up my hand. "Okay, I get the picture."

He shrugs. "I've got the tools to get info out of the laptop."

I smile. "Now you're talking my language. I would like to know what you're doing, though. As you go."

"Sure. In fact, you can be my witness, particularly if we end up firing this baby up and finding the Web site. You can testify that I took copies before we logged on to the site."

I nod. Like all things in law enforcement, this has to be done the right way. Nothing worse than knowing the perp did it, but them getting off through some legal loophole, like challenging the evidence-collection process.

Gerard starts work on the laptop. "Okay, the first thing I'm going to do is take a copy of the hard drive, as it is now. I'm removing the hard drive and I'll hook it up to my system as an external drive and make an exact copy." His hands work quickly as he talks. "For evidence we'll need copies of the files precisely as they are on the hard drive, date and time stamped, et cetera." He rubs his stubble. "It will also protect us if there are any trips or traps installed, like an auto-delete facility." He moves across to his FBI laptop. "The contents of this hard drive could be crucial to the case," he says, holding the piece of hardware up.

He's got that right.

"They've kept the hard drive pretty clean so it won't take very long."

Jonathan peers over Gerard's shoulder while I sit down, waiting.

About ten minutes later, Gerard announces that the copying process is complete. "Okay, let's fire this baby up using my Windows Evidence Acquisition Boot Disk." He looks at me, anticipating my question. "It will start the computer up using my copy of the operating system."

I nod.

Gerard inserts the disk and powers up the laptop. "Mmm…" he says.

"What's wrong?" I lean forward, worried that our only lead may be toast.

"The laptop has been set up with a BIOS password."

"Not surprising, I guess." Jonathan is obviously in the know.

"No," Gerard agrees.

"What's a BIOS password?" I ask.

"When a computer is turned on, first the CPU is started with an electrical pulse—" Gerard points to the power cable "—next the BIOS or Basic Input and Output System comes into play, to test the fundamental components of the system. It's before we even get to the boot stage, before I can use my disk."

It sounds tricky, but neither Gerard nor Jonathan seems worried. "So it's a problem?" I ask.

"No. I just need to check the FBI database for a backdoor password."

I nod slowly. "Okay," I say, feeling too much like a dumb blonde for my liking.

"It'll only take a minute or so." Gerard's already working quickly on his FBI laptop.

I stand up but resist the urge to pace. Lucky for my patience, Gerard is good to his word and roughly one minute later the laptop is whirring to life.

"Excellent," I say.

"We're not home free yet." Gerard stares at the screen. "There's probably a Windows password required."

A few seconds after he says it, an on-screen message prompts us to log in. Gerard hits Ctrl, Alt, Delete and a log-in box pops up. The username is "bunker" but the password field is blank.

"Damn," I say, sinking into the chair.

"So, what do we do?"

"We've got two options. We can get the password from the charming lady-friend of Jonathan's, if she's alive, or we can try to figure out the password ourselves."

"What about all those fancy tools you rattled off?"

"One of them is for passwords, but it takes time."

I bite my lip. "Okay, Jonathan and I will work with Detectives Carter and Stone to look for the house and the mystery woman. You can stay here and—" I wave my hand at the computer "—play with your toys."

"Gee, thanks." Gerard smiles but then moves quickly into professional mode, head down. "I want to see what's on this hard drive, too."

"Jonathan, let's go."

Jonathan pauses for a moment, looking at the laptop. I can tell where he'd rather be. "Don't worry, it's in good hands," I say.

He stays still, but only for a second or two. "Yeah, you're right."

We leave the interview room and I lead the way to the Homicide cubicles. Darren and Stone have already stuck up a massive map on a whiteboard and have circled a few locations.

Darren notices us coming toward him and looks up. "Any luck?"

I shrug. "Looks like the computer forensics could take a while."

"Whoever set up that laptop knew what they were doing," Jonathan adds.

Darren nods, and turns his attention to the map. He points to a red circle. "This is where Jonathan was picked up, on the ten." Darren's referring to the highway number. He looks at Jonathan. "You've really got no idea how long you were running for?"

Jonathan looks upset, disturbed.

"Jonathan, you've got a photographic memory," I say. "I know stress interferes with memory, but try to clear your mind and picture the house."

"You're right, you're right." He closes his eyes but his brow stays furrowed. After about a minute he opens his eyes again. "Shit, all I can think about is that woman, and Susie and Clair." He shudders as he says "that woman." He's just come off the back of a major trauma.

I could tell him that he has to remember this to help Susie and Clair, to get them out of the bunker, but I know that's part of the problem. Not only was he suffering major anxiety when he escaped from that house, but now he's also under a huge amount of pressure. Susie's and Clair's lives are in his hands, and he knows it.

"Darren, I might take a moment with Jonathan."

"Sure, use meeting room two, down the end of the corridor." Darren motions to the northeast corner of the floor. "We'll keep looking at the map."

Jonathan stares at the map, reluctant to move. "Shit!" His stress levels are peaking again.

Darren puts his hand on Jonathan's shoulder. "Don't worry. We know this area. We'll find that house. We can do sweeps in a chopper, looking for fountains." Darren smiles. "Besides, there are only a couple of areas it could be."

Jonathan nods and his brow seems to unfurrow ever so slightly.

But I know from what Darren told me about the area that it's likely lots of houses up that way have fountains. Again, Jonathan doesn't need to know this fact, not now.

I lead Jonathan down the corridor and into the meeting room. Once inside I close the blinds and shut the door.

"What's going on?" Jonathan backs into the corner of the room.

I've underestimated his anxiety. I'm closing the blinds to give us some privacy and help him relax, but it has the opposite effect. I twist the Venetians open immediately. "Sorry, I was trying to give us some privacy, that's all."

Jonathan moves away from the wall, but I can tell this one moment has undone some of the trust I've built with him. I sit down to reduce any perceived physical threat. I need to rebuild that trust, fast.

"Jonathan, I know what it feels like, I really do."

"Because you're a profiler," he says dismissively, like I couldn't possibly know what it's like to be in his shoes. "That's what you do, isn't it?"

"Yes. I put myself in the victims' and the perpetrators' shoes. I get into their skin." I pause. "But it's more than that."

He looks confused.

"I know what it's like to be targeted. By a serial killer."

He studies my face before speaking. "Really?" He sits down, not next to me, but he leaves only one seat between us—a normal distance in terms of personal space when you don't know someone.

"There was a case six months ago when things got…personal." I pause. "And others were relying on me, so I know that pressure, too."

"Susie and Clair need my help."

I nod. "But it's better to focus on what's happening here, not on them. It will do your head in."

"Did it do your head in?"

"Almost." And that is the truth. "But you know what you said before, about evil?"

"Yes."

"You're right. There is evil out there and I believe I can make a difference. And so can you. You've already made a difference."

He snorts. "How?"

"Jonathan, you escaped from a serial killer. She may be a woman and physically weaker than you, but don't underestimate her. She killed Malcolm."

"I'm no hero. To be honest, I survived through lack of ego. Malcolm wouldn't have thought it strange that some woman was coming onto him. I did."

"You saw her for what she was—a predator. And you've come to us and filled in the blanks on this investigation. My God, Jonathan, do you realize how much you've done?"

He stands up. "It's not enough. Not if…" He trails off.

"You're not done yet. You can help us, one way or another. If you don't remember the location—" I shrug my shoulders "—so what? We've got other tools at our disposal to find her, find the members of this Murderers' Club and find the bunker and your friends." I say the words to reassure him, but I know how important timing is. We need to find the house today. Not tomorrow, not next week, but today.

I continue. "Just take a few minutes to relax. And think back to what happened after you handcuffed the woman."

He closes his eyes. "Okay. Okay, I can do this." He takes a deep breath and gives his arms a couple of shakes, like an athlete about to run a race. "I handcuffed her and then searched the house." He speaks slowly, emphasizing each action. "On the kitchen table I spotted the laptop. I scooped it up and checked out the upstairs but couldn't find anything else." He pauses. "I ran out the door and slammed it shut, then down a gravel path, around the fountain. And then there was a fork." His brow furrows, as he tries to remember the details. "The path came to a fork. I knew the helipad was to the left, so I went to the right. Eventually I came to a large, white brick wall and iron gates. I ran through the gates and onto a street."

"Did you see any numbers?"

He thinks about the question. "No…I didn't even try to contact anyone in the houses around the area. I didn't know who I could trust, or if someone from the club was watching me. So I ran toward the skyline."

The skyline was Tucson. "Did the skyline look far away?"

"No. About five miles?" He seems uncertain, but distances are hard to estimate.

"Do you remember where the sun was?"

He thinks for a moment. "It was high. Nearly straight up."

"Okay." Jonathan was picked up at 2:05 p.m. The sun would have already been heading in a westerly direction. "Was it slightly to one side of you as you were running?"

"Um…yes. It was a little bit to my left and behind me."

"Okay." I scribble down *Northeast of city* on my pad.

"Did you see anything else?"

"Lots of high fences. Big houses."

"What about a street sign?"

"No."

I flip my pad onto a new page and give it a quarter turn so the page is landscape. In the center I put a square and write *House* above it. On the bottom of the paper I write *Tucson*. Next, in front of the house, I draw an arrow to the right.

"I turned left at the end of the street."

I draw a T-intersection and then mark in an arrow to the left.

Jonathan continues. "And then I took my first right."

I mark it into my mini map.

Jonathan moves his hands up and motions to the right. "Then I took another right."

"Was it the first right you came to on this road?"

He pauses, then, "No. The second."

I write it down. "Go on, Jonathan."

"I crossed over two small streets and took a left down the third street. I couldn't see the city at that point, but I just kept running. I ran into a few houses, but I guess I looked less than desirable." He looks down at his bloody shirt. "And at one point a car nearly hit me. The driver abused me and I went to ask for help, but then he seemed to notice my shirt and hit the gas."

"You watched him drive off?"

"Yes."

"Jonathan, the license plate number. Think back, use your photographic memory."

"Of course." He pauses and again I can see the concentration on his face. "It's Arizona 543K19."

Surely the driver will remember what street he was on, or at least what part of town he was in when he nearly hit a man covered in blood. "Then where did you run?"

"I'm not sure, but eventually I hit the freeway."

"The I-10. That's where the truck driver said he picked you up."

"Yes."

"How long were you walking before that?"

"I…I don't know. I was walking when he stopped. I had to, I was out of breath."

"That's okay. You couldn't have run the whole way."

"I should have been able to. I jog. Why didn't I keep running?"

Jonathan's mind is fixating on his guilt again, punishing himself undeservedly. But emotions are illogical.

"You got out, Jonathan, and now you can help the others."

He shudders, perhaps thinking of their fates, or perhaps realizing that he nearly met his end in that house.

"Look, Jonathan, why don't you sit here and take a moment. I'll talk to the detectives and see if we can't pinpoint this location." I tap my notebook and my map.

"I can't just sit here. I'd rather come with you."

"Are you sure?"

"Yes. Please let me help."

"Okay." I pause at the door. "By the way, Jonathan, how far do you normally run?"

"About four to six miles, four times a week."

I nod.

Back in the main Homicide area I look at the board and grab a felt-tip pen. "May I?"

"Knock yourself out." Darren steps back.

I put a large cross through two of the circled areas. "The house is northeast of the city let's say within five to ten miles. Jonathan saw the skyline, from a raised part of town and estimated it was about five miles away. That's probably an underestimate," I say—any landmark in the distance always looks closer than it is. "By the time he got to the freeway—" I put my pen on the freeway "—he was out of breath, and having to walk some parts of it. He normally runs four to six miles every other day, so let's estimate that he ran over five miles from the house to the freeway, but less than ten miles before he hit the freeway. I'm allowing for the fact that he was out of shape from being in the bunker but that his adrenaline would have kicked in."

Darren steps in and points to the board. "He was picked up here, and he was walking south. So if he came down onto this side of the freeway, he must have been somewhere around here." He draws a circle with his index finger around a large area of the map, capturing about eight square miles of the Catalina Foothills district. Within the imaginary circle are two marked areas.

"Are both of these areas hilly?"

Darren thinks for a couple of seconds before responding. "Yes."

"We've got a near-accident. I've got the license-plate number. The driver should remember where he was when he almost hit Jonathan."

"I'll take that number," Stone says.

I write it out again on the bottom of my sheet of paper, tear it off and pass it to her.

"Thanks," she says. "So, it would have been some time around one, one-thirty this afternoon?"

"Uh huh." I move back to the board and peer closely at the streets. I tear off my hand-drawn map and maneuver it around, trying to find a matching set of streets in one of the circled areas. But without knowing the exact distances, I find it impossible to pinpoint the location this way.

I glance at Jonathan—he's still ashen-faced and pasty, with dark circles under his eyes. Poor guy.

Jonathan moves in closer to the map.

"Anything look familiar?" I ask.

"Not yet." Jonathan shakes his head. "I didn't really look up. Most of the time I was staring at the laptop."

The laptop. I wonder how Gerard is going with our most precious piece of evidence—second to Jonathan, of course.

NeverCaught: You must have made a bundle out of this, Psycho.

AmericanPsycho: Not at all. How much do you think it cost to set this up?

NeverCaught: $100,000?

DialM: Not with all this electronic equipment. Maybe $250,000.

AmericanPsycho: That's getting closer, M. And I had labor costs, too.

DialM: You mean people know where the bunker is??

AmericanPsycho: Of course not.

DialM: Then?

AmericanPsycho: I killed them, obviously.

NeverCaught: Wicked. Bodies?

AmericanPsycho: Disposed of. Danny's with them, actually.

DialM: So somewhere in the desert?

AmericanPsycho: Yes. They should mummify nicely.

NeverCaught: Susie and Clair look so bored.

AmericanPsycho: It's amazing what people will do for money.

NeverCaught: I kinda like reality TV, though.

DialM: Television is a plague on our society and reality TV… well, that's…

NeverCaught: The man is stuck for words!

DialM: It is true. I feel very strongly about the evil of television and my feelings toward reality TV are unquantifiable.

AmericanPsycho: I can see your point, M, but you are benefiting from the legacy of reality TV right now...with Ling in that dungeon of yours.

DialM: True—but I'm the one in power.

28

Darren, Stone, Jonathan and I ride in Darren's car. We swing into the street we tracked down from our near hit-and-run and pull up. It only took us half an hour to get the driver's details from his registration, contact him and find out the street name. Jonathan gets out of the car and looks around, trying to relive the escape. The sun's setting and soon we'll be battling to find anything in the dark.

He's back in the car within seconds. "This way." He points forward and Darren takes off. Between my makeshift map and Jonathan's memory—albeit affected by stress—we piece together the way backward, back to the house. We climb up the final hill.

"It's around here somewhere," Jonathan says. "Stop!"

Darren slams on the brakes and Jonathan races out of the car. He runs back and forth along a three-hundred-foot section of the street, looking carefully at the high-gated houses. For most of them you can't actually see the house, just a walled perimeter and maybe a glimpse of garden or a rooftop.

After a few minutes Jonathan comes back to the car, shaking. "I've found it."

"Are you sure?" I ask. "It's almost dark. Things may look different."

"This is it."

I call through to the judge we had on standby and give him the exact address for the search warrant. Jonathan's statement was compelling and the judge didn't even mind that we disturbed his dinner. Darren coordinates another three patrol cars and an ambulance— for the female serial killer—to rendezvous at the club's house.

We only have to wait twenty-five minutes before the patrol cars, the ambulance and the search warrant arrive. As Darren instructed, the cars turned off their sirens as soon as they pulled off the freeway. If Chester or someone else is in there, we don't want to alert them to our presence.

"Jonathan, you have to wait here until we secure the house," I say.

He nods and seems relieved. I wouldn't want to go back into the house in a hurry either.

It's unlikely anyone except the woman is inside, but it's better to be safe than sorry. Maybe the pick-up time has been and gone, and the house is empty, or maybe Chester is in there right now, discovering the mess and trying to figure out what to do. For the sake of our case, I hope at least *she* is in there. I want to meet and cuff the woman who's inflicted so much carnage on young men over the past fifteen years. And that password sure would speed up our tech efforts.

Darren divvies up the grounds. Darren, Stone and I will take the front door, two teams will each take a side of the house, and one team will head around the back, near the helipad. We set the entry time for exactly five minutes and all head off. A house like this would have an advanced alarm system, but it should also have been disabled to allow Jonathan and the woman to walk around. Unless Chester got here before us, it should still be off.

We crouch low and move quickly up the drive, fanning out when the house is within three hundred feet. The gardens are perfectly kept and consist mostly of small trees, including lots of Japanese maples, and flowering shrubs. The house itself is set on a slight angle, with the driveway snaking around to the front, which is actually on a diagonal to the street. The three other teams head off to the left, one taking the near side, one the back and one the far side, while we follow the meandering gravel path to the front door. There are only two lights on inside the house.

Once we get to within thirty feet of the front door, we crouch behind a few shrubs. A quick glance at my watch tells me we've got one minute to go. At least two of the other three teams should be in place by now, with only the far-side team having further to travel than us. We wait the minute, fixated on our watches. We look up as the countdown ends, and nod at one another. I'm the first to move. I try the obvious first—the door handle—and am relieved when it opens. Hopefully that means the house is as Jonathan left it. I enter taking all precautions—flashlight and gun trained on the crack of the door as I push it open with my left hip. From the small gap between the door and the frame, I can see through into the large kitchen area that Jonathan described. One of the officers uses his elbow to break a glass door that links the outside to the kitchen, and we acknowledge each other. Darren slips in between me and the door, and in one fluid yet fast movement, lunges forward and takes the left-hand side of the brightly lit foyer. Stone is less than a second behind him, also training her gun to the larger space on the left. As the door opens fully, we see a black-haired woman tugging desperately on her handcuffs.

I smile at her for an instant, but it's more of a smug grin than a smile—we've got her. We check the rest of the area.

Stone proceeds up the stairs, her flashlight and gun moving in a sweeping motion in front of her. Darren and I flank her, our weapons and lights pointing outward and down to the foyer area. The other teams will finish securing the ground floor, while we head up to the second story. The wide stairway splits in two about halfway up. Darren and Stone fan to the left, I take the right. The split in the stairs is more for show than anything else, and a landing joins the two prongs at the top. Our flashlights illuminate five doors, all shut. One is directly in the center, where the staircase would have met the landing if it didn't split, and the other four doors are evenly spread on either side. I think about what went on in these rooms for an instant before I control my body's natural reaction and refocus on the immediate. Even though it looks like we got here first and the place is as Jonathan left it, I can't let my guard down. The darkness of the house unsettles me too—like the dark always does.

I reach the room and take a deep breath before gently pushing the door open. I can distinctly hear Brigitte's screams, and an image of her blood spraying over the killer replays in my mind. But it didn't happen that way. There was no blood. I push the thoughts away and move into the room, again fighting my instincts, which in this case are telling me to get the hell away from this room. But I can't. I try to ignore the sensations and concentrate purely on the search. Heart pounding, I check the room thoroughly before moving on.

Back on the landing I see Darren and Stone exiting the far-left room. I move to the second room on my side, while Darren takes the next room on the left side and Stone moves to the center room.

"Jesus," I whisper. My flashlight light catches a stainless-steel trolley with an assortment of horrors—from bondage-style to old-fashioned torture implements. I move my light beam to the bottom tray, where a selection of surgical instruments sits. But none of the victims showed any sign of torture. Maybe it was just for show, mental torture rather than physical for Malcolm, Cindy or Brigitte. Or maybe Ling's body will be different, maybe she was tortured.

I move around the room, checking all the likely hiding spots. The room has an ensuite and I check that, too. Nothing.

I emerge from the room and join Stone and Darren on the landing. The second story is clear. We move down the stairs, guns facing downward in case the teams haven't finished securing the ground floor. But before we reach the bottom, all six uniforms meet at the front foyer.

"All clear down here, sir," one of them says to Darren.

With the house checked, we turn on some lights and focus on the woman. I take a closer look at her. She's drawn her legs up toward her chest and sits sullenly, no longer tugging on the handcuffs.

I notice that her left wrist, the handcuffed one, is bruised and bleeding slightly from her escape efforts. Her face looks bad—Jonathan certainly gave her a working over. But that's what saved his life.

"What's this about?" she demands, a well-rehearsed line. She's had many years to perfect it.

I can't control my snicker. "Come on, you must be joking."

"What's your name?" Darren asks.

She turns her focus to him and smiles bewitchingly. "Wouldn't you like to know."

"Yes, I would as a matter of fact." Darren stands up. "Stone, get her out of here."

Stone flies down the last few stairs and eagerly moves closer to the woman. She's about to cuff her when she realizes she's already cuffed.

I fish the handcuff key out of my pocket. "Stone." A gentle underhand throw sends the key flying in Stone's direction. I look at the female killer. "From your friendly neighborhood..." I move down and get in her face. I won't be questioning her anyway. I push my face inches from hers to finish my sentence, "...Jonathan."

"Bitch!" she screams, unintentionally spitting, at least I think it's unintentional.

I wipe the spit off with my gloved hand. "Thanks. Just what I wanted...DNA." I stand up and smile. I must admit, once in a while I do enjoy being a bitch to the bad guys.

Stone unlocks one set of cuffs and gathers both of the woman's wrists into her police-issue. "You're under arrest for the attempted murder of Jonathan Cantor. Anything you say...." Stone continues to Miranda the woman, while Darren and I move outside.

"Interesting display in there." I know he's talking about my intimidation of the woman.

I shrug. "I couldn't help myself. You'll be questioning her anyway."

He laughs. "Why do I get the honor?"

"You know why." I move in and whisper in his ear. "You're her type."

Darren seems confused by my slightly flirtatious remark, and I back away instantly, remembering the awkward kiss we shared in Vegas. I bet that's exactly what he's thinking about, too.

An uncomfortable silence threatens to take over, but I break it by holding up my left finger. "I've got spit to get to forensics."

Darren laughs. "They should be here any second." He finally puts his gun back in its holster. "So, you're the profiler, how should I approach the questioning?"

"We need answers, fast."

"I know. We'll keep some guys on this place too, maybe catch this Chester guy coming to make the pickup."

I nod. "Sounds like a plan." I move further away from the door and Darren follows. Stone will be coming out soon to take the perp to the ambulance, and I don't want the woman overhearing our strategy. "You need to play her game. When she comes on to you, respond."

He nods. Then adds, "How much should I respond?" I hear the concern in his voice.

I shrug. "It depends on the situation."

"But we're not talking…" He trails off.

I keep a straight face and hit him gently on the arm. "Just flirt a little. Well, a lot."

"Flirt." He grins. "I can do that."

We move back inside and Darren immediately goes into action. He walks over to Stone. "You Mirandaed her?"

"Yes."

"Good, I'll take it from here." Then he leans in and whispers something quietly to Stone. Too softly for me to hear, but I bet our suspect would have heard him loud and clear. My guess is strategy.

Darren recruits one of the uniforms and heads down the driveway. I don't like the fact that Jonathan will see his attacker, but there's nothing I can do about it. I join Stone near the staircase.

"What did Carter say?" I ask, curious.

She hesitates.

"Don't worry, Stone. It's all part of questioning the suspect."

She nods. "I thought so. I mean, I was pretty sure."

I smile. "Don't sweat it." I pause. "So, what did he say?"

"He told me to take charge of the scene, and not to let 'the Fed' interfere."

"Nice. I gave the perp a dressing-down, so he gives me one in front of her. Should do the trick. Now he's just got to use his masculine charm."

Stone chuckles. "Carter? Charm?"

I'm surprised by her response. "I've always thought he *was* charming."

"I guess it depends on your definition. He's not smooth, in-control charming, more——" she searches for the right description "——boy-scout charming."

I smile. "I see what you mean."

"And that woman." Stone gestures to the pair, their silhouettes barely visible as they walk down the driveway. "Well, she'll eat him alive!"

"He may be a boy scout," I say, "but he's a smart one."

29

Darren uses the same interview room that only a few hours earlier held Jonathan. He sits across from the woman, who we've IDed as Brooke Woods from a wallet we recovered at the crime scene. She's a pharmaceutical rep who—surprise surprise—travels around the States with her job. Talk about easy victim access. We know many other elements of the profile match too. Brooke Woods is thirty-four years old, at the upper end of our predicted age range. She's single, she's got a Mazda MX5 registered in her name, and her clothes and demeanor cry out sex. On top of that she had a few arrests in her late teens: two underage drinking charges and one assault. All three times her older sister came to the rescue but a couple of years later the sister married and it looks like she cut herself off from Brooke. No doubt, as we dig we'll find out more about her family and perhaps the early sexual abuse. It's a topic Darren may broach during the interview, if we can use it to unsettle her.

Her face still looks battered and bruised, but the dried blood is no longer present and a gash on her cheekbone now sports three butterfly clips. The paramedics wanted to take her to the hospital for a stitch or two, but Darren put forward a good case against it, on the proviso that we bring her in for a CT scan later to confirm no head injury. Thank God her pupils were functioning normally. If they hadn't been, the paramedics would have taken her in and our questioning would have been put on hold. That's time we can't afford. Her right arm is also in a sling.

"I've gotta hand it to you, Brooke. I'm impressed." Darren leans back in his chair slightly, mirroring Brooke's posture.

"Impressed? With what? I've been beaten up by some guy and treated like the criminal, not the victim."

I smile. Nice tactic.

"So you're trying to tell us you didn't pull a gun on him?"

"Sure, I did. But only—" she slows down and gives Darren a metered sob "—only when I thought my life was in danger. He said he was going to rape me. Then kill me." Another sob.

If we didn't have so much evidence it would be a great line. After all, a man and a woman in a room together—it *is* more likely the male is the attacker, plus she's the one covered in bruises, not Jonathan.

"And what about the Murderers' Club?"

She hesitates only for a second. "I don't know what you're talking about." She would have assumed Jonathan told us everything he knew, but maybe she forgot she mentioned the name to him, or maybe even just hearing Darren refer to the club is enough to give her pause.

"Look, you know how this stuff works. You give us some names, we give you a break."

She shrugs. "Don't know any names."

"So, you're not the organizer, the head honcho?"

She pauses. "I really don't know what you're talking about."

"Come on, Brooke. I know you're a smart woman."

She smiles, a knowing smile. She's more than smart and she knows it.

Darren continues. "You've gotta know when the game is up."

"What game?" She shakes her head.

"Maybe the game's not up for Susie Dean and Clair Kelly." He pauses, emphasizing our knowledge of the case. "But I'm afraid it's up for you." His tone is sympathetic, not threatening, not triumphant.

"Don't pretend you give a damn about me!" The outburst is unexpected, defensive.

"I do. I respect you." He leans back. "I gotta say, I was pretty excited when we realized Malcolm Jackson's killer was a woman. It's a first for me. Tracking down a woman."

"Malcolm who? What the hell's this about?" She's saying the right words, but I can tell we're starting to get to her.

She changes tack and gives Darren a flirtatious smile. "Do you get off on the chase?"

"You bet. Don't you?"

She hesitates. "I prefer the moment of conquest." She chooses her words carefully so as not to incriminate herself. She could be talking about sex, not murder, and that's the way she likes it. Nothing admissible in court, nothing that might sway a jury.

"It's an ingenious scheme. I've got to take my hat off to the club." She's silent.

"It would have worked too," Darren says. "Except for Jonathan."

It's true. If Jonathan had the normal dose of male ego, if he'd let his body take command of his mind, he would have wound up handcuffed to a bed in that house, then dead.

Gerard enters the observation room. "How's it going?" he asks.

"Just starting out," I say.

"Do you think she'll give us the password?"

I shrug. "Hard to tell. If she thinks she can get out of the rap, she's not going to tell us anything. Why would she?" I take my eyes off Brooke and look at Gerard. "How are you doing with the laptop?"

"Okay. The hard drive's…revealing…and I've been working on the password—no luck yet. I can get the Web history from the hard drive, but we need to use that specific laptop to access the Web site."

"Why?"

"We don't know how many people there are in this club, but assuming the number is limited, say under twenty, the tech person behind this could have set up the Web server to alert him, or her, if a different IP address logs onto the site. The laptop uses a cellular modem card, like a cell phone on a card, which connects to the Internet by making a data call. The IP will always be the same, no matter where the laptop is, and it's easy to buy an anonymous SIM card, preloaded with credit so it's hard for us to track down."

"So we need the password for the laptop."

He looks at Brooke through the glass. "It would be safer. For us, and whoever's left down in that hellhole."

I nod.

"What if she lawyers up?" Gerard crosses his arms.

"She said she didn't need a lawyer because she hadn't done anything wrong."

Gerard raises an eyebrow. "Confident."

"Well, she's been doing her thing and getting away with it for well over a decade. I guess she doesn't feel threatened."

"That's her mistake."

"Yup." I smile. "Eyewitness testimony, DNA from a couple of the old cases. The results from her swab should confirm it all."

We both return our focus to Darren and Brooke.

"You married, Detective?" Brooke's natural behavior is surfacing.

"Me? Nah."

"Girlfriend?"

"Nope. You know what they say, married to the job."

"There are lots of men like you out there." She tries to struggle out of her jacket, but winces. She smiles at Darren. "Do you mind?" She tugs at the jacket, either unable to take it off by herself with her injured arm, or faking it.

"Not at all." Darren stands up and helps her take off the jacket.

She's down to her tight Super Girl top with its plunging neckline. She slips her right arm back in the sling and fans herself with her left hand. "Hot in here, isn't it?" She smiles.

Darren's eyes linger on her breasts for a moment before his eyes meet hers. "Yes, it is." He runs his finger inside his collar.

"Can I smoke in here?"

"Sorry, it's a non-smoking building."

"You never break the rules, Detective?"

Darren shrugs. "Sometimes, sure. Tell you what, how about a Coke or coffee instead?"

Brooke pulls her shoulder blades back in a casual stretch and her top reshapes slightly in response, revealing more cleavage. "Diet Coke, thanks."

Darren stands up and leaves the room, and within seconds he's standing next to Gerard and me. "This is going nowhere," he says. "We don't have time for this."

I sigh. "I think you're right."

"How'd you do with the computer stuff?" Darren asks Gerard.

"No luck on the password, but the hard drive's contents were interesting."

I forgot to follow Gerard up on that one. "What did you find?"

"The computer's only got Windows, the modem software, Internet Explorer and some default functions on it. No other programs."

"Makes sense, I guess. It was purely set up to access the Murderers' Club Web site."

"I also checked out the log files. The URL is www.murderers-club.com and it's been accessed two times, and by different users."

"How can you tell?"

"It's a secure site, but the log files have recorded two different usernames and passwords. I don't think this laptop belongs to Brooke, I think it's the house laptop."

I take it in. "What are the usernames?"

"You're going to love these." He shakes his head. "The first access was BlackWidow. Password is sexybitch, all one word."

"Brooke," Darren says, glancing back into the interview room.

"Let me guess, sometime before March twenty-seventh," I say, presuming it must coincide with Malcolm's death.

Gerard takes out his notebook and flips back a couple of pages. "Yeah. March twenty-sixth, just after 10:00 p.m. Eastern Daylight Saving Time. I tried this password for the laptop, but it's not it." His eyes move down his notebook. "Next user was NeverCaught, password is never. That user logged in at 9:00 p.m. Eastern Daylight Saving Time on April ninth."

"Brigitte's killer." I bite my lip. "They must be discussing the kill with the other members."

Gerard nods. "This laptop was kept at the house, so the members didn't have to bring their own. It gave them a way to update the others while they had the victim." He pauses. "That's not all."

Gerard has our full attention.

"Several JPEG images were uploaded by NeverCaught. He did more than discuss the kill."

"We've gotta get these bastards." Darren's jaw clenches.

We're silent for a moment.

Darren leans against the glass and looks at Brooke. "I need to get that password." He turns to me. "Go for the jugular? The childhood abuse?"

Brooke stands up and moves toward the mirror. She checks herself out and then gives us an exaggerated wave.

"She's not going to be played," I say. "Let's do it the normal way. Hit her with the facts, what she's up against, and see if we can't bribe that password out of her. Gerard, you go in, too. Tell her who you are, what you've got so far, and that you're going to get into the Web site anyway. It's just a matter of time." I turn to Darren. "Take in some of the files we found through VICAP when we were searching for Malcolm's killer." I look through the window at Brooke, who's now blowing us kisses. I sigh again. "And her Diet Coke."

A few minutes later Gerard and Darren make their entrance. Gerard carries the laptop and the Diet Coke, and Darren's arms are more than full with a selection of the VICAP case files.

Brooke laughs at Darren's burden. "Let me guess, you're going to tell me that's all the evidence you've got on me."

Darren puts the files on the table. "Actually, this is only about half of our files. Half of what we know about your activities over the past fifteen years."

Brooke gives Darren one of her seductive smiles, believing she's calling his bluff.

"It's not that hard, you know, Brooke. I'm sure you've heard of VICAP."

Her smile wavers ever so slightly. "Sure." She takes the Diet Coke Gerard offers and gives him a wink. "This your partner, Darren?"

"No. This is Special Agent Gerard with the FBI. He's a computer man."

"Is he now?" She looks Gerard up and down, her predatory nature taking over. She's probably not even aware she's doing it.

Darren and Gerard sit down and Brooke seems to shift her attention to Gerard. Despite Gerard's senior position in the Bureau, he's actually younger than Darren, at only twenty-eight, and Brooke is more likely to be attracted to a man in his twenties than thirties.

"Where did the Bureau find you?" She takes a sip of her soda and then licks her lips, slowly, seductively. I think it looks like a bad TV ad, but I guess men fall for it.

"I used to be a hacker, on the other side of the law. But I knew when it was time to bargain."

Darren cuts in by flipping open the top folder. "Cameron Michaels. Your first, yes?"

Brooke's face remains impassive, but I can see a hint of panic in her eyes, behind her mask of sexual bravado.

"If not your first, certainly one of your early victims." Darren picks up the next file. "I like this one. The Swede, Matts Jansson. Did you like the Nordic touch?" He emphasizes the word "touch."

She smiles. "I like the touch of most men, Detective." She takes another sip, but I can tell she's unsettled. A stack of files is one thing, names of her actual victims is another.

"Do you know why I especially like the Swede?" Darren continues.

"Maybe *you* like the Nordic touch?" She gives him a wink.

Darren doesn't react. "I like the Swede because that's when we first got your DNA on file."

Gerard steps in. "Is this your laptop, Brooke?"

She looks at the laptop, then at him with some distaste, her come-fuck-me image evaporated. "No."

"It was already at the house, wasn't it? The house laptop." Gerard taps the outer casing. "It's all on here. You logged on as BlackWidow around the time Malcolm Jackson was killed. And someone else with the username NeverCaught has used this laptop too. It's all recorded on the computer's hard drive."

He lets his discoveries sit, but Brooke is silent.

Darren takes the next file from the pile and fans himself with it. "Now is the time to bargain, Brooke."

"Bargain?" She looks at the stack of files. "They've got nothing to do with me."

"Really. What about the rose?" Darren pauses for effect. "We got your message on Malcolm. You didn't leave a rose, but you still marked him with one. Huh?"

For the first time she's unable to hide her shock.

I smile at Darren even though he can't see me. We've got her. *She* didn't know the rose was on Malcolm. She's been played by someone.

Darren picks up on her reaction. "Clever, I guess, giving him that small tattoo on his wrist after you killed him. But you must have known we'd figure it out."

"I don't know what you're talking about." Her words don't have the ring of confidence they did a few minutes ago.

"Like I said, now is the time to bargain." Darren drums his fingers against the stack of files. "We'd like the password for that computer."

"I will get onto your special Web site." Gerard manages a smile. "You'll just speed the process up."

"Your cooperation would be formally noted on your record." Darren scribbles something on his pad and then looks up. "Hell, it might even save you from the death penalty. The rose links you to all these cases and the DNA will be indisputable." He pats the stack of VICAP files. "The game *is* over. At least for you it is."

Suddenly she explodes. "That fucking bastard!"

"Who?" Darren's voice is casual, verging on uninterested.

"He set me up. That bastard set me up." Brooke digs her fingernails into the narrow armrests of her chair.

"Who?" Darren repeats.

She pouts at Darren, silent, for some time, before finally answering the question. "Psycho. The president." Then she shakes her head, disappointed. "You'll never catch him. He's too smart for you."

"I wouldn't bet on it." Darren's voice is full of confidence—I just hope it's not false bravado. I know one thing, I sure as hell won't rest until we get every single last member of this club.

"How many people are there in the club?"

Brooke snorts at him, like she's not going to tell him, but then she answers. "Four. Four including me."

Good, only four.

"How did you meet?" Gerard asks.

"I met the president in a chat room. He sent me a personal message and we got talking. He recruited us all like that." Her voice is angry now, angry with him. "He set up the club, then the bunker." Brooke stares at Darren intently, assessing him. "You really think you can get him?" She spits the word *him*—her betrayer.

"We get that password, we can."

Brooke gulps down the rest of her Diet Coke and slams the can on the table. "Untouchable."

"No one's untouchable," Darren says, leaning forward.

She looks at him with disdain. "*That's* the password for the laptop." She sighs. "If I'm going down, *he's* going down."

30

Gerard sits in front of the computer with Darren and me on either side, huddled in close so we can see the screen. My stomach grumbles loudly and both Gerard and Darren look at me.

"I second that," Darren says. "Chinese?"

"Sounds good. It's well past my dinnertime." I rub my stomach.

Darren stands up. "And tonight's going to be a long one. A very long one." He pauses. "Any preferences?"

Gerard and I both shake our heads.

Darren punches a number into his phone and orders enough to feed a small army before sitting back down.

Gerard puts his Windows Evidence Acquisition Boot Disk into the laptop and presses the on button. At the first prompt he types in the BIOS password and then hits Enter.

"Okay, so I'm interrupting the boot process," Gerard says, hitting a couple of keys. "This is an Intel-based computer, so I'm going to check the CMOS configuration first."

"English please," Darren says.

"Computers use a Complementary Metal Oxide Silicon configuration tool for details like the date and time, and more importantly, which drive the computer will look at first to boot the operating system. I need to check that the time is set correctly and matches the hard drive—the time stamps for when this computer was used to log on to the Web site may become crucial evidence when we're prosecuting. They correlate with your victims, but we don't want those time stamps questioned by the defense."

"Okay," Darren says.

Gerard stares at the screen. "The date looks right…and the time has been set on East Coast time and it's come across onto Daylight Saving Time correctly too. The system has been set up to check the C-drive first for the operating system. I'll change that now." Within a few keystrokes, Gerard seems satisfied. "Okay. Let's go."

The screen goes blank again, and the standard Windows operating system loading screen comes up, followed by the log-in prompt. Gerard types "Untouchable" and hits Enter.

Gerard's hands type furiously again. After a few seconds he's reaching into his bag of tricks. "I'm going to make another copy of the hard drive contents. You never can be too sure." He inserts a memory stick into the laptop's USB port and copies some files across.

Gerard stares at the screen blankly. "I'm just thinking…" He pauses and opens up a new window, letting the file copying process continue in the background. "The laptop logs confirm use around Malcolm's and Brigitte's deaths, but what about Cindy?"

I shrug. "Cindy's killer mustn't have used the house laptop."

"Maybe." Gerard pauses. "But I wonder…" Again, Darren and I watch as Gerard's fingers glide effortlessly over the laptop's keyboard.

Darren and I step slightly away from Gerard, leaving him in his own world.

"We'll go online and pretend to be BlackWidow?"

"Yeah," I say. "Maybe we can lure some information out of one of the other killers."

"I dunno. Whoever set this up is smart. Very, very smart."

"I know. The real dilemma is, do we try to delay the scheduled pick-up of Brooke and Jonathan, or do we keep someone at the house and try to intercept Chester, or whoever comes for them?" I bite my lip.

"Chester could lead us straight to the boss. Or maybe Chester is the boss."

"That's the best outcome. The worst is that he's not pulling the strings and nabbing him will then risk the lives of the other victims. And that's a big risk."

"How much will Gerard be able to get?" Darren looks at Gerard's back. Gerard doesn't even look up at the mention of his name—he's too absorbed in his work.

"On the phone before he came over, he said he'd aim to pinpoint the location of the cameras, the Web server, and the people logging on. But it won't be in the next hour."

"Do you have any *feelings* on this one?" Darren lowers his voice.

I think about it…with so many leads now I haven't tried to induce another vision and none have come, either.

"Let's stall," I say.

"Interesting." Darren and I are interrupted by Gerard's catch-cry. We move closer to the screen.

"Someone else *has* accessed the site from this computer. But they've done a damn good job of covering their tracks."

I stare at the screen, even though it doesn't reveal anything to me. "Go on."

"Someone has marked a section of the hard drive as bad. It's a common way to conceal data, even deleted data. And one of my little babies found it." He points to the disk drive, which must now hold one of the many software tools he rattled off earlier. The only one that stuck in my mind was the Forensics Toolkit. Good name.

Gerard continues. "So, that access was on April second at 8:15 p.m. Daylight Savings Time."

"You're right," I say. "Cindy."

Darren nods.

"Username, AmericanPsycho—"

"That's who Brooke was talking about," Darren straightens up. "She said *psycho*, but I didn't realize it was one of the member's log-in names."

"So AmericanPsycho is the president." I look at Gerard. "What were you saying?"

"The password. It's AD15221. Which is also interesting."

"Why?" Darren asks.

"AmericanPsycho knows quite a bit about computers. Not only did he hide his use of the computer, and very well, but the password gives it away too."

Neither Darren nor I get the significance. Our faces must show this, because Gerard explains.

"You notice that BlackWidow chose sexybitch as her password, something she could relate to and remember easily. NeverCaught used Never—very unimaginative and not very secure. You shouldn't use your username or part of your username as a password. It's one of the first things intruders try. But AmericanPsycho's password seems more random, at this stage at least. Of course, that could turn out to be his initials and part of his phone number, but I doubt it. Not when he went to so much trouble to hide his use of this computer." He looks at me. "Okay, you ready?"

I take a deep breath. "Yep. Let's log in as BlackWidow." I start to prepare myself to walk in Brooke's shoes, to become the Black Widow.

"Given Psycho's computer knowledge, I'm going to have to log in using the operating system installed on this laptop. The copies of the hard drive will have to be enough for court." Gerard doesn't seem particularly happy with this, but we don't exactly have a lot of options.

He restarts the laptop, and we're now presumably working from the original operating system. He opens up a Web browser window and types in www.mur before pausing. "Just checking the settings. You know how you can start typing an address and it fills in the rest?"

"Sure," I say.

"Well, in this case the temp files must have been set up to auto-delete, because nothing's coming up. I'll have to type in the full URL." He finishes off the rest of the address. A blank screen loads with two fields. No logo, no writing, nothing. Gerard types in BlackWidow and then sexybitch before hitting Enter on the keyboard.

"Now we get to go inside." I lean in further.

"Want to drive?" Gerard asks me.

"Good idea. Anything I need to know from a tech point of view?"

"You should be fine. I'll let you know if I see anything strange."

I switch seats with Gerard. The page seems to take a while to load. I look at Gerard questioningly.

"It's okay. It's the cellular network. Not as fast as the connection you're used to. Plus the server will be authenticating you and detecting your media settings for the video streams."

I nod, happy for the extra time to shift characters. I think about the profile, I think about Brooke's language and demeanor during questioning. And I think about all the crime scenes and what they tell me about her. I'm a predator, a female predator who has no respect for men. Men are there for sexual satisfaction and then to punish—it's all about revenge.

The page finishes loading. A small banner up the top says The Murderers' Club in red and directly underneath the banner are three menu items—News, The Contestants, All Streams and Maps. In the center of the page are two video streams. One shows two women sitting on milk crates—the bunker. The other one shows an Asian woman chained to an old-style hospital bed. She looks very, very frightened.

"Ling is still alive!" I shout, unable to contain my glee. It so rarely happens that a victim you think is dead turns up alive. I notice the chat-room lines coming up on the right-hand side of the screen and I shift my focus back to the site, back to BlackWidow, with a new sense of purpose. Ling.

The window displays three users in green, indicating they're online. BlackWidow is one of them, and the others are NeverCaught and DialM. In total there are four people icons, four usernames.

"Brooke was telling the truth. There's only four of them," I say, relief evident in my voice. Of course, it doesn't matter to the victims how many there are, but tracking down four killers is more manageable than trying to track down twenty or more. One in custody and three to go.

NeverCaught: Hey, BW. You having fun?

"You're on," Darren says.

I can't hesitate too long. Brooke would never hesitate, not when it came to her men.

BlackWidow: Oh yeah.
DialM: So, how's Jonathan? Dead?
BlackWidow: I'm having too much fun to kill him. I'd like to keep him around for a bit longer.
NeverCaught: ***ing hell. Psycho better not change the rules for you, too.
DialM: How does Jonathan compare to Malcolm?
BlackWidow: Better, actually. I prefer an understated man.
DialM: But I thought you preferred black men.

Darren's hand comes onto my shoulder. "Careful."

"Brooke must have said something about her attraction to African-American men." I pause. "But she doesn't target only them. So we should be safe." My fingers hover over the keys.

BlackWidow: Variety is the spice of life.
NeverCaught: I can't wait for the next one.
DialM: Me, too.
BlackWidow: Well, I'm done.
NeverCaught: What about some girl-on-girl action? I'd like to see that.

BlackWidow: Not my thing.
DialM: You don't give up, do you, Never?
BlackWidow: How's Ling doing?

I dangle the first bit of bait. If it's NeverCaught or DialM holding Ling, hopefully they'll respond. If not, maybe they'll make a reference to AmericanPsycho. Either way, now we need to find two locations—the bunker and wherever Ling's being held captive.

"Here we go." Darren leans in.

It suddenly occurs to me that we're flying blind and we needn't be. "Darren, can you get Jonathan in here? We may need his knowledge."

"Sure." Darren hurries out of the room.

I look back at the screen.

DialM: My darling's doing just fine. A fine specimen.

I click on the up arrow on the small scroll bar on the right of the chat area, but I can only see the past few lines. "Gerard, these chat-room lines seem to be deleting themselves."

"Whoever set this up wants to make sure no chat-room logs are kept on the site, or in this laptop. I didn't find any on the hard drive at all, and they're normally kept."

"So what can we do? I'd like to keep these conversations."

"Click on the Start icon and see if the Notepad facility is available in the Accessories."

I follow Gerard's instructions and open up Notepad. When I look back at the screen, I can see several more lines of text. I copy as much as I can and dump it into the Notepad. Then I review the last few lines.

DialM: My darling's doing just fine. A fine specimen.
NeverCaught: Not as nice as my Brigitte. You really missed out there, M.

DialM: I think I'll get my money's worth from Ling. She's got a long way to go yet. You blew your $ in one night. Not me.

NeverCaught: It's quality not quantity, old man.

"We've got some great stuff there," I say. "NeverCaught has basically admitted to killing Brigitte and we know DialM intends to keep Ling alive for some time."

· "And he's old," Gerard says.

"That or Never is very young. I've profiled him as twenty to twenty-five, given the files that came up in VICAP and the frenzy of his other victims' injuries. He attacked them with the zealousness and energy of youth."

"That and being a psychopath," Gerard says.

I smile. "That too. Speaking of psychopaths, I better say something."

BlackWidow: Age = wisdom.

DialM: Thank you, BW.

NeverCaught: I'll take youth any day.

DialM: I like my girls young but I'm quite happy with my age.

NeverCaught: Ling's the youngest, isn't she?

BlackWidow: 18.

DialM: She's legal.

NeverCaught: True.

BlackWidow: Just heard Jonathan. I'll be back soon.

NeverCaught: Have fun, BW. Don't do anything I wouldn't do.

BlackWidow: I'll do my best.

Jonathan appears behind me, accompanied by Darren. He leans in. "Holy shit!"

"I know. Sorry."

"I knew this is what it was, but actually seeing the Web site… it's…" He pauses, his eyes taking everything in. "Ling? Oh my God, she's still alive!"

"Yes. DialM is keeping her and intends to keep her for some time." I'm comforted by the knowledge that Ling's alive and in no immediate danger of being killed. But God knows what else he's done to her. And what he *will* do to her.

"He must be the one I saw."

"You saw one of them?" I ask.

"I helped Ling take her bag up to the surface. I saw him up there."

"Jonathan, why didn't you tell us this sooner?"

"I…I did…didn't I?"

"No, you didn't."

Jonathan hangs his head in shame. "It was just so crazy. I was crazy when I first escaped."

"So you can ID Chester and this DialM?"

He shrugs. "Guess so."

"That's fantastic. And we've got Brooke. At the moment for attempted murder, but as soon as the lab gets back, I bet we'll have her on murder."

"I don't care about any of that." Jonathan looks at the video streams. "That's what I care about." He jabs his finger at the streams. "Ling, Susie and Clair."

"We care about them too. Why do you think we're all still here?"

Jonathan glances at the clock on the wall. "Sorry." He pauses. "Thank you."

I point to the video of Susie and Clair. "They look bored, nothing more sinister. Their ignorance is bliss. We are going to find them, but the Mojave's a pretty big place, you know."

"But…but who knows what the sickos will do next? What if they do the food poisoning thing again, but this time someone dies? Or what if the challenges get even nastier?"

"Look, we're going to work this, and hard. But if the worst comes to the worst, we've got a few days."

Jonathan doesn't respond, but seems to accept my argument. It's not time to vote yet.

"Let's check out this Web site some more. Then I've got to find out how to extend my time with you."

Jonathan looks puzzled, and I realize he's come in at the end of things.

"In my online pseudonym as BlackWidow."

31

The Chinese food finally arrives. Darren brings us all bowls, but we keep working while we eat. I use my left hand to shovel in mouthfuls of black-bean beef, and my right to explore the Web site. The others hover behind me, also devouring the long-overdue dinner.

We check out the News section first. Roughly twenty news items are listed under date and heading, with a "More" link. I scan some of the headlines.

Welcome to the Murderers' Club

Bunker completed

Final contestants chosen

Start date set

Contestants enter the bunker

First challenge: paintball

Malcolm eliminated

Second challenge: iPod abuse

Cindy eliminated

Food challenge: reward

Fourth challenge: isolation chamber

Brigitte eliminated

Fifth challenge: obstacle course

Ling and Danny eliminated

Sixth challenge: tug-o-war

Jonathan eliminated

Three other bodies strain over my shoulder, making me a little claustrophobic. Still, if I wasn't at the computer, I'd be leaning in close, too.

Jonathan points to the challenge entries. "They seem to have something on all the challenges. Things kinda got tame in here." He points to the obstacle course challenge—compared to food poisoning and the isolation chamber it certainly is tame.

"They may have realized you were suspicious and toned it down," I say.

He nods. "It was after the isolation chamber that I really started to question what the hell was going on down there."

I click on the paintball-challenge entry and copy and paste its contents into the Notepad before scanning the text.

"It's just a summary of how the challenge went," Jonathan explains. "Who was tagged by who in the paintball, our reactions. That sort of thing."

Darren pauses mid-mouthful. "Why are they deleting the chatroom stuff but keeping these entries?"

Gerard takes the question. "The president controls the Web site, so he can pull down the news items and the whole site whenever he wants," Gerard says. "If he thought something was wrong, this site could be gone in a matter of seconds. End of story. But a chat room normally creates log files on each computer, which is something the president wants to avoid."

I nod and move to the very first news entry, titled "Welcome to the Club." I click on it and again copy and paste the text into Notepad before actually reading it.

Darren stands up. "This is sick stuff."

"Yup." The first news item talks about the launch of the Web site and the building preparations for the bunker, plus the auditioning process.

I move my cursor to the item titled "Brigitte eliminated." Just reading the entry makes me want to puke. I'm about to click on it when Gerard grabs my arm.

"This is the last news piece you can access."

"What?"

"The Web stats will show that BlackWidow has come in to visit these pages. It would look suspicious if she suddenly accessed every single News item. It's not something Brooke would do. She's presumably read all these before, and reminiscing would account for only two to three pages."

"Damn." I know he's right.

"The Web master could even have a system set up that sends him a warning signal if one of his users accesses older pages. He may already know you're in here, and be waiting for your next move."

"Would he really be keeping that close an eye on it?" Darren asks.

Gerard shrugs. "I don't know. But it is possible."

I put myself in his shoes. "I would be if I was him." I sigh. "Okay. This will be the last." I click on the entry.

We all scan the article, which includes a record of bidding on Brigitte.

"Holy shit!" Jonathan says. "Two-hundred grand."

Darren lets out a slow whistle. "Now we know how this project is being funded."

"Yes." I look up and stare into the distance. "But it tells us more than that." I look back at Darren. "It tells us that all our players, our club members, are wealthy. How many people have got $200,000 hanging around?"

"Where did Brooke get that kind of money? Last I heard sales reps didn't make millions."

"We can go ask her in a second. But either way, she and the others have money."

"Wealthy serial killers." Darren shakes his head. "Just what we need. Can you imagine the lawyers when we do bring these guys in?"

"How's it going?" We all turn around to the source of the voice—

Detective Stone. I assumed she'd gone home to get at least a couple of hours' sleep.

"So-so. What about the Catalina Foothills house? Anything?" Darren asks.

"Forensics is still there. It's going to take a while."

Jonathan can't control a shudder. I'd almost forgotten we had one of the victims standing with us. "I'm sorry. We shouldn't discuss this in front of you."

"No," he says, recovering. "I might be able to help. I want to help. And the more I know about what's been happening outside the bunker, the better. Then we know stuff from both sides."

Jonathan's hit the nail on the head. That's why I need him sitting in on this investigation. It's a very unusual situation, but he's been on the inside, he knows at least part of what the club has seen on their video streams. And that knowledge could prove more than invaluable, especially if I'm going to continue to masquerade as BlackWidow.

"Stone, Chinese?" Darren holds up the nearly empty fried-rice container.

"Love some. I'm famished." She grabs a bowl and loads up before leaving the room.

We refocus our attention on the computer. Clicking on another news item may be suspicious, but going to the next menu item— The Contestants—is plausible user behavior for BlackWidow. I click on the menu item and the page shows photos of each of the eight original contestants, four rows of two people. Most of the photos have red crosses through them, indicating the person is "out", which in this case means dead. Each photo has two links directly under it, one labeled "Bio" and the other labeled "Audition tape."

"Go to mine." Jonathan points at his photo. "*She'd* do that anyway. If she still had me."

I click on the top link, and view Jonathan's bio.

Name: Jonathan Cantor
Age: 25

Height: 6'
Weight: 185 pounds
Eye color: Green
Hair color: Dark brown
IQ: 128
Occupation: DJ/bartender
Family: None—mother dead, father MIA
Home: L.A., California
Reason entered: To support Susie and needs money.
President's take: Jonathan is an idealist, a laid-back pacifist
whose lack of ambition has seen him waste his intellect.

His father ran out on his mother and him when Jonathan
was only two, and his mother died of breast cancer three years
ago.

His existing relationship with contestant Susie Dean should
make for interesting viewing to see how they position themselves in "the game."

His anti-war, anti-violence standpoint will make for some
dynamic clashes with Danny Jensen too!

I anticipate Jonathan will go out somewhere in the middle
of the game, and that he'll raise around $50,000 for our cause.

"I wonder how much I did go for." Jonathan smiles, but it's forced.
Clicking on the link titled "Audition tape" launches a video stream.

"That's my original audition tape." He pauses. "You don't need to
watch that."

Despite Jonathan's embarrassed protests, we watch the rest of the
five-minute video.

"Susie told me to say most of that junk. I didn't really care if I got
on the show or not, but I had to pretend for Susie."

In Jonathan's case I think he's telling the truth. He went along to
help a friend, not for his own dreams of fame and fortune.

The next section of the Web site is titled All Streams, and the page
shows lots of different thumbnails of video streams.

Jonathan moves his head closer to the screen. "That's all the cameras in the bunker." He scans through them. "Jesus."

There are about fifteen streams in total, including one in the shower, one in the toilet and several others scattered around the underground dungeon.

Jonathan points to one stream of a small room. "That's the Blue Room, where we had our say after the challenges."

"It's not blue," Darren says.

"No. It was supposed to indicate blue mood—you know, sad because one of us would be going home." His fists clench. "Home. Those bastards."

I scroll down the page to the last row of video streams. "What about these ones?" I want to know the answer, but I'm also hoping the diversion will calm Jonathan down a little.

"They're from the challenge area." Jonathan looks at Gerard. "Near the main control area."

"The challenges weren't in or near the bunker?" Darren asks.

"Some of them were. The food one and the isolation chambers were in the bunker. But the others were at another location. Chester had a van, like a military van, that we'd all pile into. It was about a five-minute drive away, but we were blindfolded so I'm not sure in which direction."

"What sort of setup could you see?" Gerard asks.

"One large building, like a warehouse. But there was a big-ass satellite dish on top. My bet is that's where the Web server is. I could hear a generator going. They'd need A/C to keep that computer equipment cool."

Gerard nods. "This is a big operation. All the tech stuff alone…"

"Money's obviously not an issue for these perps," Darren says.

"True. And this president is probably very wealthy. Unless the members paid a large joining fee."

"We could always ask Brooke." Darren motions to the interview room.

"Look!" Jonathan points to the screen and a pop-up message that says *AmericanPsycho has entered the room.* "They're all online now."

"Excellent." I rest my hands on the keys, ready to start typing. "Looks like he changed the rules for Ling. Hopefully he'll do the same for me." I change my status from away to online and once more prepare myself to enter *her* mind and *their* world.

NeverCaught: Hey, BW. Did he manage another round?
BlackWidow: Sure.
AmericanPsycho: Satisfied customer?
BlackWidow: Oh, yeah. Worth every cent.
AmericanPsycho: Good to hear. So, is he dead?
BlackWidow: Well, actually…
NeverCaught: Don't know what you see in him.
BlackWidow: I'm hoping to extend.
AmericanPsycho: Why?
BlackWidow: This is my final one and I want to make it last. No more boys left after Jonathan.
AmericanPsycho: There will be a series 2, BW.

"A second series?" I take my fingers off the keyboard and squeeze my fingers into claws. "What a bastard."

Darren's hand rests on my shoulder. "At least we know this was the first time, the first series."

Jonathan's eyes are reflected in the laptop's screen and I see them widen. "God, you're right," he says. "I didn't even think of the possibility that we might not have been the first chumps."

"You're no chump," Gerard says through half a mouthful of Chinese.

I look back at the chat-room lines, but my anger is still bubbling close to the surface.

DialM: I can relate, BW. I'll still have Ling, for some time. Why throw away such a good thing?

NeverCaught: What a load of **. Psycho, the rules! Why did I have to play by the rules?

I look up at Darren. "I bet he's talking about not being able to use his normal MO, the knife. He's pissed he had to play by the rules and now others don't."

"He certainly comes across as a spoiled brat," Darren says.

"He fits the profile for Brigitte's killer."

Darren nods. "Yes, he does. And hopefully Psycho will listen to you, not him."

"Let's see how I go. I'll play to his ego…"

BlackWidow: So, can I have longer?
AmericanPsycho: DialM's extension was pre-arranged.
BlackWidow: Come on, Psycho. A second series will be months away.
AmericanPsycho: It will take a while to find eight new contestants…
BlackWidow: Please! I can't go back to my normal routines, not after you've shown me this. It's just…well it's beyond my wildest expectations. You're a genius.
AmericanPsycho: Thank you.
BlackWidow: So, how about it? Just a little bit longer?
AmericanPsycho: How much longer?
BlackWidow: Until Sunday? Then I can finish my part of the game in style.
AmericanPsycho: I thought once you had them, sexually, you lost interest.
BlackWidow: This is different. We've got this house all to ourselves. No need to rush. Not like my normal outings.
DialM: Perhaps you should let her have her fun. At least we have two more chances, with Susie and Clair still in the bunker.

AmericanPsycho: Okay, BW. He's all yours. But don't leave that house. I don't want anyone seeing you.

NeverCaught: This is bull**.

AmericanPsycho: Never, I'm the president. I decide. Besides, what you wanted wouldn't have worked with our plans, but a few extra days doesn't put any holes in the "new serial killer in town" front.

BlackWidow: Thanks, Psycho. And I've got no reason to leave the house. Plenty of food in the kitchen and Jonathan can take care of my other needs.

"I'm going to log out now. We need to start chasing down some leads."

BlackWidow: Gotta go.

DialM: Yes, you've got things to do.

BlackWidow: Thanks for the extension!!

BlackWidow has left the room.

It's time to get moving.

32

We sit in one of the project rooms, exhausted but ready to break up the leads. Around the desk are Stone, Darren, Jonathan, Gerard and myself. We're involving Jonathan in the meeting, hoping he'll provide some insight.

"So, we've got three days." I stand up and move to the whiteboard, needing the visual representation to help me divvy up the leads. "Let's start with the victims."

Stone pushes her glasses further up onto the bridge of her nose. "The guys managed to track down Danny Jensen's mother and inform her that her son is missing, believed dead. They have also contacted the Australian embassy and told them that we believe one of their citizens has been abducted."

The Australian girl... "I'll call some friends back home. Get them to pay her parents a personal visit. And I'll contact the embassy. Who did the guys speak to there?"

Stone goes through the notes that had been passed on to her. "George Keen."

I walk over to my own notepad and jot down the two tasks. Back at the whiteboard I write up Danny's and Ling's names with a little tick next to each one.

Stone continues. "Malcolm and Cindy are covered. Then we've got Brigitte Raine. Her mother lives in France and I've spoken to the French embassy here too."

I write up Brigitte's name and put a tick next to it, too.

Stone moves down her list. "Okay. Then we've got those still in the bunker. For the two women left, we've told their relatives that they're missing and that we're investigating their disappearances. So, we tracked down Susie Dean's parents—"

"Shit, I should have told them." Jonathan puts his head in his hands. "I didn't even think about that."

I put the lid on the whiteboard marker. "Jonathan, you've had other things on your mind. And sometimes it's better to hear these things from someone you don't know. It makes it…easier somehow." In my experience, people's reaction to news like this varies greatly— from total denial, to speechless shock, to violent anger. A loved one passing on the news can interfere with the person's emotional release. "Besides," I add, "if they knew what was going on, I'm sure they'd prefer you were helping us *find* Susie."

Jonathan nods.

I take the lid off the marker and write down Susie's name with a little tick next to it. I look up at Stone, ready for her to continue.

"Clair Kelly's parents live in San Diego, and we've informed them. They're going to be a tough one."

"Clair's father," Jonathan says, instantly realizing what the problem is.

Stone nods, but the rest of us are still in the dark.

"Fill us in, Stone," Darren says.

"Her father's a retired cop."

"Damn!" Darren releases his pen, which falls onto his pad with a small thud. "He's going to be on our case."

"He's older, seventy, but yeah, apparently he's already called a few times and was talking about flying over," Stone says.

"We'll deal with that when it happens." After adding Clair's name to the board, I place a little tick next to it. "Okay, the house," I say, moving along to the next part of the whiteboard and starting a new column. Again I look at Stone.

She picks up her own notebook. "The real-estate agent rented it out over the phone and received a cash payment for two months' rental. The person who rented it sent cash in the post. The agent no longer has the envelope and didn't notice the postmark."

On the board I write down *Phone, Cash* and *Two months*. "What about an ID on the caller?"

"The caller said his name was Bob Jones and supplied a fax copy of his birth certificate and a Nevada driver's license." Stone hands out photocopies of the documents. "I've checked with Nevada and both the birth certificate and driver's license are fakes."

I roll my eyes. "Great."

"The real-estate agent also remembered his voice. She said it was real deep."

"Chester," Jonathan says.

"Looks that way." I write *Chester* on the board underneath *The house* and then again as a new column. "Let's talk about Chester in a moment. What about forensics?"

"They're still processing, but they haven't found much, other than Brooke's and Jonathan's prints. Whoever was in the house before them—"

"Brigitte and NeverCaught," I say. "And probably AmericanPsycho and Cindy."

Stone shakes her head. "The place is clean. Someone's been through it with a fine-tooth comb."

"They've been very careful in every other area, so it wouldn't surprise me." I hide my disappointment. "Then again, the president was also setting the others up. He could have left their prints or DNA but he didn't."

"Why?" Stone asks.

I think about it. "He wanted to test us. He wanted it subtle. Another dimension to the game, to the bunker."

"He's setting them up?" Jonathan is confused.

"Yes." I fill him in. "Malcolm had a tattoo of a rose on his wrist and Brooke leaves a rose next to her victims. Cindy didn't have anything." I look at Darren. "I don't think we missed it. The president killed Cindy, so he didn't need to leave a clue pointing to one of his members and he sure as hell wasn't going to leave us a clue to *his* past crimes." I turn back to Jonathan. "And with Brigitte she was posed differently and there was plastic at the scene. Both elements have been linked to another killer active in North and South Dakota. The president was playing you, the contestants, *and* playing the members. He gets off on the duplicity, the control."

"Can't wait to haul his ass into jail," Stone says.

I nod my agreement. I'm also looking forward to drafting a profile. Some elements are already obvious in my mind, but I'll need to get into his head and draft the complete profile. He's going to be one tough SOB to crack. To come up with a scheme like this, his IQ must be through the roof.

Silence for a while before Stone continues. "Forensics did find a small piece of the bedside locker missing from the middle room." Stone smiles, she's got something. "The missing piece matches the fragment the ME found in Malcolm's skull."

"That positively places Malcolm at that house," Darren says.

"What fragment?" Jonathan asks me.

How much do I reveal? So far we've been pretty straight up with Jonathan and I think it's a good strategy. "A small piece of wood was embedded in Malcolm's scalp. Now it's obvious that he hit his head on that bedside table."

"Oh." Jonathan's voice is hesitant as he puts the pieces together. It was most probably an injury that happened during sex but before death.

I move along to Chester. "How did it go with Chester and the sketch artist?" I ask Jonathan. We'd managed to track down Powers and call him in for the emergency sketches.

"Great. Looks just like him."

"I've scanned it in and we're running it at the moment against the computer database," Darren says. "See what we get."

"Good. And DialM? The one who's got Ling?"

Jonathan shakes his head. "We'd just started on him when Detective Carter came and got me."

"Okay, we need to get you back on that as soon as possible." Underneath *Chester* I write *Sketch completed* and then *Database search*. I start a new column titled *DialM* and write *Sketch to be done* underneath it, with *JC* next to that.

I turn to Gerard. "Computers?"

"I want to concentrate on getting the location of the Web server and the cameras."

"They're mostly IP Webcams," Jonathan comments.

"Yup, I know."

I sigh. "And what does that mean?"

Gerard explains. "IP Webcams aren't physically attached to a specific computer, rather they have their own IP address and generate their own URL. The Web site at murderers-club.com simply includes code that calls the Web feed from the camera."

In a new column titled *Computers*, I write up *Web server location, Camera location—Ling* and *Camera locations—bunker*. "What am I missing?"

Darren answers. "The ads. Maybe we can find something out about who placed them."

I nod and write it up. "And the limo." I add that to our list too. "I know Hamill drew a blank in Vegas, but you never know your luck." I go back to Chester's column and add *Helicopter pilot*. "I don't think it's worth chasing registered helicopter pilots, but we should bear it in mind."

I study the list. "Anything else?"

Everyone's looking at the whiteboard. Hopefully we've got everything.

"What about—" Jonathan hesitates "—Brooke? We need her user habits."

"And we need to check out her house," Darren says.

Our background check on Brooke found she was currently living in Phoenix. We also discovered how she got her money—the stock market. She still works, but our BlackWidow is worth over a million.

"The laptop we've got belongs to the house, so her laptop must be at her place," Gerard says. "I could get her user habits from that. There might be other computer evidence too."

"Those Webcam locations have gotta be our priority. Your priority," I say. "Someone will have to check out Brooke's house first-hand, but you need to stay on the locations."

"Yeah, you're right."

I write *Brooke's house* on the board.

"Okay," I say. "So we've got Jonathan on the DialM sketch and Gerard on the Web stuff. Jonathan, you can help out Gerard when you're done."

"Cool." Jonathan's excitement is obvious, even for him.

"Stone, do you want to stay on the house and forensics? See if there's anything more we can get out of it?"

Stone nods at me.

"Carter, we can take the ads and the L.A. limo. See what we can't turn up."

"What about Brooke's place?" Darren says.

"I can follow up the ads and limo if you like," Stone speaks up. "I'll just be waiting to hear back from forensics on the house anyway."

I nod. "Done."

I mark in initials next to each task. Some of these will have to wait until morning, until business hours.

I feel a little strange barking out orders, but it's what Rivers wants. This is a federal case, which means it's the Bureau's baby. And Rivers just happened to nominate me babysitter.

"And we should all try to get some sleep tonight," I say, even though the thought of Ling in that basement at the hands of DialM makes me want to work everyone 24/7. But that's not realistic, even for us.

Stone, Jonathan and Gerard nod and file out of the room to their respective tasks.

With the others gone, Darren speaks his mind. "You're forgetting one thing."

"What?" I ready my pen, mortified that I've forgotten something but also relieved that Darren didn't call me up on it in front of everyone.

Darren smiles. "Your premonitions."

I lean on the table with both hands and take a deep breath. "I really don't know if I can see another person's murder and not be able to stop it." The last time I tried it was okay—even though I felt Jonathan's fear, I only saw him running through the tunnels and looking at the cameras. But what if the next one's another murder? I thought I'd gotten past this, but the prospect of what I might see and feel still frightens me.

"And you can live with the other alternative?" Darren's voice is metered and he's choosing his words carefully. But even so, I can read between the lines. The other alternative is that someone else dies and I wonder if I could have stopped it by opening myself up to the visions.

I sink into the chair. "No." Why is it that sometimes your only two options are both so unappealing?

Darren lets the silence hang heavily in the room before he finally pushes his point, and pushes me. "You have to try again, Sophie. You know that."

Even just talking about it brings on a few flashes of Brigitte's death, of Cindy in the desert…of their fear. I'm not experiencing the visions again, but the memory is so strong that I may as well be. I shudder and change the topic. "Let's get moving on Brooke and Phoenix."

Darren shakes his head and takes several breaths to speak, but each time he aborts his attempts. "I'll book the flight." His voice has that controlled edge to it again and I can tell he's annoyed with me.

"Fine," I say, happy he's moved onto the flight.

He opens the project-room door to leave. "Make your calls about the Australian girl. But then, Sophie, you need to see if you can induce another vision. You know that." He keeps his eyes on the floor, not me, and while he doesn't exactly storm out of the room, the flurry of movement and the forceful ways he closes the door make it all too obvious that he's pissed. Pissed with me. I guess even Darren has his limits. Shit.

I sit with my head in my hands. I wish Darren was wrong. I wish I could walk away from these visions and dreams, but I can't. Like he said, it's a calling and I've repressed it for way too many years. But knowing he's right doesn't make it any easier. It doesn't make me want to feel what a victim feels just before he or she is killed. It's a horrific cocktail of overwhelming panic, that sense of being trapped, and regret as they mourn what they're about to lose and what they haven't done. But the violence overshadows all of that. Most people want to die peacefully in their sleep with their family in the next room; no one wants to be raped, tortured, and then murdered. We don't want the last face we see to be that of a serial killer. Who would? And experiencing that sensation, over and over again with each vision and nightmare comes close to my idea of hell.

I wipe away a few tears that have trickled down my face, but I no longer know who I'm crying for—them or me. Maybe the tears are for everyone. I think of Ling and her parents. I have a duty to them and with Ling it's not just my duty as an FBI agent. I feel a stronger link with Ling because she's Australian. I've chosen to live and work in the U.S., but that doesn't change who I am. I love Australia and I don't want a fellow Australian to die at the hands of DialM. Darren's right, I couldn't live with myself if I didn't do everything I could to stop that. I sit back up and force myself out of my puddle of self-pity. I will try to induce another vision, but first I'll make the calls.

Five minutes later I've spoken directly to Ling's parents, catching them just before they left for Sydney airport and the first flight to the U.S. I was going to call an old colleague, get them to contact Ling's parents, but in the end I decided I owed them a direct call.

No hiding anymore. They had lots of questions, of course, and I told them everything I could. The knowledge that their daughter is being held captive in an unknown location by a killer was far from comforting, but they deserved the truth.

I look at my watch and am surprised to see it's one o'clock in the morning. No wonder I'm so tired. I bite my lip, aware that the tiredness will make me emotionally vulnerable, more affected by what I might see. But I have to do it, and it has to be now. Before I lose my nerve.

Ling is my priority, so I think about her and what we know about DialM—which isn't much. Ling is his first victim from the club, and we've got nothing to put into VICAP to even try to get a match for him. I visualize Ling's face, not from any photos but from the video stream.

I slow my breathing and take deep breaths, in and out. I try not to think about her parents on a plane, Darren and the others or what they're doing. I just think about relaxing my body and clearing my mind. I don't know how much time has passed, but it's a sound I notice first.

A heart beats, and it's not mine. It's Ling's. Her heartbeat is slow. She's not afraid, she's past fear and has moved onto acceptance. Acceptance that she's going to die. I hear footsteps and I look up. A man comes down the stairs, ducking on the top steps to avoid hitting his head. He smiles at me, but it's not a pleasant smile. My heart beats a little faster and fear rises in me. The man's in his fifties, with salt-and-pepper hair cut short. He's got soft, dark-brown eyes that are covered by round-framed glasses, but his other features are harsh. His nose is big and angular, his brow well-defined, his jaw square and wide and his lips are thin slits. He wears good clothes, like he's dressed up to go somewhere, but his shoes are boots, and covered in dust.

He moves closer to me, his thin lips still smiling at me. He sits down on the end of the bed and I ball myself up tighter and move closer to

the bedhead. But I've got nowhere to go, nowhere to run to. I bury my
head in my lap. He reaches out and touches my foot. His hand is cold
and clammy and his touch is enough to send a disgusted shudder down
my body.

"Sophie."

I look up as the door opens fully and Darren leans on the door handle, his body half in the room and half out.

"DialM's with Ling now. He's touching her." Darren's hand grips the door handle tighter.

I nod, small fast nods. "I know."

33

The alarm is set for 5:30 a.m. but I wake up with a start at 5:25 a.m. to Darren's cell phone ringing. I let out a moan—not even three hours sleep. I force myself up, and the tiredness feels worse than any hangover. My head is heavy and foggy, my mouth dry and my eyes seem to only be able to open a crack. Darren's muffled voice travels through the wall, but I can't make out what he's saying. It's gotta be about the case. I throw a fleece on over my PJs before making my way into the corridor. I lean against the wall, not willing to invade his privacy by knocking on his door. Within less than a minute his bedroom door opens.

"Shit!" he says, jumping back. He laughs, an embarrassed chuckle.

"Sorry, didn't mean to frighten you." I manage a small grin.

"I'm still half asleep. At least that's my excuse and I'm sticking to it."

"What's up?" I nod at the cell phone he's still holding in his hand.

"That was the night shift. The computer's come back with a match on the sketch of Chester. Except his name's not Chester, it's Heath Jordan. He served time for robbery and now he works in San Francisco for..." he pauses, as if allowing room for a drum roll "...a computer company."

I shake my head. "Chester, Chester, Chester."

He leans against the nearest wall. "San Fran first?"

"Yup. Phoenix can wait. Although I better go online again as my alter ego before we fly out."

I decide to jump in the shower while Darren rearranges our itinerary. Twenty minutes later I emerge from my room, hair wet, but otherwise ready to go. My dark circles needed an extra coat of base this morning and my body is already chomping at the bit for its first coffee. Darren must have sensed this, because not only is he ready, but the coffee is on, with the brewer halfway through its cycle.

"God, you're a lifesaver," I say, eyeing the coffee.

"I need my life saved this morning too." He rubs his eyes.

He looks tired, and doesn't have the advantage of being able to smother his face with makeup. He gets two cups from the press and does a fast switch so one catches the drips while he fills the other with coffee that's already made its way to the jug.

"I don't know if I can even eat this morning." I place my hand on my stomach. "The lack of sleep has made me a little queasy."

"We can grab something at the airport."

"What time's our flight?"

"Eight. That'll give you some time online, at the station."

"That'll be fun. Trying to think like Black Widow on three hours' sleep."

Darren chuckles. "Well, you can pretend you've been busy with Jonathan all night." He puts just enough emphasis on the word *busy* to imply exactly what I would have been busy doing, had I really been Brooke.

"Gee, thanks. Although I can't say I feel very sexy."

"You always look sexy." He turns away as he says it, and I'm relieved eye contact is avoided.

I try to think of something to say, some response, but nothing comes to me.

Darren turns back toward me and manages a smile. "If Heath Jordan is our guy, you might not need to be Black Widow any longer."

"True. But maybe I should take the club's laptop to San Francisco, just in case."

"If Gerard will let it out of his sight." Darren takes a gulp of coffee.

"You're right, Gerard does need that computer." I sigh. "This is going to be a tricky one to prosecute."

Darren nods. "I hadn't wanted to bring it up again. Certainly not in front of Jonathan."

"No, definitely not." I take a sip of the hot coffee. "Even if we find all the members, what will we get them on? Surfing the Net? We need to tie them not only to that Web site but to the murders. Without physical evidence linking one or all of them to our victims, we're screwed."

"The news items were pretty incriminating. And we've got the chat- room conversations you've been copying and pasting into the Notepad."

"Let's hope it's enough."

Darren takes a sip of his coffee. "We're running out of options."

"Sure are. And my vision wasn't exactly a breakthrough." I told Darren about my vision last night, but it only confirmed what DialM looks like—something we already had through Jonathan and the video stream. "We can't wait around until they kill again. And not when one of them has got Ling." I stand up and try not to think about what Ling's going through. "At least we've got Brooke on all those other murders, but if we wind up with an accessory charge for this Heath guy…"

"You're going to puncture something."

"What?"

"Your lip."

I've been biting my bottom lip as usual, a habit I can't seem to break. I release my lip and smooth my tongue over it. "I hadn't noticed."

"I notice," Darren mumbles before taking another sip of coffee. "Like I said, we've got the Web site and the chat room stuff. They've said incriminating things in there."

Darren's still looking at my lips, but I push my self-consciousness away. "Will it hold up in court? Talking about murder and actually doing it are two different things. That's the angle the lawyers will take."

In law enforcement, we have to be very aware of our actions and their repercussions for a possible conviction, but sometimes it's hard to balance that with our ultimate duty—to protect. We *could* use the two remaining contestants as bait. See who gets voted off, and wait at the house. But what if, like Ling, they're not taken to the house? God knows where Ling is being held captive. I take a gulp of coffee.

Gerard arrives at the station about five minutes after us and looks worse than Darren and I combined. He's unshaven and his more casual choice of clothing this morning—jeans and a T-shirt—further accentuates his disheveled look. It also makes him look a lot younger. You'd certainly never guess he was a U.S. government employee.

"You look like hell," Darren says.

"Jonathan and I finished up—" he looks at his watch "—all of two hours ago."

"Working on the location?" I ask.

"I was, but Jonathan was investigating a few suspect chat rooms and newsgroups I frequent."

I raise my eyebrows but figure his sentence must have come out wrong.

"I frequent them for professional purposes. It's one of our department's initiatives, to look out for potential child molesters, on-line kiddy porn and other illegal activity or violent offenders. Anyway, most of the people I've met online are into kids, that's our biggest problem in cyberspace, but a few have dubious enough connections that I thought they may have heard something about this club. Brooke won't tell us what chat room the president recruited her from, but there's no harm in looking."

"Good thinking, Gerard. Any luck?"

"Well, no, actually. I'm closer with the Web stuff, but Jonathan didn't find anything in the chat rooms and newsgroups." He sighs. "So, time to be BlackWidow?"

"Yup."

Gerard starts the computer for me. He opens up a Web browser window and logs into the site as BlackWidow. Two others are online, NeverCaught and AmericanPsycho. I wonder if that means they're on the East Coast, where it's a little bit later.

I voice this observation. "It's 6:30 a.m. here, which makes it 9:30 a.m. Eastern Standard Time."

Gerard sees where I'm going with it. "But they may log on before work. That'd cover most time zones."

He's right. "Can you get locations of where they're logging on from?"

"Yes, that's one of the things I'm working on. But whoever set this up knows what they're doing. Each computer's connection is being bounced around so many times, it's going to take a while to trace it back to the source."

I nod and bring my attention back to the site, back to BlackWidow.

BlackWidow: Morning. Anything interesting happening inside?

NeverCaught: Nope. ** it. Let's just cut to the chase. Next elimination please!

BlackWidow: I'm enjoying Jonathan too much to give up this house. Let's stick to the schedule.

AmericanPsycho: You two are still at it?

BlackWidow: You better believe it.

NeverCaught: I've said it before and I'll say it again. What do you see in him?

AmericanPsycho: I'd have to agree with Never.

BlackWidow: I like his broody look. It's sexy.

NeverCaught: I would have thought it would be a panicked look by now.

BlackWidow: That's even sexier.

AmericanPsycho: I think it's time to turn on the lights.

* * *

We watch the main video feed as the lights of the bunker come on, and the camera changes from night vision to normal vision.

"Interesting."

"What?" Darren and I ask in unison.

"I assumed the lights would be on a timer. But he turned them on at the flick of a switch, literally. Which means he's either in that control center near the bunker, or he's got electronic control over them."

"Is that possible? To control them remotely?"

"Sure. Heard of Roke Manor Research's Domestic Internet Remote Controller?"

I laugh. "Nope."

Gerard grins. "Sorry. All the doors, locks, lights and cameras could be controlled by SMS or via a customized Web page that displays the floor plan of the bunker, with controls to switch lights and other electrical devices on and off."

"SMS?"

"Yep. He could simply send an SMS with a 'lights on' command."

"Jesus," Darren says.

"I better concentrate on this again…" I look back at the screen and start typing to cover up any lag.

NeverCaught: You just want to see Susie.

AmericanPsycho: She *is* nice to look at.

BlackWidow: I'll tell Jonathan the president's got his eye on his little friend.

AmericanPsycho: Do. Jonathan needs to be put in his place.

DialM has entered the room.

DialM: Hi, all.

BlackWidow: Morning.

NeverCaught: Hi, M. How's your little pet doing?

DialM: The crying's finally stopped. She's accepted her new role in life.

AmericanPsycho: You like to break em, huh?
DialM: Yes. She lasted longer than I thought she would. She seemed such a timid thing.
BlackWidow: Looks can be deceiving.

My fingers punch the last line into the keyboard as I try to control my anger.

"She's still alive." Darren places his hand on my tense shoulder.

"For the moment." I shake my head. "I've got to get more info."

"Be careful. We don't want them suspicious."

"If AmericanPsycho is Heath, he'll be suspicious in a couple of hours anyway," I say.

"With a system like this there's a lot they can do in two hours, Anderson." Gerard seems totally awake now. "They've installed failsafes everywhere, the whole bunker could have one, too."

"Like what?" I ask.

He shrugs. "Anything could be controlled by the Roke Manor software, even explosives."

"Shit!" I shake my head. He's right. It fits with the way the whole operation has been run so far. "Maximum carnage, destroy all evidence."

Gerard nods.

My shoulders slump.

"The perfect cover-up," Darren says.

I look back at the chat room and catch up on the last comment.

DialM: Yes, they can be. Not that I mind a challenge. I'd be upset if she accepted her fate within an hour.
BlackWidow: Jonathan's accepted his part in this game.
AmericanPsycho: Really? I'm surprised, given his personality profile. Be careful with him.
BlackWidow: Don't worry. I can't play with him for much longer anyway. I've got to get back to work. Life as a ****** is flexible, but it's still work.

* * *

I look up at the screen and notice the asterisks. "Shit, what's that?"

"I noticed it before, with NeverCaught," Gerard says.

"I thought he'd typed it instead of the f-bomb," Darren says.

"So did I." Gerard leans in. "What did you type?"

"Sales rep."

"Someone's set up a filter program. Another safeguard."

"If that's the case, Brooke wasn't lying about not knowing anything about her fellow club members." Darren rubs his eyes, still trying to wake up. "None of them do."

Gerard nods. "The person behind this could have set up filters for a variety of words. Obviously it's set up for cussing and occupations."

I think about the operation. "Makes sense. Part of his control over the game. He knows who everyone is and what they do, but no one else does."

"Shall we wake up Brooke and ask her about the censoring?" Darren asks.

I shrug. "I don't know if she can add anything." I pause. "Although she has had more time to think about the president's betrayal. Maybe her lips will be looser."

Darren nods. "We can question her before we leave."

"You're on." I turn my attention back to the computer and read Psycho's comment.

AmericanPsycho: Slack of you, BW. How many times do I have to tell you to watch what you say?

BlackWidow: I know, sorry. I didn't get much sleep last night.

NeverCaught: You go, girl.

BlackWidow: I have to go. Some phone calls to make. If you don't hear from me for a while you know what I'm doing! See you.

BlackWidow has left the room.

* * *

"I give up. If the system's set up to protect their identity, I'll never get anything out of them online."

"Don't worry. We've got Heath's ass." Darren grins, but I'm not sure if it's genuine faith that the case is about to break, or optimism. I guess we'll find out soon enough.

I pace in one of the interview rooms, my mind swirling with evidence and chat-room lines, while Darren gets Brooke from the holding cell downstairs. Only a few minutes pass before he enters with Brooke, whose hands are cuffed behind her back. Her hair hangs limply around her face and she looks like she's had about as much sleep as we have.

"Hi, Brooke."

"You," she says, stopping in her tracks.

"Didn't realize I made such an impression."

She glares at me and walks toward the seat.

I lean against the table. "I guess I should introduce myself. I'm a profiler with the FBI."

She doesn't respond.

"The president of your club's done some job on you guys."

Her eyes narrow. "He'll pay."

"I'm afraid you're not in any position to make him pay." I sit down opposite her and cross my legs. "But we are."

Darren moves to the wall and leans against it. "Sure are."

"Really," she says sarcastically.

I nod slowly. "In fact, we're about to arrest one of your fellow members."

"Really?" The sarcastic tone has disappeared. "Who?"

"We know his name, but we're not sure if he's NeverCaught or AmericanPsycho."

"You obviously got onto the site okay."

"Yes. Thanks."

She leans back in her chair. "I've given you enough help."

"So you don't want to help us find the man who set you up?"

She pauses. "Like I said, I've given you enough. Work the rest out yourselves, if you can." She shakes her head.

"He planted that rose on Malcolm. He planted stuff on Brigitte, too. Doesn't that piss you off?"

"Hell, yes. Why'd you think I gave you the damn laptop password?" She sighs. "Truth is, lady, I don't have anything else for you."

Darren steps forward. "I bet she'll be more cooperative at trial time."

She smiles. "Maybe I will——" she looks Darren up and down, the sexual predator taking over again "——*Detective*."

But I think she's bluffing. She doesn't know anything more of value.

The plane touches down in San Francisco at 11:00 a.m., West Coast time. We catch a taxi from the airport directly to the San Francisco FBI field office.

I hold my Bureau ID out at the security desk. "Special Agent Anderson here to see Special Agent Dusk."

After the security guard gets confirmation that Dusk's expecting us, he lets us in. "Dusk is on the third floor," he says.

We take the elevator up in silence. I'm preparing for the eventual confrontation with Heath Jordan, and I guess Darren is doing the same. When the doors open, a short man in his early forties is waiting for us.

"Anderson?"

"Yes." I shake his hand. "And this is Detective Darren Carter from Tucson Homicide."

Darren and Dusk also shake hands.

"Has it come through?" I ask.

Dusk fishes the all-important search warrant out of his inside pocket and jostles it in his hand like a victory dance. He passes it to me and I give it a quick once-over. It's exactly what I'd requested. Jonathan's sworn statement and positive ID of Heath Jordan has given us an unlimited search warrant for both Jordan's office and his home, including all computer equipment.

"Is the rest of the team ready?" I ask Dusk.

"Uh huh. Me and my partner will go with you guys to the office, plus we've got two forensic investigators and our computer guy. I've organized four agents and four forensics people, including one computer expert just like you requested for the suspect's home address."

"Okay. Let's go."

Darren and I ride with Dusk and his partner, with forensics behind us. At Hillview Avenue we pull up right in front of SysTech, the company where Heath Jordan works. SysTech is in Palo Alto—more commonly known as Silicon Valley—about forty-five miles south of downtown San Francisco.

We're carrying out the search warrants simultaneously, so we sit in the cars, waiting until the other team is in place too. Presumably Heath is in the office, given it's Friday, but if he's at home I don't want some colleague calling him and tipping him off. This way we have the element of surprise no matter where he is.

After just under fifteen minutes, Dusk's phone rings.

"Dusk...okay. One minute from now." He hangs up. "They're in position."

I look at my watch and count down. With each second my heart beats faster, pumping adrenaline through my body. Gotta love that feeling: once again the hunter has become the prey. A buzz of righteousness joins my adrenaline surge.

We get out of the car and proceed up the stairs to the entrance.

I flash my ID at the security guard. "FBI. We've got a search warrant for Heath Jordan's office and your computer network." I hold the warrant up on the glass.

The security guard is flustered. I bet this has never happened to him before. "Um...um, let me just call the security manager."

"Do what you like, but this piece of paper gives us access *now*." I hop over the nearest barrier and the others do the same. "What floor's he on?" I demand.

"Ummm...ahh...top floor, forty-five."

I push the up button while Dusk arranges for an officer to stay with the security guard to make sure he doesn't phone Heath. The elevator travels express for the first forty floors, and when the doors open at the fortieth floor I flash my ID and tell the person to wait for the next lift.

By the time we exit onto the forty-fifth floor, only about two minutes has elapsed. Hopefully, it will still be a surprise visit. I grab the nearest person and ask them where Jordan's office is. They point me to the far corner office and we make our way to the other side of the building. As we move through the open-plan work area, people stare at us, some standing up to watch our progress. By the time we reach Heath's office, at least half the floor is up and trying to work out what's going on.

"Can I help you?" Jordan's secretary asks as we pass her. We ignore her and I fling the door open.

The secretary's behind us. "You can't just barge in like this."

I flash my ID at her without turning around.

Heath sits behind the desk, taking up more space in the room than his fancy chair. He stands up and his imposing frame makes me think about Jonathan's description, "built like a brick house." He looks more like a heavy-weight boxer or football player than a computer programmer.

"Mr. Jordan, I'm Special Agent Anderson with the FBI. We've got a warrant to search this office." I hold up my ID and hand him the search warrant. "Please step away from your desk. Now."

He backs away, reading the warrant. "I don't understand. What's this all about?"

I have to smile at his question. Why do they always pretend they're innocent? It's like bad guys belong to this club, the "deny everything" club. It's astounding sometimes.

"What's wrong…Chester?" I drag out the alias he's been using in the game. To my surprise he doesn't even flinch. Could he have covered his tracks so well that he's not frightened of being caught? Even if he has, it doesn't matter, because we've got Jonathan.

I hear the secretary on the phone, calling someone.

I get up close and personal with Heath, like I did with Brooke. I can't imagine a man Heath's size being intimidated by a five-foot-eight woman, but you never know. "Chester," I repeat. "What made you choose that name?"

His dark brown, almost black eyes move from focusing over my shoulder to making eye contact. "I don't know what you're talking about."

I laugh and put my hands on my hips. "Aren't you curious?"

"Sure I am. I'd like to know what the hell's going on." He raises his voice and looks once again over my shoulder at the agents and forensic investigators already sifting through his office.

"I didn't mean curious about what we're doing here." I pause for effect. "I meant curious about how we found you."

Still his face is impassive. It's a good mask, but it's also too impassive for a man wrongly accused. He knows exactly what I'm talking about.

I look around his office. "Nice setup you've got here." I gaze out the large window at San Francisco in the distance. Man, he must be high up in this company for a corner office with that view. "Nice view."

"I like it."

I smile. "Take a good look. You won't be seeing a view like that for some time. Forever I'd say."

"Am I under arrest?" Still no hint of concern in his voice.

He has the detached manner of a sociopath or, more likely, a psychopath. "So, are you AmericanPsycho or NeverCaught?" I know he's not DialM.

"Agent Anderson, is it?" Heath smiles at me, like we're having a normal, friendly conversation.

"Yes."

"I really wish I knew what you were talking about. Then perhaps I could help you."

I laugh again. "Carter, he's all yours." For the moment, the attempted murder of Jonathan is all we've got Heath on.

Darren takes out his handcuffs. "Heath Jordan, you're under arrest for being an accessory to the attempted murder of Jonathan Cantor." Darren continues reading him his rights.

When he's finished, I say, "Did you hear that, Heath?" I pause for effect. "*Attempted* murder." I spit "attempted", so he knows Jonathan is still alive. "And soon we'll have you for a lot more than that."

"What's going on here?"

I swing around. A man in his early to midthirties has entered the room. He's six foot and I put him at around the two hundred pound mark, but all of that two hundred pounds looks like muscle, even through his designer suit. He has dark hair, cut fairly short but slightly longer and tousled on top, and captivating green eyes. I can tell from his tone of voice and demeanor that he's a man who's used to being listened to. Obviously that's who the secretary was on the phone to.

"And you are?" I move closer to him. Behind him about ten staff members have come in for a closer look, although no one's actually in the office.

He smiles, revealing perfectly straight and extra white teeth. "Justin Reid." The smile goes and his tone becomes commanding once more. "The owner and CEO of this company. Who are you, and what the hell do you think you're doing?"

I take out my ID again. "Special Agent Anderson of the FBI." I motion toward Heath. "This man is under arrest for accessory to an attempted murder."

"What?" He's obviously shocked and, for a few seconds, speechless. "No, there must be some mistake." The certainty returns.

"I'm afraid not. We have an eyewitness. And we have a warrant to search this office and take whatever we want as evidence, including all of his computing devices."

Reid holds his hand out. "May I see the warrant, please?" He's flustered, but still commanding in his request.

I grab the warrant from the desk where Heath had dropped it when Darren was cuffing him. "You a lawyer, Mr. Reid?"

"No. But I know my rights and those of my employees." He reads the warrant. "Everything seems in order."

"Of course." I manage my most charming smile.

Reid moves over to Heath and puts his arm on his shoulder. "Don't worry, Heath, I know this is all a big mistake. I'll organize a lawyer for you."

Heath simply nods his response.

"That's a generous offer, Mr. Reid," I say.

He takes a deep breath. "Mr. Jordan has been with me for over ten years, Agent Anderson. It's the least I can do for him. Particularly when I'm sure you've got the wrong man."

Darren and Dusk's partner lead Heath out of the office. They'll take him back to the Bureau's temporary lock-up area for questioning.

"Heath!" I call before he's out the door. "Just thought I'd let you know, we've got another, much larger team at your apartment, too."

Darren pulls on Heath's arm and leads him away, past the onlookers. Talk about a walk of shame. Can't get much worse than having to walk through your office cuffed.

Reid moves closer to me. "Agent Anderson, I'd like to offer my services to you and the Bureau. I'm sure this is all a misunderstanding but I'd like to do everything I can to help you during this investigation."

"Thank you, Mr. Reid. We'll need to question you and all staff that deal with Mr. Jordan. And while we're gathering information, your staff will be locked out of their computers."

He's obviously unhappy about this, but nods.

"How about if I ask you a few questions while the rest of the team is searching?"

"Sure. Why don't we go into my office?" He puts his hand on the small of my back and guides me effortlessly out the door. "Ms. Jamble, you can return to your desk now," he says as he passes Heath's secretary. Outside he addresses the rest of his staff. "I know you're all concerned about Heath, but don't worry, I'm sure this is simply a big misunderstanding. While I sort this out, please go back to your desks; however, you'll be locked out of your computers while the FBI carries out their search. I'll let you know the minute *I* know something."

His request is actioned instantaneously. I study their faces as they disperse. If we'd traced Heath to this company, this computer with IT forensics alone, all the staff would be suspects—anybody could use his computer. But there's no mistaking a positive visual ID.

Reid leads me to the other back-corner office, but this one is about twice the size of Heath's. The office is completely glassed on all four walls, creating the illusion of even more space, but presumably diminishing Mr. Reid's privacy too. Outside the office sits an older woman, around fifty. She has tightly curled brown hair, but despite her obvious maintenance, a hint of gray around her temples makes me suspect she might be a bottle brunette. She wears a tailored navy suit, and the collar of a pale-pink silk shirt drapes across the lapel. Like Reid's suit, I get the feeling we're talking Christian Dior rather than GAP. To my surprise, she doesn't even look up as we approach. She's either deaf or has trained out all of her curiosity.

"Carolyn." Reid stops at her desk and I put the brakes on fast to keep myself from walking straight into him.

"Yes?" Now she looks up.

"Two coffees, I think." He turns to me. "We have an espresso machine. How do you take your coffee?"

"I'll have a latte, thank you. Strong."

He smiles. "Thanks, Carolyn. The usual for me."

"Yes, sir." She stands up and weaves her way out from behind her desk, revealing a knee-length skirt and skinny legs.

Like Heath's office, the floor-to-ceiling windows give a magnificent view of San Francisco.

Reid follows my gaze. "It's not often we get such a clear day. Enjoy it while you can."

I smile and manage to avert my eyes from the view to take in the rest of the office, which is tastefully and expensively decorated. To one side are two black leather couches, with stainless-steel trim and a matching stainless-steel and glass coffee table—obviously where Mr. Reid conducts his more relaxed meetings. Behind that is a modern, fully stocked bar, with three stools permanently attached to a steel plate that runs the length of the bar.

A large Japanese water feature is in the very center of the room, complete with perfectly smooth, shiny black and white pebbles. In the far corner is a life-size bronze sculpture of a naked woman. The only other art in the room is a beautiful painting directly behind Reid's desk that's suspended by wires from the ceiling. I can tell from where I'm standing that it's an original, because I can see brush strokes in thick masses of paint. The painting seems to me, an uneducated art lover, to be somewhere in between impressionism and abstract art. I can make out that the subject is a man and a woman, but that's all.

Reid's still looking at me. "Do you like it?"

My eyes drift down from the painting to Reid. "It's beautiful."

He smiles. "An FBI agent who's also an art lover."

"I appreciate art, but I'm not very educated on the subject."

"You don't have to be educated to be drawn to a piece."

"No, I guess not."

Reid motions to a seat in front of his desk while he steps around to his chair. "Do you mind if I just finish this e-mail?" He sits down. "While it's in my head."

"Sorry, you'll be locked out, too."

Reid seems a little put out, but then smiles charmingly. He stands up again and motions toward a lounge area that forms part of his office—I guess he figures we may as well be comfortable.

"So, down to business." He sits down. "This really must be some mistake, Agent Anderson."

I sink into the comfortable leather chair. "I don't think so." I pause. "You know Heath Jordan has a criminal record."

"Yes. A charge when he was much, much younger."

I raise my eyebrows. "He served five years for armed robbery."

"He was sixteen. He had it tough."

"It's not an excuse, Mr. Reid."

"No. Certainly not. Call me Justin, please."

"How long have you known Heath?"

He leans back. "I actually met him while he was serving time."

He waits for my reaction, but I give him none. "Go on," is all I say.

"I'm involved in a number of not-for-profit organizations, including an outreach program for young black offenders. SysTech runs computer classes twice a week in conjunction with the Center on Juvenile and Criminal Justice."

"A noble cause."

"I like to give back to the community."

He can certainly bloody afford to. I smile.

Reid looks up past me, and I turn around to see his PA entering the office. She places a tray on the corner of the table and unloads our coffees and a plate of biscuits.

"Anything else, sir?"

"No thanks, Carolyn."

Reid motions to the cookies but I decline the offer.

"Come on, Agent Anderson. You're a law-enforcement professional. Don't tell me you're one of these women who's constantly dieting." He manages to deliver the line with enough warmth that it's genuinely funny rather than condescending.

"No, not at all. I just don't want to spoil my lunch." It's a lie—it's unlikely I'll remember to stop for lunch. The truth is, while I'm not dieting as such, I always try to limit my sugar intake.

He eyes me suspiciously and takes a cookie. "I don't indulge much myself, I must admit."

The contrast in his personality strikes me as odd—from a commanding leader to this? At times, the way his eyes have lingered on me, it's even crossed my mind that he's hitting on me. And a man like Justin Reid would have no trouble getting a woman. With his looks and money, even if he's a jerk or already married, he'd still get women. But there's something about him that unsettles me—he's too smooth.

While he finishes his mouthful, I take the opportunity to get us back on track. "So, Heath?"

He licks his lips. "Heath showed a great deal of promise. Occasionally we employ offenders from the program, and that's what happened in Heath's case."

"Minimum wage?"

"Not at all." He takes a sip of his coffee and if he's offended by my suggestion he doesn't show it. "From memory, Heath started working for us full-time at the age of twenty-three on a salary of around thirty thousand."

I write down the details. "That is generous."

"I find if you show people respect, they do things to earn it."

"Really. You must see a nicer side of humanity than I do."

"I'm sure I do, Agent Anderson. I don't envy anyone working in law enforcement."

"I love it actually." I shrug off his comment.

He continues. "Heath went back to college part-time, and studied information technology, specializing in security. That's my company's area of expertise."

"Really?"

"NetSecure is used by the FBI. Perhaps you've noticed it on your computer when you start it up."

NetSecure…he really is loaded. "Yes, I have." I move it along, trying to hide the fact that I'm impressed. "So what does Mr. Jordan do for you now?"

"He's the head of R&D."

"So he knows his way around computers."

Reid chuckles. "You could say that."

"This crime involves computers."

"Hence the lockout." It's sinking in.

I nod.

"But I thought you were charging him with being an accessory to murder."

"For the moment. But we believe he's involved in a much broader online scheme."

"Can you expand on that?"

"Not really, no."

"But perhaps I can help." He follows the offer up with one of his charming smiles and then takes a casual sip of his coffee.

"We've got the best computer-forensics people on the case."

He smiles. "I'm sure." His response is polite, but the undertone of disbelief is obvious. A man like him probably doesn't think "the best" would work for law enforcement, earning $60,000 to $80,000 a year when they could be on $250,000 or more in the private sector. But job satisfaction's not about money.

"Have you noticed anything different about Jordan in the past couple of months?" I ask. "Particularly the last five weeks?"

"That's how long this has been going on then—five weeks?"

"I'm afraid I can't discuss that."

"Sorry." He takes a few gulps of his coffee. "Well, in answer to your question, no, I haven't noticed any unusual behavior."

"Has he taken any vacation days?"

"One or two, I think. You'd have to check with HR to be sure."

I nod. "Does your company have a helicopter?"

"Of course. We have a private plane and several helicopters across our different offices."

Silly me. Of course.

"Does Mr. Jordan ever fly the helicopter?"

"How did you know he could fly?"

I smile. "Our witness was flown via helicopter, by Mr. Jordan."

"Oh." He seems hesitant. "But that can't be right. It must be someone else. Someone who perhaps looks like Heath." Now he seems slightly upset.

"I take it you're close?"

He doesn't respond right away. "Yes. I've been his mentor, and friend, for years. When I met Heath I'd only just started this company, and was personally putting my time into the outreach program. Now I hire other people to take the classes but my dedication in terms of dollars is more than ten times greater than it was then. Heath is part of that. A good story about what a little positive intervention can do."

"I'm sorry to tell you, Mr. Reid, but I'm afraid your trust has been misplaced."

He shakes his head. "I just…I can't see it."

It's time to disclose more information to Reid—he needs to realize the seriousness of the situation. "I know this must be hard. I mean, serial killers are able to hide their activities even from a wife or partner. It's common."

"Serial killers? You're not saying…"

"Heath is mixed up in something very big and very bad. If he hasn't personally killed himself, he's been actively involved in at least six homicides."

Reid stands up and walks toward the window, sipping his coffee and staring absently at the view, trying to absorb this bombshell. But it looks to me like he's in denial.

34

As soon as I arrive at the field office I go straight to the interview room and call Darren out.

"Anything?"

"He's not talking. At all."

"Shit. We need to find that bunker. And Ling." I twist the ring on my little finger. "How much have you told him?"

"I've been bombarding him with the evidence we have against him. The laptop, Jonathan's ID of him, the Web site, the name of the club, everything. I even told him that Brooke had rolled on him and said she'd testify against him."

"And still nothing?"

"No." Darren rubs his face. "I don't think we're going to get anything from him."

"Okay," I say, but it's not what I want to hear. I bite my lip. "Let's leave him in there for a bit and see what the computer geeks have found on his office and home computers."

We make our way downstairs and are just about to enter the computer lab when my cell rings. I flip the phone open and look at the number.

"It's Gerard," I say to Darren before pressing the call button. "Agent Gerard, tell me you've got something."

"I've got something."

I smile and grab Darren's arm. "Yes?" I say.

"I've managed to get the location of the Australian girl's Webcam."

"What? That's fantastic news!" I think about Ling's parents, somewhere in the middle of the Pacific now. What parent could sit in another country knowing that their child was missing?

Gerard's voice is full of confidence and excitement. "She's close, too."

"To you or us?"

"You."

"Where is she?" This time I'm going to make it in time, in time to save Ling. It's not going to be like Brigitte and the others.

"She's on a property just outside of Red Bluff, California."

"Red Bluff?" I ask Darren, having no idea where it is myself.

He nods. "North. Not far."

"Go on," I say to Gerard.

"I've been able to triangulate the signal to within about fifty yards. I checked out the property on one of our birds, and she's on a horse ranch. You got a pen?"

"Hold on." I think about the dust I saw on DialM's boots in my vision. It was dust from his ranch. I pat down my pockets and then look around until I find a pen and paper on a nearby desk. "Shoot." I take down the address. "This is fantastic, Gerard. You're a genius!"

"That, I know. Do you want some more good news?"

"Sure." The location of Ling was enough, but I'm certainly not going to complain about more leads.

"Jonathan's getting closer with the Web server location. And that should mean the bunker location."

"Thanks, Gerard. Call me when you've got something new."

I hang up and fill Darren in on the details. I go back upstairs to put in place all the arrangements for the bust, while Darren covers our original plan and checks in with the San Fran IT guys. I also get Dusk on a background search of the property and its owner.

Twenty minutes later we meet up.

"Well?" Darren says. He's got a cheeky smile on his face, like he's holding a royal flush against my pair of nines.

"What?"

He shrugs. "How'd it go?"

"I've got the warrant, and the SWAT team is assembled and waiting downstairs. We should be able to make DialM's place in about an hour. You?"

He grins again.

"Spit it out!"

"Heath Jordan is AmericanPsycho."

"What?"

"Log records on his laptop indicate access to www.murderersclub.com using the ID of AmericanPsycho, and the computer also has that Roke Manor software installed. We've got the president."

I give him a hard punch in the arm. "You bastard. I bet you've known that for nearly all of the last twenty minutes."

"Pretty much. I was waiting for the right time to tell you."

I shake my head, but I can't help grinning. "We've got the president." But even as I say it, I feel uncertain. Could it be this easy? Could we really have the mastermind behind bars?

"What's wrong?"

"Nothing." I shake the feeling away. Evidence doesn't lie—we've got Psycho. And soon we'll have DialM. I look at my watch. "That leaves us with only NeverCaught to find, and getting the girls out of the bunker." I turn around and we make our way to Dusk's desk. "How'd you do?" I ask Dusk.

"A title search found the owner—one Victor Petrov. I've looked him up on the system. No criminal record, but we do have some info on him." Dusk shuffles some papers. "Russian heritage but born here. He's semiretired. He used to train racehorses and now he uses his fifty-acre property as a small breeding ranch. He's also extremely wealthy according to his IRS records."

"A prerequisite of the club," Darren says.

* * *

A couple of miles before the turnoff to Petrov's ranch, the SWAT van and the Bureau contingent pull in. The SWAT team is led by Rhode, a young man who looks like a stereotypical marine. Dusk, Darren and I join Rhode and his men inside the van for the final review of the plans. I've given Rhode the lead on the bust—he's certainly more prepared for this kind of a takedown than I am.

"Okay. Our latest satellite picture confirms two heat signatures. This one is weaker." He points to the map. "And we're assuming this is our hostage. She's in the barn, possibly underground, which would account for the lower heat-source reading."

The other option is that Ling is ill, maybe dying, but to my relief he doesn't even mention that possibility.

"She's being held in a barn. Here." Rhode points to an aerial photograph of the ranch house and surrounding buildings. "I've just had confirmation that the other heat signature is still in the main house. Here." He points to the front of the ranch house. "So, our plan remains the same. Anderson, Dusk and Carter will drive up to the house and distract the suspect, while we come into the property from this back road here." He runs his finger along a line on the photograph, a dirt road. "We'll go straight for the barn and the hostage, and on our signal you—" he nods his head in our direction "—can make the formal arrest."

While the SWAT team is decked out in their usual gear, Carter, Dusk and I wear casual clothes with vests underneath. This way, Petrov will have no warning that a team is taking over his property. If we really do have the president behind bars, there's no way he could have warned DialM or any of the other members. He wouldn't have had time before our grand entrance. Which means as far as DialM and NeverCaught are concerned, the game is still on.

"Okay, let's go." Rhode rolls up the maps and photos and gets back into the front of the van. We pull away and they stay put to give us a couple of minutes' lead.

Five minutes later Dusk, Carter and I are turning into the dirt driveway of Petrov's property. The place is well kept, with high wooden fences splitting the front area into several large paddocks. A statuesque black horse with a small white patch on its nose watches our approach and then starts running next to the car, stopping only when the paddock ends.

The driveway takes a sharp left and snakes its way up to the house. The residence is quite simple, especially considering Petrov's earnings for the past twenty years. The wooden house looks like it's been recently painted, and a wide veranda extends across the front and the left-hand side. A wind chime hangs over the two steps up to the veranda and sways in the breeze. It's the perfect image of a peaceful ranch. Before we bring the car to a halt, a man steps outside onto the veranda.

It's the man from my vision and as soon as I see him my body reacts, my heart racing and anger swelling inside of me. A slim build, Petrov wears black pants and a long-sleeved shirt, and it strikes me as rather dressed up for sitting around watching television or whatever else he was doing inside. Just like in my vision and on the sketch Powers and Jonathan drafted, he wears small, wire-framed glasses. We pull the car to a stop and approach him.

"Can I help you?" His voice is friendly, welcoming, and, like Heath, he shows no sign of concern or guilt. I wonder if my FBI badge will change that.

I go through the practiced routine of showing my credentials and announcing myself as FBI, keeping my voice flat and neutral. He doesn't seem surprised or perturbed by our presence.

"So, in what way can I service the Bureau?" He smiles.

I pull the warrant out of my pocket. "We have a search warrant. For your house and all the associated buildings."

"What?" Now he seems surprised, but still not concerned. "What for?"

"We have evidence that indicates you've been holding an Australian woman by the name of Ling Gianolo hostage."

"What?" he repeats, then he laughs slightly. "Why, that's preposterous!"

"Really?" With one hand behind my back to hide a clenched fist, I move toward the house. "If you'd like to step inside, Mr. Petrov."

"Certainly, anything I can do to help you, or this poor young woman." He looks around, showing me the first chink in his armor. "What did you say her name was?" He forces a casual tone into his voice.

He's trying my patience. "Ling."

"Yes, Ling."

"If you'd like to help, you can show us to your computer."

"I'm afraid I'm not very computer literate. I did purchase a laptop recently, but I think I may have broken it." He shakes his head. "Like I said, I'm not into computers at all."

"Do you like movies, Mr. Petrov?"

"That's a curious question, my dear."

"It's Agent Anderson, Mr. Petrov. The question relates to this investigation, and you know it."

"I'm sure I don't know what you're talking about, but in answer to your question, yes, I like some movies."

"How about an Alfred Hitchcock one called *Dial M for Murder?*"

"That's a classic. Of course I know the film." He smiles. "I'm glad you know of the original, not that remake. Especially given your youth."

I smile. "It's a good movie, but I quite like the Noir films that include a femme fatale." I widen my smile and keep eye contact, ready to observe his reaction. "Where the woman is a bit of a Black Widow." I pause. "You've heard of the spider, yes?"

He keeps the smile plastered on his face, but I can tell it takes more effort now. "Yes, I know of the spider." He retreats into the house and we follow.

Inside, the place is pristine and old-fashioned. The walls are painted white, with photographs of horses scattered around the place and the furniture looks mostly antique, old-world English. He takes us through to a back room and unlocks the top drawer of a large wooden desk. He pulls out the laptop, but as he hands it to us, a small stream of smoke comes from the back of it. We back away from the hissing sound.

"What the...?" Darren stares at the computer.

Petrov smiles, a more genuine smile now. "Like I said, I think I broke it."

Booby trapped it is more like. Heath must have installed a fail-safe on the computer, something Petrov triggered—maybe a button somewhere? The good news is Petrov is definitely surprised to see us, which means Heath didn't have time to log on and warn him.

"It doesn't matter," I say. "Our computer forensics team will still be able to read the hard drive." I don't know if I'm bluffing or not, but either way I don't like the look on Petrov's face. By now his feathers should be more ruffled. Unless he has a plan...at the moment he thinks he's only against the three of us. He doesn't know that the SWAT team is currently searching the barn, presumably about to discover and rescue Ling. Once they've got Ling out, we can formally arrest Petrov for her abduction.

I focus on Petrov again, not Ling. What would I do if I were him? I put myself in the perp's shoes, just like I do whenever I draft a profile.

Petrov moves toward his desk and I bring my right hand closer to my gun. I know what I'd do if I thought I was facing three people who knew way too much.

I decide it's time to let him know that we're not alone. "Mr. Petrov, we've—"

But it's too late. In one swift movement he lunges and reaches into his desk. Everything goes into slow motion.

Petrov pulls a gun out, but my hand is already close to my Smith & Wesson. I pull it out of the holster.

Darren and Dusk are both pulling out their weapons, but Petrov's got the jump on them. He aims his gun at me, the person who can take a shot at him now, right now.

"Stop!" I cry. But he's not going to stop.

The sights of my gun are lined up, aiming for his chest. I hesitate for a millisecond, wanting to somehow confirm that my instincts are right—that if I don't fire right now, he will. But there's no time—

I squeeze the trigger and drop down so I'm on bended knee, ready to take another shot.

My first bullet hits him in the chest, but not right in the heart. The bullet would have blown a lung, but probably isn't fatal.

His eyes widen from pain and shock and his gun lowers, but he doesn't drop it. He brings his weapon upward again...

Shit!

Now Dusk and Darren are both aiming their guns at Petrov. He must know he hasn't got a chance. If he'd got his shot off first, got me, then maybe he'd be able to shoot fast enough to get Darren and Dusk, but now he's got three guns trained on him.

It doesn't stop him. The gun keeps coming back up, and he readjusts his aim, targeting me again.

I start to squeeze the trigger, ready to release my second shot, when the gun to my right goes off—Darren.

It's almost as if I can see the bullet streaking its way across the room and toward Petrov's heart.

Bingo. Petrov drops the gun and falls to his knees. He hangs in limbo for a second and then falls forward. His eyes are still wide open and he stares past us to the door.

I hear footsteps, running, and I swing around. Two SWAT team members enter the room, guns held high, ready to take a shot.

Darren and I look at each other in shock, and relief. We're the ones standing and Petrov's the one on the floor.

Dusk knocks the gun away from Petrov so it's no longer within his reach and the SWAT guys lower their weapons.

"The girl?" I look at the SWAT guys, hoping one of them will have an answer for me.

"Rhode sent us up here as soon as we heard the shot. The team was just about to enter the barn."

I run...past the SWAT guys, out the front door, down the veranda steps, and then do the three-hundred-feet dash to the barn. I push the door open and seven guns swing around in my direction.

"Sorry." It sounds lame; I should know better than to run into an area the SWAT's in charge of, but now all I can think of is Ling. Maybe if we've saved her, if we've got here in time, it will make up for me failing Brigitte and the others.

The guns go back to their original position, covering the entire barn even though heat signatures indicated only one person in this area. You can never be too sure.

Rhode gives me a look, and then drops to his knees. He uses one hand to clear away dirt from a trapdoor. I move in closer. Ling's down there.

Rhode motions to his nearest team member and nods at the door. The guy raises his rifle and points it at the trapdoor. Rhode lies on his stomach and slowly, gently opens it a couple of inches. He's checking for booby traps, but my guess is the door is safe. Petrov never thought it would come to this, never thought he'd be suspected, let alone caught.

My patience wears thin in the next few minutes, as Rhode checks the trapdoor from every angle, and even looks around it for trip wires. I consider telling him that Petrov isn't the type to set up a trip wire, but I hold my tongue out of respect for Rhode and what he does. This is his specialty and I wouldn't like anyone telling me how to profile, so why should I tell him how to secure a room?

Eventually, Rhode is satisfied and pulls the trapdoor all the way open, while his SWAT team continues to cover the barn. I move closer, keeping my gun drawn, just in case.

The trapdoor leads to a steep wooden staircase. Rhode goes down the stairs, gun first, hunched over so he doesn't hit his head. One other SWAT guy follows him, and I'm hot on their heels. I can barely see past the bulk of the two heavyset men, but within a few steps Ling comes into view. She's cowering in the corner of the old-style bed, her hands covering her face. She's heard us on the stairs and assumed it's him. God knows what he's done to her.

"Ling," I say, knowing a female voice will reassure her.

She instantly looks up and her crumpled face relaxes ever so slightly. Her shoulders drop, but she can't manage a smile—I don't blame her. She moves toward us, but is restricted by the chains. Even this doesn't dampen her obvious relief. Two men with guns and a woman.

"I'm FBI, Ling. Is this room safe for us as far as you know?" Safe... what a bad word to choose on my part. It certainly hasn't been safe for her.

Ling seems confused by the question.

"Did Petrov booby trap the room?"

She shakes her head but points up the stairs, and directly above my head. I look up warily—the Webcam.

Shit! How did I forget about the video stream? I see a switch and flick it. There's only one member of the club who could be watching, NeverCaught, and now we've announced our presence to him.

35

We load Ling into the ambulance and as soon as the doors shut I call Gerard, just like I promised I would.

"Gerard, it's Anderson."

"Yes?"

"We got her. She's okay."

His voice relaxes. "That's awesome news."

I can hear Jonathan's voice in the background.

"Yes," Gerard says, obviously not to me. He tells me to hang on and I listen as he tells Jonathan that Ling is okay. No doubt Jonathan will be as relieved as Ling was when I told her Jonathan was safe. That he'd escaped.

"Sorry, back again now."

"Any tech news from your end?" I ask.

"We found the Web server. I tried to call you about half an hour ago, but your phone was off. I was right, someone has been moving the Web server. But it's stopped and I've tracked it down."

"That's fantastic."

"Kind of. They're using a server in the University of California."

"What? How the hell is the university involved?"

"Hold on," Gerard says. "It doesn't work like that. Lots of hackers get into a network and use computer storage space. They hide their hacks or special programs there in case they ever get caught. Then there's not much evidence on their computer, because it's all sitting on a server—and only they know where."

"Oh…clever."

"Hackers *are* clever. Anyway, the college server will be calling the video feeds, so now I'll be able to trace the IP addresses of the Webcams pretty easily."

"How easily?"

Gerard gets my drift. "Give me a couple of hours."

"That's what I like to hear. And what about NeverCaught?"

"Hold on a sec."

I can hear Gerard's fingers tapping furiously on a keyboard. After less than a minute the sound stops.

"He's not online now. Last log-on time was about fifteen minutes ago."

"Shit!"

"What?"

"He saw us online. He saw the SWAT team rescuing Ling."

"So he'll be covering his tracks. If he knows how to."

"I think Petrov's laptop was booby trapped because when he passed it to us the whole thing smoked and fizzed."

"He burnt the hard drive." Gerard pauses. "We might still be able to recover something from it," he says, but he doesn't sound too hopeful.

"It doesn't matter for Petrov. He's dead."

"Oh…oh." He pulls himself together. "No loss, right?"

Gerard isn't used to dealing with death. He's more used to credit-card scams, identity theft and online porn. This is different. It's probably the first case he's worked on where anyone's died.

I reassure him. "The world's better off." It's harsh, but true. "DialM, Petrov, was in his fifties… God knows how many lives he's taken." I never like death, regardless of the circumstances, but at the moment my biggest regret is that we can't question him.

I let the words sink in for a few seconds before continuing. "So, how are we going to find NeverCaught? I can't tell you how much I want to catch this bastard."

"Me, too. Me, too." He sighs. "If he saw you guys, he's not going to log on again. Chances are, he's destroyed his computer already—"

"And he's probably destroying any other evidence as we speak."

"Guess so." Gerard doesn't deal with other evidence, so his focus is on the computer forensics. "Do you think he'll go after the women in the bunker?"

"No. Brooke doesn't know where the bunker is and I'm betting NeverCaught doesn't either. It was the president who was pulling all the strings. And we've got him."

"Good. Good."

"So, how can we find NeverCaught?"

"I might be able to trace back his IP address from the Web server, but I get the feeling Heath will have thought of that."

"Okay."

"There's something else, too."

"Yes?"

"Clair Kelly's father is here."

"Oh."

"He's been hounding me for your number for the last half hour."

"Give it to him. At least I've got some good news for him."

"It's not his daughter you've found."

"No. But *his* daughter is better off than Ling. At the moment Clair just thinks she's part of a reality TV show. She hasn't been tortured for over a week like Ling."

"No. I guess you're right."

I sigh, trying not to think too much about what Ling's been through. I have to remind myself that we worked as quickly as we could. Another few hours and her parents will be here, helping her through this in whatever way they can. "Listen, call me when you get something new. Carter and I will stay in San Fran for the moment. Until we find out exactly where this bunker is in the Mojave. Who knows, maybe we'll have some luck with Heath," I say, even though I don't believe it.

"Okay. I'll be in touch."

I hang up and hop in the car with Darren and Dusk. Rhode's staying until the coroner and forensics arrive, while we head back to the San Francisco FBI field office.

I get less than five minutes to myself before the phone rings. I take a deep breath, preparing myself for an anxious parent, who also happens to be an ex-cop. Great.

"Agent Anderson speaking."

"Agent Anderson, it's Will Kelly here, Clair Kelly's father."

"Yes, Mr. Kelly, Agent Gerard told me you'd be calling."

"So, where are we at?" He delivers the line easily—he's said those words many times before and phrases the question more like a colleague than a victim's father. It could be intentional in an attempt to catch me off guard, or it's possible the cop in him never went away.

"The case is going very well, Mr. Kelly. We've just—" I search for a word other than killed "—*intercepted* one of the suspects and rescued a young girl."

"The girl alive?" This time I hear emotion in his voice.

"Yes. She'll be okay." Physically at least.

"And Clair? Do you know where she is? Where she's being held?"

"No, not yet."

"So you'll question this latest suspect?"

I pause. "No. He's dead."

"Oh."

Being in the law-enforcement business I know Mr. Kelly is experiencing two contradictory emotions. Firstly he's happy that a monster has been erased, literally, but he's also aware that dead men can't talk.

"We have other suspects in custody and we've got leads on the location of where your daughter is being held." I don't tell him that Gerard is working on those leads, that he holds the key to his daughter's location. I know Gerard will work better without someone breathing down his neck. Besides, it's easier for me to keep Mr. Kelly at bay long distance than it would be for someone who's in the same town.

"What leads?" Mr. Kelly presses.

"I'm afraid I can't discuss that. You know how it is, Mr. Kelly."

He's silent for a few seconds. "Mmm, maybe I know how it is, but I don't like it."

"And I don't blame you, sir."

Silence again. An impasse.

"So Clair is being held captive somewhere in the Mojave Desert?"

He knows the answer, but he's going through the facts again out aloud. Maybe in the hope that I'll give him extra information, or maybe just to let it sink in.

"Yes. She and one other woman are being held in an underground bunker. But Mr. Kelly, I must stress, they do not realize they're even in danger. As far as they're concerned, they're part of a reality TV show. To date, your daughter has not been hurt in any way." I don't mention some of the cruel challenges Jonathan told us about. Better to dwell on the positive—Clair's alive and is not aware of what's really going on. In this case the saying "ignorance is bliss" is certainly true. I know Malcolm's parents would do anything to trade places with Mr. Kelly. Even Cindy's neglectful parents would prefer it if their daughter was still alive.

I continue. "I know it's probably not much comfort to you—"

"It is. It is, but…"

"I know, Mr. Kelly. You want us to find her."

"Yes."

"There are four perps in this case, Mr. Kelly. One's dead, we've got two in custody and the fourth is probably unaware of the location of the bunker. We will find your daughter."

"Thank you, Agent Anderson. I appreciate your candor. I'll be staying in Tucson for the moment."

"Of course, Mr. Kelly. As Agent Gerard told you, I'm in San

Francisco, but feel free to call me anytime. And I will, of course, call you as soon as we have word on your daughter."

"Okay. Thanks." He says the right words but I know he doesn't feel any sense of resolution.

For the rest of the drive I think about our plan of action—or lack thereof. Brooke's a dead end; Petrov is dead; NeverCaught is on hold; and Heath seems intent on keeping his mouth shut.

When we get back to the San Francisco field office at 7:00 p.m., I'm surprised to find Justin Reid waiting for me by the security desk in the foyer. I tell the others to go on up while I talk to him.

I take his outstretched hand and shake it. "What can I do for you, Mr. Reid?"

"I'd like to see Heath."

I don't respond verbally but my look says it all—you can't always get what you want.

"I want to help, Agent Anderson. I know Heath can be stubborn. But he knows me, he trusts me. Maybe I can help you."

"So you believe us now? Believe that he's involved in multiple murders?"

He's silent at first, and then he shakes his head and leans on the desk behind him. "I don't know what to think. I just…I can't imagine Heath hurting anyone, letting alone killing someone. This doesn't feel real."

I study Reid for a moment. He's a smooth operator and an incredibly successful businessman—he lives in a world so different than mine. A world where the news that one of your employees is a killer *is* totally surreal.

"I understand." I look at Reid, deciding whether to grant him his wish. I'm left with one overriding thought—I want to catch Never, and if Reid can help me… "Okay, Mr. Reid. I'll let you see him. We will, of course, be monitoring your conversation."

"Of course."

I organize a visitor's badge for him and we wait for the elevator.

"Tell me about yourself, Agent Anderson." He leans against the wall and looks intently at me.

"Excuse me?" Reid's small talk is inappropriate, more like a pick-up attempt.

"I'm just curious about what brings an Australian to the U.S." There's no hint of coyness or embarrassment in his voice—he's a man who's used to getting what he wants.

I roll my eyes in my imagination. Like I haven't heard that before. Still, I guess it's better than him pumping me for information about the case. I will have to give him some details if he's going to get Heath to talk, but I'm happy to postpone that tricky subject.

"I came out for this job. To work as a profiler in the FBI."

"Admirable."

"It's good work."

"Serve, protect, uphold the peace."

"What about you, Mr. Reid. What drives you?" I keep my voice polite and open.

He shrugs. "Recognition, I guess."

I'm thrown by his honesty.

He laughs. "Surprised? Well, it's the truth. Given you're an FBI agent, thought I better tell the truth, the whole truth and nothing but the truth." He holds his hand up in a mock oath.

I smile, immediately relaxing. "You better watch it, I'm a trained psychologist and if you're not careful I'll be asking you what happened in your childhood to make you crave recognition."

The elevator arrives and we both hop in.

"You've certainly got recognition now."

He nods slowly. "Yes."

I get the feeling it's not enough for him. It's the same for all ambitious people—you set a goal, reach it, and then set your next goal, forever raising the bar. And that's how Justin Reid has got where he is today.

"You must be extremely happy with SysTech." Who wouldn't be?

The market share for the NetSecure product alone would be enormous. He's the Google of software security.

"We've done well. The company's done well."

He's a complex creature. At times his arrogance is overwhelming, but now I've given him the opportunity to stroke his ego and he's backing away.

He looks past me and stares blankly at the doors before focusing on me again. "So, Heath. What do you want me to say to him? I don't even know anything about what you think is happening. What you think he's part of?"

I notice *think*—he still can't accept Heath's crimes, but I'm not going to debate his word choice. "I'm afraid he's more than part of it." I sigh. "Heath is the president of an online club. The club has been holding several people hostage and killing them off, one by one."

Reid's jaw drops. It's nearly a minute before he speaks. "Heath?"

"Yes. He's been positively IDed by one of the victims."

"Someone escaped? What a relief."

"Yes. A young man was taken by a female killer, but he escaped."

"A female killer? That's unusual isn't it?"

"Very."

"And you've got this woman too? This female murderer?"

"Yes. There's one suspect still at large and we'd like Heath's help finding him."

"I see. Did any of the other victims survive?"

"We believe there are still two alive. We'll have their location shortly."

"Congratulations, Agent Anderson. You've caught your man."

I smile. I hadn't thought about it much—too focused on getting the two women out of the bunker and finding NeverCaught. Reid's right though, we've done well. "Yes. But I want the fourth member."

"I admire you. Ambition and perfectionism…it's a good combination."

Back to the hint of flirtation.

"Thank you," I say.

The doors open and we make our way through the corridors to the interview room.

"So, you want me to convince Heath to give up this fourth member. You don't know anything about him?"

"Only his online username...NeverCaught."

"Never caught." He shrugs. "I'll certainly give it a shot."

When we reach the observation area that adjoins Heath's interview room, I fill Darren and Dusk in on Reid's presence.

Reid looks at Heath through the glass. "Is he okay?" I hear concern in his voice.

"He's fine," Darren says. "We've even given him a cup of coffee." He points to the empty cup on the table in front of Heath.

Reid doesn't smile. "I may as well go in."

"Do you want someone to go in with you?" I ask quietly.

"For my protection?" He shakes his head. "No, I don't need that."

I show Reid through to the entrance, but I stay out of Heath's line of sight. I scamper back to the observation room to listen.

"You know who you're dealing with there?" Dusk asks me.

"Sure, respected businessman, owner of a big software company...that provides important software to the Bureau. Don't worry, I'm being polite." I tune into the conversation on the other side of the wall.

"Heath, how are they treating you?"

Heath stands up and even though the pair doesn't touch, I get an instant feel for how close they are.

"Fine, Justin, fine."

They both sit down and are silent for a few moments.

Dusk looks at me. "You might want to stay in his good books. He's the most respected and powerful businessman in this community. I sure as hell wouldn't want to get him pissed."

"I'll keep that in mind," I say.

Dusk chuckles. "Not to mention *Cosmopolitan's* most eligible bachelor five years running."

"Really?"

"Bet that got him notches on the headboard," Dusk says.

"I bet." I observe Reid through the glass.

"I've called Harry Strongson," Reid says to Heath. "He'll be here soon."

"Thanks."

Darren looks at me. "Know who Strongson is?"

I shrug. "No."

Dusk's voice is grim. "He's only the best criminal lawyer in the city." He shakes his head. "If Reid's going to foot the bill, he certainly must believe the guy's innocent. Reid's got his reputation and that of his company to protect."

I shrug. "I guess money's no problem for him."

"Nor for Heath. Reid pays him $200,000 a year and the bank statements the team found at his house are impressive in terms of his savings."

"He is the president of the club," I say. "It's an elite group."

We focus on the interview room again.

Reid's talking. "I...I don't know what to think, Heath. The FBI are saying terrible things about you. You've been charged with accessory to attempted murder."

"Yes, I know."

"And they've got evidence that you're part of some online club of killers."

"They told me that too."

"So you know the position you're in?"

Heath nods.

"If you know something, Heath, you should tell them. There are two people who can be saved, and one killer, someone who uses the pseudonym NeverCaught, is still at large. I'm sure the police and FBI would appreciate any information you have."

Heath crosses his arms across his bulky chest. "I'm not saying *anything*. I don't know anything."

I shake my head. It's the same line he's been giving us.

Reid tries again. "Come on, Heath. This is your life, your future.

Helping them now will make it easier for you. Maybe reduce your sentence."

Heath doesn't respond.

Reid spends the next five minutes pleading with Heath to come clean if he's involved, to say something, but Heath does not break his silence.

"It's useless," I say. "I may as well get him out."

When I open the door to the interview room, Reid looks up at me. "I'm sorry." He holds his hands upward.

"Thank you for coming down, Mr. Reid." I hold the door open and he stands up. He holds his hand out to Heath, who shakes it with a smile, before Reid leaves the room.

As soon as I shut the door he turns around. "I'm really sorry, Agent Anderson. I was hoping he'd say *something*. But Heath can be a stubborn man."

"Yes, I can see that." I walk Reid to the elevator. "So, you've organized for Strongson to represent Heath?"

"Yes. That's right." When we reach the lifts Reid doesn't push the down button. "Look Agent Anderson, I know you think Heath is guilty, but I still think you've got the wrong man. I want justice served, but I'm going to support Heath."

I sigh. "You've got to do what you think is right." There's no point arguing with Reid. At some stage, when we've got all the evidence together, he'll realize that Heath is guilty. Then perhaps he'll change his tune. But I won't waste my energy on him now. "Thanks again for trying, Mr. Reid." I push the down button for him.

He nods and we stand in awkward silence.

A wave of dizziness threatens to overcome me. It could be the lack of sleep, but it's also a symptom I often get right before a premonition or vision. I fight it off, closing my mind. The last thing I want to do is collapse in a heap in front of Reid.

"Are you okay?" Reid touches my elbow but I pull away instantly.

"I'm fine." My repression is successful and the dizziness stops. Finally the elevator arrives.

"Goodbye, Agent Anderson." Reid extends his hand and I shake it. He moves into the lift. "Maybe next time we meet it will be under more pleasant circumstances." The flirtatiousness returns, accompanied by a grin.

I smile. "Maybe," I say, even though I'm convinced the next time I see Reid will be in the courtroom when I give evidence against his favorite employee.

36

Gerard's estimate of a couple of hours turned into three hours, but we're not complaining, not now that we have the location of the bunker. He managed to trace the cameras to a remote part of the Mojave in California, about forty miles west of Barstow, between the 15 and the 40. We then used the nearest satellite to pinpoint the exact location by scanning the one-square-mile Gerard had given us. It took us another half an hour to find two faint heat signatures—the two women are alive. It would have been faster if the bunker wasn't buried so deep underground, if we didn't have to scan each square foot so carefully, looking for even the slightest blob of heat and ruling out local animals. About three miles west of the heat signatures, we found the structure Jonathan described, the control room for the whole operation. Now we have detailed satellite photos of that too.

Gerard has moved his attention to tracking NeverCaught, while we organize the rescue from San Francisco. We set the operation's take-off for 5:00 a.m., giving us time to get a few hours' sleep. It'll also give us the daylight needed to carry out the bust. We have two bomb squads and two SWAT teams ready to accompany Darren, Dusk and me to the bunker. I've prepared for the worst—thinking about the computer fail-safes and what might be waiting for us in the Mojave.

Five choppers in total, all Black Hawks, carry us toward the Mojave. It takes about three hours and one fuel stop to reach the specific GPS location of the control room. We continue on to the bunker's GPS, leaving one bomb squad and one SWAT team at the control room. For the moment, their instructions are to simply secure the area. Gerard has a full computer forensics team en route from FBI headquarters in DC, but they're about two hours behind us.

Our choppers set down about two hundred and fifty feet away from the coordinates. The SWAT team, bomb squad, Dusk, Darren and I all file out of the two large choppers and I use my GPS device to lead the teams to the exact location. Several of the SWAT members have metal detectors that they run over the desert floor, looking for the steel trapdoor. After about five minutes one of the metal detectors goes off, and we soon discover the doorway to the bunker.

The bomb-squad leader, McCoy, ushers us away while they check the metal. Eventually, satisfied it's safe, they enter the code Jonathan gave us, but it doesn't work.

McCoy looks up. "That's okay. We can get around it."

McCoy and his men work on the door, while the rest of us look at the barren land surrounding us and feel pretty useless. The sun already has a kick to it and the desert landscape seems to make the sun's rays even brighter, so it feels more like midday than nine o'clock in the morning.

It only takes the guys ten minutes to open the metal door, but it's an hour after that when McCoy emerges from the desert floor. The bomb squad has been in the belly of the desert, doing its thing while we restlessly soaked up the rays.

McCoy walks toward me, his face a stone mask.

"Well?" I ask, as soon as he's close enough.

"We've worked our way down the levels to the last door." He wipes sweat off his brow. "The place is wired all right. We've found five charges so far."

"Shit." I think about Susie and Clair—there must be some way to get them out without setting off the bombs.

McCoy holds up his hand. "It's not as bad as it sounds. There are no trip wires and the charges are on radio control. You've got the person who set this up?"

He needs confirmation that no one's going to be hitting that radio control button.

"Yes," I say, now more confident of the capture. Even though I was cautious about admitting we had the president, the digital evidence proves that Heath is AmericanPsycho, and we know from Brooke that AmericanPsycho's the president. On top of that, the president would have blown this place, and the evidence, if he could have.

McCoy gives me a short, sharp nod. "Then we're ready to go through the final door and get them out. You can come down now."

"Great. Let's go."

I walk with him back the few feet to the door but we're stopped in our tracks by an almighty bang. I instinctively look in the direction of the control room and sure enough a blaze of red can be seen on the horizon. Everyone looks uncertainly at each other, thinking about the teams over there. What went wrong? Are they okay?

"Sir!" One of the bomb-squad specialists pops his head out of the trapdoor. "We've been triggered."

What the...? The radio trigger? How can it have been triggered? Could NeverCaught have access too?

We run to the trapdoor. "How long have we got?" McCoy asks.

"Three minutes."

"What do you want to do?" He looks at me.

It's my call—do I risk the lives of our team to save the two women? Can we make it in time?

I hesitate, but only for a second. I don't have time to mull the decision over. "We've got to get them out."

"Swanston, open that door, now!" says McCoy into his comms device.

The SWAT leader is right behind me, signaling to his team. But we don't need SWAT and I'm not willing to risk their lives too. I turn to him. "Keep your men up here, and get some distance between you and the area." The SWAT leader breathes in, ready to protest, but realizes there's no time for discussion. I look at Darren and Dusk. "You guys too."

Darren smiles. "Not on your life."

I shake my head, but there's no time to argue. I throw myself through the trapdoor feet first, and slide down the outside of the ladder. Darren and McCoy are hot on my heels.

We move quickly down the next ladder and get to a long corridor. It's the corridor from my dreams. As we pass the rest of the bomb-squad members, who are scattered at various points along the tunnel, we send them up to the surface. The fewer people down here the better.

We sprint toward the end and we're about halfway down the last corridor when we see two of the bomb-squad members coming toward us with two very confused women in tow. The bomb guys are literally dragging them along, and Susie and Clair are scared—but not of bombs, of the men who are trying to save their lives.

"It must be part of the show," Susie says, but there's uncertainty in her voice.

"Stop it, you're hurting me," Clair says.

Jesus Christ. If only they knew. I run down toward them.

Susie tries to plant herself firmly on the ground. "I'm not going with you. Who the hell are you anyway?"

"We told you, San Francisco Bomb Squad, now move it." The guy holding Susie tries to pull her harder, his patience wearing thin. He knows what's about to happen if we don't hightail it to the surface.

I reach them and grab Susie's other arm. "Susie, I'm FBI, we've been working with Jonathan to try to find you."

"What? Working with Jonathan?" She's moving, but only just.

Clair turns back. "Jonathan?"

"You have to move!" yells one of the bomb squad members. But his words have the opposite effect, and now Clair begins to struggle more, too.

McCoy pushes us all past him and now we're all heading back toward the surface. "Pick 'em up!" he yells. "We've got one and a half minutes before this place blows."

His team members follow the order and sling Susie and Clair over their shoulders in the fireman's lift. Surprisingly, it does seem to speed us up.

We reach the first ladder. "Susie and Clair, you have to run. Up the ladder," I say, knowing that the fireman's lift will be too awkward for the ladder. "Trust us, please."

Clair's guy reaches the ladder first and pushes her up. Finally the urgency of our voices and our official appearance seem to be sinking in and Clair moves quickly up the ladder. Darren goes up next, but while Clair and her guy are moving up to the second ladder, Darren stays in the middle section and helps to haul everyone up. Again, I'm surprised by the strength in his wiry frame as his hand clasps my left wrist and he heaves me upward. I'm followed by Susie and McCoy.

"Come on, Susie," I yell.

She seems to speed up somewhat but not as much as we'd like. We both realize that this one woman may cost us all our lives.

"Go!" Darren says to me.

I look at him but shake my head. "Not on your life."

He reaches down and grabs Susie's arm, which is now within reach. I hold Susie back and let McCoy and the other bomb squad team member pass us. They make quick work of the final ladder.

"How long?" I yell.

McCoy keeps climbing, but calls back over his shoulder. "Fifteen seconds."

Darren manages to push me up the ladder first, then Susie, then himself. I move much faster than Susie and I'm at the top and out while she's only two-thirds of the way up. "Come on, Susie," I plead, thinking about Darren trapped below her.

I look past Susie to Darren. He seems resigned to the fact that he's not going to make it. "Come on, Darren."

He comes out of his stupor and starts pushing Susie with his left hand, while holding on with his right.

"Move, Susie, move!" I yell.

On the surface, the others have run in the opposite direction to the underground corridors, getting away from any blast sites that might be underneath and cause a cave in.

"Go!" Darren yells at me from behind Susie.

I ignore him and stay put.

Susie's only got a few rungs to go when the ground shakes. She releases the rungs but Darren, who's literally right up her ass, manages to support her weight. She grasps onto the ladder again and pulls herself up the final rungs. She throws herself on the desert floor and while Darren takes the last few steps out of the trapdoor I manage to pull her up to her feet and drag her toward the others.

The ground shifts again as another charge goes off. The blasts are getting closer to us. We keep running, listening to each pop and feeling the ground shudder as the sequence continues.

Finally, six explosions later, we're standing with the others, all safe. Hopefully the team at the control room shares our fate.

Susie and Clair are different shades of white-gray, still not sure what's going on.

"Goddamn it!" Susie yells. "How can we keep doing the show now that the bunker's gone?"

37

The SWAT team leader comes up to me, one of our SAT-phones in his hand. "I just heard from the other team. Everyone from the SWAT is okay, but…" he pauses and looks at McCoy "…we lost some of the bomb-squad members."

"Shit." McCoy rests his hands on his thighs and shakes his head.

"How many?" I ask, my voice threatening to crack.

"Four dead and three injured. At least that's what they think. It sounds messy over there."

Four? That takes the toll of this sick game to nine—Malcolm, Cindy, Janice, Brigitte, Danny—whose body still hasn't been found—and now four of ours. The fucking bastards.

"What happened?" I ask, balling my hands into fists and hitting them off my legs.

"They think there must have been a trip wire, and when they set that off, it triggered the timer here."

I nod, barely absorbing the information. Four people I led into this rescue mission are dead. Our evidence is blown—literally—and we've still got one member of the Murderers' Club at large, doing God knows what.

"Sophie?" Darren puts his hand on my elbow.

Clair pulls away from the others and looks directly at me. "What's going on?" Her father's a cop, she's not as naive as Susie.

I guess now's as good a time as any to tell them what's really been going on.

I look at the SWAT leader. "Tell them to head to the nearest hospital. I want the injured attended to. I'll organize forensics."

"I'll wait for forensics," Dusk says.

I nod my thanks and turn back to Clair. I walk toward Susie and Clair follows. I feel like I should tell them to sit down, give them a shot of whisky or something, but we're in the middle of the desert. There can be no props for the telling of this story.

I look at them in turn. "Susie, Clair."

They look expectantly at me.

I take a deep breath. "This is not a reality TV show."

"What?" Susie blurts, while Clair looks puzzled.

"But...I don't understand." Clair's voice is uncertain as she tries to piece together the events of the last ten minutes. She's just been saved by a SWAT team and a bomb squad. She's probably overheard us talking about people dying. Perhaps the penny is dropping, perhaps it's starting to hit her that the bunker was something sinister.

"This was all a setup," I say.

Susie brushes some hair off her face. "Like a *Punk'd* type of thing?"

"No. Not like that at all." Where do I start? "I'm Special Agent Sophie Anderson. I work for the FBI as a criminal profiler."

"Criminal?" Clair is, once again, picking up the right words.

"Yes. I profile killers, mostly serial killers." Here it comes... "And I'm afraid this was set up by a group of serial killers who call themselves the Murderers' Club."

Susie's hands fly up to her face. "What?" It's finally hit her. "What are you saying?"

"The others, except for Jonathan and Ling, are—" there's no easy way to say it "—dead."

"Dead?" Susie begins to shake. "But... How? And what about the audience?" She's still having difficulty absorbing the information and navigating through the repercussions.

"The only audience was the four club members. A woman, who killed Malcolm but failed in her attempt to kill Jonathan, and three men. One of the men is in custody, one is dead, and I'm afraid we still haven't caught the other one."

"The others...the other contestants...they're dead?" Clair suddenly has difficulty accepting the severity of the game's stakes.

I take her hands. "Yes."

"But not Ling? Not Jonathan?" she asks. Her voice when she say's Jonathan's name has more emotion in it, more desperation.

"Jonathan escaped. That's how we found out so much about this club. And Ling was being held captive by one of the club members, but we rescued her a few hours ago."

Clair sinks to the ground, collapsing into a cross-legged position. "Daddy always said people could be evil."

I purse my lips together, but resist the urge to say, "He was right." Instead, I grab a SAT-phone and dial Mr. Kelly's cell-phone number. I hand it to Clair. "Your dad wants to speak to you."

She looks up at me with wide eyes and takes the phone. "Daddy?...Yes, I'm okay." The tears start and she stands up and walks away from us for privacy.

Susie shakes her head. "So we weren't really on TV?"

"No. You were being watched, via a Web site, by the club members."

"And Chester?"

"His real name is Heath. And he's behind the whole thing. He's the president of the club."

"And Jonathan. Is he okay?" Susie asks. She rubs her hands up and down her forearms, almost clawing at her skin.

"He'll be okay."

"Was he..." Susie bites her lip "...was he hurt?"

"No. He managed to overpower his attacker. And he's been instrumental in helping us track you down."

Susie manages an ironic smile. "Thank God for Jonathan's conspiracy theories."

Clair comes back with the phone and hands it to me. "I...I don't know how to thank you. I don't know how we could be so stupid."

"You weren't stupid. It was a good scheme, a brilliant scheme. If it hadn't been for Jonathan..."

She tries for a smile but it's more of a wince. "And for you. Thank you."

I smile—this is the reason I'm in this work. To save women like Clair and Susie and to put men like Heath behind bars—preferably forever. But truth be told, I don't know how this would have gone down if Jonathan hadn't escaped. Would my visions have broken the case? Would we have found Brooke or DialM some other way? I'll never know.

We instinctively look up as the noise of a police chopper interrupts us. It lands and Jonathan runs out. He throws his arms around Susie and Clair.

After nearly a minute the three release their grip.

"I can't believe..." Susie starts.

"I know." Jonathan holds her hands. "They've told you about... about the others?"

Susie drops her head. "So it really is true."

I guess she needed to hear it from her best friend.

"Yes." Jonathan swallows hard. "They're all dead. We *were* the game."

I tear myself away from the reunion and focus on Gerard. "Any luck on NeverCaught?"

"No. He's gone. He hasn't been online and I can't track him through his IP address." Gerard puts his hand on my shoulder. "I'm sorry."

"It's not your fault. At least we got them." I look back at Susie, Clair and Jonathan.

He nods, but I can tell he still thinks he failed.

"Don't worry, Gerard, we'll get him."

He sighs. After a moment he asks, "Have you guys checked out the shack a few miles back?" He looks up and thumbs in a southerly direction.

"What shack? We flew in from the north."

"It's a small hut of some description."

It doesn't take us long to assemble a small team of Darren and I plus two bomb-squad members. Flying south in the police chopper, we spot the shack within a few minutes. As soon as we're out of the chopper, Darren and I draw our guns. This could be part of the Murderers' Club or it could be unrelated.

The two bomb-squad members complete their sweep on the sparse, hastily erected wooden structure. It looks new and the door is padlocked. Already I've got that sinking feeling that we're about to find something horrible. Who knows if it's logic, cop intuition or psychic knowledge. I decide it's probably logic when I see Darren's face—he's preparing himself for something too. Like me, while his gun is pointed at the ground, his grip is two-handed and I can tell he's ready to fire. We look at each other, but don't need to voice our concerns about what might be in the shack. Another booby trap?

Once we've got the all clear on the building's exterior, I put my gun's muzzle against the padlock and squeeze the trigger. The gun jumps from the recoil, but the lock is broken. I pop what is left of the padlock off the door frame. Again, I stand back and let the bomb squad check around the door. They give me the nod and I push the door open. It creaks and I open it slowly, holding my gun out in front of me. I take one step inside and my senses are immediately assaulted. I don't know which hits me first, the ungodly stench or the visual of a large pit. Even though it's dark, the smell tells me what's down there. I teeter on the edge, but Darren grabs my hand to stop me from falling into the mess. I peer into the darkness and my eyes adjust fully. Finally they can see what I know is there, and I'm staring at bodies, piled into the pit in a mass grave.

Darren's eyes adjust at the same time as mine. "Jesus," he says, peering over my shoulder.

Most of the bodies are partially mummified from the desert heat, but on top is a fresher corpse and it's this one that's the source of the smell. Bile rises in my throat, but I swallow the bitterness down.

I back away. "Shit!"

"What is it?" asks one of the bomb-squad techs.

"Bodies," I say. "More bloody bodies." I move away and can still smell decomposing flesh, the stench clinging to my nostrils. I take in a few deep breaths of fresh air, trying to get rid of the sensory memory.

"You okay?" Darren asks.

"I'm mad as hell is what I am." I force myself to put my gun away, even though all I can think about is killing whoever put those bodies in the ground. I take another deep breath, finally rid of the smell, and open my comms link. "We've got bodies over here."

It's Dusk who answers me. "What?"

"Looks like maybe eight or nine," I say, but I'll be damned if I'm going to take another look and confirm numbers. It's not that they're dead, nor is it the smell that really bothers, it's the fact that they've been thrown into a pit on top of one another, with such obvious disregard for human life. I know that shouldn't surprise me, I've seen bodies treated worse, but the image of them piled on top of one another is a visual I'll never forget.

Two days later I sit in one of the meeting rooms at the FBI's San Francisco field office, finalizing my last report before heading back to DC. The door opens and Darren strides into the room, a file in his hand. "We've got some IDs."

"And?"

"Danny Jensen was the most recent body in the pit. Bug activity puts his death at around ten days ago."

"That's in line with Jonathan's statement. Danny was taken a week before him."

"Yes."

"And the others?"

Darren opens the file under his arm. "We've got IDs on five of the eight victims. Four of them had a record and one was ex-army. All were truly down and outs." He sits down and passes me a photo of a man in his army uniform; he looks about twenty-five. "This is Corporal James Cook. Served in Iraq but was dishonorably discharged for misconduct. He had alcohol and drug problems and was broke, so he'd certainly hit rock bottom." Darren passes me another photo, this time of an older man, around forty, but it's a mug shot. "Richard Steiner, served time for armed robbery but was living on the streets for the past six months." Darren looks up at me. "You getting the picture?"

"Yeah. Easy targets, high-risk victims. The three we can't ID were probably homeless too, invisible in the system."

Darren nods. "But I know what they were doing there." A slight smile plays on his lips.

"What?"

"They built the place. We found Cook's prints on some of the debris from the control room."

"He could have been in on it. Or maybe these vics were some kind of test run."

Darren shakes his head. "I don't think so. Dusk just got off the phone to Steiner's parole officer and he said that the last time he saw Steiner was three months ago. Steiner told him it looked like he had a real job in construction and that he'd give him all the details in a day or two. But the parole officer never heard from him again. I mean, think about it, the place had to be built somehow and I can't imagine Brooke, or even Heath, out there swinging a hammer."

Darren's got a point, especially given Heath was the only member of the club who even knew where the bunker was.

Another part of the mystery solved. It certainly was a well-thought-out scheme.

38

Two weeks later

I sit at my desk back in DC and stare at the photos of the victims of the Murderers' Club. I'm supposed to be working on a profile of a serial rapist in Indianapolis but I keep drifting back to the case. I close my eyes but still see the victims. It's hard to forget. I remember the pit of bodies, the smell, as if I was still there. And the memory of Brigitte being dragged down the corridor by her hair, screaming, will never leave me either…another permanent reminder of the case. I shudder.

I focus on the positive, on the outcomes. We got almost all of them. Brooke's DNA matched the three early crime scenes in which DNA was found and with the evidence in front of her she finally confessed to all the murders over the past fifteen years, including her most recent victim, Malcolm. She'll probably get the death penalty, but one way or another she'll be in jail for the rest of her life. Hopefully that's enough justice and vengeance for the Jackson family.

DialM, Victor Petrov, is dead and out of the way for good. I knew it wasn't his first murder, and a thorough sweep of his property, including imaging of the ground, revealed bodies in the barn. Forensics started digging and found the remains of twenty young girls. They're still identifying the victims, and hopefully that will bring closure to their families. Sometimes it's better to know your loved one is dead, than to live in hope.

Then there's Heath, AmericanPsycho. Heath still isn't talking, but Brooke wanted her vengeance, too. She's signed a witness statement that AmericanPsycho was the mastermind of the whole thing, the president. She's also pinned Cindy's and Danny's murders on him. Her statement, coupled with the computer evidence that identifies Heath as AmericanPsycho, should be enough for a jury. No doubt his fancy, expensive lawyer will have a few tricks up his sleeve, but all we can do is wait for the trial and trust our evidence and the court system.

I'd like to be content with three out of four but it's not in my nature. I flick over to a photo of Brigitte. I'll get the bastard—one way or another.

AmericanPsycho has entered the room.
Killer4Ever: Hi, Psycho, long time no see.
AmericanPsycho: Yes, I've been busy.
Killer4Ever: Don't make me jealous. I'm still pissed I didn't get into your club.
AmericanPsycho: Sorry, Killer. Maybe next time.
Killer4Ever: So it's finished?
AmericanPsycho: Yes.
Killer4Ever: Fun?
AmericanPsycho: You've got no idea.
Killer4Ever: My name's definitely on the list for next time?
AmericanPsycho: Yes.

EPILOGUE

He looked at each of the photos and smiled, reliving each moment. Things hadn't played out exactly the way they were supposed to, but he'd still had his fun. Soon he'd destroy the photos—too much of a risk. But by then he'd have studied them enough that he could easily recall their faces, just like he could with all his victims.

What a world he lived in, a world where he could successfully lead a perfect double life. Not only was he able to fit into society, but he was revered by the business community, who were completely ignorant of his true nature. And that's what he got off on. He loved keeping such a deep, dark secret. Not ten minutes went by when he didn't think, even fleetingly, of murder. Past or future victims, methods, facial expressions, famous killers, famous victims. God, he loved it. He loved the power of his secret, loved knowing how vulnerable everyone really was.

It was a pity the game was over. A pity not all the victims had been killed—he'd been especially looking forward to Susie. She'd keep though.

He locked the photos away in his personal safe and took out the speech he'd prepared for the fund-raiser. He went over the main points. He enjoyed these functions. They either paid him or persuaded him to speak about himself—and who wouldn't want to talk about themselves to a captive audience for thirty minutes? But he couldn't concentrate on the speech.

He put the cue cards away and let himself think of the club. He'd had fun manipulating everyone—the contestants, the members of the club and, ultimately, the cops. That was the true challenge for him. How he'd enjoyed coming up with the appropriate calling cards for each murder—just enough to point the cops in the right direction without being too heavy-handed. He smiled, thinking about how BlackWidow must have reacted when she found out about the rose tattoo. He controlled everyone and that's just the way he liked it. They were all puppets in his private play.

There had also been pleasant surprises in the plot, such as the captivating Sophie Anderson. Now that would be a conquest. She wanted her man—and he could give him to her. Although perhaps not in the way she wanted. He sighed and let his thoughts linger on Sophie, replaying the way she moved, the way she smiled. But the feature he loved most about her was her over-developed sense of justice, of righteousness. He smiled, smug in the knowledge that right now she'd be stewing over the one that got away. If only she knew the truth.

And she would feel guilt over the toll in the desert, the law- enforcement toll. It was her case, her call, and people had died. He did feel sorry for her, knowing she'd take it hard—that sort always did. But it had been fun setting off the explosives. He'd had to wait, of course, had to make it look like it was triggered by the bomb squad, not him. Otherwise the cops and FBI would have known. How could Heath Jordan, the president, warn the other members or set off the explosives if he was in prison? To keep his secret, he'd had to bide his time.

"Are you ready, sir?"

He looked up. "Yes."

She was invaluable to him, essential for his public face. She didn't know his secret, and never would. Heath, on the other hand, was essential for his darker side. He was a good scapegoat, and he knew he could trust Heath to never, ever talk. His little visit with Heath had reassured him of that fact. He would never reveal his true involvement, nor would he resent that he'd taken certain liberties to make sure the evidence pointed to Heath. He'd been good to Heath in more ways than one, and Heath would repay that debt now. Besides, they both knew the FBI didn't have enough for murder, not enough to put Heath away forever. And he'd be there for Heath when he got out. The only murder Heath did commit, Janice Dust, they'd never get him on. He'd taken care of business and followed orders, like any good sidekick.

He buttoned his double-breasted Armani jacket and straightened his tie. He looked at the handsome reflection in the mirror and smiled. "You truly are the American psycho, Justin." Reid's smile was ear-to-ear.

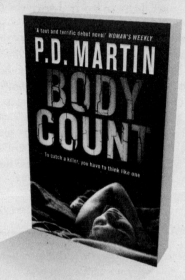

If you enjoyed this book, then make sure you also read these other titles by Mira Books! Order direct and we'll deliver them straight to your door.

Book Title/Author	ISBN & Price	Quantity
Body Count P.D. Martin	978 0778 301882 £6.99	
Dangerous Deception Beverly Barton	978 0778 302247 £6.99	
Lost Chris Jordan	978 0778 302261 £6.99	
A Necessary Evil Alex Kava	978 0778 301073 £6.99	
The Venus Fix M.J. Rose	978 0778 301424 £6.99	
Last Known Victim Erica Spindler	978 0778 301622 £6.99	

TH0708

Please add 99p postage & packing per book
DELIVERY TO UK ONLY
Post to: End Page Offer, PO Box 1780, Croydon, CR9 3UH

E-mail: customer.relations@hmb.co.uk

Please ensure that you include full postal address details.
Please pay by cheque or postal order (payable to Reader Service).
Prices and availability subject to change without notice.

Order online at: www.mirabooks.co.uk

Allow 28 days for delivery.

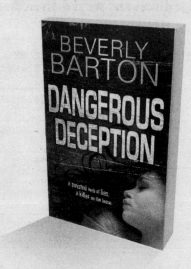

HURRICANE-SAVAGED NEW ORLEANS HAS A NEW DARK FORCE TO FEAR...

For police captain Patti O'Shea, the discovery of a dead body is shocking, but part of the job.

A dead body with the right hand severed is disturbing.

But when a corpse is discovered with the police badge of her murdered husband, she is pushed over the edge.

Driven by revenge, and working outside the law, Patti vows to track the monster responsible. But as the killings continue, it becomes clear that she is not the hunter – but the hunted.

MIRA